VASILY MAHANENKO

I0562113

IN SEARCH OF
THE ULDANS

*Books are the lives
we don't have
time to live,

Vasily Mahanenko*

GALACTOGON
BOOK #2

MD
BOOKS

MAGIC DOME BOOKS

IN SEARCH O THE ULDANS
GALACTOGON, BOOK TWO
COPYRIGHT © VASILY MAHANENKO 2019
COVER ART © VLADIMIR MANYUKHIN 2019
ENGLISH TRANSLATION COPYRIGHT ©
BORIS SMIRNOV 2019
PUBLISHED BY MAGIC DOME BOOKS
FIRST PAPERBACK EDITION 2019
ALL RIGHTS RESERVED
ISBN: 978-80-7619-047-4

ALL BOOKS BY VASILY MAHANENKO:

TABLE OF CONTENTS:

PROLOGUE

"WHAT CAN I SAY?" drawled Galactogon's owner. "The score is 8–0 in your favor."

He stepped away from the large screen displaying a room with two capsules and three bodies lying on the floor. In the image, the doors of the room burst open and a medical team rushed in to save the victims.

"How do you do it? I simply cannot wrap my mind around it..."

"I'll repeat it for the hundredth time: Even when you push them to their limits, humans remain human," said the President, rubbing his hands with a pleased expression. "When will you finally agree with me?"

"Never. You're just lucky when it comes to the people you find."

"But it was you who chose this couple, like the seven others earlier. And you were the one who came up with the script, worked out the backstory, and brought it all together. Eight out of eight—don't you think that the problem lies not in people, but in your philosophy?"

The mogul made no answer, nodding instead at the monitor and addressing a question to the dark corner of the room, "What about them? How are they?"

"Subject 'Eunice' is alive. The bullets did not hit any vital organs," came the reply from some invisible aide. "She is in a state of shock. The sequence of events involving Subject 'Eunice' unfolded in accordance to the plan. Subject 'Alexis' is alive, but in critical condition. The bullets fired by Constantine before the attack did not hit any vital…"

"Before or after—what's the difference?" the President interrupted the report. "Will he live or not?"

"He requires a heart transplant, but he will live. The last bullet perforated the left ventricle. Currently, the medcapsule is supplying his brain and body with oxygen."

"Please, avoid any unnecessary details," the President interrupted. "What do you need for the operation?"

"Permission and money. Thirty million, according to preliminary estimates. Subject 'Alexis' needs his heart replaced. He will also need prosthetics for his arm and leg."

"We'll assume that he won then," the owner of Galactogon said, displeased. "The money shall be wired to the settlement account. Do everything you must to keep him alive…There are too many casualties as it is."

One of the doctors on the screen raised his hand to his ear, taking the call, nodded in agreement, and two medical teams surrounded Alexis Panzer.

"What about our assassin?"

"Severe wounds, fatal. We lost him."

"A fourth one down." The President simpered as if the situation amused him. "Four of the warriors who agreed to participate in your play are already dead."

"Our play!"

"No, Sergei, in yours. You saw the psychologists' report: Alexis and Eunice have grown too immersed in virtual reality. They had reached the point of recklessness. When all the bridges were burned, this couple had nothing to lose. They—or he, it no longer matters—decided to become heroes. It happens. Accept it."

"I admit that I chose the wrong subject. The bond between this couple was too weak, not strong enough to take care of each other. You saw yourself that he did not consider what could happen to the girl. He saw only that he would lose the fight and his only thought was how to kill the shooter. We need something more powerful, something that will compel a person to submit to his basest instincts."

"You want to play again?"

"Why not? Do we not have more subjects? There are three hundred in the project. I won't only catch up to you—I'll beat you yet, Maxwell." Galactogon's owner turned back to the dark corner. "Develop and implement a scenario that will extract this couple from the project. And without any unnecessary verbiage please. They are no longer of interest to us."

"And what is of interest?" The President arched an eyebrow.

"I propose we consider our options. For instance, what would a mother do if she had to choose between her children? If she could choose which one was to die and which to live? As I recall, there are several suitable subjects for such a scenario in our project. Again, I wager that the mother would choose her firstborn. My data people tell me that firstborns are more loved."

"You don't know people at all." The President shook his head. "But I agree. I just saw you have a bottle of Maison Garlonde from the 2045 vintage. You can say goodbye to it because a loving mother would…But, hang on, let's consider the other options too. Maternal instinct is too close to the most basic of instincts and the wager seems to me too dull and easy to predict."

"As you like. Anyway, it is your turn to choose."

CHAPTER ONE

IF YOU HAVE EVER BEEN KILLED BEFORE—in real life, I mean—then you have my most sincere condolences. There is nothing pleasant about this procedure: It is frequently painful, unnerving and scary. Accordingly, if you are not partial to masochism, I recommend you avoid psychos and serial killers. Otherwise, my advice is grin and bear it and hope that if paradise awaits you after death, it will be like the one I'm currently in.

The sun in this, my personal paradise, is always at its zenith, but you don't have to worry about heatstroke or sunburn. Comfort here is paramount. I blinked blissfully, staring straight into the disk of hot light and savored the sea breeze along my skin. Warm, emerald waves lapped at my feet and tickled them like a playful girl. The sweet chirping of exotic birds behind me mixed with the surf to form a tranquil music. Everything around me dispelled any possible cares and submerged me in nirvana—

which is what I concentrated on, letting my mind enjoy a moment of peace. In precisely ten seconds I will give myself a mental kick and remind myself that these are nothing but illusions, digital decorations, plastered upon the walls of the medical diagnostic center. In precisely ten seconds—and not a second more. I have to remember who I am and why I am here.

My name is Alexis Panzer. I am a pro gamer who specializes in Galactogon, although at the moment, I'm in a therapeutic VR scene generated by my medical recovery capsule. The world around me is a projection created to deceive my mind. I have to feel whole and healthy. Only then, according to the doctors, can I recover from my surgeries.

Three days have passed since I regained consciousness and found myself on this beach. Since then my physician has dropped in to visit me as well as to check in on my psychological recovery and discuss my physical condition. And, the physician pointed out, my physical condition was pretty poor. My battle with the final boss, Constantine, cost me an arm and a leg, literally, and then some: I needed a heart transplant, three synth-tissue patches on my lungs, and prosthetics for my arm and leg. There is still no prognosis and all my questions receive the same boilerplate answer: 'Your current state is satisfactory.'

But it's the not knowing that hurts most. I don't know how my struggle with Constantine ended, and I constantly ask myself: How did I end up in the capsule? How long was I unconscious? What happened with Eunice and our child? Every attempt to learn anything from the doctor ended in failure. Doc claimed he knew nothing and told me to shut up. I obediently kept quiet, followed his instructions and waited. The important thing was to live. I hadn't the strength to do anything more.

My eyes began to ache from staring at the sun for too long. Squinting, I brushed away the tears. The discomfort was pleasant, if only because it took my mind off my anxious thoughts. Suddenly I heard the rustle of sand, as if someone was walking along the strand, but I was not worried. My doctor always appeared like that, gradually, instead of materializing beside me so as not to scare me. Delighted by the company, I greeted him warmly without opening my eyes:

"*Guten Tag Herr Doktor! Buen dia! Buon giorno!* I hope, Patient Panzer has managed to demonstrate a healthy spirit?"

"And then some, in my view," answered an unfamiliar voice. "But I lack the medical expertise to declare it with any authority." I opened my eyes and tried to look at the stranger through the dark spots and the sun's blinding rays. From my position on the sand, all I could make out were some expensive leather shoes.

"Good afternoon, Alexis. It is extremely inconvenient to speak when you are in this position. Could you stand up please?"

While I silently got up, my information-starved brain worked at a frantic pace. The doctor had always showed up casually: sandals, canvas shorts and a cheerful shirt covered in multi-colored pills like he was Dr. Mario, so as not to disturb me. This visitor though had appeared in his finest dress: A strict business suit, a leather case and name-brand accessories. Either this is a representative of the corporation's legal department—people who tended to sleep in their suits and trousers—or he's a junior detective who wants to frighten me. My intuition screamed that the second option was more likely, but my experience insisted that this man had some power behind him. His commanding demeanor did not suggest he was trying to make an impression on me.

"Thank you. Have a seat." An office table and two chairs materialized right there on the sand. The man took off his sunglasses, opened the suitcase and, undoing the bottom button of his jacket, sank into one of the chairs. While I silently occupied the other chair, he took out several sheets of paper from a suitcase and arranged them on the table in a neat pile.

"My name is Reynard the Fox. My title and responsibilities do not matter at the moment. What is salient here is that I can help you resolve the difficult situation you find yourself in," the man looked at me expectantly.

"Could you explain what that situation is?" I asked. "I'm a little detached from reality at the moment, for reasons of health."

"I understand. The law enforcement investigation believes that you intentionally moved to a dwelling equipped with special security and hacking equipment. The owner of the house you rented has already been charged with illegal use of specialized equipment. You hacked the tracking system, tricked one of the competitors and killed him. Having made sure that Constantine was dead, you tried to get rid of Eunice, reckoning that she and her child were a burden. Thus, you faked an assault on yourself and falsified evidence in order to frame Constantine. This is currently the official theory of how the crime was committed. Do you have something to say?"

IN SEARCH OF THE ULDANS

"Are you insane?!" I jumped to my feet from the madness I'd just heard. "It didn't happen that way at all! He was the one who threatened us with a gun. He shot Eunice in her legs and arms! He threatened to kill her and then bring the child to term inside of her like…like she was some kind of incubator! I did what I did because I feared for our lives!"

"Please, take your seat! I understood you. The doctor does not want you to grow agitated. I agree that the official theory has some flaws. That is why I'm here. Tell me your version of events. According to official information, Constantine should have been in a coma under the supervision of doctors at the time of the crime, but instead he was found shot dead in your house. Cameras in the street have him coming to you independently and fully conscious. Is that so?"

"It is," I agreed, taking my seat again and with a hollow voice asked, "Are Eunice and the child still alive?"

The sensible part of my mind quickly took hold of my emotions, isolating the important from what Reynard had said: 'You tried to get rid of Eunice.' This could mean different things.

"They are alive indeed, but they are in intensive care. She has lost a great deal of blood and the child's life is in danger. The doctors are doing everything they can, though Eunice's life is not in danger." These words took a great weight from my chest. "She is being maintained in a medically-induced coma and no one is allowed to see her. Consequently, you are the only witness in the investigation at the moment. Let's return to the purpose of my visit. I'm listening to you."

Trying not to omit a single detail, I told Reynard about

---

everything, starting with the exit from the game cocoon, Constantine's appearance, his threats, the shooting, my desire to save my child—and me throwing the weight plate from my barbell. I had nothing to hide because I am a law-abiding citizen and was confident that the experts would draw the right conclusions. Thinking, I decided to add an important detail:

"He jammed my smart home system, but he couldn't know that mine occupied only half of our resources. Eunice had control over the other half. She could have recorded a video. Here is the access key to the system. Check it out."

Reynard nodded and disappeared into the air where he sat. A second later, his belongings disappeared along with his chair and table, leaving me sitting alone in the middle of the beach. I stroked the upholstery of my armrest and made sure that Reynard the Fox had not been a figment of my imagination. I felt a little bit of ease—my family was alive, so the rest was unimportant.

Once more time turned to molasses. An hour passed, another, a third, but no one was in a hurry to drop the charges against me. In the end, I got up and, with almost Olympic calmness, returned to my main activity, swimming laps along the waves.

Almost a day had elapsed before I finally received the long-awaited news. No matter how hard I tried to anticipate my guest's reappearance, Reynard managed to catch me off guard, materializing right beside me.

"Good afternoon, Alexis. On behalf of the corporation and law enforcement, thank you for your cooperation. The incident has been fully reconstructed. There was indeed a video. All the charges against you have been dropped."

"Thank you," I nodded, relieved.

"Certain decisions have been made and I have been tasked with acquainting you with them. Sit down, this conversation will be long and difficult."

The desk and chair reappeared, once again recreating the seaside corporate office. I sat down in my old chair, which had remained after the last visit and therefore become my 'seat of meditation' over the last 24 hours.

"Let's get right to the point. In view of the circumstances, it was decided to terminate the scenario you were involved in ahead of schedule. This was done pursuant to clause thirteen of the contract you signed, the 'Force majeure' clause. You may reacquaint yourself with it if you like." Reynard handed me the signed document and I read over the standard force majeure boilerplate.

"You might agree that this is the only reasonable solution. All project participants have already been notified of the closure and..."

"What participants?" I stopped him. "Has Eunice woken up?"

"Not yet. Constantine killed only six," Reynard replied. "Your friend, whom you asked us to take care of, is alive. Constantine was bluffing when he said that she and her family were dead."

Alonso and Lucille are alive! I even pumped my fist from joy. I had spent my time here tormenting myself for not being able to save them and here it turned out that it had all been in vain. They were alive!

"Permit me to go on. My...employers...have instructed me to destroy the prize planet and everything that is somehow connected with this scenario—so that human greed does not cause more people to suffer. Yet, it would be unfair to leave you without any reward, since you lost your opportunity to find the prize even as you were so close to finding it. As compensation for the loss of profits for reasons beyond your control, you have been allowed to retain all the rewards you received in the course of your attempt."

"Rewards?" The word caught me off guard.

"You sound surprised...Why? Galactogon is a commercial project aimed at generating income. Maximum profit is possible only if the internal game balance is respected. No players may have an unfair advantage—or disadvantage—relative to the others. Everyone is equal, within limits. The exception are those individuals who spend their real money in Galactogon, but they are treated as a discrete playerbase that requires its own balance. In the case of the competition you took part in, the contestants were initially placed in conditions that were radically different from those faced by ordinary and commercial players. The corporation therefore instituted a reward and penalty system and applied it to the decisions you made in the course of your attempts. I could furnish some examples to explain better."

I nodded, unable to hide my chagrin and trying to dampen the fire which had just incinerated all my professional self-esteem to a sad heap of ash. Stupid old me had assumed that I had earned what I had. I thought I was cool, smart, unique.

Reynard, meanwhile, took a document from the suitcase

and read:

"If you care to examine this—here are all the rewards. Item: You received compensation for meeting the conditions for starting your search. Specifically, you could not know anything about the game, you could not prepare for it, and you had to make your choices based on your intuition. Item: You helped another player fulfill his long-cherished dream of becoming a pirate. You could have escaped from the Training Sector on your own, but took the player with you. For this, you received a frigate and engine prototypes. Item: You filed a formal complaint against the hacker Dan Cormak, as a consequence of which he was sentenced to twenty-two years and had his illegally-acquired property confiscated. For this, you received your own planet. Item: You tried to warn your fellow contestants and competitors about impending disaster, in particular, Lucille and Eunice. For this, you received an orbship with a full crew. Item: You agreed to marry Eunice, putting the interests of the child above yours. For this, you were granted access to the Zatrathi orbital station. Throughout, all your decisions and actions were considered by a special commission and found worthy of encouragement. Due to the project's termination, this commission has been dissolved and there will be no more rewards. Now you are a regular player in Galactogon, but, as I said, you are allowed to retain all of the rewards listed above. And with them you have the chance of ensuring substantial profits for the owners of Galactogon."

"If I return to Galactogon," I muttered angrily. Keeping calm was proving difficult. My professional self-esteem had just suffered a significant blow. Everything was bubbling inside of me. It turned out that they had helped me out all along my way. I had played with a handicap. And now that their little betting game was done with, the mighty of this world had folded up the board and placed the pieces back in their case.

"There is little doubt that you will return. Your injuries require lengthy and expensive treatment. You must spend the next six months in a medical recovery capsule. And as luck would have it, your medical bills cost about as much as a couple high level spacecraft in Galactogon, while your current financial situation leaves much to be desired. Take a look." Reynard handed me a sheet of paper. "This is your balance sheet: Your assets and accounts. That red number is the balance owed by you as of today, minus the costs of treatment and rehabilitation in the clinic for the current month. Do not forget that from now on you are responsible not only for yourself, but also for your spouse and child. Even if you liquidate all your property, there is enough money for only two months, no more."

"And you won't help us? We didn't end up here because of our own mistakes. We are here because two fat cats decided to have a little fun! They are liable for our condition and must pay for the treatment. It's spare change for them."

"Mr. Panzer…Mr. Panzer…" Reynard shook his head. "Be careful about what you say. I understand that you are upset now, and I will pretend that I have not heard anything, but keep in mind that I represent the legal interests of my clients. You are an intelligent man. It is foolish to blame anyone for the actions of a maniac. Do not take this as a threat, but no one except you is responsible for what happened. Let me remind you that you signed the contract voluntarily and, as a result, accepted all the risks and consequences. But...my employers are ready to offer you a helping hand. Your medical capsule will be connected to Galactogon, giving you the option of playing the game and therefore earning money to pay for your treatment. First, we will connect you. Later on, when she is feeling better, we will extend the same offer to Eunice."

I pulled the document over to me dramatically and rubbed my nose. Treatment and rehabilitation in a private clinic really cost a lot.

"What about transferring us to an ordinary clinic?" There had to be some way of severing all ties with Galactogon.

"The choice is yours," Reynard did not try to dissuade me and pulled out another sheet. This Fox character seemed loaded with boilerplate for any occasion. "Here are the findings from the medical commission. Without the current medical capsule supporting you, you have two days to live. Public clinics, unfortunately, are not equipped with such modules, and it's not for me to tell you about the quality of their services."

I felt like a hunted quarry which had only one way out—to surrender. And the truth was that I myself would customarily go to private doctors and clinics as soon as I felt under the weather. The public healthcare was free and very good, but it was twenty years behind the private sector in terms of medtech.

"So what is your decision?" Reynard hiked an eyebrow. He gave me next to no time to think.

"As if I have a choice...Very well. I agree to your terms."

"I figured you would. I won't occupy you any further. Rest

assured that your oral consent is sufficient for your capsule to be hooked up to Galactogon. You'll feel right at home—the weather's quite hot in there too at the moment. All the best!"

Reynard vanished, taking his office furniture, documents and the still open briefcase with him. Caught off guard, I collapsed into the sand and swore long and hard, feeling even more angry and humiliated.

Will you just look and see how quickly the bettors pulled the plug on their entire wager as soon as the results had become clear! At least I can be happy that we got off so easy—along with the prize and the planet, they could've just as easily 'pulled the plug' on all the survivors as well.

"We need to run some tests, Alexis." The doctor appeared immediately after Reynard left and seemed already up to date. "We must check to see how your time in Galactogon will affect your body. We will start with a few seconds and then gradually increase the interval. We're connecting you to the test server now."

The seascape around me drifted and reformed into a colorful spaceport. I managed to make out several docked frigates before I returned back to the beach. The doctor was nearby. The medical capsule gave him a full account of my physical condition, but the doctor himself wanted to monitor my emotional stability.

"Excellent. There is no adverse reaction. We will increase the immersion interval to a minute. If you feel sick, simply sit down on the ground. This will serve as a signal to stop the test."

The interval kept increasing: first a minute, then five, ten,

---

half an hour, an hour, three. The next two days for me turned into a series of spatial jumps from the beach to the unfamiliar spaceport in Galactogon. There were no other players on the test server and the NPCs offered few dialog options, so at first I wandered aimlessly amid the empty buildings. Then it occurred to me to take the opportunity and look for non-trivial ways to get into the command center. I figured that most of the Galactogon spaceports were created using the same templates, and as a pirate in training, it was useful for me to know the ways of getting into the planet's holiest of holies.

"The tests have been concluded successfully, you are ready to enter Galactogon," the doctor announced after the second day. "Any requests before we send you to the game?"

"Yeah. I want to connect the capsule to my smart home system."

I would be lost without Stan to guide me along. Information analysis, web search, a sensible adviser—the personality matrix of my home AI suited me like a glove and I was not about to give it up. In addition, it was unwise to allow yourself to leave reality for half a year without maintaining your business IRL. Stan would be my eyes and ears in the real world.

"Our clinic does not have its own technicians, nor the capability to do this, but for an additional fee we can contact your home AI's service department. Will that suit you?" It did not suit me one bit and in fact it annoyed me even more, but also there was nothing I could do about it. After a long and ornery conversation with a clinic representative, I felt like twisting the neck of the thin-necked extortionist. It should be legal to sign

---

contracts with tears, as if to say: 'I agree with the terms, but I ain't happy about them.' I was forced to pay an amount with five zeroes to expand the clinic and install extra broadband channels. The clinic director was unmovable: Either I pay the specified amount or I don't get Stan. The bank terminal appeared as soon as I hollered my consent and kicked up a cloud of sand in exasperation. Those bastards. I don't even want to imagine how much it costs to integrate a banking module into a medcapsule.

"Good afternoon, Master, what are your instructions?" Stan could not speak, only write to the chat in the interface, but even this was enough for me to break into a wide grin. My heart immediately warmed up.

Saying goodbye to the doctor and agreeing to weekly check-ups, I found myself in complete darkness, barely diluted by a loading bar. Galactogon was slowly seeping into my medical capsule. The loading bar reached a hundred percent and the game opened its arms to accept me. I had been gone a mere six days, but it felt as if I had lived an entire life during my absence.

I spawned in the palace of the Precian Emperor, in one of its myriad guest rooms. I made a few familiar movements to check my new hardware's performance and collapsed in my bed as I was. Now it was possible to relax and sleep—my own caring doctor had injected me with a mild tranquilizer. My last thought before shutting down was that I should forbid him from doing this the next time I saw him.

IN SEARCH OF THE ULDANS

"Captain Surgeon, an official reception with the emperor will take place in four hours." A soft knock and a polite voice broke through my sleep. A Precian noble stood in my room's doorway. "Would you like to freshen up before the audience?"

This offer came in very handy. Having caught up on my sleep, I was ready to calmly figure out what had happened in the game since I left and where the hell my damn ship was. I could not contact my crew: The NPCs did not respond to my comm, and I still hadn't gotten my marine armor back, so I started with the most important thing: integrating with Stan. There was no voice feature for communicating with third-party software in Galactogon. The only way to communicate was to chat through my avatar's PDA. This turned out to be very inconvenient, and it was Stan who found a solution. He began our communication with several detailed reports about how he missed me, how he had waited for me, how little resources he had left, and how brazen, evil law enforcement officers had rummaged through his databanks. Listening to his litany of complaints, I made a mental note to lower his emotion settings. Stan seemed to be trying to match the behavior of a person, and forgot his main duty—to provide me with analytical data. At the first attempt to gain an answer, my patience failed. Stan came to the rescue. His next message contained instructions for setting up voice input and audio playback in the PDA interface. The only pity was that the PDA only had a loudspeaker option which everyone around me would hear. This would constrain what I could say to Stan.

"Home construction is currently at 70%; all systems have been connected. What are your instructions, Master?"

"All right. I need the following information…"

It took Stan some time to amass the data on the current state of my finances, the location and operation of my clinic, the recovery technologies in my medcapsule, the limitations and negative consequences of my six-month convalescence in it, as well as the cost of such a model for personal use. The problem had to be considered from all angles. Stan assured me that his data collection would be assigned the highest priority, wished me a speedy recovery, reminded me to do my morning workout and disconnected. I already felt like I was at home—a week without a loyal assistant was an eternity.

While I was dealing with urgent matters, two Precians drew a bath and waited to help me wash and then have a massage. Too bad that Galactogon had a 12+ age limit. Everything was by the book, decorous and noble, with no hint of eroticism, let alone happy endings. Eh…A pleasant languor spread through my body, and I had to force myself to look through my current list of missions:

The Imperial Gift: You have been given a unique opportunity to meet with the emperor of the Precian Empire and receive from him a reward for uncovering information about the KRIEG.

The Stork and the Fox: Notify Alviaan, First Councilor of the Delvian Emperor, that the princess is pregnant.

IN SEARCH OF THE ULDANS

Meet Tryd: Meet Tryd, Hilvar's contact, hand him the envelope and receive his instructions. Return to Hilvar with his reply.

A Pirate I was Meant to be. Part 1: Destroy 150 interceptors (12 of 150 destroyed) or 125 scouts (0 of 125), or 100 shuttles (0 of 100), or 75 monitors (0 of 75), or 50 frigates (0 of 50), or 20 albendas (0 of 20), or 10 cruisers (1 of 10).

Treasure Hunter: Find your way to the secret Uldan base, located on a moon of the planet Zalva. Required item: Orbship Warlock.

On top of this, I had earned two audiences with the emperor of any of Galactogon's empires for earning the 'First Defender' and 'Semper Fidelis' achievements. In total, three meetings with the masters of this universe. Not bad, though it'll go sour quick if the system decides that this one meeting with the Precian Empire counts for all three. Just in case, I better extract the utmost from this one, which means I need to thoroughly prepare and call my partner.

"Marina, how are you? This is Surgeon speaking. Do you have any interests in the Precian Empire?"

"What the hell, you weirdo! You just call me as if nothing's happened?! Is this some way of making fun of me?" the girl yelled in response to my greeting. I was taken aback, not expecting such a turn. "Or is your ball sack too small to show up in person? 'Cause if so, sew yourself a bigger one, you *surgeon*, and we can talk when you've made yourself a big boy!"

"Wow." I couldn't help appreciate the state that the typically-restrained captain of the Cruiser *Alexandria* was in. Most likely, Kiddo was pissed about the disappearance of my planet, which served as the homeworld for her cruiser. If that was the case, I'd better not keep the truth from my partner. "Marina, I've been away from the game for six days due to health problems. I almost swapped this metal box for a plush wooden one. I have no idea what happened during that time. You are the first person I called because I still assume we're partners. Let's not start fighting right away. What happened?"

A noisy exhalation in the mic and a long pause suggested that Marina had switched her mental tumbler from the 'pissed' to the 'cogitating' setting. After a short while, she managed to calm herself:

"Last night I attacked Shylak XIV, the Qualians' trade planet, overwhelmed the Grand Arbiter and destroyed the planetary command center. Basically, the raid went off better than we could have expected. But then the aliens showed up out of nowhere and attacked *Alexandria*, destroying her. That is to say that they appeared on the opposite edge of the galaxy from where their invasion is supposed to be happening! The binding to your planet vanished and so did the planet itself. Hell even the star system, no longer exists! Without a homeworld, *Alexandria* respawned in Qualian space. And those buggers boarded and captured her. So what am I supposed to think, partner? I trusted you and now I am stranded without a cruiser! And what the hell did the devs get involved for?"

IN SEARCH OF THE ULDANS

"Did the Zatrathi attack everyone in the system or your ship alone?" I frowned, hearing her account. As I had assumed, Marina's troubles stemmed from the devs' having moved Blood Island. If I understood Reynard correctly, the planet was still in Galactogon, but only Brainiac, my ship's computer, would know its coordinates. But anyway, what were the Zatrathi doing in Qualian space? My many years spent playing Runlustia paid off—the plot twists remained similar. If the invaders attacked only Marina's vessel and ignored everyone else, then the Galactogon playerbase had some merry times ahead of it.

"Is that all you care about?" came the indignant cry from the comm. "I lost my ship! What's the difference who else the aliens attacked?"

"You haven't lost anything yet!" I snapped back. "In a couple hours, I have an audience with the Precian Emperor, I will ask him for help. They are in the same alliance with the Qualians. Let me ask you one more time, did the Zatrathi attack only you or everyone?"

Kiddo did not hurry to reply, seemingly mulling the ambush over in her head.

"You're right, they only attacked us. They didn't bother with the other players raiding Shylak. What does this tell you?"

"What does it tell me?" My fears had been confirmed. "Do you have assets with the Qualians?"

"Oh only my legendary cruiser!"

"Aside from the ship. Other ships, mining facilities, valuables? Everything you can take with you."

"Suppose I do. What's it to you?"

"Get it all out. Logic dictates that within the next week, the Qualians will announce their withdrawal from the Alliance and join the Zatrathi. First of all, the Qualians have lost their prince. Second of all, there is news that the KRIEG has been completed. Third, the players are being pushed to fight on two fronts, just the way the developers like it, and now there's this Zatrathi ship ambushing you. All indications are that the Qualians are about to start a power struggle for mastery of Galactogon. I'll figure out what happened to my planet and try to get your ship back. By the way, where are you now?"

"I'm in prison on Raydon, the Qualians' second largest trading planet. I'm under arrest until the investigation runs its course."

"So sit tight and wait quietly. What about your business in the Precian Empire? Don't hold back. Consider it compensation for the loss of your ship. I have the audience with the emperor coming up and I don't really have anything to ask him. Just some trifles. It would be foolish to waste such an opportunity."

"Precians, you say? Yes, there is one piece of business. There is a corporation called Hansa that's based on the planet Belket in Precian space. Hansa specializes in weapons, ammunition and high-end ship weaponry. They are the best gunsmiths the Precians have and by extension the Alliance as a whole. Their services cost astronomical amounts of money, but their products are always singular. You can't buy them from players, even after the latest update. It would simply be the bees' knees if the Precian Emperor grants me permission to work with them and throws in a discount for the cooperation, of say, twenty percent. I know plenty of people who are ready to purchase Hansa products, but who don't have the chance due to the current limitations. If we manage to set ourselves up as middlemen, the income will be modest but stable. We can go in fifty-fifty if you like. Galactogon's accountants can generate the relevant reports. What do you say, partner?"

"I say I look forward to doing business with you, partner," I replied. "You've got a deal. Do you know where Wally and the team are right now?"

"I don't know for sure. I don't keep track of them, but I think they're out hunting small ships. All right, I have to go. They're about to take me on my daily walk. Call me in about four hours and let me know how it went with the emperor."

Marina disconnected and I grinned. Naturally, Kiddo had no reason to track my ship herself, since Wally would do that for her. Every chance he got, he sent reports about what was going on to his true boss.

"Mister Surgeon, it is time." A Precian appeared next to me with clothes for me to wear. "You are already expected in the audience hall."

Compared with its analogues in Runlustia, the emperor's ceremonial hall in Galactogon could be called ascetic. I was used to the fact that every detail of the palace interior had its own history—everything had artistic and, most importantly, material value, which meant it could be stolen and sold for a profit. Here, however, the eye had nothing to latch onto. The place was like any other ordinary gray room that had been labeled the ceremonial hall and which had a psychedelic throne in its center. It was an odd approach on the part of the devs to the design of a location that many players wanted to get into. But it should be noted that the palace matched its owner. Outwardly, the emperor differed little from his subjects. He was a blue-skinned humanoid wrapped in a legendary suit of armor and therefore looked more like a space marine than one of the twelve most-influential NPCs in Galactogon. Only the hologram of a crown above his pointy-eared head and long, thin neck suggested his higher status.

There were about twenty attendees in total, but I was the only player among them. Standing last in line for my reward, I realized the reality of what was going on. Reynard warned me about this—there would be no more concessions. If I had met the emperor before Constantine's attack, this reception would have been in my honor. Now I have to stand and wait for my turn. It was boring to watch the NPCs receive orders, titles or planets. Finally, the celebration reached my end of the woods.

"Outlaw of the Qualian Empire," announced the court clerk, "gifted with the grace of our emperor, witness of the heroism of the Precian prince, the first to destroy the ship of the Zatrathi, the first to kill a Zatrathi in melee combat, who set forth upon the path of piracy, captain of the Orbship *Warlock*: Captain Surgeon!"

The emperor nodded, allowing me to approach.

"I'm glad you could recover from your illness, Surgeon," said the head of the Precians, officially restating the reason for my five-day absence from the game. "You were able to obtain the orbship and showed that the Uldans are not a myth. I heard

IN SEARCH OF THE ULDANS

rumors about the search for this amazing civilization, but I thought it was a fairy tale. Now, I am overwhelmed with contradictory feelings. I am both unhappy and pleased that I was wrong. Tell us all about your adventures. How did you manage all this anyway?"

There were no other players around, so I freely recounted how I had received *Warlock*. I kept the drama to a minimum and emphasized my fortune. My professional self-esteem squealed from the effort. I had lucked out so many times that anyone with a modicum of humility should have put it together: Something was going on. Ordinary players don't get their hands on special prototype engines while still in the tutorial.

"Now I understand how you learned about the KRIEG," the emperor shook his head and said instructively: "Remember this lesson for the future, Surgeon, luck is a fickle mistress. Do not imagine that she will hold true."

The developers had just used the emperor's mouth to inform me that my walk in the park had brought me to uncharted waters. And I was yet to find out exactly what lay in store for me.

"The Precian Empire is grateful to you for the information about the KRIEG and my son's actions," the emperor continued. "The prince did the right thing in killing the traitor. Accept this gift as a reward for the news."

One of the Precians gave me a small piece of paper on a golden platter.

"A check for two hundred tons of raq," the emperor solemnly declared. "You may redeem it in whole or in parts on any of the planets of my empire."

I accepted the emperor's first gift, bowing my head gratefully. Two hundred tons of raq at a cost of fifty credits per kilogram made me the owner of ten million GC. My current balance barely exceeded one and a half, so this generous gift from Galactogon would be very useful. I guess they decided to finally give me some money.

"You were the first to destroy a Zatrathi ship, proving to the skeptics that such a feat was even possible. Accept this gift as a reward for your valor!"

Again a Precian with a golden tray approached me.

"A ship that has achieved such success should be rewarded. This is permission to contact the Hansa Arms Corporation and an order to upgrade one of your vessel's systems. Hansa should find something that will please even the owner of an orbship."

It's a good thing that Kiddo had told me about Hansa, otherwise I would not have realized the value of the second reward. Happy, I bowed my head again, accepting the document.

"You were the first to kill a Zatrathi, demonstrating that the enemy may be killed not only in space, but also on the planets it has captured. Accept this gift as a reward for your courage!"

Instead of a golden tray, a cargo drone flew into the hall, hauling a sparkling suit of armor in its tractor beam. The properties of the gift were hidden, but one glance turned out to be enough to understand that the A-class Qualian marine armor that I had never received was an ancient prototype compared to the sleek killer in front of me.

IN SEARCH OF THE ULDANS

"Armor and arms are the alpha and omega of any marine. This legendary marine armor and ranger's blaster will allow you to more effectively vanquish our foes. Wield them with honor!"

A solemn fanfare followed, marking the end of the award ceremony. I took a step back to take my place, but a light tap on my back indicated that the emperor had not yet finished.

"Once you have visited Zalva's moon and received your upgrade from the Hansa Arms Corporation, you shall be expelled from our empire. Pirates have no place in the Precian Empire! I cannot trust someone who voluntarily chose the path of piracy. From now on, and as long as you remain a pirate, you shall find no safe harbor in Precian space. Escort Surgeon to his ship and see that he leaves Zalva immediately."

This marked the end of both my audience with the emperor and my walk in the park. Two armored marines appeared on both sides of me and unceremoniously turned me to the door. My eyes followed the drone with the armor suit, which turned around after the escorts. It looked like 'the alpha and omega' of any Precian marine would be delivered directly to my orbship.

Until I reached the spaceport, I still harbored some hope of secretly meeting the emperor. Things like that happened in Runlustia all the time—when it was possible to solve problems with the rulers behind the scenes, bypassing the officially announced political course, or even get non-trivial tasks. But this time, there was no miracle forthcoming. As the dock with the now-kindred *Warlock* loomed on the horizon, it became clear that the Precian Emperor did not entertain any intrigues. If I wanted to stay on Zalva, then I had to give up on Hilvar's

---

mission. It's a shame that the issue with Kiddo's ship remained unaddressed. My mission log appeared before my eyes and I cursed. It was impossible to cancel the mission. My choices were either to slink back to Hilvar and confess my inadequacy or wait a calendar year until the deadline expired. There were no other ways of quitting my path to piracy.

Yet the nearer I came to the dock, the calmer I became. The mere sight of *Warlock* dispelled my doubts. Come what may. I could of course, fly to Hilvar, abandon piracy and join the glorious horde of those fighting against the Zatrathi. But why not try to live the Pirate Dream? The Confederacy did not refuse admission to freelance privateers. If I joined them, there would be no obligations and, therefore, neither foreign allies, nor foreign rivals. I would be the only one to decide whether to attack a ship that came across my path or not. The more worrying question was how I was going to make my living. Although, on the whole, it wasn't such a pressing one for the moment. There was even time to consider my other missions.

Thinking these thoughts, I stepped onto the dock. Thanks to my rhino marine, a desolate zone had formed around my *Warlock*. Watching the maintenance men cautiously skirt in an invisible circle around my ship, I realized that my cryptosaur had already become infamous on Zalva. I jumped off the platform and waved to the rhino. He roared menacingly and rushed straight towards me, paying no attention to the technicians and repair equipment in his way. It was petty, of course, but still nice to see the Precians jump out of the way at the last moment, abandoning their instruments in their flight. Oh, what a pity! I was not going to reimburse the cost of the equipment. That's what you get for exiling me.

The cryptosaur rushed up to me like a locomotive at full steam and, ignoring all inertia, stopped dead in front of me, blasting me with hot air from his flared nostrils. I patted the marine on his nose and climbed onto his back, which had morphed into a comfortable saddle.

"Wait, Surgeon! We need to talk..." was all I heard before my mount brought me to my ship. I was in such a hurry to get back that I paid no attention to the voice.

"Our lost lamb has returned!" It may have seemed that the ship herself had greeted her captain in a deeply-buried voice, but this was really my engineer who dwelt in the vessel's depths. Of the entire *Warlock* crew, she was the only one who could speak. I dismounted my rhino and waited for the engineer to crawl to the surface. "We thought you decided to settle here, Cap'n. To sprout roots, find yourself a blue wife and make some blue kids. You surrendered to the blue meanies without a struggle or a fight?"

"Don't hold your breath," I smiled, affably patting the head of the slizosaur who had bent down to my height. My engineer and permanent shieldsman was a huge and extremely snarky serpent. "Someone needs to captain this tub. You lot would grow rusty without me. Then I'll have to go about sanding everything back to order."

"Surgeon! We need to talk! Don't leave!" sounded the voice again. The rhino marine snarled menacingly, cautioning the stranger from approaching. I turned around and saw a player in a typical suit of armor with Precian insignia. It was the kind of insignia you got for grinding rapport with the empire. The man was standing beside a tent, pitched right there on the dock as if he had been camping out waiting for me for a long time. Such perseverance should be rewarded, and I was curious to hear what he wanted from me.

"I'll listen, but not for long," I glanced over at the Precian guards. The marines' postures suggested that they were ready to see their emperor's orders performed to a T.

"Mr. Eine wishes to speak with you. If you could wait for a half hour—he is on his way here as we speak."

"I don't think I can spare even five minutes." The guards had perked up noticeably. "At ease, fellas…I'm going, I'm going…"

Before entering my ship, I turned and yelled to the stranger:

"Sorry, if I don't go now, these courageous fellas will blast me to pieces. So take care and don't hold it against me."

"This man is under the protection of Mr. Eine!" The stranger turned to the guards and flashed a sparkling badge. "Leave him."

"Emperor's orders. The pirate must leave Zalva immediately!" One of the guards replied in a metallic voice and knocked the player away with a single blow.

I had no desire to get into a fight with the Precians, so I ordered:

"We are leaving! Everyone aboard! Space awaits us!"

This was mostly addressed to the cryptosaur, who had decided that the guards were posing a threat to the ship and was about to attack them. A platform extended from the bottom of *Warlock*, and the rhinoceros stalked inside with a business-like

---

snort as if to say that if it hadn't been for my orders, he would have wiped the entire dock clean with the Precians. The ship's hull meanwhile wavered and parted, forming an entrance for me.

"Welcome back, Captain!" the ship computer greeted me.

"Hello, Brainiac! I need a full report on the current status of the ship, crew and equipment."

"All systems are operating normally. Crew readiness is at 100%. The droid squadron is back at 100% as well. We have two suits of armor, one of which we received a few minutes ago. I am currently running diagnostics on it. There are ten tons of elo reserves, forty tons of raq and two tons of tiron in our holds."

"Send the new armor suit to the bridge and synchronize it to the ship. Anything important that I should know about before blast-off?"

"Unauthorized persons made twenty-eight attempts to breach the ship's security perimeter. I deployed the marine to protect the perimeter and hull integrity. In response, the enemy detachment set up a camp at the far end of the dock and engaged in intelligence gathering until you appeared. The guards were changed around the clock, every two hours. An enemy parliamentarian requested permission to speak with you several times. That is all. The new armor suit has been synched to the ship. I congratulate you on your new equipment."

My curiosity subsided, sending a fiery farewell to the stranger picking himself up out on the dock: just another hunter of rarities, trying to get into my orbship. The hell with him. And yet...well, if he's a potential buyer, I should sound him out just in case...

"Stan, I need information about a player named Eine. This process is high priority. Have you finished collecting data for the previous process?"

"I have. The information has been uploaded to your PDA. New process accepted. Getting started on it now."

The handheld computer squeaked, displaying an incoming message icon. Reminding myself that I needed to take time to assess my situation out in reality, I turned my attention to the new armor. Its properties exceeded all my expectations. It was like the Christmas gift of a lifetime. The emperor's generosity impressed me! The legendary class gave the armor 21 stats with the option of replacing or integrating blasters, active shielding, a jetpack and a bunch of extra components that basically made whoever donned the suit into a good old tank. With this kind of gear, I could calmly go toe to toe with a Zatrathi, without any fear of failure. Brainiac could project the ship's control systems directly into the suit's HUD, turning it into a kind of personal captain's chair. I designated one of the screens as a channel to Brainiac and adjusted my captain's chair to the suit's dimensions.

"Brainiac, I ordered you to compile a list of the crew's abilities. How are you doing with that?"

"The process has been completed. The compiled data has been sent to your armor's computer."

"Excellent. Let's take off then. Set course for Zalva's second moon."

"This is Orbship *Warlock* requesting launch clearance," Brainiac addressed the control tower.

IN SEARCH OF THE ULDANS

"Launch clearance granted. Follow corridor 2-2-5 to rendezvous with Grand Arbiter *Intrepid*. Your ship must be inspected before leaving planetary orbit."

This was unexpected but reasonable. What if I was about to smuggle some dangerous outlaw out with me? I'm a pirate, after all. It's something I'd do. Just in case, Brainiac assured me that there was nothing illegal or prohibited aboard.

Warlock took off and a countdown timer appeared to indicate the time left before we docked with the Grand Arbiter. This was enough for me to read over Stan's report.

Reynard hadn't deceived me—there wasn't much of a silver lining in our situation. We had been justifiably admitted to one of the most expensive clinics on Earth. It was a very private facility, yet Stan managed to dig up something about it. My personal assistant managed to download the data from the medical capsule directly. There had been no exaggeration—without constant stimulation of my heart muscles, I would be a dead man. The implant worked well, but it would take time for it to merge with my system. My prognosis was good on the assumption that I would spend four or five months in the medical capsule, and then another month for rehab. Eunice's condition was stable, but she remained in the coma. Stan reassured me that the critical threat to the child had passed and now the doctors were just playing things as safe as possible. That was it for the good news. Even though Eunice and the baby were basically all right, I was still in deep trouble. There was no alternative, cheap treatment in my situation. My insurance payout for the destroyed house and the money that I had

---

managed to earn during my search for the prize planet made it possible to pay the medical bills, but I would have nothing left. There was one loophole. Although there was no official system for converting Galactogon Credits into real ones, there were quite a few third-party resources offering exchange services. The rate was naturally unprofitable, but, in an extreme case it would provide at least some money. So, I would need to increase the amount of raq I had on board and periodically exchange it for loans of real money. Piracy was beginning to look better and better.

"We have docked, Cap'n," the engineer notified me. There followed an unpleasant metallic sound. The docking mechanisms of the Grand Arbiter had grown rusty from disuse, the hatch in my orbship took shape, and a team of customs officers stepped on board. Having made a cursory inspection, the underlings lined up, waiting for management. After a minute or so, a Precian in rather elaborate armor appeared in the hatchway—an Imperial Adviser.

"According to regulations, the ship inspection should take five minutes, so we will not waste time. His Imperial Highness instructed me to accompany you to the moon, but only if you agree to take me with you." I had no chance to respond to this because the adviser immediately raised his hand, calling for silence. "Do not rush to refuse! The palace is rotten with spies; the emperor made a public show of exiling you for their benefit. Consider your exile a guarantee of your safety and relative freedom in Galactogon. We suspect that the Qualians are collaborating with the Zatrathi. They plot to eliminate the ruling dynasties of all the empires, including the allied ones. Thus we are on the brink of hostilities with the Qualian Empire. The margin for error is very small. When the problem with the Qualians is resolved, the Precian Empire will show its appreciation for you. I am asking you to take me with you at the behest of the emperor. I am the keeper of knowledge about the Uldans and would very much like to enter their base."

"Well, your words explain a lot, and it is possible that I don't mind taking you along, but after searching the moon, I have to leave imperial space," I clarified an important point. "What am I supposed to do with you then?"

"I would be quite happy if you set me down on Belket, where you will receive your reward from the Hansa Corp. If that does not work, any other planet of the Confederation would do. The Precian Empire has consulates on all inhabited planets. I am not a pretentious person and when it comes to my life's work and passion—the Uldans, that is—I can abide some inconvenience."

"I bet," I muttered to myself, thinking and watching the adviser's small beady eyes scrupulously crawl over *Warlock*'s interior. Still, if the NPCs themselves decided to visit my ship, it means that they are ready to make concessions. "What will I get in return? I was kindly awarded an exile earlier. I would like something more beneficial to my person."

"Oh! The emperor anticipated such a development." The beads flashed knowingly in my direction. "People, especially pirates, rarely adhere to the principles of charity. The Precian Empire is prepared to share with you the Uldan technologies that it has. I'm sure your ship's computer can figure out what to do with them."

Brainiac drew my attention with a blinking message:

"I recommend we accept the offer! There is a critical dearth of information about the Uldan base. It is reliably known that it is located deep below the surface of the moon, and our ship serves as an access key. There are no exact coordinates. Let me remind you that the orbship is a reconnaissance vessel, not a research vessel. New information may be hard to come by and therefore very useful."

"I see no reason to refuse, especially since we could use the help," I agreed with my ship's computer and nodded to the adviser, while swiping away the warning that had jumped out:

Mission updated: Treasure Hunter...

"Write in the inspection report: Orbship *Warlock* has no prohibited items for export," the adviser ordered, and the customs officers left my ship. The inspection regulations had been executed immaculately.

"Brainiac, set course for Zalva's second moon. Maximum acceleration. Adviser, we have a few minutes of flight ahead of us. Could you share with me what you know about the Uldans in the meantime?"

"Unfortunately, there's not much to share. The technology employed by our winged ancestors strains the limits of our understanding, but you yourself no doubt already learned as much from your ship and crew. We don't even know how they disappeared. There is a theory that a war broke out between the

IN SEARCH OF THE ULDANS

Uldans and an unknown race, and ninety thousand years ago one of the parties used forbidden weapons. Analogs of the KRIEG, only on the scale of Galactogon. Both sides of the conflict were destroyed, and other races took the leading positions in our galaxy."

"Hold on. The KRIEG. What can you tell me about it?" I seized an unexpected opportunity.

"I'm sorry, Surgeon, but I cannot reveal classified information. And the KRIEG is very classified." The adviser spread his hands helplessly.

"I'll trade you some info about the Uldans for some answers about the KRIEG," I said, pushing the Precian's sore point.

"It all depends on the question." A transparent film descended over the adviser's beady eyes and he began to thoughtfully stroke his long neck. "If I can answer it, without violating confidentiality, I will gladly exchange the information. I can say one thing right away, the aftermath of using the KRIEG shall be terrifying for everyone."

"Yes, I already realized that the KRIEG is a weapon of mass destruction. What I am interested in is its area of effect. If the Qualians decide to use it, I'd like to know how far to jump from the epicenter."

"Two hyper-minutes," the adviser replied after a bit of thought, making me whistle in surprise. In two minutes you could fly through a dozen star systems and that's only in one direction. If a KRIEG detonates in a sphere, then a vast region of Galactogon would be laid waste.

"The Uldans fought against the Vraxis," I handed over the

information I had received from Warlock and now it was the turn of the adviser to show surprise by preening his neck in my direction.

"Is this information reliable? As far as I know, the Vraxis is a race of hypertrophic insects with a very rudimentary intelligence."

"You could not find a more reliable source. I heard it directly from the last Uldan commander of this very ship. And, in my opinion, the intellect of the Vraxis is a bit higher than rudimentary, since their queen had a dangerous army which was guided by generals," I replied.

"Yes you are right. It is likely that our information is not accurate," the adviser muttered thoughtfully. "I was present at the audience where you told the emperor about how you acquired the orbship. It is unheard of and incredible, yet I both believe and envy you. You had a chance to see a living Uldan. Everyone else has had to content themselves with rare images."

"I am picking up a weak distress signal," Brainiac interrupted suddenly. "The signal is coming through in the Uldan language. Its transmitter seems to be located below the moon's surface. ETA is thirty seconds."

"Route the signal to the cabin speakers and ready the cryptosaur. We will land. Translate the signal into the common language."

A noisy hiss sounded in the speakers and gradually gave way to a monotonous message in a foreign language:

"Mayday. Mayday. This is base 20-449. We are under attack and require assistance," Brainiac translated out loud. "The message repeats. This is an emergency recording, Captain."

IN SEARCH OF THE ULDANS

But that was already clear. Neither the timbre nor the pitch of the voice has changed. No matter how incredible they are, it's impossible to wait for help at the microphone for a hundred thousand years.

"That's enough. Crew—any suggestions for where to look for the entrance? Any ideas are welcome."

"Here is the location where the signal is strongest," Brainiac poured forth new information like fuel onto the fire.

"So the entrance is in another place," the snake remarked in a business-like tone.

"What? Why?" I was surprised at the engineer's certainty.

"The first thing the enemy would do is target the transmitter, to prevent the defenders from calling reinforcements. Therefore, the transmitter must be able to withstand any bombardment and continue its transmission. That is, the best place to install a transmitter is where the crust is thickest, while the best place to enter the facility is where it's thin. But I am assuming here, Cap'n. You should orbit the moon to make sure. The ship can track the signal and the base might react to our appearance and open the door itself. There are many possibilities to consider."

After thirty minutes of flying around the moon, it became clear that neither the base nor the ship were about to enter into an intimate relationship without our encouragement. Zalva's second moon proved to be a huge barren rock that was entirely unattractive to the mining corporations yet highly sought after by the Precian nobility. It was dotted with pompous palace architecture: The entire moon was like a gated community for the cream of the Precian Empire. Brainiac kept reporting that we were being tracked by ground batteries, but no one dared open fire. The Grand Arbiter *Intrepid* had guaranteed our security.

"I have discovered a large area that contains no settlements or buildings. Flora and fauna are likewise absent. The signal is reading the strongest from the center of the location. Transmitting the area to your visors now." Brainiac modeled an excellent projection of the moon on the second lap and filled it with as much detail as possible.

"This is called the Barrens," the adviser explained, having carefully studied the map. "It is a bit of a local natural reserve at the moment. At one time, various attempts were made to build on this territory, but for various reasons it was not possible to complete the work."

"Candidate site number one," I reasoned. "We'll touch down in the center. Brainiac, send the cryptosaur to scout. We don't need to run into any strangers right now."

"Roger. Executing orders." The orbship banked sharply and plummeted to the moon's surface. A slight vibration of the floor indicated that the rhino had disembarked. One of the screens began to broadcast the surface through the eyes of the cryptosaur. Gray stone and dust as far as the eye could see. The atmosphere analysis showed a complete absence of oxygen. Nothing extraordinary or unusual.

"Landing zone is clear." Brainiac reported after a minute. The marine was running around the wasteland in circles, looking for potential enemies. There was no one.

"Let's go. Adviser, will you be joining us?"

"Indubitably! I would be happy to show you the places where

I spent my youth. Every rock here is like an old friend." The desire to be useful vied with the Precian's excitement and eagerness.

There was no particular reason to leave the ship, but I was impatient to try out the new armor suit. Brainiac did not land *Warlock* entirely, allowing me to glide down to the surface from a five-meter height. The adviser did not lag behind, but it was evident that he had a hard time, and this was alarming.

Recalling the pretentious castles of the local rich, I asked for the sake of interest:

"Do you have a 'Xanadu' here too?"

"Sorry, what?" the adviser did not understand my terrene vocabulary.

"I mean, a place to rest. A palace," I explained, feeling uncomfortable.

"If you mean…an extra-planetary…residence, then…yes." The adviser sounded short of breath. "But for the most part…only my mother lives here at the moment. She is…she is always throwing parties…living the high…life."

"That is exactly what I meant," I grunted, wishing to get away from the topic of someone else's wealth. It seemed the Precian picked up on my embarrassment because a guffaw cut through his panting.

"You, Surgeon, are a human…and you see things from a human point of view. Humans boast and show off…their wealth, so you think…that this place is just a bunch of creatures competing in luxury. This is not true. The emperor cares…about the welfare of his people. For us to build a manor…and equip it with advanced innovations is not so expensive…Consequently, there is nothing to be proud of…The other factor is that not everyone is…allowed…to settle here. This…is a privilege that must be earned…Only the Precian…who can climb…to that point on his own, earns the…right to live on the moon…" The adviser nodded to the top of a nearby hill, catching his breath. "That is the 'Peak of Valor,' the central point of the Barrens…You need to climb up there…alone, using a lowly D-class suit. Do not think that it is easy for us…Even three hundred years ago…quite a few Precians would die…here…Now the test of valor takes place once a month…It is monitored and insured…Yet still, some…die. Those who are weak in spirit feel death…almost immediately…The strong have time to reach the peak."

"Why?" I asked surprised. "What's so deadly here?"

"No one knows." The adviser was pausing ever more frequently, his movements slowing down. "The barrens…have an op…pressive effect on all the races. A team of our scientists surveyed the crust…throughout the territory at a depth of one…kilometer but never found anything. No…radiation, no emissions…no mys…terious fields. The Barrens do not tolerate the weak. They checked using members of other races…as well. Qualians, Vraxis, and even Anorxian synthoids all…experience the same symptoms—shortness of breath…dizziness, loss of consciousness and death. However, Pyrrhenians…Delvians and all the others are completely unaffected by the Barrens…Like humans…Such is the phen…ome..non…"

"Are you okay?" I grew worried. "Maybe you should return to the ship…" The last thing I needed was to have an Imperial

Adviser die on my watch.

"Do not worry," the adviser grinned with exertion. "I am here…because of my job. An imperial order: The weak…have no place in the management of the empire, all the advisers…are tested three…times a year. I can't boast that I'm used to it—it is difficult every time…like the first…but there's no cause for concern."

"Your scientists are a bunch of lazy nerds!" *Warlock*'s engineer came on the comms. "There can be no enlightenment without sweat and perseverance! There is a void at a depth of 1.5 kilometers below the surface. My scanner's power is not enough to establish its full dimensions but the area seems to have active protection. Nature is extremely creative, but it could not create this without sentient help."

"Your ship and crew are…a true treasure," the adviser almost whispered. "How lucky you are! The empire…thanks you for this vital information. We will…survey this area further."

"Let's go to the 'Peak of Valor.'" I pointed to the hill. "We'll see what's up there."

I was forced to help the adviser. The Precian tried his hardest, but the closer we came to the top of the hill the more jumbled his movements became and the more his step faltered. The cryptosaur kept watch over the perimeter of the Barrens, scaring away any real or potential witnesses, so I decided to solve the problem on my own. Despite the proud Precian's objections, I grabbed him by his slender armpits and activated my thrusters hauling him straight to the top. As soon as I landed, my companion went limp, fainting. This was the last thing I needed!

"Brainiac, extract him!" I ordered, activating the recovery mode on the Precian's armor. In the blink of an eye, *Warlock* appeared above our heads. The orbship descended smoothly and gradually until instead of setting down on the stony surface...it passed straight through and went on descending! Before my eyes, the vessel was submerging into the stone, as if there was nothing there! I stood gaping from a distance of one meter, the ground beneath my feet quite firm...

"Brainiac, ascend two meters and hover in position. Open the hatch!"

Grabbing the unconscious adviser in my arms, I jumped inside the orbship in one leap, having noticed that the stones under the ship did not differ from those anywhere else in the Barrens. Either this was some high-quality camouflage or this is what Brainiac was talking about when he said that the orbship was the key to entering the base. But there was no time to test this theory right now. We had to save the Precian. The last thing my pirate's status needed was having a Precian adviser die while in my care. No one would bother one bit about the reasons he'd kicked the bucket on my ship. The hatch closed, and before I could even give the order to leave, the health indicator on the adviser's suit changed from red to green...and after a few seconds went out completely. The Precian regained consciousness; he seemed perfectly fine. It did not take him much time to understand what had happened.

"It is time to tender my resignation," the adviser remarked wryly and with an effort threw back his helmet. He was unable to move. Dark blue circles had formed under the eyes so that, with the rest of his Precian appearance, he looked a bit like a plucked turkey that had managed to escape death at the last moment. Brainiac took pity on our guest and without being ordered to, applied a restorative injection to the adviser's neck. His eyes brightened, the dark circles disappeared, and his skin regained its healthy bluish tint.

"*Warlock*'s hull insulates from the effects of this place," I guessed the reason for the Precian's quick recovery. "Brainiac, extract the cryptosaur. It is time for us to visit the Uldans. A kilogram of raq to anyone who guesses where the entrance to the base is."

"Cap'n, did you see how we passed through the stone?" The engineer dangled his head into the deck. "Wasn't that a thing, eh?"

"I am being asked this question by a talking two-handed snake-engineer who works alongside a four-handed orangutan and transforming rhino onboard a flying balloon ship?" I asked sarcastically. "And yet, it's not a bad question at all. The Uldans are a real fairy tale!"

"We are also Uldans," Brainiac spoke up for his crew. "But the information available to us is not enough to scientifically explain how one solid body can pass through another without breaking the bonds of the molecular lattice. This cannot be camouflage either. I already ran a soil analysis."

"You spent a hundred thousand years with Warlock on Blood Island. Much has changed during that time. Is the cryptosaur back on board? Excellent. Begin the descent. Start with a meter per second, then gradually increase the speed. Let's see what these space fairies have in store for us."

There was no objection. *Warlock*'s contact with the Peak of Valor went unnoticed in the ship. All of the systems went on functioning as usual and the hull sensors reported no pressure. Brainiac plunged the orbship halfway in, waited a few seconds, as if gathering his courage, and then plunged us into the stone completely. Descending the first hundred meters caused no problems whatsoever. It was as if the ship were moving through empty space. The only downside was that we were blind—the screens showed nothing but solid stone all around us.

We moved on in complete silence, afraid that a single word would jinx our luck. This game is a game and all, but my adrenaline and excitement from the descent into uncertainty grew steadily so that when a system notification popped up before me, I started from the tension…

Mission accomplished: Treasure Hunter. Reward: Next quest in chain.

New mission available: Treasure Hunter. Part 2. Enter the base's command center and gain access to the mainframe.

Our internment in the moon's crust ended unexpectedly and was accompanied by a loud exhalation from the adviser. Before and below us stretched the Uldan base in all its glory. The lights had gone on working without a hitch during the intervening hundred millennia, so we could regard the panorama before us in full. From above, the base resembled an integrated circuit, beautifully precise in its layout, but as soon as we descended some more, the flat grid acquired an unimaginable verticality. Intricate designs intertwined, penetrating the space in all directions. The tall spires and steeples resembled the Zatrathi ships I had seen. They were just as ungainly, spiky and odd to the modern eye. Brainiac made several attempts to chart a route through the architectural jumble of glass and shiny metal, but was forced to give up. It would be impossible to navigate through this thicket.

"There is a dock a hundred meters below us. We'll land there." I ordered, deciding to act. I had already understood the most important thing—the base's command center was located diametrically across from where we had entered. I imagine this was done to force the player to take in the designers' work. My hunch was that it wouldn't take more than 2–3 minutes to fly there in my armor suit—assuming I could pilot it well. And since I wasn't sure I could pilot it that well, I decided to try and render a 3D map of the base first.

"Brainiac, is there a way to survey the full base? I'd like to have all the info we can get. If we can generate a map that includes as much detail as possible, our job will be a lot easier."

"The orbship is equipped with four reconnaissance drones. They can fly around the base and survey it. We can use their data to render a 3D map. Shall I activate them?"

"Send two. Have them fly in a circle. Adviser, I'm afraid you will have to remain aboard *Warlock*. The local radiation can kill you."

The Precian's sour face was so eloquent that I felt like

---

cheering him up:

"I will stream to the ship, so you will see everything that I see. The base will be studied."

"Drones have been launched. Estimated time of flight...Warning! Attack detected!"

Warlock immediately readied her entire arsenal of beam cannons, but there were no targets to be found. The Uldan base remained below us in a deep slumber.

"Brainiac, project the drones' video recordings to the screen," I ordered. The two recordings were almost equally useless because they had been recorded from the drones themselves. They emerged from the orbship, made a pass around the ship calibrating their flight modes to the local environmental conditions, traveled a few meters from the ship and then the recordings broke off. One more recording was available from *Warlock* herself. Both drones were visible on the screen. After calibration, they scattered in different directions and crossed a trigger field that had remained utterly undetected until that point. The trigger field flickered, revealing its existence, and then went out having done its bit. Two plasma shots were fired from opposite sides of the base, aimed directly at the drones. The explosions that followed didn't leave so much as a piece of plastic. Brainiac figured out where the fire came from and highlighted cannons all over the base. I couldn't help but whistle—the chances of crossing the base and not catching several dozen salvos from those guns was about zero point zero.

"Cap'n, I have some bad news for you," the engineer said

pensively, assuming the role of Captain Obvious. "We can't fly here."

My frustrated sigh was also my answer to this. It looked like we had a fight ahead of us, and to say no would be equivalent to losing my reward.

"We have landed. Attention! The docking module has sent a connection request."

"Accept it. Set the cryptosaur to battle readiness. Activate the droids. We'll have to fight our way to the command center."

"You are going to fight the Uldans?" the adviser gasped with surprise.

"No. I'm going to fight the ones who captured the base and have managed to survive here for the last hundred thousand years in hibernation. I assume they will be the best warriors that the Vraxis have."

CHAPTER TWO

THE HULL OPENED GENTLY, forming an exit to the dock, which was well illuminated and ended after ten meters in an imposing steel door. Having learned my lesson by losing my recon drones, I sent a droid ahead this time. I could spare one easily. Fortunately, the droid reached the door without incident and stopped, waiting for further instructions.

"Brainiac, have you connected to the base's local network?" I held a high opinion of my ship's computer, but this time I was getting ahead of myself.

"Negative. There is no terminal in the dock. Attempts at establishing a remote connection have failed. The network has complex, multi-layered security which uses encryption algorithms that are unknown to me. I have not been able to detect any vulnerabilities."

This was an unpleasant bit of news. It would be foolish to send out another reconnaissance drone. All the unexplored areas around us harbored the threat of respawn or total destruction. The developers had not created this base for robots and drones to go strolling around it. The earlier loss had taught me that much.

"Brainiac, recall the droid. I'll go myself."

"I'm coming with you," said the adviser, his face a mask of determination. "And do not try to dissuade me. This is perhaps my one chance to touch eternity. Moreover, I am bound to the planetary spirit, so death for me will not be an obstacle. The emperor expects me to bring back information!"

"All right, but on one condition. If you lose consciousness, you will return to the ship." It is foolish to argue with NPCs whose actions are subject to strict algorithms, but I didn't want to have to drag him around either. "Brainiac, assign two droids to escort the adviser. Make sure they stick with him and protect him."

Automatons #29 and #30 took up positions next to the adviser, and I mentally said goodbye to my property. There was no chance that they'd survive, but I had no other choice. I can buy more droids, whereas my rapport with the Precian had to be earned.

"Really, it isn't worth the trouble. After all, you are not obliged," the adviser complained sluggishly, but a notification told me that I had done the right thing.

Your rapport with the Third Adviser of the Precian Emperor has grown. Current Rapport: 3.

"Stay behind me. Heed my orders. Do not run ahead," I ordered, arming my blaster. There's no time for formalities during combat, my orders had to be executed immediately. Otherwise, even my desire to grind rapport with the adviser would not save him. I'd 'accidentally' shoot him while fighting off an enemy and continue the expedition without him.

The Precian seemed to understand everything and agreed without saying anything. I entered the docking area slowly expecting an attack any second, but nothing happened. After waiting another couple of seconds, I waved to the adviser. He hesitated before leaving the ship, perhaps worried like I was that he would faint, but after a second his boots touched the hard floor.

"Looks like there's nothing to worry about, Captain Surgeon," he said with a sigh of relief. "I believe that the walls of the base block the effects of the Barrens."

Delighted with the good news, the Precian rushed towards me, but I cautiously raised my hand:

"Maintain a distance of five meters. Get ready, I'm about to open the door."

Without waiting any further, I crossed the docking area. Behind me came the noise of blasters being cocked. Brainiac unloaded the droids to provide fire support and now *Warlock*'s exit hatch looked like a bristling porcupine. I really hoped that there was nothing on the other side of the door because otherwise I'd be in the line of fire between the droids and the enemy. The massive door to the Uldan base opened smoothly, soaring upwards. I remained on the threshold, staring into the darkness. The light from the docking area ended abruptly at my feet, jealously guarding its every photon from the voracious darkness before me. It was odd—during our overflight, we could clearly see the panorama of the base and the lighting working fine all over it, but this building was entirely dark. Taking a step forward, I plunged into the viscous gloom. Before my eyes could adjust, the armor suit automatically snapped on its built-in floodlights and I involuntarily shut my eyes for a moment.

The lights turned out to be useless, however. Instead of illuminating the room, the cone of light encountered the darkness—and the darkness absorbed it. Squatting down, I shined the light flush against the floor and swallowed nervously. My spatial sensor managed to render a 3D model of the chamber we were in quite admirably: The floor, walls, and ceiling were covered with a thick carpet of organic matter. The spot I was staring at was an unpleasant brown color and covered with mucus, as if we were in the stomach of some leviathan. Above me, I could see tendrils or tentacles dangling from the ceiling, which, judging by every horror movie I had seen, meant trouble. I transmitted the picture of the room to the adviser still in the docking module.

"Any idea what this is?"

"None whatsoever. We know little about the Uldans, but I can say for certain that they were highly-organized and salubrious creatures. This…room…is not suitable for work. It is difficult to imagine that this is the product of one of their technologies."

"Maybe this is all for show—to scare away uninvited guests?" I proposed a theory I didn't believe in at all. "Brainiac? What do you say?"

"A visual inspection of the premises suggests a hypothetical approximation with a probability of sixty percent that, given the presence of…"

"Can we do this without the unnecessary jargon?! Clearly and to the point, please!"

"The organic layer covering the room resembles the uterine tissue. The data I have on hand indicate that the Uldans would not use living tissue as a construction material. This was entirely out of keeping with their worldview and as the adviser pointed out, they were extremely sensitive about cleanliness."

"Cap'n, I have a bad feeling about this," the engineer interrupted. "Maybe we should look for other options?"

Personally, I agreed with the snake. I suspected something was wrong the moment I saw this…this 'creep' (to borrow a term from an old classic) where it wasn't supposed to be. But my excitement did not permit me to retreat. If this were reality, Zalva's second moon would already be growing small in *Warlock*'s rearview mirrors. But this is a game where you just need to grit your teeth and try at least once.

I gently stepped onto the floor before me. It was indeed organic instead of the typical plastic. The creep did not react to my touch. Squatting again, I prodded the creep with the barrel of my blaster, pushing it a couple of centimeters into the organic carpet. Again nothing.

"Adviser, please step back to the ship," I asked and fired a couple plasma shots at the floor. The armor suit's sensors identified the ensuing smell as burning flesh, but I did not wait for the consequences. The organism was alive, but silent and still.

IN SEARCH OF THE ULDANS

Brainiac's request and the next salvo of plasma at the floor, walls and ceiling, again had no effect—the base did not respond to my aggression.

"I'm going in!" I announced, more for my benefit than my crew's. Standing on a living organism was unpleasant, like on a slimy, plush carpet. Wishing to feel a hard floor under my feet again, I stepped onto the spot that the plasma had scorched. It was a typical steel floor of all facilities in Galactogon. I allowed the adviser to return and as soon as he stepped into the room with me a system notification appeared:

You are the first player to visit the Nahami base.

Scenario activated: Uninvited Guest. Scenario requirements have been met.

Have a nice game!

"This is a historic event!" said the Precian reverently, sliding his flashlight along the walls. "Never before has a Precian been so close to…"

The adviser did not have time to finish.

"Cap'n, it's a trap!" screamed my engineer. Fleshy tendrils dropped from the ceiling, closing the passage and entombing the adviser and me in the creep. I readied my blasters but didn't have time to start shooting: The creep covering the floor began to move and I almost lost my balance. The suit's inertial blockers helped me keep my feet, but my stomach sank from the feeling of free fall. Another wall of organic matter shot up between me and the adviser, blocking my sight of him.

"Brainiac, report!" I yelled, firing wildly with my blasters and causing a local mini-Armageddon. The bars forming my cage scattered in burnt lumps, but new ones immediately grew to fill their place. After the tenth time, it became clear that I wasn't going to shoot my way out.

"The entire base is moving. Every part of it is transforming and shifting in all three spatial axes. The purpose of the transformation is incomprehensible. I have launched *Warlock*. The dock is no more. This was an ambush!" If Brainiac weren't a ship AI, he would no doubt be panicking by now.

"What is the adviser's status?"

"He is alive. I am able to track his movement. You are moving in different directions. There seems to be no passage between you any longer. The sector you are in is surrounded by a forcefield with unknown characteristics. It prevents us from reaching you. Attention! The base has stopped moving."

I felt this last observation myself, since the floor had suddenly stopped sliding beneath me. I fired another shot and the smell of burning meat again enveloped everything around me. This time my cage did not regrow, freeing me. It remained as pitch black as before around me, though I was comfortable in the armor suit. A 3D image of the room I was in appeared before me. This time there was an open corridor leading out of it—and in this corridor, there was a mob of living creatures heading in my direction. The suit's sensors managed to render various details of the swarming mass: sharp, thin limbs, a thicket of antennae and jointed appendages. I had encountered the Vraxis before and now had no doubts—a horde of insects was coming

---

to greet me. I snapped both blasters into combat mode and prepared to return the hospitality. Maybe it wouldn't be as spectacular as the reception they had planned for me, but I'd do my best. As soon as I got a lock on a target, green pulsating plasma flew in the direction of the unexpected guests. Meanwhile, I felt a surge of adrenaline. This was the first time I had used the legendary blasters that the Precian Emperor had gifted me. The power was unimaginable! Each shot unloaded two or three insects from the system resources, turning them into flickering crates of loot. There were no remains—only more and more lucre and the blasters' slowly growing XP bar. A couple minutes of fire only increased the bar by a fraction of one percent. The insects had nowhere to go in the narrow corridor, so they surged forward to quickly get to me and crush me in their endless stream. There was neither counterfire, nor defensive maneuvers—just endless bodies barreling down on me. At the moment, my blasters were winning however.

I took a breath and changed powercells. The new suit had its blasters mounted on the shoulder pads, which freed my hands. The disadvantage was the limited aiming radius and activation time. Deactivating the built-in blasters, I removed the prize blaster I'd gotten from the Zatrathi. While the main ones are activated, I will have time to use it as a club. Plus, I feel better when my weapons are in my hands.

The torrent of insects temporarily dried up, and I contacted the ship:

"Brainiac, give me a sitrep."

"We lost both of the droids assigned to guard the adviser.

I'm sending you the recording now."

"And the adviser himself?"

"He is alive but isolated by a forcefield. I cannot get in touch with him. I am sending you a recording of your movements which includes your current locations."

The adviser had found himself in the same mess as me. His droid guards tried to hold back the insects, but their B-class blasters could not cope with the onslaught. The Vraxis had torn the iron guards to shreds and captured the Precian. Or that's what I assumed. The recordings ended with the droids' destruction.

The other file I received was no less interesting: Brainiac located me in a spire which was equally distant from the base's center and the adviser. After I finish conferring with my crew, I'll have to decide where to go: Rescue the adviser or head for the mainframe. Although, to continue on without the adviser was not an option. It was his appearance that launched the scenario.

"Brainiac, have you analyzed the forcefield around the ship? Can you disrupt it?"

"Oh we analyzed it all right, there's just not much to say," the engineer spoke up. "It's holding us nice and tight. Its generator is in the base. We can't bust through it with anything. I have already tried. So you'll have to figure it out on your own somehow. You'll help us out too in the process."

I grinned. Whereas Brainiac bore this fiasco stoically, the snake spoke for everyone. Wishing the ship good luck, I scanned the room I was in one more time. Nothing. No niches, no doors, no windows—just the ubiquitous creep covering every

IN SEARCH OF THE ULDANS

surface with itself. After the firefight, the corridor remained clear and offered nothing of interest. For the hell of it, I shot at the walls of the room without much hope of finding a secret area. Everyone knows that the goodies aren't located at the dungeon entrance. And this Uldan base is nothing other than ye olde dungeon of yore.

"Stan, I need a summary of the Vraxis race. Species, stats, abilities, weapons. Short and to the point please."

"Understood. Regarding my search for the player named Eine: Please note, Master, that there are more than a thousand players with that name in Galactogon."

"The player named Eine is a collector of rare Galactogon items. There shouldn't be many like him."

"You are correct, there is only one player named Eine that matches this profile. The search is complete. All available information has been sent to your PDA. I have started the next process. I hope you recovery continues well."

I decided to acquaint myself with the collector trying to steal my ship at some later time. The first flickering loot crate dissolved in my hands, rewarding me with a bone token. An exact replica of a sheriff's star from the ancient American Wild West. The Zatrathi dropped these kinds of tokens too, only metal ones. Even back at the orbital station, these tokens seemed strange to me: They came with no description, no system warning, no item counter. All they did was take up inventory slots and weight. And now, here again, I was staring at 250 or so bone tokens without any indication of what I could use them for. Stan ran a quick search through the fora, but found nothing.

Either they were useless flair or they were so valuable that everyone stayed quiet about them.

I contacted my ship again.

"Brainiac, have you analyzed the information we downloaded from the Zatrathi? Did you find anything of value?"

"I received no such process request," the ship replied predictably, assuming a defensive tone. Like any good crew, in the absence of direct orders, mine preferred to loiter and lollygag.

"In that case, get on it. As I recall, you downloaded the menu from the cafeteria, so systematize everything that you managed to collect about the Zatrathi. What they eat, what they drink, how they get sick, how long they live. If you find something useful for us, send it over to the engineer and see if he can do anything with it. Just because I'm not on board doesn't mean that you can relax. I want everything organized and cataloged by the time I return. Any questions?"

"There are a couple," spoke up the engineer. "If we don't find anything useful, can I launch my prototypes?"

I took a deep breath, smothering my annoyance. What a Snorlax this snake is! Without my orders, no one takes any initiative, and I got so carried away with the game that I completely forgot about updating the ship. I don't know whom to thank for the hint, but this is just in time.

"I'm granting permission to upgrade the ship. You can use up to a third of the available raq."

"Any priorities? Weapons, defensive systems, speed, auxiliary functions, ergonomics? I have a lot of stuff in the works."

"Speed. That's the most important thing right now. The Zatrathi caught up with us as if we were standing still."

"Roger that, Cap'n! I have a couple ideas. Once I'm done, we'll win all the space race prizes. Over and out!"

The first twenty meters of my journey down the corridor brought an unpleasant discovery: My energy consumption was exceeding all imaginable calculations. Each meter of hallway came with great difficulty. Tentacles kept shooting out from the ceiling like tendrils of snot. One of them caught me and jerked me up like a feather, ignoring the weight of my armor. I had to constantly shoot back and dodge, dive to the ground, rise to my feet and move on to the next little bit of hallway. A complete sweep of the ceiling bought me some breathing room. The attacks stopped, but not for long. In exchange I got to watch as the creep grew back over its territory. It all started with the floor. It buckled, surged and sent a wave of organic matter shooting up the walls. Once the creep had covered the walls, it moved on to the ceiling. Tendrils of the stuff intertwined, united and filled in until the room's fauna had returned to its original state. I calculated my energy reserves and decided to experiment. What if I completely cut the creep from the center? If I was in a spire, it would have no connection to the rest of the organism in the base. Maybe the creep will die and I'll have some time before it grows back from inside the facility. No sooner said than done! I scorched a good two meters of the corridor, preventing the snotty organism from reuniting with the part I had cut off. As soon as the last clot of plasma severed the organic matter, the isolated part of it stopped. The mysterious organism in the rest of the base throbbed but didn't start regrowing the cleared area. Perhaps it was gathering its strength. Meanwhile, the isolated creep began shrinking and curling into itself until at last it formed an ugly, pulsating cocoon. The cleared section of corridor had excellent lighting, and I saw with my own eyes how something stirred inside the cocoon. It seemed that I have just prodded the mysterious organism that had seized the base into reproducing itself.

The cocoon grew rapidly in size. By the time it came to term, I was ready. The cannons took their places on my shoulders, ready in one instant to turn the creature into a charred nugget. Were this IRL, I would not have waited long enough to acquaint myself with the newborn but in VR we were accustomed to dull the instinct of self-preservation for the sake of profit. Experience, loot, knowledge, quests. Everything that can be sold for real or in-game money, always keeping our daily bread in mind. All that remained us was the most valuable, but unsellable thing. Emotions. Strong and real, albeit generated in an artificial world.

The cocoon twitched one more time and opened like a flower, spitting something in my direction. My inertial dampeners howled, but withstood the impact of the warrior that came slamming into me. Quick and purposeful, he did not resemble a helpless newborn at all. Deftly dodging the plasma from my blasters, he began frenetically shredding my armor with his sharp claws—and quite effectively too. I had nothing to protect me from physical damage except for the armor suit itself, and with every passing second I felt more and more like the last

IN SEARCH OF THE ULDANS

Vienna sausage in a tin that a meth-head was trying to eat after a 48 hour binge. The creature attacked relentlessly with terrible purpose, which was its downfall.

Having coped with my initial shock and realizing the uselessness of shooting the thing, I opened my inventory. Here it is. Its time has come. My first piece of loot in Galactogon. A present from the bettors for meeting their conditions—one of my two ZPEF-Manipulators. Jokingly referred to by the gaming community as the pacifier, this incredibly useful device looked much like an ordinary police baton. And yet, a single manipulator's mini-tractor beam was enough: Squealing amusingly and jerking its limbs helplessly, the warrior dangled in midair, allowing me to examine him at my leisure.

I was utterly ignorant of insects, but even in my inexperienced view, this little critter didn't have much in common with the current citizens of the Vraxis Empire. Stan sifted through the Galactogon insect reference wikis and found nothing like it. Four upper limbs with three elbow joints attached to an unnaturally thin body at an angle of ninety degrees to each other. Three legs provided stability and instantaneous movement in any direction, and a freely rotating head endowed the creature with frightening mobility and awareness.

"Can you talk?" I asked, already knowing the answer. Foot soldiers had no need of this ability. There was no use for it. All the Vraxis were ruled by their queen. And she saw and felt what was happening through each of her subjects. A convenient way to ensure social order, what can you say. The main benefit was that all orders were executed without questions or objections, no matter how suicidal.

Bringing the warrior closer to me, I said as clearly as I could:

"I am not your enemy. The war between the Uldans and the Vraxis ended ninety thousand years ago. My ship is a trophy. The Uldans are extinct, while the Vraxis thrive and prosper. There is no reason to fight. Allow me to reach the command center, pick up my Precian and leave the base. In exchange, I will report that you are alive to your current queen. She will send help. I am not an enemy."

My blasters erupted and I lowered the manipulators—all that remained of the ancient creature was a flickering crate. I was talking to myself. All that time, the insect did not give up trying to escape from my tractor beam. Soldiers are not called upon to think, their job is to obey their orders. There are others who think for them.

Scenario update: Uninvited Guest.
You have cleared 0.01% of the base from its invaders.

I read the message with a grin. The base-clearing mission wasn't meant for a lone player. Without a party and a ton of powercells there was nothing to do here. Frustrated, I reached out for the loot crate and picked up the golden token. The only difference to the ones I'd gotten from the Zatrathi was the dark border.

The creep did not dare try to seize the corridor again, and I was able to appreciate the devs' plan. The walls, the floor and ceiling consisted of irregular segments, interlinked with clockwork precision. My spatial sensor did not detect boundaries between the segments and perceived the room as one whole. Visually, however, the segments had clear boundaries and differed from each other in their patterns, finish and even material. The strange organism that had occupied the base could reconfigure it at will, separating and recombining the facilities as it saw fit. Now I understood how I had been separated from the adviser: The dock we had landed in had been taken apart and reassembled. If so, then it was useless to search for armories or warehouses filled with outlandish items. The loot in them would have long since been mixed throughout the base.

I was about to get upset when an interesting detail drew my attention. Before the transformation of the base, I had been in the landing dock. After the rearrangement, the segment in which I had been had moved along with its walls and ceiling. Now that I had cleared the creep from it, a barely noticeable inscription had appeared, scrawled hastily right there on the wall. I came closer. The symbols were unfamiliar, but this did not prevent me from understanding that they constituted only the end of the message. Someone had clumsily written this in a hurry and perhaps with multiple interruptions. Out of curiosity, I tried to scorch a furrow into the wall with my blaster, but nothing happened. Hoping that the inscription said something more substantial than 'Phileros is a eunuch,' I contacted my ship. I needed to know whether the first part of the message was located where the Precian had been.

"Brainiac, what's the status of the adviser?"

"There have been no changes to his status. The data of his armor suit show that he has not moved since the base's metamorphosis."

"Keep monitoring him. And if anything changes, let me know."

Now I sent an image of the strange inscription to Brainiac:

"Can you read what is written here?"

"You're into graffiti?" the snake popped up. "This particular sequence of numbers does not make sense, Captain."

"So these are numbers?"

"Yes, these are Uldan numbers. Uldans use a digital alphabet like this one. You humans are used to positional number systems. One, two, one hundred. It is frighteningly inconvenient. We prefer a non-positional adaptive system, tied to the position of the stars relative to each other. It is especially convenient when talking about galactic coordinates or information that must be kept secret. Every thousand years, the system is updated. New symbols are assigned to new meanings and everything started anew. To understand which millennium's numbers are written here, you need to find the beginning of the message. This is but the end. This fragment may be translated as '3' in your language as well as '10' and even '98989.'"

"How interesting," I said, fascinated. "The first half of the message should be where the adviser is right now."

"Perhaps, but let's not celebrate prematurely, Cap'n," the serpent latched onto me. "Even if you find the beginning, we're not sure that we can decrypt the data. A hundred thousand years have passed. The ship's memory banks contain the key for its

---

millennium. We downloaded the current coordinates of the planets from your ship and corrected our data. But if this inscription was made in an earlier millennium, then we will not be able to translate it without its key."

"Why the hell would someone even come up with a system like that?" I objected.

"With all due respect the system is very convenient, but yes, requires one to get used to it and receive updated keys—once every thousand years. At small values, the positional form is good, but when it is necessary to calculate a distance of hundreds of thousands of light years to jump to a specific point in space without error, our system works much better."

"So there's no point in even trying to collect the full inscription?" My enthusiasm evaporated, replaced by another disappointment.

"Why? Once upon a time there were drives that automatically received updated keys. If the message is dated to an earlier millennium than we have in the databases, there is always the chance to find a drive from that epoch and get the necessary data. You should look around the base if you get the chance. All I can say is that this inscription seems very much like some coordinates."

"And what could be there?" I asked, referring to the encrypted location.

"Why anything at all! A ship, a planet or all the treasures of the galaxy! Use your imagination, Cap'n! Imagine a dying Uldan, with his last breath and at the cost of tremendous effort scrawling these symbols on the wall in the hope that we will uncover them…This must be something of worth at the very least…Anyway, Cap'n, you're keeping me from my work. I am about to improve our ship's speed by an order of magnitude and here you are with your archaeology."

"Over and out," I snapped. The snake was out of line naturally, but it really was silly to get distracted right now. I had photographed the inscription so it wouldn't be going anywhere and who knew how much time I had to complete the scenario I was in. What if the adviser will be devoured in twenty minutes while I'm sitting here meditating on numbers?

Nevertheless, before moving on, I made sure to get my prize. Walking up to one of the walls of the hallway, I grabbed onto a thick segment of piping running along its length and tore it off. A pair of simple crimps with my hands and I became the proud owner of a weighty two-meter lance, suitable for stabbing enemies. In order to avoid wasting energy, I decided I'd play as a medieval knight for a bit. As soon as a tentacle appeared, I stuck it with my lance, piercing it. The wounded tentacle slithered out of sight, allowing me to move a couple meters down the hall.

Using this simple technique, I reached the next room. There were no significant differences from the first one here—the same creep carpeting the floor, the ceiling and the walls. The only difference was that it didn't try to attack me. At the far side of the room, I saw two more corridors leading in opposite directions. I was drawn to them, figuring that they must lead to sweet loot and lucre, but overruling my desire to turn off my path I decided to keep moving forward. Ruthlessly scorching a broad swath in the organic matter, I separated the room from the main base.

IN SEARCH OF THE ULDANS

The separated creep acted as before: Once again, it shrank and shriveled into a cocoon, only this time one that was twice as large. The four-meter colossus rested against the ceiling, expanding with every beat of its pulse. I aimed at it with my blasters and fired. I wasn't about to let this monster hatch when it was ready. Lumps of the cocoon scattered across the room, spitting out three warriors who were not quite ready to be born. Their transparent bodies had not yet acquired their chitinous armor and the light passed through them like x-rays. The heads of all three twitched more reflexively than consciously, but it seemed to me that this frenetic motion was their fighting spirit not allowing them to die in peace.

I didn't get a chance to enjoy their death animations for long. The bits of creep that had scattered from the explosion began to slink back together. There was an unpleasant crunch as the congealing mass of organic matter crushed the warriors' bodies. Less than a minute later, a huge pulsing cocoon stood in the room, whole and ready to spit horror at me.

I shot it again. The number of creatures produced was the same. A countdown counter appeared before my eyes marking 90 seconds. I used the time to rewatch the video of the first battle. Back then I hadn't noticed where the warriors came from, and I needed to remedy that. The video showed how the cocoon had swelled, its upper part opened with a loud bang, catching the eye and distracting me from the important detail—the warriors had actually emerged from the cocoon's lower portion. The end of the recording. Bunch of goddamn sleight of hand artists, those devs.

GALACTOGON BOOK TWO

The third time around I didn't rush things and studied the pulsating cocoon in detail. Three conspicuous spots darkened the segment near the floor. I walked around the cocoon. The spots followed after me. Either the cocoon or the creatures inside of it could sense me and were aggroing already. Well, let's try it differently. I pointed my manipulator at the central hole, and aimed my blasters on either side and waited. A second. Another. The cocoon twitched for the last time, and out of the corner of my eye I noticed a bud beginning to open. I forced myself to keep my eyes fixed on the dark spots and ignore the fancy show above. Everything was decided in a split second, although it felt like time had stopped. The lower slit flashed like a camera's shutter, firing three charged torpedoes to meet an inglorious death. I set my blasters to autofire and easily turned the two warriors into shimmering loot crates. The third one I caught with my manipulator. Born for valor and glory, the warrior squealed in protest. I slammed him into the ceiling several times for good measure. The insect went limp, but not dead, surprising me with its vitality. Taking the two golden stars, I decided not to kill the creature. He'll make for some poor form of booty to make up for the lack of lucre on this base. He can eat flies in *Warlock*'s cargo holds until I sell him on the black market. Surely there are some entomologist-collectors here in Galactogon. I bet the same Eine would be interested in this specimen.

Summoning *Warlock*, I asked my crew to assess the viability of keeping our hostage. Brainiac meticulously examined the sharp limbs, but, in the end, reluctantly agreed that my idea was feasible enough. Having dealt with this question, I decided to explore the right corridor. It was very short and ended in a barren room, empty, like the head of its designer. No inscriptions, no secret compartments, nothing to plunder. My internal kleptomaniac, so carefully cultivated and nurtured over my gaming career, couldn't help but feel a deep disappointment. What kind of game is this anyway, if there's no loot? I even considered becoming a slave trader and filling my holds with insect warriors.

By the time my captive came to and began struggling against the manipulator's beam, I had managed to examine the entire left corridor. I didn't knock the warrior out against the ceiling this time: I prefer to treat my possessions with a bit of care. Dangling the critter in front of me, I secured the manipulator to the front of my armor suit: This would keep the insect in my field of view and free my hands to do other stuff at the same time. Adjusting the distance to three meters, I moved into the corridor with the live weight and prepared for an attack from the air, but everything was quiet. The rabid warrior was waving his limbs frenetically and in the process severing all the tentacles that tried to descend from the ceiling. I took a few steps deep into the corridor and received a system notification:

Scenario updated: Uninvited Guest.
You have cleared 0.04% of the base from its invaders.

A quick calculation suggested that the Uldan base contained about ten thousand such rooms. Each one spawned a warrior, which led me to the sad conclusion that I would not have enough energy to deal with all of them. Even if it takes one shot to kill one enemy, I'd only have enough to turn 70% of the enemies here into golden tokens. And that was the best case scenario. When I considered the worst case, I ordered my ship to self-destruct if it lost contact with me. The last thing I needed was to lose my ship in this place.

The amazing thing was that all it took was me accepting the reality of the matter and it was as if a mountain had fallen from my shoulders. Clearing the base was too much of a task for me.

I activated my suit's thrusters and launched myself a half a meter into the air, getting used to moving along the corridors. It no longer made sense to save energy, but I still had to find the adviser. My captive insect did a good job of clearing my way and I calmly flew deep into the base. Soon the number of alternate paths began to increase and there were even corridors with their own adjacent areas. Unable to resist, I cleared one for the sake of experimentation. Having killed the warrior in there, I was informed that the base was now 0.05% clear. This told me that the percentages did not depend on the size of the room cleared, which was a bit surprising. Reaching the next fork in my path, I understood that I would need some help.

"Brainiac, where should I go next?"

"The beacon shows that you are here," Brainiac sent me an updated map. The red dot indicating my location was in the main building, a couple minutes' flight from the adviser's blue marker. My blasters snapped to combat readiness—the demise of my droids told me that I shouldn't expect a warm welcome. A few turns through a few small rooms—and I flew into a huge chamber, the size of a hall. My spatial sensor could hardly gauge its size. If all the rooms I had previously seen had a height of four meters, the ceiling here was no less than fifty meters overhead, while the rest of the hall stretched away like a football field. I opened the image broadcast by Brainiac. If the scale is correct, this hall occupied more than half of the central base complex. A thousand squealing voices and the rustle of many legs made me start from the map: A swarm of insects was scurrying towards me from the other end of the hall. Before my arrival, the creatures were occupied with some kind of spherical forcefield against the far wall. The adviser was nowhere to be seen, but his marker told me that he was located over there. I had not deactivated my thrusters and quickly soared upwards to look around. The first thing I noticed were two shimmering crates that served as my droids' tombstones—the insects hadn't left so much as a piece of metal. Turning on my floodlights, I flew over to the forcefield. The adviser! Two twisters of energy spiraled from the Precian's hands channeling a spherical shield. Brainiac, who was tracking me through my video stream, reported that the adviser's strength was running out—in the few seconds it took me to assess the situation, his shield had shrunk by a couple of millimeters. He had no more than fifteen minutes left before his shield would collapse.

I took out the second manipulator and lifted the insect closest to me. It bore a passing resemblance to a praying mantis with hypertrophied lower limbs and a disproportionately large head. As soon as I directed my floodlights at it to get a better look, the creature began to twitch and make unpleasant sounds.

Then its compound eyes popped with a wet sound and the insect went limp. The manipulator entered standby mode while the creature was replaced by a loot crate.

The funniest thing was that my suit's floodlights actually gained experience from this kill. An ordinary D-class lamp, which no one thought of upgrading, turned out to be a powerful weapon against the local fauna. Pulling up another mantis, I repeated the execution. From a distance of three meters my floodlights exterminated the next member of the ancient insectoid race in a flash. Delighted, I pulled out the third insect, lifted it and my earlier captive to the maximum height to keep them out of my way and descended to the floor. The bright light of my floodlights illuminated the room. The creatures struggled to absorb the rays of light without any luck. The morass of insects rushing onto me was mercilessly burned by my lamp. I felt like some paladin of the Holy Lamp.

"Adviser, you may remove your shield. I have cleared the premises!" I shouted, actively raking in the flickering loot crates. It looks like the bone tokens would be my only reward on this base. In total, this room yielded four hundred and twenty of them.

"Surgeon?" sounded the adviser's frightened voice and another searchlight beam pierced the gloom.

"In the flesh. Turn off your searchlight. I've taken a prisoner here and the light kills them."

"A prisoner? Where?" The Precian looked up swinging the beam with him. A shimmering crate instantly dropped to the floor from the dead mantis. Maybe this was the game telling me that these insects were not supposed to serve as my loot.

"I apologize on behalf of the Precian Empire," the adviser shrank into himself and shut off the light. "We shall compensate you for your loss. Thank you for saving me from rebirth. It is not the most pleasant procedure."

"What was that forcefield you used? I've never seen that before."

"A personal shield. It is issued to officials of the highest ranks. It is extremely power thirsty, but invaluable in a pinch when you need to wait for help. Unfortunately, it does not last very long."

"You are lucky. Brainiac said you had about fifteen minutes of energy remaining."

"Once the domestic problems of the empire have been resolved, I will be happy to welcome you and your crew on Zalva," the adviser said. "You shall be my cherished guests! I look forward to our conversations about the Uldans."

"Thank you, adviser, I will be glad of that too. And now I have a question for you, where were you when the base completed its metamorphosis? I need the exact location."

"Does that mean that I was right and the base really did transform? Fascinating! Once more, Uldan technology exceeds all expectations!"

"These aren't Uldans. These are their foes." I kicked the living carpet of creep under my feet and nodded at the struggling warrior: "The base has been taken over by some mysterious organism, which spawns these insects. I'm afraid we won't find anything here. Where were you when the metamorphosis began?"

"Let me think…The attack came swiftly. First I ran, then I fell and tumbled… The droids were shooting back as I was backing away and…It seems here, but I'm not sure." The adviser pointed to a place located almost in the center of the room. But he was wrong. I remembered exactly: When the ambush began, the Precian had been standing next to a wall.

"Did the droids move?" I stepped over to my fighters' remains. Two elo powercells, one blaster and one piece of armor—that was all that was left from two A-class pieces of hardware.

"Yes, they were swept away in the onslaught. They were standing elsewhere initially."

"Brainiac?" I had one last option available, but even this failed me. From the ship's perspective, the adviser had not left his initial coordinates, since the distance between us and *Warlock* was too great. Giving the adviser two powercells, I gained some more rapport with him.

"We'll have to clear the hall," I said, assessing the work ahead of us with foreboding. I didn't even want to imagine how big the cocoon in this place would be. It was like the devs had made the room incredibly huge to tell the players: If you want to get the first part of the inscription, you'll have to fight for it. I didn't want to shoot my blasters at the walls, for fear of destroying the inscription, and the creep grew back faster than I could finish. A flight around the giant hall uncovered a small corridor. Straight, long and no more than two meters wide. It was a perfect chokepoint for defending against the enemy's onslaught. There could easily be over a dozen warriors and either they will have to attack one by one or at the same time interfering with each other. Both would suit me fine. The warriors would become excellent targets for two, no, for three blasters. I would hand the manipulator and my prisoner to the adviser. It is unlikely that an NPC of such a rank would fight alongside me.

I still had to decide the most important thing however: What happens if I start cutting off other rooms? Will the cocoons start spawning too? If so, will the warriors come running to me here or will they hang back where their cocoon spawned? Lacking any theory on the matter, I decided to turn to empiricism. The corridor allowed me to defend myself from either side.

"Adviser, I have an important mission for you. Do not lose this specimen. It must be delivered to the ship and studied. Aren't you interested in the anatomy of these ancient warriors?"

I knew what buttons to push. The adviser grabbed the manipulator and prepared to guard the POW. I was sure that he would not have released the warrior even if faced with death. Freed of my captive, I got comfortable in the corridor and burned a broad swath into the creep.

The blaster did not have time to return to its original position before the base started shaking all around us. We barely kept our feet as the floor trembled beneath us. The creep under our feet began to shrivel, contracting to the center of the room and dragging us along. An unpleasant loud rustling filled the whole space as the creep from the rooms I had passed through earlier began to draw into the new cocoon. Goose bumps ran down my back—the small corridor I had chosen seemed to be the link between the organism's brain and body. I pursed my lips in displeasure, anticipating a quick outcome. The cocoon had already reached the ceiling and went on growing in mass and girth. I had no good arguments against such a giant.

"What is this?" whispered the adviser, dumbfounded, as I dragged him from the moving creep to the clean floor. Most of the premises had already been cleared and illuminated by an array of white lights.

"Get in the corridor this second!" I had to drag the adviser by force. Once he was safe, I activated my jet thrusters. I had one piece of business left. The first part of the inscription was to be found on the opposite side of the hall. Once I sent the photo to Brainiac, he announced that the inscription was now complete. I still had to locate the converter, but I could easily accomplish this task in the outside world. Every little part of my body that had any knack for prophecy was screaming that I had completed my mission on the Uldan base and that I needed to get out of here. I flew back to the adviser as quickly as I could. He had remained exactly where I left him—immobilized either by his fear or his curiosity. Transfixed by the action, he neither moved nor heard me. The pulsating cocoon was already fully formed. We had no more than thirty seconds left.

"Adviser, wake up! We have to go!"

This did not jog the Precian from his strange stupor and I hadn't time to be polite. Mentally saying goodbye to all my rapport with the Precian Empire, I snatched the manipulator from the adviser's hands and threw the best right hook I could muster. Amplified by the suit's servomotors, the blow knocked the adviser clean against the wall—where he slumped to the floor. Grabbing his limp body, I aimed the captive warrior down the corridor to clear the dangling creep and rushed in his wake. We did not get very far—the adviser turned out to be more resilient than I expected and came to after a couple of seconds. He twisted in my embrace, blocking my hand, and even my suit's servomotors could not cope with him. Finally I dropped him to the floor and received a notification that I had lost rapport. I dismissed the message, set my blasters to combat mode, and looked at the adviser sternly. He looked quite peaceful.

"Don't lose it!" I held the manipulator out to the Precian. Without arguing, he took the device and crawled aside. I guess he was starting to realize that I stunned him for a reason.

I managed to fly about half the length of the corridor, which gave me the sliver of hope. I assigned the second manipulator as my primary weapon, abandoning the blaster—the creatures died of it instantly and without remains, which didn't suit our position. My plan was to obstruct the passage with bodies, complicating the advance of the rest of the swarm.

The entire base began shaking once again, signaling that the fight was about to begin in earnest and I opened fire without having seen the enemy. By the time the plasma reached the end of the corridor, the first warrior appeared. He had no chance to react to the fatal shot with his companions pushing up behind him. One-zero in my favor. The adviser grunted in amazement at the impending avalanche, and my rapport with him returned to its previous value. The Precian had forgiven me my rude treatment.

"Fall back!" I ordered, still pumping plasma bolts down the

corridor. The insects died one after another, yet their torrent did not let up. There were very many this time around. Two things, however, were working in my favor: the narrowness of the corridor and my constant use of the manipulator. Whatever insects made it through my blaze of plasma I would immobilize and hurl under the feet of the ones coming up behind. Since the manipulators would periodically gain XP, I figured that the swarm trampled these unlucky ones to death and slowed down as a result. One shot—one dead pest. One step back—minus a dozen pests. My powercells were running out at a breakneck pace—in effect the only thing I was really doing was switching them out between throwing the overzealous warriors under their fellows' feet. My shoulder-mounted blasters did most of the work.

Scenario update: Uninvited Guest.
You have cleared 50.16% of the base from its invaders.
Launching second part of scenario.

I don't even remember when the insects ended. There was nowhere to retreat, we have already reached the edge of the corridor. Exiting was tantamount to certain death, so the adviser and I dug in with all our limbs, firing at the warriors. At some point he joined me, armed with a blaster. We had just enough powercells to power one manipulator and three blasters long enough to manage an army of insects.

When the system notification popped up, the remaining creep under our feet suddenly began to flow deep into the base. Somewhere in there another giant cocoon was brewing.

IN SEARCH OF THE ULDANS

Whereas initially I had had to methodically and progressively clear the entire territory before releasing the adviser, this battle would surely be the last one. But I had neither the time nor the powercells, which meant that we had no way of fighting this next wave of chitinous assholes. I grabbed the adviser by the shoulders and took off, bouncing along the creep. In the next couple of seconds, it dissolved completely leaving us in front of an illuminated and pristine base. We both realized the inevitability of respawning.

"These trophies are rightfully yours. Collect as many as you can, while you have time. I will try to buy more time for you," said the adviser and pointed to the flickering crates. I nodded my thanks and rushed to fill my inventory with golden tokens. I had at most a minute before the new army would be spawned and another thirty seconds before it tore us to shreds. The adviser would be good enough for a few moments, so I should collect as much of this loot as possible.

Four minutes passed without any rustling. A third of the corridor was empty, but no one hurried to meet us. After nine more minutes, I had collected all five thousand golden tokens and approached the adviser.

"They aren't coming," the Precian stated the obvious.

"Then let's go take a walk," I suggested. "Maybe we'll make it to the ship. It's stupid to stand here and there's no help coming. Let's at least go check out the Uldan base in its normal state. What if we find something interesting?"

"Only a pirate thinks about loot even as he ascends the scaffold. You have chosen the right profession," the adviser

---

laughed, returning the blaster to me.

I didn't bother explaining to the NPC that every player was just as greedy as I was, pirate or not. We were the real swarm of locusts in this game. It didn't matter if an object was misplaced or mishung or even just in its right place doing what it was supposed to be—if it looked somewhat valuable, we players would try to appropriate it to our inventories. Everything that could be filched would be filched. Everything that could be pawned would be pawned. Out in reality, such behavior was looked-down upon and punishable by law. In the game, however, it ensured success and profit. In this regard, the utterly barren Uldan base could be viewed as a bit of pure mockery on the part of the devs. But I had something to be proud of—I was going to sell my captured spear to Eine as an artifact of unprecedented rarity.

We walked on foot in order to avoid wasting powercells on my thrusters, paying attention to each dent in the hope of finding at least something sensible. Even the base in the test server that I had been sent to before being reconnected had not been this empty. There were always some objects or equipment lying around. The only thing here were bare walls. Even the lights could not be dismantled—I had checked.

So on we went, confidently to meet our destiny. We came to a turn and entered a narrow corridor, which turned again and ended unexpectedly. An enormous stadium stretched out before us. Or perhaps it was an amphitheater, judging by the round shape of the chamber.

"Now we know why the mountain didn't come to

Mohammed," I said, stunned. The adviser made no response and I understood him. The horde of insects that the enormous cocoon in the center of the stadium could hatch would demoralize anyone. This time, however, our mysterious enemy bet on quality instead of quantity.

"Brainiac, are you seeing this?" I asked as the cocoon opened and the final boss emerged.

"Uh-huh. We are currently working on how to unsee it," the snake replied in his stead. "We don't know what it is and we don't want to know, Cap'n. And anyway, isn't it time we got out of here? Your blasters will be like cap guns against this thing."

The engineer was right—my blasters might serve to tickle this monster—and I didn't even have the powercells for that. It was ten meters tall with a barrel for a torso and completely covered with a brown layer of chitin. Its neck, half a meter in diameter, bore a funny and disproportionately small head, similar to a human one, which gave it a terrifyingly comic appearance, while its two, long, twisted horns only added to this impression. A broad tail and three lower limbs allowed the creature to keep itself in an upright position, ridiculously dangling its short arms like a T-Rex. And as if for the sake of contrast, two enormous, iridescent wings stuck out of the monster's back. They flapped powerfully, washing us with gusts of air.

The monster butterfly rose into the air, shifted a meter to the side and collapsed again on the floor, leaving a rainbow egg in its earlier place. And there were many such eggs throughout the amphitheater.

Gazing at this mutant, I thought about genetic experiments.

Had this monster spawned from the forbidden love of the Uldans and the Vraxis queen? It had the head and wings of an Uldan and the body and tail of a Vraxis. Only its upper and lower limbs didn't match my theory, but this could be attributed to the difficulties of symbiosis.

"*Hrsha anshta gring hrsha!*" shrieked an unpleasant metallic voice. The creature had noticed us.

"It's speaking in Uldan!" the snake's voice sounded dumbfounded: "'Your path ends here!'"

"I'm patching you through my speakers. Translate for me. Broadcast the translation to the adviser too," I ordered. "The war is over! The Uldans were defeated."

You couldn't call the Uldan language melodious and in the snake's hissing pronunciation, you could probably use it to torture a confession out of someone.

"The war will never end!" the creature responded angrily— and laid another egg. "It will go on until the last defender falls and I shall spawn them by the millions! The base will never surrender—neither to the Vraxis, nor to the humans, nor anyone else. I am the queen and I shall annihilate everyone!"

My conjecture no longer seemed so wild—the monster seemed to identify as Uldan. I decided to try and exploit the boss's talkativeness and began asking questions:

"I am here because my ship picked up a distress signal. What happened here?"

"Distress? How would you—a human, the lowliest of races—help me in the unlikely circumstance that I even were in distress? By the time *you people* had evolved enough to pick up a stick, we had already conquered space and time! Why, we created your friend right there, next to you, the one who cannot understand the true speech. Precians, Qualians—they are all our creations. They were supposed to be the finest species the galaxy had known. Now we must rule Galactogon relying on their power!"

"The Vraxis turned out to be more powerful still. You Uldans lost the war. Your civilization is dead, as are all members of your race. The Uldans are an ancient myth, a fairy tale. If you do not need help here—then turn off the distress beacon. Galactogon has enough problems without you crying wolf."

"That is a lie! A lie as arrogant and stupid as you are, pathetic little human!" the creature did not take to the news calmly. "The Uldans shall prosper and multiply! You came here aboard an orbship and not in those ancient troughs that swarm this moon's orbit! And if it weren't for your orbship, you wouldn't have gotten within a mile of this base."

"One of your own, Warlock, gave me this orbship, ever heard of him? He was a guardian. His world was located far from the fighting, which is how Warlock survived for so long. He gave me the ship and faded into the ether. He was the last living Uldan. The rest are dead."

"I am an Uldan! And I am alive!" A screech verging on ultrasound pierced my ears, but the armor suit's sound system filtered it. "The war is not over yet! Look around, human, what do you see? Does it seem to you that the Vraxis has won? No! It was I who defeated them. They invaded the base, and the queen began to lay her cursed eggs, devouring my fellows. But I managed to swallow her! I merged my mind with the Vraxis queen and exterminated the invading army! I saved the base and began to wait, warding away the curious. What was I waiting for? I waited for the distress beacon to do its work and it did—it brought you. Now I have a ship. Now I can leave this place and continue my war."

"Red alert, Cap'n! Brainiac is being hacked! Do something, Cap'n!"

"It is too late. I sense your bond to the planetary spirit and I have already rechanneled it." The monster did not even consider hiding its cards. "From now on you shall be bound to this base! Your fate shall be to remain here as witnesses to my triumph."

A shimmering field absorbed the salvo from my blasters. The dungeon boss was too well-protected. In response, the monster emitted a shockwave that knocked the adviser and me against the wall. This was immediately followed by an immobilizing field that pinned us in place and blocked both my blaster fire and the manipulator's tractor beam. Next to us, my 'Uldan' POW sprawled against the wall in a field of his own. The game must have interpreted him to be my property.

"Adviser, I need your help!"

"What can I do? I am plastered to the wall just like you are!"

"The Grand Arbiter *Intrepid* is in orbit above us. One and a half kilometers of crust is nothing for its beam cannons. Order a barrage on our location. We have to kill this monster!"

"Did you hear what it said about the binding? This is our homeworld now!"

At this moment, the first terrible offspring of the Uldan in many millennia began to hatch from its egg. In its gaunt neck and skull, I could vaguely make out the features of my rhinoceros marine. The egg tumbled over with his knees half-hatched and the pup raised his horned head and uttered such a baritone groan that an animal fear stirred in my stomach. Twitching its head, the creature began breaking out of its egg. The shell cracked and warped and fell away in pieces as the marine hatchling grew in strength and armor.

"What is there to consider, adviser?! We are losing time. This thing is hacking my ship! Imagine what an ancient, evil monster that can spawn an entire army can do! Let me remind you that this moon is inhabited by Precians—and they will be eaten first! Either we destroy this damn mutant now or your own mother will become its breakfast! And if you're not so fond of her, think of all the other Precians that will suffer and all the other star systems with all the other races!"

The adviser made no answer. He stared at the struggling Uldan hatchling and came to only when his brother began hatching beside him. A red light began blinking on the Precian's armor—the encrypted comm indicator. The ugly, mutant butterfly no longer wanted to talk and began laying more eggs from a semi-transparent sack in its abdomen. Meanwhile, Brainiac was fighting with every byte he had and panicked pleas for help from *Warlock* filled the airwaves. The mutant had easily breached Brainiac's IT defenses and was steadily making its way to the CPU. By his own estimate, Brainiac had no more than a minute left before he would lose all control over the vessel...But then nobody was about to let the mutant have its way. The heavens (if you could call the stadium's slate gray ceiling the heavens) parted and a deadly downpour of artillery beams, columns of pure plasma miles tall, burst forth from above. A shield flickered on around the monster, refracting and splitting the plasma in every direction. If it weren't for the shield that the Precian cast just in the nick of time, I would have instantly evaporated in the obliterating sunburst. The Vraxis warrior was less fortunate. The energy currents encaging us collapsed under the firestorm, the wall behind us evaporated, but we continued to hang in the air as if caught in a tractor beam. Our shield began giving way, shrinking, and I began rabidly shoveling my remaining powercells from my inventory to the adviser. The plasma did not let up, too blinding to look at, but the mutant somehow managed to hold on, a buckled silhouette amid the light. At least it didn't have the strength to attack us anymore.

In the next instant, I saw a shadow flicker down among the white columns—and the white surged and I simply went blind. A sun detonated where the mutant had been and flooded everything in white light. When my vision returned, I found myself in my underwear standing alone in the middle of a huge molten pit. The base's metal had melted to the surrounding crust. My respawn had taken ten minutes and the rock and the steel still glowed red around me. A timer labeled 'invulnerability' hung before my eyes, counting down the time I had to return to my suit—which hung a couple of meters ahead—and escape this lethal area. I dashed forward and the marine armor admitted its rightful owner. Unfortunately, it had lost one class. A quick review of the logs revealed that the Precians in the Grand Arbiter had taken the adviser's orders very seriously. When they saw that their beam cannons could not kill the monster, they hit it (and us) with an orbital torpedo. There's no arguing against a weapon like that, even if you are an ancient mutant butterfly. I looked in the direction where my ship had been. There were only traces of molten metal there. My chest grew tight and cold. Had *Warlock* really been destroyed? Was she really going to have to respawn?

"Cap'n, are you awake? If you hear this, say something! Come in!"

The happy message warmed my heart. My ship was alive!

"Yes! I'm okay. Brainiac, what is the status of the adviser?"

"We picked him up a few minutes ago. Stay where you are, Cap'n. We'll be there in a jiffy!"

There was a screech. The ship descended through the burned hole, continually clinging to the stone and metal. Soon enough, the orbship hung before me with its hatch open.

"We can't fly through the crust any longer, so we're back to the tried and true method of using holes or making them," the snake explained, welcoming me aboard. "Do you know that we are being blamed for an attempt to destroy the moon? Let's get out of here before it's too late!"

I stopped right there in the hatch, perplexed. The snake laughed in response.

"Relax, the adviser is already on it. There are many casualties and the powers that be need a culprit. The nearby haciendas have been leveled, but outside a radius of five kilometers it's not so bad. Everyone remembers seeing us flying around. You should listen to the radio—they are going to call the emperor to account for the atrocities of pirates. Basically, we are not welcome here."

"How did you survive?"

"As soon as things started shifting and collapsing, I immediately understood that it was time to get out of here. You distracted the monster's attention just in time. The blocking field vanished and we pulled up so hard that we made a click and a half in a couple seconds. If you'd been aboard, you'd have been turned into a pancake. Then came the explosion—and that was it. The passage down from the surface collapsed, but the beam cannon tore a crater so big you could call it the new main entrance. We doubled back carefully and picked up the adviser on our sensors. His forcefield had held out, barely. So we picked him up and began waiting for you. There is nothing more to do here. There is nothing left of the base."

"So there's nothing to plunder?" I asked, causing the adviser who had just approached to burst out in laughter.

"You are a true pirate indeed, Surgeon. We circled the entire base. There is nothing left. It's a shame, but you were right: Such a monster has no place in our galaxy. Let the Uldans remain a myth. Pretty and harmless for us and our descendants."

"I think I'd prefer to take a look myself. Where would you like us to drop you off? Here or on…Sorry, let me just answer this call. This is Surgeon!"

"Hi, this is Marina. How did your audience go?"

I looked at my watch. That's right! I promised to call her in four hours. Six had passed since then and, fed up with waiting, Marina had dialed me first.

"What's up! The audience was a flop. They kicked me out of the empire without any discussion. It turns out that pirates have no place in the Precian Empire."

"Damn. How do I get my ship back now?"

"Don't you have some acquaintances that can make a deal with the Qualians?"

"You think I haven't tried that? The Qualians flat out refuse to discuss me! I am now enemy number one. I destroyed their command center! Those imbeciles still have another four hours to rebuild it and get their Grand Arbiters to combat readiness."

"The Grand Arbiters are incapacitated? Are you trying to say that the Qualian Empire is currently defenseless?"

"Discounting the protection provided by players—yes. Do you read the fora at all? There are such crazy things afoot. The fora are all flame wars and rustled jimmies. The emperor has ordered the guilds to block all approaches to the capital and trading planets. In short, read it for yourself! I have my own problems to solve. Luckily it isn't the first time. Good luck!"

The PDA went blank as Marina hung up. I guess I wasn't the only one having a bad day.

"How long will it take to fly from here to Raydon?" I asked the adviser pensively, rejecting one idea after another. I should find some way to help Kiddo. It wouldn't do to abandon her. But how?

"About 30 minutes. But if you show up in Qualian space, they will immediately arrest you!" The adviser could see my utterly negative rapport with the Qualians.

"Technically, there is no one to arrest me at the moment. The planetary command center is down."

"What do you want with the Qualians anyway?" the adviser asked, surprised.

"I think it's the Qualians who want me. Yesterday, they captured a friend of mine. Because of those stupid Zatrathi, by the way. That's right! A Zatrathi ship appeared out of nowhere in the Shylak system and focused entirely on the Cruiser *Alexandria*, my friend's ship. That's how the Qualians got her."

"Your friend is Captain Kiddo?" the adviser asked flatly as if he knew the answer.

"The very one. She is currently imprisoned on the glorious planet of Raydon, awaiting her fate. Whatever you think about pirates, they don't abandon their own. It is a matter of honor! I admit I don't know how we'll get her out yet, but I'll think of something on our way."

"The mere suggestion that the Qualians are working with the Zatrathi is a serious accusation. At the moment, absent any substantive evidence, these are but rumors. And if you are mistaken, the Precian Empire will be closed to you forever," the adviser warned sternly. It seems that the conflict between the Precians and the Qualians had reached its peak and even high-born NPCs had grown interested in such an insignificant topic.

"Adviser, I have grown accustomed to trusting my partners. If my partner tells me that a Zatrathi vessel appeared and attacked her cruiser and no other ship in the vicinity, then that is the way it is."

"I need to contact the emperor. This information cannot wait."

A few minutes of conversation and the adviser stunned me with the news:

"The Emperor offers to work with you. You must verify your claim."

New mission available: Deep Recon. Mission description: Travel to the Qualian Empire and investigate the collusion between the Qualians and the Zatrathi. Do you wish to accept this mission?

There was nothing to think about so I accepted immediately. The adviser continued:

"I'm going with you. The emperor ordered to personally verify the veracity of your claim."

"No problem," I grinned, already forming a plan of how to infiltrate Qualian space. "Brainiac, lift off. Set course for Raydon."

CHAPTER THREE

"STAN, I NEED A FORUM SCAN ASAP. This process is top priority. I need to know the top hundred guilds in the Qualian Empire and the sectors they're currently operating in. Send all the coordinates to Brainiac as soon as you get them. The Qualian Emperor would have sent them to the frontiers to defend the empire. Brainiac, if we head for Raydon from the moon's orbit, will we fly through any sector on this list?"

"Just a minute," Brainiac paused, analyzing the data Stan had sent over. "Quadrant 2256-9967. The Ozark System."

"Stan: The Black Sails—they're a guild that plays for the Qualian Empire—I need to know everything there is about them. Who their leader is, what their rapport with the emperor is, how many ships they have. And you, Brainiac: Start calculating the hyperspace route to Raydon. Have us jump through that sector."

The Black Sails had deservedly earned their eighth place in the guild rankings. Their fleet contained fifteen cruisers of the latest type, most of which were either B- or A-class, two hundred destroyers, a limitless host of frigates, corvettes, monitors, carracks and other heaps of metal capable of moving quickly from one planet to another. The Black Sails owned six planets in the Qualian Empire and several officially sanctioned mining sites for elo, tiron, shlir, and even raq. Stan couldn't find anything about their membership but it was evident that this guild had a lot of people in it. That was exactly what I was counting on.

"Adviser, I need your help again," I explained the essence of my plan, and the somber Precian broke into a broad grin. The adviser knew about the Black Sails and did not understand how I planned to break through their picket. Assuring me that he would play his part perfectly, assuming his emperor permitted it, the adviser went off to consult the emperor. I took advantage of the lull to open my PDA and familiarize myself with my warriors a little better. A detailed description of the crew members and the ship took several pages of fine text, but the main points were easy to identify:

Orbship Warlock: Classless reconnaissance vessel. Dimensions: Spherical, with a diameter of fifty meters. Analogous vessel category: Between frigate and destroyer. The engineer had modified the two gravity engines, increasing our speed by almost seventy percent. The Warlock had her own research and repair facilities, a hangar for thirty-two assault droids and a hold with a cargo capacity of 850 tons. She was armed with six beam cannons that could pivot around the ship to fire in any direction, four EM cannons for stripping shields from enemy vessels and 22 A-class torpedoes. With enough resources, it was possible to manufacture a new torpedo in five minutes, so it was unlikely that we'd ever be unarmed. For defense we had standard shields and an anti-torpedo system, popularly known as the flycatcher. On top of this, our torpedoes had proximity fuses which meant that we could use them as improvised mines. A useful bit of hardware.

Cryptosaur: The Warlock's personal marine. And the ship's harvester. A universal device without class—in his default configuration bearing the resemblance of a rhino with three eyes, but capable of transforming into a variety of configurations. Equipped with three A-class blasters, that could move freely around his body, though their default positions were in his eye sockets. Capable of transporting two players, the rhino could accelerate to a very high speed at tremendous fuel costs. His horn was a reinforced ram capable of piercing a frigate's hull. The cryptosaur could extract any type of resource in Galactogon, with a hauling capacity of 5000 units. He was equipped with active and passive armor. There was also the option of mounting either the strabosaur or a beam cannon on the cryptosaur, losing thereby one of the player mounts.

Strabosaur: The ship's gunner. A universal device without class—in its default configuration bearing the resemblance of an orangutan with four arms. Equipped with four blasters, but with an option of wielding a beam cannon, though that would occupy his lower pair of arms. Capable of integrating with the cryptosaur

---

into a combat unit. His main role was to tetra-handedly handle the ship's armaments.

Slizosaur: The Warlock's engineer and shield operator. A universal device without class—in its default configuration bearing the resemblance of a ten-meter snake with two hands. The only member of the crew who could talk. Fully integrated with the ship's hull. In charge of making repairs, developing new ship systems and updating current ones. In charge of the ship's defensive systems—the energy shields and the "flycatcher." Current list of inventions, ready for implementation: (expand to see list).

The abilities of all the team members were divided into levels and could be used depending on their functional state.

"The emperor agreed to my participation in your adventure," the adviser had finished his private conversation a long time ago and waited patiently while I did my reading. I nodded, and Brainiac told me what I had expected:

"Active hyperspace scan detected."

The Qualian Emperor had contracted the players to protect his empire until the command center was restored. The players agreed, dividing the space into sectors and concentrating all the ships at their disposal. The defenders' targets were players instead of NPCs—since only the former could be yanked out of hyperspace. Players could not be allowed to reach the defenseless planets. Shylak's fate clearly showed the result of such an oversight—that which the marauders could not drag off, they would annihilate with their torpedoes, turning the trading planet into ruins.

Their hyperspace scanners found us three seconds before their hyperdrive disruptor beams pulled us out. Brainiac started the countdown.

"Three. Two. One. Leaving hyperspace lane. Warning! Warning! We are under attack!"

In an instant a myriad blinking dots filled the blank screen.

"Shields are up. I am picking up 120 large bogeys and 720 minnows. We are being targeted with EM cannons. Our hyperdrive has been disrupted and there are fifteen tractor beams trying to lock onto us," the slizosaur summarized our unhappy situation.

"What about the torpedoes?" I asked. If the Black Sails decide to attack right away, my entire plan will be toast.

"Why waste the credits? They'll wipe us out as it stands."

Agreeing with this assessment, I activated the public channel and announced:

"Attention! I am carrying an adviser of the Precian Emperor on board! We are a diplomatic mission headed to Raydon. I repeat, I have a Precian, imperial adviser on board! We are diplomats on our way to Raydon. An attack on the adviser will be regarded as an act of aggression against the Precians! Can anyone hear me?"

The EM salvo, capable of demolishing all our shields and the ship with it, never came. Someone could hear me.

"This is Bones, first deputy of the Black Sails. State your name."

IN SEARCH OF THE ULDANS

"Captain Surgeon. I am escorting the imperial adviser on a diplomatic mission," I repeated my initial message.

"Since when do Precian advisers fly around in bowling balls?" The orbship's unusually perfect form drew the usual questions—which I wasn't about to answer.

"If you don't stand down and allow us to pass on our way in five minutes, I will self-destruct this vessel. You can deal with the consequences yourselves, Bones. Are you sure you have a good explanation for why you refused a diplomat passage to a trade planet? Send an inspection team over if you like. There's no one on this ship but the adviser and me. We can wait!"

"I understand, Surgeon! But it will take us some time," Bones seemed torn between getting rid of us or giving me a chance.

"I have thirty minutes left. It's a mission with a time limit. Either I complete it, or you'll be to blame. If you want to start a war with the Precians and become infamous, go right ahead. The timer's counting down. Over and up."

I sat back and waited. Come on now, Bones, don't let us down! The more time passed since our exchange, the more confident I felt. A guild wouldn't risk attacking the adviser and spoiling relations between the empires. Everything else was a formality. I was confident about the adviser. He would play his role of an arrogant bureaucrat—who considers it below his dignity to communicate with the plebs—perfectly. So anyone who'd come to check my ship wouldn't have much to do but shut up and go back.

Meanwhile the comm channel was abuzz with offers to work

with the Black Sails, sell my *Warlock* or even just sell information about her.

After re-reading the description of the Precian mission, I inquired:

"Adviser, I have a question. How can I prove to you that the Zatrathi were indeed involved? Would the logbook from the ship they ambushed help you?"

"Are you talking about the cruiser *Alexandria*?" asked the adviser. "If the logbook contains information about Qualian ships in the system and their actions during the ambush, I believe that would be enough. Does *Alexandria* maintain such logs?"

"Just a second!" I dialed Kiddo on my comm. "Hey Marina! This is Surgeon again. Do you miss me?"

"Get to the point." Incarceration had not improved the girl's mood.

"I need a complete extract from your cruiser's logbook during its battle with the Zatrathi, along with the actions of the other Qualian ships in the Shylak system. That's the first thing. The second thing is you should get ready for some guests, Kiddo! I don't leave my people behind. In an hour or two I'll be on Raydon. First, there'll be carnage and destruction, and then I'll drop in for you. Send me your coordinates so I don't accidentally raze your prison. If your crew's not with you, tell them to find a transport and load up. I will fly in, pick you up, then stop by the ship graveyard for your cruiser—and then you can be on your way. All I need are the logbook excerpt. By that point in time, your people have to be ready. There will be no second chance."

"There won't be a first one either. You won't make it

through. The emperor's gathered all his heavy artillery here—they won't let anyone close to Raydon."

"Let's each be responsible for our own part of the plan. Is that all right, Captain Kiddo? You just send me your coordinates, get your people ready and wait for an hour. Maybe even less, if the locals get a move on. I'll do the rest."

"The hell with you," Marina agreed wearily. It took her a bit to process what I was telling her. "I'm in here with Anton, my XO. They didn't lock up the others. In an hour the crew will be at the graveyard's wharf."

"What about the logs?"

"That depends on what you need them for. There is a lot of confidential data in there. Neither I nor my crew would be happy if it leaked."

"Nevertheless, you're going to have to share it with me, Marina. I am currently on my way to Raydon with an adviser of the Precian Emperor. The extract is for him, so he can use it as evidence that the Qualians allowed the Zatrathi to ambush your ship. I have a related mission with the Precians. Will you help me or should I leave you to your solitude?"

"Let's say you've convinced me. However! The Precians must know that I helped them voluntarily."

"Anything you say." Anytime there was a chance of stealing a bite, Kiddo was as eager as a school of piranhas. "I'll be waiting for those coordinates. Get ready to break out of the slammer. We'll make some noise soon."

I hung up and apprised the adviser of my conversation. Repeating, just in case, that pirates had no place in the Precian

Empire, he enthusiastically took to Kiddo's quandary. Time ground on once again. In order to somehow pass it, I studied Stan's intel about the mysterious Mr. Eine, who was so eager to meet me. Stan had not managed to dig up the true identity of this player. In the real world he was known only as Mr. A, apparently a translation from German. Eine was one of the most famous collectors of unique things. He collected everything from unique forks with six tines to abandoned orbital stations. The gossip on the forums painted him as a decent, albeit somewhat stingy, independent businessman. Eine haggled to the last GC, irrespective of the item's value. He had his own website where anyone could submit a description of the unique item they had, to see if he was interested. Eine, or his employees, responded to everyone. I opened the inventory and looked at spear I had fashioned from the piece of pipe on the Uldan base—my only prize from that raid and an excellent bargaining chip to start negotiations with.

"Surgeon, get ready for visitors. We are about to dock."

Twenty minutes later, a Qualian official showed up in the system. I hesitate to imagine where they got him on such short notice. After giving Brainiac permission to dock, I warned the Black Sails that only the inspector with bodyguards and two players would be allowed aboard my ship and any attempt to plant a bug would end painfully for the culprit. The Qualian official assured me that there would be no problems on their part, and a few minutes later, *Warlock*'s cabin had grown a bit crowded. Designed for four passengers, the captain's bridge could hardly accommodate guests who wanted to see the adviser of the Precian's emperor. In fact, there was only one person—the head of one of Shylak's trading guilds. The players with him were only interested in my ship and how to buy it from me. Five bodyguards scanned the ship and confirmed that there were no living creatures besides us on board.

"What is the purpose of your visit to Raydon?" The Qualian decided to take the bull by the horns, but the adviser, having a wealth of experience at the highest level, avoided direct answers. Looking at the upstart, he chewed his lips and after a hefty pause, deigned to reply:

"Did the emperor authorize you to conduct an interrogation on behalf of the Qualian Empire?"

The adviser said this with such disdain in his voice that the Qualian's face twisted in humiliation. At this level, however, the official was powerless. Still, when it came to us players, he was not bound by official protocol. The Qualian pointed a finger at me and spat out:

"Arrest him! He is an enemy of the empire! A pirate's place is in prison!"

The guards were about to rush in my direction when the adviser raised his hand in warning.

"This human is here on official, Precian business and enjoys my protection until his work is complete. Any aggressive actions against him will have consequences. He is to escort me to the embassy on Raydon and then you will be free to do with him as you please."

I winced at the last sentence, yet the adviser was right. He could not show any friendliness to a pirate who had been

---

officially exiled from his empire.

"In that case, if this pirate commits any unlawful acts on Raydon, it shall be you who answers for them, adviser!" the head of the trade guild clarified prudently.

"Only if I am on board his ship!" the adviser budged only a little. "Do not insult law enforcement, my friend! Surely you can cope with a lone pirate and arrest him on the spot?"

"Welcome to the Qualian Empire, adviser," the merchant had the sense to understand that he had no answer to this. Turning to the players, he ordered: "Allow them to pass on to Raydon and send several ships as escorts."

With that, the NPC left my vessel. The players accompanying him, however, didn't hurry to follow him out.

"Surgeon, a few words," said a player named Gammon. As this was more a statement than a question, I assumed he was the leader of the Black Sails. "If you think anyone buys your story about going to Raydon so they can arrest you as soon as you complete your quest, you're sorely mistaken. You're going to break out Kiddo. You're counting on the defenses being down. Correct? But what'll you do if I send two cruisers that way? You know, just in case."

"You'll leave your sector defenseless. The emperor won't like it," I shrugged, showing no emotion. But Gammon continued:

"The emperor won't like it if a pirate shows up at the second-largest trading planet and starts doing his dirty laundry there. So the idea of sending the two cruisers is not a bad one. But I'm ready to change my mind if you give me a description of your ship, its performance characteristics, expansion possibilities, where you got it, as well as ten million credits and…everything else too, perhaps."

"Oh really?" I didn't even know what to say. What an excellent negotiation tactic. I used to behave the same way back in my Runlustia days, so now instead of being irritated, I was eager for the upcoming duel.

"There's not much to say here. You can say yes and that's about it. It's really a lovely deal." I couldn't see Gammon's face for his helmet, but I could hear his cheeks crackling from his grin.

"A deal? Well, heck, I like deals. They're very good for my health and my wallet," I replied in kind. "My offer is you pay me ten million and leave off all the cruiser talk. In exchange, I'll tell you why the Precian adviser is heading to meet the Qualians. For now, take my word for it, this info is the bees' knees! Now that's a lovely deal."

"You are joking?" The upbeat tone seemed to evaporate from my adversary just like that.

"Gammon, I'll be happy to see the Black Sails' ships in orbit around Raydon. It won't interfere with my plans at all. Do you really think that the adviser of the Precian's emperor has come to do a pirate's business? Ho hum. I won't lie about Kiddo. She is a nice bonus. If I get her out, all the better. If I don't, I won't spill any tears over it. They'll let her go sooner or later anyway. This is a game, after all. Now, gentlemen, please forgive me—I have pressing business. Which is to say: Get the hell off my ship."

Behind my bravado, I was doing my utmost to smother my panic. The latest updates had turned the cruisers into real

---

headaches. Even one of them near Raydon would dash my plans. Stubborn math showed again and again that my entire ship couldn't output the energy to take down a cruiser's shields. There were torpedoes of course, but the preconditions to using them effectively were more numerous than fleas on a stray dog. Maybe if my enemy sat still and did absolutely nothing, the torpedoes would work. In that case, yes, there'd be a chance of winning.

"Stanley, send me an analysis of the cruiser class. Can they attack ships on the surface of the planet?"

"Cruisers may bombard the planet with orbit-to-surface torpedoes. They do not carry beam cannons capable of penetrating planetary atmospheres. Only Grand Arbiters are large enough to carry such weapons systems."

"How many fighters can one cruiser carry?" For a moment, I saw a small glimmer of hope for getting out of this mess safe and sound, but it faded instantly with Stan's reply:

"The average cruiser has berths for six hundred fighters, the number may vary depending on the purpose of the ship."

"We will be leaving hyperspace in thirty seconds," said Brainiac, forcing me to make up my mind.

"Battle stations. Bring the ship to full combat readiness. Our main objective is to blow up anything we come across. Don't get distracted by the little stuff. Gunner, the ships are on you. Brainiac, start scanning for any stockpiles near our landing zone and send the harvester there when you find it. Are we pirates or what? We'll land the adviser and raise hell!"

Gammon hadn't bluffed—the promised cruisers were

already waiting for us when we popped into Raydon's system. Their new upgrades had allowed them to beat my ship by a couple of minutes, enough to take up strategically important positions and get ready for battle. Braniac announced that *Warlock* was in the area of effect of their hyperdrive disruptors, but this didn't change much, merely piled on the pressure. As soon as I land on the planet, the disruptors won't do anything anyway. The engineer counted 107 fighters and 22 frigates. As I had figured, not all of the Black Sails' players were online. The guild charter was serious business and all, but it was also voluntary. It's not easy to get an armada together when one guy has to visit his grandma, another's wife is threatening to leave him, a third is sick and a fourth is depressed. Everything as usual.

"Orbship *Warlock*, follow landing vector 1-1 to dock 1."

I grinned. I wish they'd always greet me like this, without AA fire and with a welcome mat at the best dock in town. It's a pity that I won't be able to keep this adviser with me much longer. Everyone seems to treat me so nice when he's around. Braniac banked the orbship and dived straight down, forcing a dozen or so Black Sails fighters to flap their wings in irritation and head to alternate docks. They weren't allowed to dock at ours.

"There is a welcoming party for me," the adviser nodded at a small procession of Precians lined up at the entrance to the dock. "On behalf of the emperor, I remind you that the Precian Empire does not condone piracy so the moment I set foot on the planet, you will lose diplomatic immunity. You are free to do as you please; we are not responsible for your actions."

As soon as he spoke this, the dispatcher confirmed our landing and announced that we were exempt from the customs inspection. The adviser disembarked and the dispatcher's voice again sounded in my headphones:

"Pirate Surgeon, you are prohibited from taking off! Remain where you are and await further instructions!"

I wouldn't call his tone friendly but then again I am not a submissive sacrificial sheep. Getting comfy in my captain's chair, I called Marina:

"Did you figure out your prison's coordinates?"

"Quadrant 769, the second underground level. I can't do better than that."

"Brainiac?" I asked for help from my ship computer on the internal channel.

"Route calculated. Flight time is ten minutes."

"Surgeon, there are two cruisers from the Black Sails hanging over Raydon. Do you know about this?" Kiddo asked just in case.

"Yeah, those are my new buddies. I've already landed. Sit tight. I'll be there soon."

Disconnecting, I called the dispatcher:

"This is Captain Surgeon. I have important information about the prince's death. I know who killed him and why. I will only speak with an official imperial representative!"

I would always have time to take off and raise hell. Since the NPCs keep saying I'm a pirate, I feel I should act the part. What do pirates love more than raising hell? Pillaging and cheating! And that's what I was going to do now.

IN SEARCH OF THE ULDANS

"This is the imperial viceroy speaking," said a new voice after a few seconds. "Where did you get the information?"

"I saw it myself. The Zatrathi didn't do it, but I know who did, why and who the other witnesses are."

"I demand you immediately provide me with this information!" the viceroy said with such menace that a shiver ran down my spine. If it weren't for the hundreds of hours I'd spent talking to the high-ranking NPCs in Runlustia, maybe I'd even have told him…

"Not so fast, Mr. Viceroy. I'm not about to negotiate with a barrel pointed at me. Order the Black Sails' cruisers to leave this system. Also, I want thirty tons of raq and ten tons of elo delivered to my ship. You have ten minutes. All further negotiations will commence only after you have met my conditions. Otherwise, I'll self-destruct the ship. I'm not afraid to lose a class, but if you refuse, your rapport is sure to suffer. Time is money, Mr. Viceroy!"

I didn't raise my bet too high. Thirty tons of raq at the current price of fifty GC per kilogram would make a nice addition to my retirement fund but not so large as to draw the curiosity of the game admins. The Qualians did not bother arguing and exactly ten minutes later, the raq and elo were in my hold and the Black Sails' cruisers had left the system. Surely the Qualians' generosity was down to the fact that the NPCs weren't about to let me leave this planet alive. And if my ship is destroyed, the entire contents of her holds will remain at the place of her destruction. If I linger here long enough for them to rebuild their command center, they'll get all their raq back with a single blast from the Grand Arbiter. Only I wasn't about to linger anywhere. I'm a pirate after all. I don't have to keep my word.

"Brainiac, did you find the stockpiles?"

"I have located three. All of them are between here and the place of Captain Kiddo's detention. Two contain resources, the other one is for equipment."

"Well, we're good on resources so send the marine to harvest the gear. He should plunder anything that's legendary or A-class and leave the rest of the rubbish in peace. Understood? Good. In that case—blast off!"

"Captain Surgeon, turn off your engines! You are violating our negotiations! Abort launch procedures!" The dispatcher began to chatter anxiously, but it was too late. *Warlock* tore away from the docking platform.

"Communication center straight ahead!" reported the snake, expecting orders. Each order had to be barked, wasting precious fractions of seconds. But it wasn't hard say three simple words:

"Fire at will!"

A surge of plasma rushed forward, crashing into the supports holding up the huge transmitter. Before it even hit the ground, a blanket of AA fire broke out all around us. The maintenance personnel, the security guards, the small beam turrets mounted on roofs—everything that could shoot opened up on *Warlock*—yet it was useless against the orbship's shields. The Qualians had not counted on such base treachery and so hadn't prepared any heavy weapons.

"Gunner, destroy everything you can! Do not spare energy, we have enough elo in our holds!"

IN SEARCH OF THE ULDANS

The orbship rushed forward, leaving behind a flaming inferno. The first platform, the reception area for various dignitaries visiting Raydon had already ceased to exist. It was followed by another dozen or so platforms that hovered in our flight path. After a few minutes of havoc, Brainiac announced:

"Multiple small targets at 8 o'clock. They are security personnel."

"So fast? Well done boys!" I respectfully shook my head, paying tribute to the speed of the in-game brethren. They rushed to defend the planet as soon as the viceroy called them.

"Security personnel are target number one. Kill them." I ordered. Respect is not the same thing as care. To respect something in pirate fashion means to first suppress the enemy with a couple of shots from a cannon, and then finish him off from a distance—so the blast wave won't rattle the teeth you have left.

"Roger that. Multiple targets at 6 o'clock. Multiple targets at 12 o'clock. We are approaching the warehouse. The marine has been deployed."

A light vibration passed through the hull. I looked at the screen and watched as my rhinoceros, flailing his legs in flight, slammed through the roof of a large gray building and disappeared inside. This did not impair his functionality even by a percent. These kinds of maneuvers didn't bother the marine one bit.

Mission updated: A Pirate I was Meant to be. Part 1: 17 of 150 interceptors destroyed.

The gunner meanwhile was ruthlessly mowing down anyone who wandered into his sights. At my order he focused on the players, sometimes raining damage on the larger buildings as well. My ship-to-ship torpedoes were useless planetside, so I could only use my cannons. Ten tons of elo would allow me to shoot all week on full auto—and still have enough energy to power my shields. The light fighters and scouts couldn't say the same and so I kept swiping away the same notification time and time again:

Mission updated: A Pirate I was Meant to be. Part 1: 8 out of 125 scouts destroyed.

The first responders now clearly figured out that until larger ships arrived, tangling with me would be dangerous. The players among them flew off to a safe distance and, having nothing better to do, started to bombard me with their comments. I turned off the comm so as not to listen to the flow of abuse. By this time, the rhino had trampled apart the warehouse guards and meticulously fulfilled its goal, searching for items of the desired class. The Qualians didn't allow the players into the warehouse, fearing that instead of defending the place, the defenders would start looting it and later just blame me.

"I have intercepted some important information," Brainiac was listening in on the background chatter. "They will be able to bring heavy equipment to the stockpile in fifteen minutes."

Damn, I better go rescue Marina and Anton or I'll lose the cryptosaur! I immediately activated my armor's combat mode and set a fifteen minute timer in my HUD.

"Brainiac, set up a security perimeter. Don't let anyone near the ship!" I ordered, as soon as the orbship stopped above the prison. The floor disappeared beneath me and I jumped out, picking up speed as I fell. I had managed to figure out how to fly the armor suit back at the Uldan base, so now I merely concentrated on clearing the roof of enemies. There weren't much: Several beam turrets and a couple Qualian corrections officers who hadn't the time to react to my appearance over the prison. Anything I couldn't destroy, I buried in rubble. Without slowing down, I slammed into one of the walls, smashing through to the next floor. In this manner, I quickly found myself on the top floor of the prison.

"Halt!" someone yelled and my HUD informed me that the suit had blocked a manipulator beam. I shook my head, recovering my senses—the landing had been rough and for a couple of moments I had lost my breath. Stretching my limbs, I jumped up and looked around. The two guards were looking with puzzlement at the remains of their manipulators. They obviously did not expect to meet someone who was encased in an armor suit on the top floor. Two blasts of plasma quickly cleared the corridor, turning the guards into flickering boxes of loot. I did not receive any alerts about losing rapport with the Qualians, since I no longer had any.

Afraid that I would lose the element of surprise by running around in search of stairs or an elevator, I pointed my blaster at the floor, pulled the trigger and went plummeting down to the floor below. If I had more time, I would definitely wander around the cells and free whoever was being held here. Maybe I'd even earn a couple unique missions for my blatant rudeness toward the Qualians, and yet the timer was counting down before my eyes, reminding me that I might lose my marine soon.

When the dust settled, I pulled off the same trick, leaving behind another pair of twinkling crates. The enemies had no chance. Kiddo and her XO had no protection. One random shot from the guards—and our entire escape would go to hell.

It took me a good while to bust down to the second underground level—the prison had seven floors. Having blasted the guards, I called through the external loudspeaker:

"Marin-a-ah!"

All I heard in response, was a rustle from the vertical tunnel I had made in the floors above. Apparently, the guards who approached the noise tried to figure out what was going on and how to react to it. I also realized that prison cells could be soundproofed, and Marina did not hear me, as I did. So I had to call her on the PDA:

"What cell are you in?"

"I don't know! You're already here?" Marina couldn't wait to get out.

"Uh-huh. Do you hear anything?" I bashed in the nearest door and looked inside. Empty.

"No. I mean, I can hear you smashing pots and pans into the mic, but otherwise nothing."

"That's too bad. I'm here on the second underground level, looking for you and your prince. Step away from the cell door just in case. We wouldn't want any workplace accidents occurring.

Safety first and all that."

"Okay, okay. Make some more noise." Another door flew off its hinges, and again there was no one in the cell. "No, I don't hear anything. The cell must be soundproofed."

"In that case, just sit tight and wait. Warn Anton so I don't crush him with the door either."

I busted down another door and quickly glanced inside. And having grown accustomed to finding nothing, I almost jumped back as I encountered a pair of frightened Qualian eyes. This race even kept their own people in their dungeons. Cursing and telling him to scram, I tore the next door off its hinges. Empty. There were about fifty cells on this floor. It seemed my search could go on for a long time.

I ended up stumbling across Anton first. The Qualians had left him in his clothes, confiscating his armor suit, as I expected. Squinting from the bright light, he was about to go outside, but I stopped him:

"Stay here a little longer. I'll come pick you up after I've found Marina. It's dangerous to go without armor."

I found the girl next door. Leaving her with Anton, I returned to the shaft I had made in the prison building and patted myself on the back for my foresight: The overhead floors already bristled with the reinforcements' blasters. A short flight upward and several salvos from my blasters cleared the way. Remaining at the first underground level, I hung my head down and yelled:

"Get out! Quickly! Grab my hand. I'll haul you up one at a time."

Marina climbed up first and demanded a blaster. I winced—

this was a shameful oversight in my plan. I knew that the players in prison would be without armor or weapons, but didn't think of this trifle—a small shield generator and spare blasters for the fugitives. It was a good thing that my inventory had a couple forgotten assault blasters lying around. Kiddo hissed something with displeasure but took the weapon.

I reached in to extract Anton but encountered the Qualian prisoner I'd just released instead. He was dangling in the hole, trying to clamber up to our floor. I couldn't care less about his fate, but he was getting in the way of my escape. So yanking him up with a quick jerk, I hauled up Anton after him. Marina immediately aimed her blaster at the Qualian.

"Don't shoot," I ordered, about to jet up to the ground floor.

"What do you need him for?" Marina hissed through her teeth.

"What do you need to shoot him for? Do you miss your pirate ways?" The girl's reaction surprised me. Her voice had anger in it and her look didn't bode anything nice for the ex-prisoner. It was the kind of look you give to your sworn nemesis. The last thing I needed was for Marina to start losing her mind, confusing the game with meatspace. I wonder when the last time she exited the game was…

"They must be crushed like the cockroaches they are," Captain Kiddo's demeanor confirmed my fears. Damn, why now? I hate potential problems. The girl really was immersing herself into Galactogon much deeper than was good for her. Then again, I wasn't about to lecture a grown woman about the dangers of VR immersion. If Marina wanted to drive herself mad, it was her brain to do with as she pleased. At the same time, at the moment, any problems could grow to become critical.

"In that case, this cockroach is a pet of mine and only I have the right to crush him. Let's not tinker around each other's brains and business, partner. Okay? Good. Wait for me here, I'm going to climb higher."

We passed through the next two floors without incident and I let my guard down. There were no guards to be seen. Marina had silently acknowledged my point about my 'pet' and stopped aggroing the Qualian. Having reached the second floor, I barely had time to assess the situation when a large clump of plasma smashed into me. I was thrown back a few meters, slamming into the concrete wall. The next blast came flying quickly after the first, wanting to make friends with me too. I looked at my screens: A beam cannon stood at the far end of the corridor, firing in tandem with the Qualian squad manning it. In this production I had been cast as the target. There was nowhere to go.

Yet my armor held. The red plasma bursts tossed me around, but they couldn't breach my shields. My blasters locked on and the Qualian beam cannon lit up with a flickering shield, blocking my attack. The reply came instantly, but the wall behind me backed me up again. Noticing some movement on the right, I realized that things were getting worse. Four Qualians were bringing up a second beam cannon. My armor suit wouldn't survive fire from two of those at once. Meanwhile, their shields blocked my attempts to defend myself. Without waiting for the second gun to be installed, and taking advantage of a pause in the first one's fire, I darted into the doorway, retreating to my party. The way up was closed.

"Security?" Marina had already guessed what was going on from the plasma flashing in the hole in the ceiling. Knocking down one of the cell doors and killing the prisoner within, Marina drove everyone in, stuck her blaster out into the corridor and began to pump suppressive fire down its length. Nodding, I raised my blasters to protect us against any kamikaze attempts from above and called my ship:

"Brainiac, I need fire support ASAP. We are located on the second floor under the ship. The Qualians are on the third floor, about twenty meters south of our position. We can't break through. Blast the walls and pick us up."

"The probability of collateral damage to the captain of the ship are at least thirty percent. I strongly recommend leaving the corridor," Brainiac wouldn't shut up with his recommendations.

"If you don't blast these walls, the probability of collateral damage will be 100%!" I yelled, shooting into the opening. The building around us shook and the opening filled with Qualians with beam cannons. These boys weren't wasting their time! If we don't hurry, we're doomed! The building shook a few more times. The opening began to widen as hunks of concrete fell away. Screams sounded from above and dust filled the corridor. Unable to think of anything better, I covered my party with my suit, shielding them from the flying fragments.

"Is everyone okay?" I asked, as soon as the shards stopped spattering my shields. Our visibility was no more than a meter because of the dust, and my spatial scanner showed nothing but a hodgepodge of debris and ruins.

"So far, yes, but we can't breathe," Marina croaked and coughed. Activating the armor suit's medunit, I injected all three of my companion's with an equine dose of restorative solution.

"Get us out of here, Brainiac. Right this instant!"

"The passage has been created. I can see you, but I cannot extract you without the marine. Please follow my instructions. I will guide you to the extraction point. Leave the cell and move ten meters to the left, walking as closely to the wall as possible—there is a hole in the center of the corridor."

"Get on my shoulders!" I ordered the Qualian, picking up Marina and Anton with my arms. They couldn't hear Brainiac and I wasn't about to waste time explaining what was going on. If they wanted to live, they would do as I say.

The Qualian wanted to live it seems. With the agility of a mongoose, the gray-skinned humanoid instantly climbed up onto my shoulders, shifted, settling more comfortably, and, went still, clutching my helmet. The armor suit's servomotors howled from the load but went on functioning. I went out to the corridor, squeezed against the wall, and almost fell: The floor collapsed beneath me unable to withstand my weight. The stabilization system automatically fired the thrusters, allowing me to hover over the collapse. Very carefully, like a sapper in a minefield, I leaned forward, forcing the armor suit to fly straight. The floor was streaming under my feet but I didn't dare step on it again.

"There is a cell door to your right. Go in."

The door was locked, and my hands, like my blasters, were occupied with my passengers. I asked Marina to deal with the door. Sick of having nothing to do, Marina didn't have to be asked twice. She aimed her blaster and unloaded its entire clip until a gust of fresh air cleared the dust around us. Waiting for further instructions from Brainiac, I was not ready for the panorama that opened up—the prison ended on the other side of the doorway. Brainiac had demolished half of the building to save our skins. Now *Warlock* hung hovering three meters ahead of us, her entrance glittering amiably. I leaned forward again and slowly dragged my rescues toward the ship.

"We will reach the end of our service life and get scrapped before you reach us, Cap'n," the serpent gibed poking out from the orbship. Grabbing my suit, the engineer adroitly but carefully pulled us inside. "Okay. These three are coming with me to the medbay. Their condition is almost critical. You should have warned that they were without armor, I would have sent over a spare. Why save them if you're going to finish them off yourself? Ah, young people."

"Brainiac extract the cryptosaur!" I ordered, ignoring the snake. "It's time to get off this planet."

"There might be a problem with that." Despite the fact that the engineer was occupied with healing the escapees, he did not stop monitoring the situation around the ship. "A few seconds ago, four cruisers ships entered the Raydon system. Either we make our getaway now or we won't get away period. They'll be in orbit in five minutes."

"Can we bind all the passengers to the ship?" I asked pensively. The players had found their bearings too quickly and reinforced with capital ships. I'd only been gone about ten

---

minutes!

"Are you in the mood for reassurance or sincerity?" the snake maintained her wry tone no matter what happened.

"Keep it up and I'll sell you to the Zatrathi," I growled angrily. The snake sensed I was not in the mood for her jokes and replied strictly to the point:

"Negative. Binding to the ship is not feasible due to the absence of the planetary spirit. The marine needs help, Cap'n— the number of items he has harvested is too large for him to carry back to the ship on his own."

"If he needs help, then we can go help him. The important thing is we do it in time," I muttered to myself, reloading my armor suit's powercells. My blasters had spent half of the suit's energy.

"Get the droids ready. We have to retrieve the marine and the loot he's found!" the ship banked sharply, landing right at the entrance to the stockpile. The gunner cleared the area of Qualians, allowing me and the droids to leave the ship. The front door had bulged from inside like a burn blister. As I looked on, it bulged and buckled and then burst, spraying us with shards of steel. My marine's snout appeared in the newly-formed hole. All three eyes of the rhinoceros glowed with happiness from his successful mission as he dumped the loot in a huge pile right at the entrance.

"Let's go!" I ordered the droids and flew into the breach. Grabbing the first item, which looked like an engine component, I dragged it back to the ship. The marine came trotting behind me, holding a square-shaped object of a mysterious purpose in his teeth. The properties dialog informed me that this was some A-class item, but I didn't bother delving further. The engineer can figure out what can be used and what can be consigned to the cargo holds. In the meantime, we better be praying to all the gods of Galactogon that we can get off this planet.

"The loading is complete." One trip by the droids was enough to secure the loot. I flew back to the ship, ordering:

"Emergency blast off! Set course for the ship graveyard."

"ETA is one minute thirty seconds." Despite my armor suit, I felt all the momentum of the abrupt launch, which pressed me so hard against the floor that I couldn't even take a step.

"How are the passengers?" I inquired anxiously. Such inertia could have a bad effect on their health—up to the point of forcing them to respawn.

"First he picks up a bunch of stowaways and then we're the ones who have to nurse them." The snake returned to her normal mood, not passing up a chance to complain about the captain. "Your passengers are fine. I've placed them into medcapsules. They have another twenty seconds of rest ahead of them."

"Send them to my cabin when you're done." I could not help smiling. If you forget for a moment that the snake is a regular NPC, you might imagine that she is a grumpy woman who's married some poor oaf and is now constantly unhappy with him. Either the door in the kitchen creaks too much or he earns too little money, or he's leaving his socks everywhere. And at the same time, she's ready to bite the head off anyone who suggests that her husband isn't the greatest man ever.

IN SEARCH OF THE ULDANS

"What's new?" Marina appeared after a minute.

"There are four cruisers maneuvering around Raydon. They are on the hunt for a terrifying and insolent pirate. They've brought fifty carracks with them. Several guilds have gathered here, but they haven't yet decided who the leader is. I think that should gain us a couple of minutes. The ship graveyard is straight ahead. I have a spare armor suit ready for you. Gear up as fast as you can and go get your cruiser. To be frank, Marina, I don't know how we are going to get out of here."

"What class are the cruisers, Frank?"

"One C-class and one B-class." Ignoring her bad pun, I checked the data. "We should have a fight on our hands."

"We'll see about that. Stay near the hull, and don't do anything crazy. I'll figure it out myself, just let me get home."

"Don't forget about the logs for the Precians. I need them immediately, as soon as you reach your ship. Everything else is secondary," I reminded her about our earlier agreement.

"I'll send you the logs." Marina had already climbed into the suit and adjusted it to herself. "Thanks for getting us out. Do you have a suit for Anton?"

I shook my head without looking up from my screens. I didn't have any other armor suits. Marina wanted to add something else, but the floor beneath her disappeared, and with a trailing cry, the girl fell out into space, choking on the phrase she had begun. A robotic arm grabbed the indignant pirate and placed her on a small platform. She shook her fist at me from there.

"The ship graveyard," the snake announced. "I'm picking up

---

several hyperdrive disruptors blocking our hyperspace jump. There's also an EM cannon locking onto us. Warning! 25 torpedoes inbound."

I am ashamed to admit, but instead of thinking about torpedoes flying at me, I stared at the graveyard. Lestran had taken *The Space Cucumber* and *Warlock* had never been destroyed yet, so I had never been here before. A graveyard as such did not exist. In the middle of space hung a small platform with a control panel. Captains and their crew approached and entered an access code for their destroyed vessel, which would then materialize immediately behind the platform. The joyful players quickly clambered inside and went off in search of adventure. In order to steal something from the graveyard, you had to not only know the code, but also the ship's homeworld and status—that is, whether it had been destroyed or not.

Alexandria appeared all at once as if a magician's handkerchief had been whipped off of her. The huge A-class colossus was a cruiser of the latest type. The hatch opened, and the crew of the cruiser filtered in to man their stations. Twenty seconds passed and the ship lit up with a myriad lights like some deepwater leviathan opening its eyes. A shield flickered to life around the cruiser, protecting my own ship just in time. Marina was about to settle some accounts. The torpedoes were approaching, and *Warlock* sidled up to the cruiser's hull as close as possible, looking for protection from her big sister. There was a deafening roar, and all twenty-five torpedoes evaporated from a well-coordinated salvo of my partner's point defense guns. If I didn't know that a fourteen year-old boy was managing the

---

cruiser's weapons systems, I'd imagine that a team of artillerists had pulled off such a feat. As it stood, the boy was Kiddo's pride and joy. She had trained him herself, hovering over him day after day to ensure that her gunner's skills grew appropriately. As soon as they had picked up Anton, Marina's joyful voice broke the air on the common frequency:

"Attention all ships! This is the captain of the cruiser *Alexandria*! I am declaring this system a no-weapons zone. Any further aggression will be regarded hostile and met with live fire! You had your chance to get rid of me and you blew it, you goons."

The obscenities that erupted in response to this suggested that there were few gentlemen in the system. And while a majority resorted to their well-worn memes and insults, a small handful tried to get Kiddo to see the reason of their actions.

"We have orders from the Emperor!"

"We can't let you out of the system, Captain Kiddo!"

"We have to shoot!" I think these were the only responses that didn't contain swearing.

"Bad try, guys," I muttered to myself, amused by the circus. At the moment Kiddo was disposed to tear to shreds anyone who stood between her ship and her freedom.

"I said my part. Surgeon, we're leaving. Set bearing to two-two-zero, speed twenty. Anyone who gets in the way gets no quarter. I've announced my course. You can choose what's more important to you on your own: the Emperor's orders or your ship's current class."

Marina cut off her broadcast and called me up on our closed

channel.

"I can jam the disruptor beams long enough for us to jump out of system, but it'll take time. I have no way of knowing if the Qualians will rebuild their command center ahead of time. We can't handle a Grand Arbiter. I won't be able to take it out a second time. Let's leave the system first, then deal with the hyperdrive disruptor beams and discuss the jump coordinates. At the moment, we can't hyperjump outside the empire. A single cruiser doesn't scare me, but if we run into a guild acting like a team, we will be overwhelmed. I'm sending over the logs. The full account of the battle is in there. Over and out."

Having instructed Brainiac to follow the cruiser, I dialed the adviser back on Raydon.

"Pirate Kiddo gave me the logs, please accept the transfer from me. Analyze the data. If the Qualians' plot is confirmed—I would like to consider my mission accomplished."

"I confirm the transfer. I need about half an hour to analyze this data. Our signal quality is deteriorating; are you moving away from the planet?"

"Yes, in about a minute our connection will completely disappear. It is unlikely that the Qualians will permit us to use their comm relays," I confirmed as Brainiac explained what was going on with my HUD. The ship computer could participate in my conversations with NPCs.

"I won't manage in a few minutes." The adviser did not sound happy. "If the data is not confirmed, I will return to the emperor with nothing and you will therefore lose access to the empire. These were His Imperial Majesty's conditions."

IN SEARCH OF THE ULDANS

I repeated to myself several curses I had just heard directed at Kiddo, but then a notification that the mission had been updated flashed before my eyes.

"I have nothing more to do on this planet. In five minutes I will be delivered to your ship. Please delay your departure." The adviser's tone did not brook objections.

"Marina, I have problems. I need to wait for the adviser. Five minutes."

"We ain't got five minutes!" barked the girl angrily. "In a few minutes the best Qualian guilds will send their cruisers into this system. At that point you may as well self-destruct. I'm not about to go up against an armada."

"If I leave, I will lose a very nice mission sequence. And I'll lose access to the Hansa Corp. And also…Well, look, I'll just lose too much!"

"Goddamn it, Surgeon! We'll wait five minutes and drift slowly out of the system. Tell your adviser to hurry up. And don't leave my security perimeter. It's about to get hot around here. And one more thing, if we get out of here, I don't owe you anything more for the rescue or my ship. Over and out."

Alexandria's shield flushed a deep purple color, warning anyone concerned that the ship was charging up for something. Renewed shouting and swearing filled the comm channels. The ships around us rushed to get as far from *Alexandria* as possible, but not everyone could make it in time. *Alexandria*'s bow erupted in a flash as bright as a sun, emitting a fireball half its size at the nearest cruiser. Several torpedoes sallied from the enemy ship to meet the ball of plasma, but it only swallowed them and grew in size. When the enormous ball of plasma reached the enemy ship, Galactogon froze for a moment—the game servers were calculating the damage and rendering the ensuing picture.

The remains of the Qualian cruiser remained in place. The mysterious weapon did not blow the vessel to the other side of the galaxy, nor disintegrate her into its constituent atoms, nor collapse her into a black hole. The ball of plasma simply burned its way through her hull, leaving a perfectly tidy tunnel of an immense width. But Marina was in no hurry to enjoy her victory. The next second, about fifty torpedoes shot forth from *Alexandria* in search of their targets. Seeing the players in the smaller ships get distracted by the cruiser's demise, Kiddo made good use of her chance. The price for gawking turned out to be steep: Fifty bright flashes signaled fifty lost classes and fifty lost ships.

"If you lot don't show me your stern and jet in the next two minutes, I'll repeat that trick again," Marina's cold voice cut through the racket of abuse—causing it to stop all at once. The players were quicker on the ball now. One by one, the scouts, frigates, and even carracks turned tail, calculating their hyperjump routes. The three remaining cruisers, however, looked like they were planning on attacking Kiddo together.

"Request to dock incoming," Brainiac announced in the ringing silence. The adviser had reached us in just three minutes. Distracted by his arrival, a few minutes went by before I looked at my screens again—by then, the Raydon system was clear. The cruisers thought better of it and hurried off.

"I'm sending you the coordinates. We're leaving," Marina

commanded as soon as the ship undocked. The Precian took the passenger seat and immersed himself in his analysis of the logs from Kiddo's ship. Brainiac began crunching the numbers for the hyperjump, displaying a countdown timer in the meantime. It looked that we were going to get out of this mess after all...

"Good mooorning, Galactogon!" Gammon's voice burst in over the public chat as the engineer said sadly:

"A hyperdrive disruptor beam is painting our vessel. We won't be able to enter hyperspace. Ten cruisers have entered the Raydon system."

Spending time on negotiations was not Marina's preferred M.O. *Alexandria*'s engines flared and the cruiser rushed forward at such a speed that I was forced to thank my snake engineer for upgrading our engines in time. The upgrade was the only thing that allowed me to keep up with my partner.

"Kiddo, where are you off to? I came here to chat with you— even brought some cruisers—and you show me your stern. Watch out, I might mistake that for flirting," grunted Gammon and then guffawed at his own wit.

"Am I missing something? Do we have some kind of business to discuss?" Marina deigned to answer, ignoring the dubious urgency.

"None with you, but some with that little birdie that's tucked under your wing there. Sur-geon...Oh, Sur-geon...Be a man and step out from that gal's skirt, will you? You owe me. Captain of *Alexandria*—you are free to leave the system as soon as you stop shielding that UFO. His destiny lies in the jurisdiction of the

Qualian Empire. Or mine. I haven't decided yet."

"And then what? You'll let me go? With no double-crosses or anything? The pirate that's escaped your masters?" Marina clarified with notes of distrust, and my stomach sank unpleasantly. My hand automatically crept to the self-destruct button. Even if all the electronics on the ship were knocked out with an EM blast, the button would work.

"I'll let you go on principle. It's more profitable for me if you owe me one. I can afford to do a favor for a nice lady instead of fighting her."

"Noble of you…but hard to believe."

"Let's be honest, Kiddo. If the Qualians hadn't sent away my two cruisers, you'd still be in your cell. And that's the Qualians' problem. But leave Surgeon. What do you need him for? I have ten cruisers, two of them can jump ahead of you. What are you going to do? The fireworks just now were impressive, but you won't be able to shoot that thing more than three times. You have three more charges at most. I am ready to sacrifice three cruisers. What about you?"

"Surgeon, we must return to Zalva urgently!" The adviser said excitedly, distracting me from the dialogue that was deciding my fate. "There is proof that the Qualians were complicit! The Emperor must see it with his own eyes. He will declare war!"

Mission accomplished: Deep Recon.
Report to the Precian Emperor to receive your reward.

A saving thought flashed through my head, and I jumped after it, praying that the Precian wouldn't refuse immediately.

"Adviser, I understand that you don't work with pirates. What would you say if the Black Sails switch allegiance to the Precians? With all their resources and ships?"

"That is a very interesting proposal," the adviser answered interestedly. "It would be foolish, of course, to refuse the support of a guild of this level. But I am afraid that after we submit our memorandum of protest to the Qualians, we will no longer consider any changes of allegiance between our empires. If the Black Sails do not submit their application in time, we will not be able to help. Neither we nor any other empire in Galactogon. The Black Sails will have to work their way up from the bottom, proving their usefulness to their new empire. They will receive neither planets, nor mining concessions."

"They could apply to you now, guaranteeing a significant contribution to the development of the empire. They might take an active financial role in the restoration of Zalva's second moon, for example," I tossed out the bait and realized from a red flashing light bulb that the adviser had already contacted the emperor about the deal. The number eight guild in the Qualian Empire is nothing to sneeze at, especially with war around the corner.

"If they swear allegiance to the Precian Empire now, the emperor will make an exception and accept them," the adviser said, giving my hope of salvation a real footing. I had lost the thread of negotiations between Kiddo and Gammon in the meantime, but now it was unimportant:

"Kiddo, stop haggling. Our suspicions have been confirmed. The adviser just acknowledged them. Gammon, my offer still stands. Ten million credits for info that is worth much more than that and directly concerns the interests of your guild. Captain Kiddo will confirm that I am not bluffing."

Marina instantly got her bearings in the situation.

"Gammon, the information that Surgeon is offering you really is valuable," she said. "You know me—I value my reputation. If you let us go and pay us, you'll reap immense profits later."

"What is this some new con?" The guild leader snorted. "You two found yourself a new sucker?"

"Attention, we are slowing down," Kiddo announced publicly and *Alexandria* fell abruptly behind *Warlock*. I slowed down after her and returned to the cruiser's stern. Naturally, Kiddo was risking it, allowing the enemy ships to encircle us, but it would be difficult to win the confidence of the head of the Black Sails in some other manner. "Gammon, I'll wait for you on my ship. Surgeon, you should join us. Let's not be kids about this and play the believe-don't-believe game."

Ten minutes later, *Alexandria*'s comfortable cabin played host to a meeting of five: Marina and Anton, Gammon, his deputy Bones, and me.

"All right, get on with it," Gammon grinned, scooting his chair closer. The head of the Sails still thought he was wasting his time, but curiosity had prevailed for the moment. "When will I get a chance to hang out on *Alexandria* and listen to two hucksters persuade me to waste ten million credits?"

IN SEARCH OF THE ULDANS

"We're offering you a deal. We'll give you the information first and if you see its value, you'll transfer the money and release us. As you can see, there is no risk for you," I radiated goodwill and self-confidence.

"And if I don't see the value in it?" Gammon exchanged glances with his deputy.

"Then you become renowned throughout all of Galactogon as the last little shit without honor and dignity. And I ensure that this renown is carried far and wide," Kiddo replied seriously.

"What poor hospitality, Kiddo. Instead of offering tea you treat us with bile. Well, let's have your secret then," said Gammon.

"The Qualians are working with the Zatrathi, violating their treaty with the Alliance. The Precians have irrefutable evidence of this fact, and as soon as the adviser returns to Zalva, no matter whether on his own or after respawning, the Alliance will announce an embargo. Relations between empires are strained as it is, yet now war seems inevitable."

"Yeah and so what?" Gammon snorted. "The Qualians were always obsessed with the Zatrathi. Everyone knew about it, and it didn't bother anyone before that, why start a war now?"

"Because before no imperial adviser received orders to acquire irrefutable evidence personally for the emperor. Are you following this or not? I'm sure these are new scenarios. You can see for yourself how an NPC reacts to your well-known news."

I sent Gammon and Kiddo a short clip in which the very animated adviser babbled about his findings in *Alexandria*'s logbook. After the video had had its desired effect, I continued:

"Now try and imagine, Gammon. At the moment you have six planets, good connections within your empire, your own space mines and hold eighth place in the rankings. What will happen to all that once the combined forces of all the players from all the other empires set upon you? The Zatrathi are far away and they're plenty powerful. The players will welcome an enemy nearby, a smaller fish to gobble up. Why aren't you a suitable minnow?"

"We'll see about that! Let them come. I'll have some things to tell them of my own," Gammon said through his teeth. The guild leader quickly understood the ramifications and could probably envision his future better than me.

"Nobody's saying the war won't be long and valorous but you already know the final outcome. The Qualians will be crushed—sooner or later, but they will be crushed. The players will start fleeing like space rats from a sinking ship, but it will be too late. You will lose everything. Now look here—I specifically asked the adviser about you and the possibility of your guild switching to the Precian Empire as mercenaries."

Here, I sent another clip to Gammon and Kiddo of the adviser discussing the conditions for the Black Sails' change of factions.

"As you can see, under normal circumstances, without our blessing and cooperation, the transition from one empire to another is strictly regulated. You simply won't have time to retrieve all your assets from the Qualians otherwise. Now try and tell me that I don't deserve freedom and the reward I asked for. Especially when I went out on a limb and got you an imperial guarantee. Here—take this as proof of my goodwill to you."

I sent off the last clip, in which the adviser confirmed on behalf of the emperor the transition of the Black Sails to the Precian Empire, under the condition they did so immediately. Gammon's opaque visor kept me from seeing his reaction. All I could do was wait until he had finished discussing the offer with his guild and deputies. Marina meanwhile was conferring with Anton, paying us no attention.

"I won't have enough time to liquidate all our assets while you're on your way to Zalva." It took Gammon about five minutes to come back to us. I had even begun to worry. "I need three or four hours."

"No problem," Marina came to my aid, for I had no idea how to persuade the adviser to postpone the report. "If you can make it worth the adviser's time to wait, he will give you the extra time."

"With what? Another ten million? I don't even know yet how much the reconstruction of Zalva's moon is going to cost our guild," grumbled Gammon.

"It's not money. I have something else in mind. You said yourself that everyone knows about the Zatrathi. Help me find the ship that ambushed me, promise to deliver it to the adviser and he will happily wait as long as necessary. And it will further persuade the Precians to break off relations with the Qualians."

"You want me to help you get even?" Gammon instantly understood what Kiddo was getting at.

"You bet. The Zatrathi attacked us from behind, taking out our cannons. I barely managed to hit her with twenty torpedoes of my favorite design. The Zatrathi ship is still somewhere around here being repaired. It shouldn't be difficult for you to find her. Grant Surgeon and me safe passage, pay us for our help with the Precians and the adviser is yours. I value my good name too much to allow some scum to ambush me on own raid. Surgeon, are you with us?"

"You'll have to do this without me," I had to refuse. "I plundered so much loot from Raydon that I need to lie low and sort through my holds. I don't much feel like going after the Zatrathi that managed to take you out. Let's do it without my involvement."

"I agree to the terms," Gammon, putting everything at stake. "Bring the adviser here."

"No, my dear!" Kiddo smiled crookedly. "First, we have to draw up a contract and sign it. I don't like surprises. Anton, show him our draft."

So that's what they were up to while I languished in anticipation. That's a bit of prudence I should learn from.

CHAPTER FOUR

"S URGEON, I HAVE ACCEPTED THE OFFER OF THE HEAD OF THE BLACK SAILS. The additional evidence of the Qualian's betrayal will not be superfluous when war is at stake. I must see the Zatrathi ship for myself and, if possible, interrogate the crew," the adviser announced, as soon as I returned to my *Warlock*.

The guild leader had something to be happy about. Having taken his oath of allegiance, the adviser welcomed the idea of hunting down the Zatrathi ship, thereby granting him time to settle his accounts in the Qualian Empire. I imagine that the market for valuable planets was blowing up right now from the unique offers coming out of the Black Sails. Any more or less serious guild would be agonizing over the question of why the Sails were selling off their best assets. Gammon will dump them and will make sure to throw in some tidbits of info to the more generous buyers. The head of the Black Sails received an additional bonus from his meeting with the adviser in the form of a guarantee that the Precian Empire would reimburse any losses his guild sustained in this raid.

I looked in the direction of the Black Sails cruiser and winced at the idea that some got off lucky and others got shafted. Judging by the adviser's speech, I was in the latter category.

"I was informed that you do not want to go with the Black Sails, but I have to insist on your involvement. Despite their oath of allegiance, Gammon has not been officially presented to the emperor, and the guild had not yet proven that the Precians can trust them. I cannot board their ship, much less *Alexandria*. In fact, in the case of *Alexandria* there is nothing to speak of! It is a pirate flagship after all!"

I really did not want to join the new raid. This wasn't my fight and quite simply, I was tired.

"Adviser, I have already done much for the Precian Empire and…"

"Just as the Precian Empire has done for you and Captain Kiddo!" the adviser interrupted me.

"Agreed," I conceded the obvious. "Our dealings have been mutually beneficial, but still hear me out! The Zatrathi ship destroyed Kiddo's ship on its own. A single hit on my ship and we'll be stardust! It would be safer for you to travel aboard the Black Sails' cruiser. Is the emperor so scrupulous in adhering to the protocol that he will risk your safety?"

"It is not for you, pirate, to question the orders of His Imperial Majesty!" It looked like I was going to lose rapport with the adviser if I continued to argue. "Like any scallywag, all you worry about is your plunder. We understand this and therefore the Precian Empire is ready to compensate you for any losses of cargo. The orbship is not in danger of losing a class. It cannot lose that which it doesn't have. What else holds you back?"

Besides my childish stubbornness—nothing, I guess. Reluctantly, I called Kiddo and announced that I would join her revenge mission, though without any particular enthusiasm. I agreed to come with but refused to get involved in any fighting.

As soon as the adviser was sure that I had accepted the mission, he began making calls and no longer replied to me. NPCs were convenient partners in this regard—they never interfered in the players' gameplay when it came to trivial matters.

Angry and irritated, I was looking for someone to take it out on and found a suitable victim:

"Tell me, oh miracle of Uldan technology, of the stuff we worked so hard to steal, what can we actually use?"

"So we don't lose it when we respawn?" the snake understood what I was getting at instantly. "I suppose I can integrate just about everything. If you give me some time, there won't be any extras on board. But it will take about six hours. Does that suit you?"

"I think I'm going to rename you Zoe," I muttered. "No that doesn't suit me. Integrate all the legendary modules, and we'll see about the rest when you're done."

"Why Zoe?" the snake stuttered.

"Ah cause I feel like it. Don't get distracted!" I cut her off.

"Legendaries then. So, right now I can add a repair kit, an

additional power unit and an automatic target locking system to your suit. As it happens, you have three slots free. The latter is necessary, otherwise you'll miss more often when you shoot."

"That's it! You've gone too far, Zoe," I got angry.

"Why Zoe? What is this? Human humor?" the robot snake asked with surprise.

"Yes. It's a joke. Zoe's short for Zoetrope. An ancient device that created the illusion of motion, activity, work. Get it?" I explained. The slizosaur had gotten to me with her constant lip. "The repair unit isn't necessary. Mount that on the second armor suit. Is there anything that'll increase damage output? My blasters couldn't handle the Qualian shields. That won't do."

"There is an EM cannon, but I can only mount it to an arm. It won't have auto-aim." Satisfied with my explanation, the slizosaur dropped the topic of my bad puns. "I can also increase the power of your blasters by forty percent, but I will have to sacrifice something. There are no more available module slots. I propose we sacrifice the autopilot. You don't seem to use it anyway."

"Do it!" I ordered and my cabin grew cramped. The snake popped out of the hull and began to work on the armor suit. After a long pause, she called out:

"Cap'n, I was thinking about your Zoe jest. I get the humor...And maybe I even like the reference. I could even attach some devices that will make the reference better. It'd be nice after all. But this irritation of yours...Well, to wit, don't call me Zoe. I have a long metal tail and you are soft and fleshy. A fight won't make our ship better."

IN SEARCH OF THE ULDANS

"All right. You've convinced me," I laughed as my bad mood dissipated. Calm now, I returned to my preparations for the raid.

Then my PDA vibrated—it was Kiddo.

"Surgeon, I'm sending you the coordinates. We'll be jumping in a couple of minutes. We will go in first and provide you with protection. Just don't do anything on your own."

Having assured Marina that I hadn't the slightest inclination for heroism in this case, I finally remembered my stowaway: the Qualian I had broken out of prison was still in the medcapsule—mostly so he wouldn't get underfoot. I asked the engineer to take a break from updating my armor suit, release the guest and prepare my old armor for my guest. When the Qualian appeared, I nodded at the suit prepared for him:

"Gear up. This ship has no inertial dampeners."

I didn't have to ask twice. The Qualian quickly put on the suit and began adjusting its settings. It looked like he knew what he was doing.

"So what were you in prison for?"

Unlike the prisoner back on the Uldan base, the system let me bring this character back to my ship. All I had to figure out was what I needed him for.

"For violating Qualian law," came the vague reply.

"Well, that much is obvious," I muttered to myself. "Okay then, violator of Qualian law, I don't need you on this ship. If you want to stay, you'll start by answering my questions properly. You make that mistake again and I jettison you. Show him, Brainiac."

The next instant, the Qualian went flying into space just like

143

Marina had earlier. Once he had had a chance to enjoy the delights of weightlessness and cosmic radiation, I had Brainiac bring him back.

"Next time I'll leave you there, only without the suit. Should I repeat my question?"

"No," the Qualian was impressionable, but also intelligent. I don't know what impressed him more: the prospect of a long sojourn in outer space or the sudden appearance of holes in my ship, but he reported diligently. "Trespassing on the property of the Duke of Dalerno with the intent to steal some family ornaments. Sentenced to death."

"How dull. A bungling burglar," I summarized.

"I'm not a burglar. I'm a thief! And I had right good standing in the thieves' guild too."

"The keyword being 'had.' Thieves in good standing don't get caught."

"Thieves in good standing are sometimes set up by dummy clients and end up in prison or the gallows. I had just gotten into the palace and they were already waiting for me."

"Everything's clear with you then." My curiosity in the hapless thief subsided, and I began thinking where I could get rid of him. "I'm heading out on a raid with an adviser of the Precian Emperor. After that I plan on jumping to Belket. I can drop you off there."

"Why? Just kill me here," the thief snorted. "Or toss me out to space. I'll stand no chance in Precian territory."

"I don't have a reason to kill you. And I won't throw you overboard with armor. I could use the suit. But I don't need an extra pair of lungs on this ship either. Any suggestions? Maybe I can take you back to your colleagues?"

"The thieves won't take me back. I'm a dead man for them. No one will want to do business with me. As for the empires, well, I've already mentioned the Precians, and the others are no different. Better, drop me off on any planet of the Confederation."

An outcast? My interest in the Qualian spiked again. It was always a nice boon to meet an outcast in any game. They make good party members but they also almost always have some kind of unique skill or ability. My suspicions about the coincidence of encountering this passenger couldn't help but stir in my head. The Qualian could well be some hidden reward from the developers for breaking out the pirates. According to the script, Kiddo should have been rescued by the other pirates. And this guy was right there in the neighboring cell. That's the first thing. His specialization was thievery. That's the second thing. And he had no kith or kin. Thoughts whirled through my head, and I realized that I was ready to make this fellow a lucrative offer.

"There is another option. It seems like I've saved you twice already and so feel some sort of responsibility for you. Providence indicates that our destinies should be linked," I paused, hoping that I did not overdo it with the fatalism, and finished: "You can become a member of my crew if you take an oath of loyalty. I am a pirate. Pillage and plunder is my trade. A good thief can come in handy in my line of work."

"And will you bind me to the planetary spirit?" the thief inquired, incredulously. His question only confirmed to me that he truly was an outcast. He had no homeworld so any death would be his last.

"As a captain, I have to look out for my team," I confirmed. "I have my own planet with its own spirit, so there shouldn't be a problem with this. But I'd like to know I can trust you. I only met you a few hours ago. You could be lying about everything. What if you decide to steal my ship and hand it over to your guildmates? What if you betray me at the most inopportune moment? If you want to join my crew, prove to me that you deserve to."

"We can both play that game," the Qualian scoffed. "I will prove to you my usefulness, tell you of some nice places and passwords of the thieves' guild and in the end I'll find myself in space without an armor suit. You humans are very unreliable partners in this regard."

"Are you sure you're not confusing something? It was your reliable Qualians who betrayed you and sentenced you to death, while this unreliable human saved you twice, gave you armor and offered you a homeworld," I didn't mind putting the screws to the Qualian a little. The stakes had been voiced so it remained only to nudge the character in the desired decision. "If you do not believe me, then you have only one way out—the first Confederate planet we encounter."

The Qualian was silent and I pointedly gave an order to the ship computer:

"Brainiac, adjust the permissions on his armor suit: no thrusters, no weapons, no ship integration, no attempts to leave the suit. Monitor everything that our guest does aboard our ship.

I won't tolerate sabotage or theft. By the way! What do they call you, thief?"

"Jacques Sebastian. Hereditary smuggler and master thief. Former adviser of the Raydon thieves' guild. The only one who made it through the Lazarus pyramid," the Qualian answered haltingly, padding his worth.

"That bit about the pyramid probably sounds real impressive, but it is lost on me. I have no idea what the Lazarus pyramid is. I'll have to take you to Hilvar. He likes smugglers."

"Wow! You know Hilvar?" Sebastian asked sarcastically.

"Yes, and you're wasting your sarcasm. I'm not the last pirate in this galaxy. Those two people that I broke out of prison are the captain of the cruiser *Alexandria* and her chief mate. Ever heard of them?"

"I heard that she's with the Corsican. People like that are just as bad for me as for you. The worst of the pirates."

"You're mistaken, thief. She wouldn't have anything to do with you for any price. And the 'worst of the pirates' did not kill you at my personal request. In general, have a think before we meet Hilvar. I've got a Zatrathi ship to deal with at the moment."

The hereditary smuggler exhausted me with his stubbornness, so I decided to let him stew about his unenviable fate. The possibility that he would choose to be left on a Confederate planet was gradually melting away. My offer was the best one and, most importantly, the only one. The thief had just tried to sell himself as expensively as possible and I, in turn, had haggled to bring down the price.

Kiddo's and Gammon's cruisers blinked and disappeared.

The players went to fight the Zatrathi and it was time for me to join them.

"Let's go Brainiac. Have you updated the armor suit, snake?"

"Yes, but one of the upgrades is a Qualian prototype that doesn't quite work yet. It has a critical bug so make sure not to fiddle with it. Otherwise, you'll be respawning before I can correct it."

"Well that's just great," I said sarcastically. "You said that there were only three free slots left."

"Yes, three. I removed the sonar module since it seemed redundant. The space scanner manages all right in the water anyway. In exchange you get an additional argument in the form of twenty surface-to-surface missiles. Don't mistake their small size. They'll smash a marine walker to bits. I wired them to the blasters' targeting system, so the whole thing should work like a charm—err, when it works, that is."

"And will I have to wait long for you to fix the bug?" I really liked the sound of the new weapon and wanted to try it out as soon as possible.

"I don't know. I need time. A couple of days. So if you launch the rockets and they accidentally detonate during launch, it's not my fault. You've been warned."

Having reckoned the pros and cons, I did not refuse. Nobody forced me to use rockets for a couple of days, and then the engineer would fix everything. And if that Zatrathi ship sank us, this nice attachment will remain mine anyway.

"We have arrived," said Brainiac and the long glowing lines

once again turned into twinkling stars. A three-dimensional map of the star system appeared on the screen—a red giant with two barren moons that had been mining planets once upon a time. Several astronomical units from us, I could make out *her*—an unearthly alien ship. Outwardly, she looked more like a virion of the flu, albeit three times larger than a cruiser. It was no wonder that such a large vessel had destroyed *Alexandria*. But the best part was the detachment of Qualian repair ships attending her. When I emerged from hyperspace, some of them were engaged in repairing the Zatrathi vessel, while the other part was busy screening it from Kiddo's and Gammon's attacks. The Allies had attacked as soon as they entered the system.

"This is unfathomable treachery!" exclaimed the adviser, who had spent this entire time conferring with the Emperor and only now ended his private conversation to rejoin me. "This is war! The Qualians must pay for their perfidy!"

Your rapport with the Precian Empire has improved. Current value: 30.

Twelve cruisers were pouring all their fire on the Zatrathi shields without any effect. The enemy's defenses handled both the EM and beam cannons without much trouble, regenerating their shields on the fly. Torpedoes were completely useless—the Zatrathi had no problem intercepting them a good distance from their ship. All this gave rise to an interesting impasse: The players were attacking as hard as they could, while the enemy defended as hard as it could, which meant that it couldn't counterattack. I could safely go heat up some popcorn and wait for one of the sides to run out of energy or else change their battle tactics. The Zatrathi ship really did look terrifying and menacing with immense arcs of current sparking periodically among its myriad spires.

"Marina, if you have a Plan B, now is the time," Gammon's voice came on the comm. "What was that BFG you used on my cruiser? If it's a matter of elo, I'll help you out."

"The Yamato Cannon. It's a prototype. Firing it disabled it and it'll need repairs. Let's push! They can't defend forever! Launch your fighters!"

No sooner said than done! Maybe out in meatspace the players had been knocked about the ears for missing too many days of work because now at least a hundred small points instantly scrambled from each cruiser. In open space, they looked like a dense cloud of insects. The fighters, which could ignore the energy shields quickly passed this barrier and rushed to the body of the enemy virus. It seemed as though a little more and we'd gain the upper hand, but I was wrong. An EM salvo from the Zatrathi ship knocked out our fighters' electronics, turning them into space debris for a short period. While the pilots were resetting their systems, their fighters drifted in space without any control, bumping into each other. Curses and complaints filled the airwaves. Meanwhile, hangar doors opened in the Zatrathi ship unleashing squadrons of enemy fighters already familiar to me—no one was about to let the players reset their ships quietly. Here and there, our fighters began exploding into short-lived balls of fire that rolled into themselves—and left small shimmering crates. With one attack the Zatrathi plunged hundreds of fighter owners into despair, quickly and accurately knocking down their hard-earned ship-classes.

"Send the frigates to defend the fighters!" Kiddo instantly reacted to the change in the situation. Each of the cruisers could accommodate up to three frigates, but not all of them responded to the girl's orders. Only a dozen or so rushed to the Zatrathi ship. The EM cannons fired again but the frigates' anti-EM systems did their part. Only one of the ships shut down and the enemy fighters immediately blew It up. The survivors took up positions, defending the larger concentrations of our fighters. Sometimes they fired torpedoes, but they were easily intercepted—the Zatrathi ships had excellent point defense gunners. Our side had one effective weapon remaining—the beam cannons. Even if they couldn't penetrate the enemies' hulls, they did manage to keep away the Zatrathi from our fighters. Space again began to light up with short flashes, most of which were red this time around. The enemy was beginning to suffer losses.

"Two questions for you, Brainiac. The first is why is that the EM cannons have no effect on the enemy fighters? The second is what will happen to us if we fly closer?"

"You sure do like to ask difficult questions, Captain," the snake answered instead. "There is no answer to the first one. The second answer is only a hypothetical one. Our shields should hold, assuming the Zatrathi don't have any further surprises, but the torpedoes will give us trouble."

Torpedoes? I frowned, peering into the screen. Hundreds of

Zatrathi torpedoes were making their way towards our fighters and frigates. It looked like we had made them angry. If this is only part of their arsenal, then Kiddo, with her thirst for revenge, has set everyone up. Barely having time to reboot, our fighters rushed back under the protection of the cruisers. The frigates remained on the front line, trying to use their maneuverability to evade the torpedoes. But casualties were unavoidable. It took just a few moments for the battle to shift the other way. Four frigates and more than a hundred fighters had already set off to the ship graveyards.

The second wave of Zatrathi torpedoes came too late. All the surviving ships disappeared under the reliable protection of their cruisers, passing the baton of active combat to their teams. The guys on the cruisers extinguished the enemy's torpedoes as soon as they left the Zatrathi ship's shields. It was pleasant to watch the players coordinate to destroy the torpedoes. These boys weren't playing for a top guild for nothing.

Once the Zatrathi fighters had no one to fight with, they turned back and disappeared into the bowels of their fortress.

After that the battle unfolded without any further climaxes or unexpected turns. Every thirty seconds the Zatrathi fired a salvo of torpedoes, our guys shot them out of the sky and then it was our turn to hit back. Nobody wanted to give up.

"Surgeon, we're changing plans. We need you," Kiddo said over the air. I immediately dialed her on my PDA.

"What did you want?"

"I want to sink that Zatrathi ship. Will you help me?"

"It depends on how." The stubborn struggle had not

persuaded me to join Kiddo and Gammon.

"I want you to board them."

Hearing the offer, I snorted skeptically:

"Kiddo, that wasn't in our agreement."

"Yes, I know. But you can see for yourself—we can't break through. They're knocking out our torpedoes before they can close the distance. And they're disabling our fighters. The only sensible option is to board them. Look, they haven't had the time to fix their hull. This is our chance!"

"Brainiac, move the ship as carefully as possible to this location." I indicated a point on the map from which I could assess the damage to the Zatrathi hull. One of the spires was peppered with numerous holes. The orbship could well slip inside. Assuming I wanted to.

The Qualian repair ships were working on restoring the outer hull and shield. The innards were being repaired by the Zatrathi themselves—they crawled with slug engineers.

"Surgeon, are you going to say anything?" Marina was waiting for my assent and pressured me on the public channel instead of the PDA. "We will provide fire support. And we'll give you our best marines. Come on, I know you! You're a true professional, not some wuss who sits behind the lines. Make up your mind!"

"Let's dispense with the crude flattery, Kiddo," I winced from the stupidity of what she had just said. Her attempt to put me in the public limelight hadn't gone as she had planned it. "In theory, I can survive the fire from the EM cannons and sneak in there. But I will regret losing my cargo if I something happens."

"Surgeon, we are partners and can always come to some agreement. Let's do it this way—you can keep sixty percent of the loot from your boarding action. The rest will go to the marines."

"That's more like it! Now you're talking like a business partner, partner! Let's wait for the next wave of torpedoes. As soon as you knock it out, I'll fly into the breach. We'll need fire support; otherwise they will immediately knock me out. The marines are all equipped with legendary gear, I assume? I can carry about thirty men in my holds. We will break through to the flight deck and blow the ship up from the inside." My inner pirate child was already looking forward to the next adventure and would not forgive me if I missed out.

"Great. Fly over to me, the men are already ready. Plan to close on the right, but stay behind. The main cannons are located in front."

"Kiddo, I hesitate to ask, how did you determine where the Zatrathi front and back is?" To my uninitiated eyes the Zatrathi ships had neither bows nor sterns like my orbship.

"Once you lay into them several times with some high-caliber weaponry, you'll figure it out. The blue lights there are their bow; their fighter hangers are on their flanks. Any other questions?"

"Will you take my guys? Bones is itching for some hand-to-tentacle combat," Gammon interrupted. "He will come in useful."

"No more than two and they have thirty seconds to get ready. Marina, I'll head to you first," I replied, turning towards *Alexandria*. At this moment, the Zatrathi ship fired another spread of torpedoes. Maneuvering among the beam cannons and carefully destroying the deadly missiles, I sidled up to the cruiser. The marines were already waiting in open space. Holding onto each other like kids in kindergarten, the living chain floated into my hold. It was harder to fit Bones and his partner in the crammed space, but I'd never promised anyone five-star accommodations either.

"Brainiac, do you have any idea of where their bridge might be?" I asked my ship computer. But the snake answered in his stead:

"No. It could be located in any of the spires as well as in the internal compartments with equal probability."

"I see. Everybody get ready. We're going in. Fire support only at my command!"

I flew up as close as possible to the shield, inviting the enemy to attack me. The Zatrathi did not need to be asked twice—a salvo of torpedoes rushed in my direction as well as in the direction of our fighters.

"Full throttle back!" the engineer ordered and a torpedo came flying out of *Warlock*. The snake's distinguishing feature wasn't greed but thrift over the ordnance entrusted to her care. If she decided to part with a torpedo, it meant that there was good reason for it, and the Zatrathi would suffer the maximum possible damage from the shot. Our side's torpedoes did not allow the beam cannons of the Zatrathi to destroy mine, which played into our hands. Heeding the engineer's order, we hurled abruptly away from the Zatrathi. At the same moment, my torpedo's fuse ended its countdown and the missile exploded in the midst of the

Zatrathi. Since most of the warheads fired by the bombers were aimed at me, they could not avoid the explosion. The enemy's torpedoes detonated in a chain reaction, trapping the Zatrathi pilots.

"Wonderful!" Brainiac reacted to the outcome of the maneuver that had cleared the way to the Zatrathi ship.

"Cover us!" I ordered into the comm and *Warlock* rushed forward at full thrust. Everyone who was on the ship felt the EM blast, but Brainiac handled it well—the reactor came back up in a split second. The auxiliary power unit worked perfectly.

"Gunner, clear the way for us!" I flew right up to the hull and the orangutan swept away the black clumps of antennae and radar dishes with fire from our beam cannons.

"The package is out for delivery," said the snake, referring to the torpedo, but then immediately hissed angrily: "They've intercepted it. They're deflecting it. Those package thieving bastards!"

The second torpedo came too close to the hull, and the Zatrathi did not dare to use their point defense cannons, wary of further damaging their own hull. Instead, they launched their version of the flycatcher and simply guided the missile away. The timer finished counting down and the warhead detonated in a brief fiery inferno. A damaged spire appeared ahead of us surrounded by repair ships. A jungle of scaffolding filled the intervening space.

"I have sight of the LZ. Gunner, make us a passage."

All of a sudden something shook our ship.

"They're trying to trap us with tractor beams, like a torpedo," the snake explained. "The active protection is working but we won't last long. It's time, Cap'n! They're about to hit us with their EM. Our shields will dissolve and then we're as good as dead."

"Copy. Marina, where are you?"

"Relax. We're here," came an unfamiliar male voice and a fighter flew past me. The player banked sharply, unloading all the elo in his beam cannons—and then rammed the Zatrathi hull at full throttle. The hull gave in and spewed debris into open space. That which could not be opened with beam weapons, could be rammed, opening a way in for us.

"Get the Precians to reimburse your pilot," I advised Kiddo, flying through the opened passage. The gunner was blissfully pouring plasma onto anything around us and updates about my mission for Hilvar kept flashing before my eyes. A squadron of Zatrathi fighters left the ship on a course to intercept us. But they came to their senses just in time.

"Torpedoes away," announced the snake, and the surface of the nearest spire exploded into a ball of fire. The munitions had reached their target. Enough time to assess the diversion and make a decision. I banked and was about to crash through the still burning opening. The engineers were close at hand and no doubt there was already some troops waiting for us—unless that part of the ship was completely isolated from its main areas. I decided to break through on the other side.

"Where are you going?!" I did not have time to answer Kiddo as *Warlock* gnawed into the insides of the Zatrathi ship. If it weren't for my seatbelt, I would have been flattened against the wall of my cabin. The ship was shaking, the lights went out and sprays of sparks were raining all around us. There was a terrible screech and I began to worry that my ship wouldn't survive the landing. Or the marines. But after a couple of seconds, everything went quiet.

"Is everyone okay? Go! Go! Go!" I yelled, swallowing, to moisten my throat which had gone dry from excitement. The maneuver had not come easy to my ship: The anti-EM paneling had suffered greatly and all the external sensors had been lopped off as Brainiac hadn't had time to retract them. Without them, *Warlock* was deaf, blind and dumb. But at least the raiding party had reached the dungeon.

"Engineer, commence emergency repairs. Spare no supplies," I ordered and opened the hold. The marines were all there, healthy, locked and ready. Pouring out, they scrambled to take up their positions.

"Brainiac, start hacking the local network! Gunner, cover the entrance. Don't let anyone get close."

"Set up a perimeter," a male voice came on the air. "We'll take it from here, Surgeon."

"I have connected to the network. I am sending you a map of the spire we are in. I have located the communications relay to the mainframe. Plotting a route now."

"I have received the map, thank you! Squads one and two move forward. Squad three maintain overwatch."

"I can overwatch myself; don't waste your men. I have thirty droids on board."

"Roger. Squad three—the lower three decks are yours. Squad one—you have the central three decks. Squad two—the top three decks. Safeties off and don't hoard the powercells if things get hot. Let's go!"

It was pleasant to observe the marines' well-coordinated boarding procedure. Kiddo's assault team specialized in ship-to-ship combat—they weren't so fit for surface action. Each of the marines had a directional shield integrated into his armor. His flanks were supposed to be covered either by a fellow marine or a wall. Even my scant knowledge was enough to understand that they wouldn't be able to fight very effectively in the open.

Bones and his partner were asked to open the doors and advanced after the landing party, choosing the central decks. They had already accomplished their main purpose—the Precian adviser had witnessed them enter the Zatrathi vessel. As always, the guild's business came first.

"Surgeon, I have to go with you," the adviser reminded me. "I must see the Zatrathi ship with my own eyes!"

"So go see it," I said without much protest. "Brainiac, send out the droids and the marine. Tell them to look for the nearest stockpile. Detail two droids to guard the adviser!"

"Acknowledged," the ship computer replied. "I have located a resource stockpile. According to the primary analysis, the length of the route will be one and a half kilometers. Access is through the third, fourth or fifth decks. There is a complex system of corridors here. Precise calculations will take a long time."

While the special forces were capturing the ship, I could plunder some gear and resources from the Zatrathi.

"How far is it as the crow flies?" I asked.

Brainiac sent me a simplified map of the ship. The treachery of the Zatrathi seemed evident in the corridors' myriad twists and turns and dead ends.

"Two hun-hun-dred meters," Brainiac replied with a little stutter. The slizosaur had begun repairing the ship. "Shall I run a detailed analysis of the co-co-corridor system?"

"No. It has been designed to make life complicated for people like us. Think of it as the labyrinth of the Minotaur." Let the devs think that they've stumped us, while I think of some other way to do this. "Send the rhino. We'll head along deck four. We'll see if he can break through the wall."

The marine went rushing out of *Warlock*'s hull and slammed straight into the wall. The metal panels gave way, opening a passage to the neighboring corridor.

"Good boy," I praised the rhino, causing him to wag his tail. "Demo all the walls between here and the stockpile. Crush any Zatrathi you encounter."

I turned to the Qualian.

"Sebastian, get ready. It's time for us to do some larceny and thievery. Brainiac, grant him pilot access to his armor suit."

Surprised by my offer, the thief instantly became excited and jumped to his feet. "Excellent! What are we going to steal?"

"Anything that's not bolted down. We'll start by ransacking the crew cabins. Anyway, it's not for me to teach you. Kiddo, marines, how's it looking out there?"

"They've stopped shooting torpedoes at us and the fighters have retreated too. Everything's quiet, though they're holding their lines," reported Marina.

"Minor local resistance," replied the assault leader. "Slugs and a couple of warriors. Nothing serious, we are clearing the corridors. The layout in this place is incomprehensible."

I could get behind that. Judging by the map Brainiac had sent me, the marines had delved fairly deeply. The corridors were constantly looping, crisscrossing and diverging. The levels kept overlapping and then splitting again. As a result, the marines had to pause and clear out the pockets of resistance they encountered. Leaving enemies behind your back was stupid and dangerous.

"I cannot gain access to this compartment's mainframe," Brainiac suddenly declared. "There seems to be an advanced anti-intrusion system in place. I would need to connect directly to the control circuit. Warning, I am detecting movement at the sector's perimeter. Five hundred warriors. They are moving along three decks at once."

"Roger! Thank you!" answered the assault leader, who incidentally had never introduced himself to me. "How long do we have before they get here?"

"About five minutes if they follow the corridors. About thirty seconds as the crow flies," I reckoned.

"As the crow flies?" the marine asked.

"Through the walls. If you ask me, it's faster to demolish them than to go around."

"Well, we have a lot of numbskulls here, but no sledgehammers," the officer replied. "Blasters won't do it."

"Pity. It's a good idea. If you come across something you can use, try it. You have guests on the way, over and out." I disconnected. It was time to check out the tunnel the rhino had made and come up with a reasonable explanation for this and other holes. No doubt the grunts will have some questions. No one's seen the rhino before. Although…I can just order the gunner to blow up the deck and that will be that. No deck, no questions.

Sebastian jumped out of the ship, approached a wall and began touching it confidently. Out of curiosity, I also approached. In some way known only to him, the thief determined the exact location of the cache and, prying off a barely visible panel with the blade of his knife, tossed it aside. A small safe stood behind the panel. I whistled with admiration. Sebastian unceremoniously yanked the steel box out of the wall, set it on the floor and with a hefty blow, dented one of its edges. The metal cracked, allowing the thief to insert the knife into the slot and enlarge it to a decent size. Squatting down, the Qualian ran his hand inside and pulled out three sparkling crystals.

"Anything valuable?" asked Sebastian in bewilderment, handing me his find.

I took the crystals and shrugged. I'd never seen items like that before. Brainiac ran a rapid analysis and determined that they were made of ordinary glass. No inscriptions, no codes or anything like that—just faceted glass crystals. They were at first, and even second glance, no different than cheap plastic trinkets.

"Let's move on. Maybe we will find something valuable further on." I had no idea what to do with this kind of loot, so I tossed it in my inventory. Just in case. Sebastian showed no interest in these 'treasures' either. The next room was an exact copy of the previous one, only with less destruction. This time, the thief carefully tapped the walls, found another safe, and added two more crystals to my inventory. I even felt a little bad, considering the possibility that these 'crystals' could be the Zatrathi crew's savings.

"Brainiac, send two droids to strip the furniture from the Zatrathi ship," my pirate's conscience did not allow me to leave empty-handed. Then again, the furniture here looked so odd that I couldn't even be sure that it was furniture. At first glance, I couldn't identify the purpose of many things here, so I would just have to hope that the droids didn't pick up a toilet in the process. Who knows how the slugs handle that business. And I wouldn't put it past the devs to put a clip together and call it 'The Heist.' Either way, it was a risk I was willing to take to avoid passing up something interesting!

I had just approached the next breach in the wall when the rhino's satisfied mug popped up in it. Having gotten soused to his nostrils on raq, he had returned to unload the loot and was on his way back. I checked the logs: Twelve slugs had breathed their last breath under my marine's feet. He didn't even have to shoot—he just trampled anything without armor as he went.

"Brainiac, is there anything valuable at all in this spire? Beside the stockpile you found earlier, I mean."

"Negative. These are the crew compartments for the maintenance personnel."

"Ah, all right. Have you noticed any technical gadgets? Maybe someone took their work home with them?"

"I have only been able to access the cameras around the

spire's perimeter. I obtained the schematic from the internal network. I have no other means of surveying this vessel's interior. It is not even known how many living enemies are in this compartment. I am hampered by my lack of knowledge about Zatrathi shipbuilding practices."

"Have you been talking to that snake again? Stop moping. Remind me, do we have a holding cell for a hostile prisoner? I want to try and capture a slug. Can you provide him with living conditions so he won't die right away?"

"The answer is affirmative. The Zatrathi eating habits are known. *Warlock*'s microclimate will permit us to sustain one specimen."

"Good. Order the marine to take one slug prisoner. Have the droids do the same. They should avoid killing anything unless they have to, and call me immediately if they succeed."

"Understood."

"How are the repairs going? Is there any estimate about how much longer they will take?"

"Two hours and thirty minutes," the snake joined the conversation. "During this time, I can launch the ship and safely send us to the base. It will not be possible to repair it completely."

"The hard part will be getting out of here," I muttered and returned to the adviser. He had remained standing beside the ship. "You wished to examine the Zatrathi ship? We have cleared the defenders from this area."

I added this detail on purpose—our assault force had wiped out all of the Zatrathi warriors. The players were currently celebrating like kids (many of them were, after all), collecting the golden tokens they had earned. They were especially happy that they didn't have to waste time gathering loot from a myriad crates. All a player had to do was open one and he would automatically receive his share of the reward for killing five hundred Zatrathi.

I couldn't help wondering whether I could get some too if I hurried over to where they were. Judging by the map, they weren't that far, so maybe it made sense to go get some tokens. I'll ask Kiddo what they're worth at some later point…

I pulled out my manipulators and lifted a massive construction that resembled a bed into the air. I wanted to make an appearance in front of the marines. Hadn't they said that they didn't have anything to knock walls down with?

Swinging the bed back as far as the room allowed, I slammed it against the wall. The manipulators fell silent as the 'furniture for slug lewdness' shattered into pieces. Let's just say that this wasn't the saddest possible ending for a bed and we can even rejoice that it didn't go in vain—a small hole had appeared in the place where I had struck the wall. I couldn't wriggle through it nor make it larger, but I refused to despair.

"Engineer, drop everything and make me a good battering ram from some raq. It has to be light enough for the manipulators to pick it up and heavy enough to bust down the walls around here.

"Why even get your hands dirty, Cap'n? Give me a sec and I'll make you a ram with its own thrusters. All you have to do is aim it and the devil will do everything on its own."

"That a snake! How long will it take?"

"Ten minutes. It's not complicated. Let's see—I assume the demolished area has to be large enough for your armor suit to pass through? Did I understand correctly? We have enough raq and I have some mini-thrusters here. I was just racking my brain for what I could do with them. It'd be a pity to throw them away. Now they'll come in handy. Just wait bit! It'll be ready to go in a jiffy."

"I don't understand. Why go through such difficulties?" the adviser stopped beside me watching the snake work. The engineer had set up outside of the ship so there would be less work getting the ram out later. "Why can't we walk down the corridors?"

"Because no one keeps their treasures in public passages. And it'll be faster this way too." I explained and received a look of approval from one side and a look of disapproval from the other. Sebastian silently agreed me, while the adviser muttered something disparaging about pirates. I forced myself to keep my mouth shut about the Precian's hypocrisy. When the matter concerned traveling aboard a pirate ship to the Zatrathi, his attitude was quite different.

The snake did not let me down—ten minutes later a demonic battering ram named 'Knock Knock' hovered before us. The short time available for building it had affected the ram's outward appearance. Crooked, it bobbed in the air, firing its thrusters and waiting to be pointed at some wall. I turned it in the right direction and pressed the control button. Ba-da-boom! My ears rang from the crash. I appraised the new hole in the wall. It was just the right size. I climbed through first and patted the battering ram, which fired its thrusters in anticipation of further action. It's true what they say about appearances being deceptive.

"Hang on just a minute." The engineer slipped busily behind me and circled around her creation, meticulously inspecting the dents. "I suppose I am willing to give you a warranty good for four hundred blows. After that, it'll need repairs. The engines are welded in there. I won't be able to extract them later. So use her for all she's got, Cap'n. No need to be sparing."

"Understood, thanks. Get back to the ship repairs. It's time!" I ordered and stepped back to let the snake go and let Sebastian in. When the thief found the next safe with a glass crystal, he grew despondent. The heist seemed to be boring him.

"Let's go that way," I checked the map and began calculating a route to the marines. They had managed to come very close to where the spire we were in joined the rest of the Zatrathi fortress ship. There wasn't any chatter on the open channels—the party had switched to a third party voice chat, making it impossible to intercept their communications in-game. Obviously, no one thought of inviting me to that group.

Over the next seven rooms, I received a small but welcome gift—an enemy slug of my own. An engineer, he had no weapons or shields and had camouflaged himself to blend in with the interior so effectively that if it were not for Sebastian, I would never have seen him. I aimed my manipulators and levitated my captive into the air.

Closely examining the prisoner, the adviser said, "Are these the terrifying invaders of Galactogon?"

"Not quite," I replied. "This is an engineer. There are also warriors and a mysterious black fog among their ranks. Typically, these fellows only deal with repair and maintenance, but they can sometimes help the warriors too. They're slow but industrious. Back at the orbital station, the warriors used them like sappers to drive me out of cover."

"We heard that the Delvians captured a couple of warriors, but they did not have time to share a description or image with us. The aliens attacked the planet where the prisoners were being held and severed the lines of communication. Until now, we have not known what our enemy actually looks like. Thus, today is a landmark day for the Precian Empire: The enemy has finally revealed its face. Tell the Black Sails that I will expect all their battle recordings with Zatrathi warriors aboard this ship. For a reward, of course."

I sighed enviously. Gammon was simply rolling in the bacon. His rapport with the Precians will go through the roof and the ten mill I charged him will seem like spare change in retrospect. A real bargain. I should have asked for fifty.

Thinking such morose thoughts, I returned to the ship, holding the slug in front of me. Brainiac assigned the prisoner a compartment and administered a sedative just in case. We had no way of knowing the effect it would have, but thankfully the devs didn't come up with any surprises when it came to racial pharmacology. The slug went limp instantly and I loaded him into the cell. He can sleep tight until I find a willing buyer for him.

"We're at the entrance to the spire," the marine officer said over the comms. "The doors are locked from inside the main compartment. We are expected and not welcome. How are things going outside?"

"There are a lot of fighters circling around the spire, but they are not trying to attack," Kiddo replied. "Can you knock down the door or demo it?"

"We're about to try it. Hang on, I can hear a strange noise from the other side. Captain—it sounds like sawing."

"Blast! Guys, they are sawing the spire off! The fighters are there as a screen—so we wouldn't see anything." Marina veritably erupted in anger. "Oh those sly Zatrathi bastards! I'm going to let them have it! Hang on a moment!"

The news made me hurry up. The assault force was trying to blast the doors down with their blasters while Marina concentrated on the fighters in an attempt to interfere with the work of the engineers as much as she could. The comms went silent for a minute in anticipation of the resolution.

Checking the map again, I aimed the ram at the next wall. As we bashed our way towards the marines, we encountered another slug that I dispatched with a shot from my blaster. A silver token and a piece of raq were my loot. It was time to move on. Sebastian had no reason to hurry. He tarried behind me, exploring the crew's quarters, pilfering the glass crystals from the safes as he went. As for me, I needed to get to the marines as fast as possible. Although, that's not true. First of all, I needed to reach the place where the marines had killed the five hundred warriors. The marines had sounded too satisfied collecting their loot.

Twenty demolished walls brought us to our destination. The crates flickered, waiting for me to open them. Without further delay, I opened the closest crate and my UI went nuts with system notifications. There were so many of them that for a second I thought that Galactogon might not cope and crash. Reflecting whether to contact technical support or not, I scrolled down to the bottom of the log where the totals would be printed:

New items: Gold token (500)
New items: Raq (350)
New items: Powercell (120)
New items: Armor shard (37)
New items: C-class Zatrathi combat blaster (5)
New items: B-class Zatrathi combat blaster (2)

Was this junk worth all the hype? I'll try and remember to write to the devs. The functionality for picking up multiple items clearly needed fixing, since it was clearly designed for small quantities. When it came to large volumes, the interface glitched and confused the players.

The tokens, the raq and the powercells went into my inventory, while the armor and blasters remained where I found them. My current carrying capacity was only one thousand one hundred kilograms, and eighty percent of that was already occupied. There was physically no place to store further weapons and armor and I didn't need to anyway. These items' class was shamefully low.

I moved further down the corridor. The map indicated that

there was a right turn a dozen meters ahead. Reaching the location, I ordered:

"Everyone move away from the wall. Stand by the door to the central compartment. Raise your shields just in case too."

The marine officer ordered his men to comply in a slightly ironic voice. I couldn't care less about the irony as long as he did not ask any questions.

The ram slammed into the wall, blasting a big old hole in it. I stepped through it, smiling triumphantly and relishing the effect on my audience. Two players had suffered collateral damage despite my warning—in the cramped room there was simply nowhere to go. Somehow I did not consider that, but both were alive and could continue on.

"I told you to hurry up," I said and began moving through the squad, getting them to clear the way. The marines stepped back from the sturdy and tightly locked doors. Judging by the burn marks on it they had tried in vain to punch through the doors with blasters and beam cannons. Alas, the blast doors had been well designed. If I tried to demo them directly, my ram would simply break. It seemed more sensible to try to go around through the wall.

"Step aside. Let's try the tried and tested method. Get ready to fight just in case. Who knows what's on the other side."

I aimed the ram away from the door. The immediate wall around them was sure to be reinforced. But a bit further on, the panels should be the normal kind used aboard this ship. Also made from raq but not as thick. The players silently split into groups and cocked their blasters for battle. I suppose their commander had issued them orders on their own comm channel. It grew quiet and now I could make out a subtle buzz from the other side of the door. The operation to saw off the spire seemed to be still under way, albeit with interruptions. The ship was about to jettison one of its spires like a lizard's tail. Aiming, I fired the ram, hoping we weren't all about to get sucked out to space.

There was a dull thud and three dozen blue plasma blasts flew into the hole that had formed.

"Hold your distance! Advance!" Combat orders seemed to come in the public chat, since three of the players didn't have access to the private channel. Bones and his partner hadn't been invited to the private comm either.

I waited a few seconds until the last of Kiddo's marines had gone in and then carefully peered into the opening. Hmm. The engineer's brainchild had definitely met its match and end but it had also earned a posthumous reward. The demolished wall consisted of ten standard partitions. The depth of the funnel formed was about two meters. Each next hole was smaller than the previous one, and the players had to go through a small window to get inside the central part of the ship. But, trained to fight in tight confines, the marines infiltrated with the agility of cockroaches.

Having no such skill, I slowly climbed into the hole and looked out. My wrecked ram stood sad and alone, its engines charred and blown, as around it the air sizzled from the bolts of blue and red plasma being exchanged between the marines and the Zatrathi. The metallic buzz was much louder now, even with

---

the sounds of the shootout. I guess the Zatrathi were sawing the other levels, not knowing that their efforts were already in vain.

"You may enter!" came the order and Bones and his partner squeezed past me to join the assault team. The adviser noted the courage of his new allies, ignoring the fact that it was Kiddo's pirates and me who had done most of the work.

Having made it to the Zatrathi ship's main compartment, I contacted my own ship:

"Brainiac, can you see us?"

"No. You have left the area of survelllance. I require a new uplink to see you."

"Sure thing. Just tell me how I can do that for you."

"Find a network jack and then simply touch your right glove to the connector. The system will identify the interface and adapt its connector accordingly."

I found a network socket close by. Squatting down, I brought my hand up to the strange connector. A plug extended out of my glove's index finger. It whirred growing larger and smaller until it found the right dimensions. Then Brainiac directed me to stick my finger into the socket. The plug with the transmitter and the integrated carrier disconnected from the armor suit and lit up red: Brainiac had started the connection procedure.

I looked around, contemplating where to go. Long corridors stretched in all directions. The players were hunched in the middle shooting at the Zatrathi coming from all directions. One flank was doing much better than the other. In the former case, the assault team had penetrated a good distance from the breach. By the time the Zatrathi manage to saw off the spire, we should be well clear of it. Good luck digging us out of this base then.

"Ready!" said Brainiac and the LED changed to green. I retrieved the connection device. "I have gained access to the ship's parameters...data on its crew and personnel...as well as the Zatrathi locator beacons. Sending the data to your HUD now."

A 3D schematic of the Zatrathi vessel appeared before my eyes. The players were marked with sparse blue dots on the map, while the swarms of red dots indicated the Zatrathi. Even in the spire, which we had allegedly cleared out, there were still many living slugs left. The engineers had simply hidden in the cracks and crannies, understanding their role. Studying the schematic, I called the marine officer.

"Sergeant, can you spare a minute?"

"You think I have one to spare?" he snapped back, but asked: "What's up?"

"I have gained access to the Zatrathi network. There's some info I'd like to share with you. If you give me the access codes to the marines' armor suits, I will synchronize with you and share a 3D map of the ship with live enemy locations. Might be something else too."

"Do as he says, Graykill." Without giving the marine a chance to reply, Kiddo entered the conversation. "Surgeon, my network guys will see to it that your smart ship doesn't go where he shouldn't be before Graykill changes the codes."

Graykill muttered something about my ideas of OPSEC but had to do as his captain told him. Half a minute later, the PDA peeped, announcing that all thirty access codes had arrived.

"Brainiac, synchronize with the armor suits and send them the map and enemy positions. All transmissions have to go through me. If you detect any attempts of hostile intrusion, shut everything down, wipe the memory banks and burn the hardware. Are those orders clear?"

"Affirmative," replied the ship computer and the enigmatic cackle following the exchange suggested that the most trusting relationships are built on mutual threats.

Graykill received the map and rearranged his fighters. Reinforcements were pulled from the corridor where the marines were winning and sent to the one where they were losing. They took the Black Sails with them. I agreed with the adjustments—a blizzard of red was moving in from that flank. Our frenetic assault now gave way to a stubborn defense, with three beam cannons appropriated from the marines' inventory. Their coordination was impressive: Six manned the cannons, five maintained the shields and the rest of the brethren poured suppressing fire down the corridor, barely peeking from behind their cover.

"Engineer, what's the probability of my surface-to-surface rockets exploding at launch?" I wouldn't say that I didn't have faith in Graykill's men, but it didn't hurt to be safe. Engrossed in the battle, I'd forgotten all about my thief. If he dies here, then all my long-term plans with him will go the way of the Zatrathi grandmother.

"Captain, I told you. It's fifty-fifty. Either they'll blow up or they won't. The technology is crude and unreliable. I wouldn't bet one way or another, but it'd be a shame to waste them. Leave them alone. I'll fix the ship and then fix the rockets. In a day, maybe two, they'll be ready."

"This thing can be useful today. Would I survive the malfunction?"

"No. No chance."

The marines meanwhile were trying as hard as they could. Graykill slowed the attack in the second corridor and returned the fighters to their original positions, leaving only five to cover that approach. Everyone else was playing the 'who has more powercells' game. The cannons were thumping off deadly clumps of plasma into the ship, the marines manning the shields were swapping out powercells every 10 seconds, ignoring the shooting around them, and yet the storm of red dots was growing larger and larger. It got to the point where several Zatrathi managed to get close to one of the shield operators, snag him, and simply toss him somewhere deep into the ship. The player had no defense against physical damage, but for a few seconds the wave of attackers ebbed: Before dying, the marine had detonated the grenades he had. A rifleman took the place of his fallen mate, but the Zatrathi managed to repeat the maneuver—a couple suicidal warriors came running in, snagged two marines, hurled them towards their lines and the corridor shook from the grenades' explosions. The raid had ended for another two players.

"Captain, how about some reinforcements?" Graykill understood our prospects perfectly well. Sooner or later, the steady torrent of red dots would overrun us. Brainiac had counted 24 thousand Zatrathi on the ship, who knew how to use weapons. We had managed to get rid of only a small part of the total horde.

"Can't do. It's hot here too. Their fighters have blockaded us entirely. We can't break through. The Qualians even tried to fight us in the open. We blew up two. But sooner or later, their Grand Arbiter will show up. Gammon, are you picking up anything on their comms?"

"Nothing. We've been kicked from…Oh shit! Bones!"

On the one hand, I didn't feel so bad because Bones' partner had gone the way of the two marines. An agile Zatrathi warrior managed to jump over both the shields and cannons and, before turning into a loot crate, grabbed the Black Sail and threw him towards the wall where Bones had just fallen. On the other hand, I didn't have time for schadenfreude. The Precian adviser rushed to rescue his new ally and almost fell to friendly fire. The marines stopped shooting just in time—no one wanted to be the one to kill an imperial adviser.

"Maintain your fire! The adviser has shields!" I shouted, but it was too late. The Zatrathi warriors poured out of the corridor overwhelming the marines. Each player found himself in a melee with an enemy. Close combat was the deadliest thing for our raid. The end would be an inglorious one. The time had come to use my secret weapon.

Two enhanced auto-locking blasters had so far kept me from hand-to-hand combat with the Zatrathi. When the adviser reached Bones, shielding him with his dome shield, I realized that the moment had come. Sebastian had long since appeared behind me and was keeping safe in the rear. The remaining marines refused to give up, scrabbling for every kill. Their constant maneuvering and well-coordinated changes of tactics delighted me. It seemed that everything was going as it should, but the map showed that the main course was still ahead. A myriad enemies were already en route towards us.

As soon as Brainiac accepted the order to self-destruct if I went to respawn, I pulled the trigger, firing my rockets. With the reticle, I had marked the far end of the corridor. First, as a welcoming gesture for the Zatrathi reinforcements. Second, as a way to keep the area of effect further from us. I heard a click above my right ear. I flinched and prepared to respawn. The subsequent bang was so immense that my ears shut themselves on their own. A ringing filled my head, I felt a frenetic shaking, but the picture before me didn't change. I was alive! A salvo of rockets flew off from my shoulders and zoomed off trailing smoke and flame at the point I had aimed at. What a wonder! I'd managed to shoot them once and live to see it. Russian rocket roulette is a game for psychos…or desperados!

"Everyone behind cover!" I yelled without being able to hear myself. The shockwave reached us just as I turned to cover Sebastian. But my armor suit failed—I fell almost flat to the floor despite the inertial dampening system and crushed the Qualian under me. Seeing the jet of flame rushing above us, he stayed still. My shields' energy level began to plummet, yet I couldn't even move to replace the powercell—without letting Sebastian be incinerated. I watched the numbers count down irrevocably: 30% of energy available, 20%, 10%…Pulling out one hand, I reached for the powercell but then saw that the counter had

---

stopped at 5% and the jet of fire had slacked. The suit had activated every single emergency indicator there was. However, replacing four powercells didn't take too long and I managed to do it even without getting up. Someone knocked from below the armor suit and I rolled over, freeing the Qualian. Finally I could take a look around the battlefield too. Sebastian was alive and even almost entirely healthy. Then I caught a glint from the adviser's dome shield, which meant that he and Bones were also okay. As for the marines...I still couldn't see because now a long system notification obscured my field of view:

New level reached: Fire Flower Personal Rocket Artillery (Legendary) has reached Level 3. Durability, number of rockets and energy have been restored by 30%. Device modified: 3 (of 25) defects eliminated.

Achievement unlocked: 'Liberator' (Rank 3). Your group has destroyed more than ten thousand Zatrathi warriors in open combat. −30% to XP needed to level up your items.

"What the hell was that?" Graykill suddenly appeared in front of me, jerked me to my feet and shook me like a dusty kitten. He looked angry.

"What's the difference?" I was taken aback by his overbearing tone. "It worked didn't it?"

"Worked?! I lost almost all my men!" roared the marine. "Why didn't you warn me?"

He wasn't lying. Out of Kiddo's thirty marines that had joined our raid, only five had survived. The only thing that saved them was their legendary armor.

"I couldn't. Did you see the horde moving toward us? It was time to shoot, not talk!" I snapped. "This is a game. You can't win without taking casualties. Your losses are 24 marines...the Zatrathi losses are more than half of their army. You should be celebrating."

"Surgeon, we have to secure our advantage! Hit 'em one more time, will you?" Kiddo suddenly popped into our exchange. "Graykill, work with what you have. We've managed to punch through their defenses. We've made another big round hole in their ship's hull. Hah! They reduced their shields and are using the Qualian repairmen as cover! Let them have it, guys! Signing off!"

"Do as your captain orders," I wrenched myself from Graykill's grip and shook myself off defiantly. Telling him to go to hell (mentally), I began to collect the loot. As always, a wall of text scrolled past my eyes. Skipping down to the totals at the bottom, I clapped my hands in satisfaction—I had managed to wipe out not only the Zatrathi and engineers but a bunch of black fogs as well. Those were the ones who dropped black tokens:

New items: Gold token (11522)
New items: Black token (94)
New items: Silver token (443)

...

I did not bother picking up the raq, armor, powercells and heap of Zarathi blasters and clothes. I didn't have any more space. After a second thought, I did pick up the loot that the black fog had dropped—flasks full of black powder. They weighed nothing at all and didn't take up much room.

Only then did I notice the strange silence: The sawing had stopped and there were no further attempts to restart it after my rocket attack. I figured this was good news. The bad news was that the explosion had damaged the corridor so much that it had become impassable. I opened the map to look for alternate routes and saw our blue dots but no red dot at all. The hell…

"Brainiac what's wrong with the map?"

"The comm nexus for that part of the ship has been destroyed. There is no longer a connection to the ship mainframe. My space scanners can detect no further nexuses at your location. I cannot update the map."

"Let me see what you have from the locator beacons a second before the rocket attack, only erase the dots in the detonation zone. Send this to everyone in the party."

"Affirmative." A map of the ship appeared on my HUD with the locations marked.

"What now?" Graykill had not gotten over losing his squad. He also distanced himself from the decision making, implying that I was now in command of the parade. Cushy job. Never had the opportunity before. If we fail this mission, Surgeon with his caprices will be the one to blame. Graykill will never admit that his marines would've fallen without my involvement too.

The adviser turned off his shield and approached us.

"Nothing new, Graykill. We get to the center, kill the main boss and we scram. Kiddo will finish what she has to do. Judging by the map, the command center of the ship is located here," I pointed in the direction of the new breach. "The enemies were coming from there."

"What a brilliant plan! First you blow up the corridors to Kingdom Come, wipe your party and now you want to go take on the final boss. There's no other way to the central compartment. Didn't you notice? Your little fireworks display caused a collapse! It's a dead end now!"

Kiddo had ordered her marine to work with me, not obey and respect me. However, oddly enough, Graykill's anger didn't bother me. In view of the 26 empty armor suits strewn around us, I understood him. Five class-A, twenty class-B and one class-C. Kiddo and Graykill had lost an entire assault team in one fell swoop—not to mention, Bones' partner. You can't take items that have lost a class with you, so I'll have to leave them here...Hang on! Why can't I take them?

"Brainiac, send over twenty droids to my position! We need to pick up 25 armor suits from Captain Kiddo's marine squad. There's also one that belonged to a Black Sail. Let them grab a few tons of raq with them while they're at it. Or whatever they'll carry."

"Roger. ETA is ten minutes," replied the ship computer.

I used an internal, private channel to communicate with Brainiac, so I didn't have time to calm Graykill down after I hung up. The new wave of Zatrathi reached the collapse and froze, generating an algorithm for what to do next. The NPCs' code didn't take into account the possibility of an obstacle onboard their own ship.

"Everyone drop to the floor or get behind cover," I moved away from the surviving fighters, took aim and, almost without flinching, pressed the rocket launch button.

But instead of the expected click, I heard Graykill's angry hiss from somewhere among the rubble.

"Goddamn you, Surgeon, what the hell do you need to shoot your damn rockets for again? You'll always have a chance to shut us in! They won't reach us anyway."

I ignored the marine, not understanding why nothing was happening. I pushed the button a couple more times.

"Engineer, why isn't the rocket arty working?" The snake had promised me that either I would explode or the enemy would. But everyone was alive.

"I warned you: It's unreliable, unfinished. You shouldn't have used it to begin with. Anyway, pursuant to game rules clause 335.3, this weapon is being disabled due to upsetting the game balance. Thank you for taking part in testing a prototype, your costs for the revision and modernization of the Fire Flower Personal Rocket Artillery will be reimbursed. We wish you a pleasant game."

"I see. Okay. Get back to the repairs. Over and out," I said, frustrated.

I can't believe they took my toy away! Oh you bastard developers. They popped in and quickly cleaned everything up, covering their asses. It's clear as day that they had designed the arty to be used in open space, and didn't consider that the specially gifted might employ it during a boarding operation. Now they had deleted the item from the weapons database.

I am not malicious, naturally, but I like to keep things formal and exact damages when damages are due. The lingering Zatrathi allowed me time to open a feedback form and file a complaint about "interference with the game process by the developers." I can't just let them mess with me like that unchallenged. So... "*Changing battle conditions affected the balance of power. We were faced with a huge enemy army and found ourselves at an immense disadvantage. It was impossible to hold our lines, so I resorted to a weapon that I had received legitimately in the course of normal gameplay. I consider its confiscation illegal. I demand compensation and am ready to pursue my claim by any means available to me.*"

"Your complaint has been received and is awaiting moderator verification."

"And?" Graykill climbed out of his foxhole and approached me. "Are we going to spend a long time crawling around the cracks?"

"Get out. Armageddon II isn't coming. The devs have taken away my new toy. You can rejoice," I explained. "But I have another idea. Look, the Zatrathi have come up from the two lower decks, while the top one is clear. If there is no further damage on that deck, we can try to clear it and use it to get to the center. Shall we risk it?"

"Clearing it is not a problem but we are space marines, not ground infantry. We don't have jetpacks."

"But I do. I'll take you with me and the rest can head back to the ship. The party has nothing more to do here anyway."

"Do you propose that we just abandon all these armor suits

here?" Graykill grew even more annoyed.

"No. I have some droids coming over to pick them up in 5–7 minutes. I'll return the suits to you after the raid, so stop worrying so much," I reassured the marine. "Have your boys help us clear out what's left and then they can take some time off."

I cocked my blasters. Several nimble Zatrathi warriors had begun to clamber through the debris. A dozen shots suppressed them, but new ones followed shortly. The NPCs had calculated their further behavior and respawning no longer scared them. It is a pity that the NPC warriors had no instinct for self-preservation.

Graykill began conferring with his team and a minute later, two beam cannons had been set up at the edge of the opening and began pouring fire on the Zatrathi on the lower decks. The return fire didn't bother us much: The players spared no energy on their shields, nullifying the enemy's numerical advantage. Before my droids arrived, I managed to clear and unlock the doors to our bay. The idea of stuffing armor suits through a tiny opening in the wall was a questionable one. The automatons brought with them a large panel to carry the goods. This was the engineer's solution to the problem of transportation.

The marines' comments grew markedly less subdued as the heap of equipment and materials on the improvised stretcher grew higher and higher. I unloaded all six hundred kilograms of raq from my inventory and opened another shimmering loot crate. Altogether, I had amassed several tons of lucre, which was now loaded on the panel. The droids yoked themselves to the load, and slowly, straining and with difficulty, dragged the lot of it back to the ship. That snake and her frugality had a greater influence on me than I could imagine.

Bones and the adviser, I sent back to *Warlock* as well. There was no point taking further risks. Bones helped the droids haul the armor suits and soon the metal convoy disappeared in the doorway.

"Why aren't you going with them? Do you have a death wish, Sebastian?" I asked the thief as he was watching the convoy leave.

"I'm coming with you. Maybe the command center will have something more interesting than glass to steal," the Qualian said stubbornly. "What kind of a thief am I if I pass on such a chance? This armor suit can fly, so I won't be a burden to you."

"You have no homeworld," I reminded just in case, but the thief was no longer listening. He stepped over to the point where we would set out from. The two cannons did their work well—the lower decks were already empty. There wasn't much loot, however, which indicated that the AI had improved and the majority of the Zatrathi were looking for other ways of reaching us. And if that was the case, we didn't have much time.

Graykill ordered his guys to close up shop and head back to the ship with my droids. Then I picked him up and we jetted up to the upper deck. The marine definitely weighed a lot. Twenty meters of flight expended half my fuel. At least there wasn't anyone upstairs and I could calmly replace the expended powercells. Sebastian, meanwhile, had some problems with flying. He hovered for too long, took overly complicated trajectories and managed to collide with things that were difficult to collide with. I was about to rise to meet him and tow him upstairs, but I didn't feel like spending the fuel. In the end, the thief got close enough and Graykill and I managed to catch him and drag him to us. The suit's medical unit considered it necessary to restore the Qualian's strength. The thief gasped when the needle entered the neck.

"Forward now, on the double!" ordered Graykill, feeling himself in his element. I fell in behind, knowing full well that the marine had much more experience than me fighting in close quarters and I had better listen to him. Activating the suit's afterburners, I tried to keep up with the commander. As he ran, Graykill set such a pace, you'd think there already was a pack of Zatrathi on our heels. Sebastian was not used to such exertion and his suit had no afterburners so he fell behind immediately. I fell back with him a little later too. The marine clearly had an advantage when running in a straight line.

"Commander, you run fast but you'll just leave your squad behind you," I called out to Graykill, huffing and puffing.

"Why you've already lost me my squad. Come on, rookie, put some effort into it!" I could hear by his tone that the marine was enjoying himself.

"I put in the effort on the toilet! What'll be the benefit if I have to fight the Zatrathi while crawling from exhaustion? Slow down already. They're not going anywhere," I got completely angry.

The marine commander broke out laughing but slowed his pace.

"You're a hell of a sprinter, marine. What's with your handle though?" We still had another five hundred meters to go and I wanted to take the player down a peg. "Do you run better than you kill?"

"Meaning?"

"Gray—as in without pleasure or fantasy," I continued.

"Gray, you say? Well, that depends on how you look at it." Instead of taking offense, Graykill seemed to cheer up. "When you have fifty shades in your arsenal, you will have both pleasure and fantasy."

"You're not a web designer by any chance?" I frowned. "They are experts in shades."

"Uh-huh, you're a surgeon and I'm a web designer. Let's just leave it at that."

"I have identified a network outlet," said Brainiac, who had been scanning the space around us in the meantime. After a short break we had reached an immense hangar. It was empty because all the fighters had scrambled. We encountered a hollow echo, scattered parts, repair equipment and a pair of small reconnaissance ships scattered among the flight deck's bright markings. I connected to the network so that Brainiac could update our map.

Now it displayed the damaged areas as well. There were red dots all around us, filling all the available space. The blue ones, symbolizing our players, were slowly creeping towards my ship. It was clear that they wouldn't make it back in time.

"They forgot to shut the doors," I commented on a trickle of red dots catching up to our blue ones. As if hearing me, one of the blue dots stopped and doubled back. Minus one legendary armor. A voluntary sacrifice from Graykill's squad for the benefit of the rest of the team.

"Brainiac, calculate a route for me to the command center and, as soon as everyone is on board, blast off and head for cover with our cruisers! Kiddo, I'm going to need fire support for my ship! Graykill and I will stay behind. Do what you must but the ship and your men must survive!" I once again estimated the number of red dots and gave up on any hope of coming out alive.

"Process acknowledged. Here is the calculated route!" Brainiac paused for a while trying to come up with some reason not to abandon me, but in the end he couldn't think of anything. The dotted line led us through the hangar to the far door. It wasn't far at all from there to the center. The last obstacle looked to be the fat red dots that stood at the end of the path. Clearly these weren't ordinary warriors, which were much smaller. But before I deal with them further, I had better check in on my Qualian thief...

"Sebastian, do you see that ship?" I pointed at a spiky Zatrathi scout standing nearby. "If you want to survive, you'll start it up and get out of here."

"You want me to hack its security, start the engines without an access card and take off without hitting anything?" the Qualian echoed. "There may be problems with the latter."

"Just take care of the first two things first," I encouraged the thief. "Mind you, Zatrathi tech may be different than what you're used to. Once you figure it out, let me know that you are ready. Now get to it!"

Sebastian clambered up the scout and disappeared in its

cockpit to sort out the controls. The marine and I moved on. It was a longer run this time, but Graykill matched my pace. The door on the other side of the hangar had a sensor so that as soon as we approached, it opened on its own, allowing us to pass without difficulty. Full auto from my two blasters killed the black fogs hovering near the ceiling, but the loot didn't fall and stayed up there. We went through several long corridors with turns and forks, and finally saw the goal of our entire enterprise—thirty meters ahead, a pair of brightly painted doors suggested that the command center was located right there.

"Well I'll be...It's like the nightmare of a drunk illustrator," drawled Graykill, appreciating the obstacle between us and the doors. We'd never tangled with Zatrathi like this...It was clear now why the map showed a fat circle instead of a small dot for these creatures. Their three-meter-round torsos were supported by four elephantine legs. Their arms were thin appendages but their seeming weakness was compensated by quantity and dexterity. I counted six and each monster wielded them in addition to a pair of beam cannons. Their small chitinous heads whirled briskly right and left and were completely dotted with small black dots, which could be eyes. I had a vague suspicion that I had seen something like this somewhere. Brainiac came to my aid:

"I detect a resemblance to the warriors we encountered on the Uldan base. These specimens are larger in size, however, and resemble a crude Vraxis prototype."

Indeed, looking at these creatures, I had the impression that a child had drawn a Vraxis warrior from memory and their overzealous parent brought the picture to life. Only, there was nothing childish about what these comic-looking warriors could do to us. They had shield generators in addition to their beam cannons too. Using the weapons we had on these boys would be a waste of time.

I opened my map in the hope of finding a detour. The dashed line, charted by Brainiac, led obstinately to the door, suggesting that it would not be possible to bypass the obstacle. Well, if we have to go through the door, we'll go through the door.

The entire interior of the Zatrathi ship was a classic silver color, so the colorful doors seemed like an artifact. There was no symmetry or logic in the ornament to an outside viewer—there were just abstract blots of color, a bit reminiscent of lens flares IRL. The odd and unexpected flight of designer fancy only seemed to extend to the door and its guards. The Zatrathi did not react to us in any way, waiting either for us to approach them or attack them.

"Are you sure we have to go in there?" Graykill suddenly turned to me.

"The flight deck is behind those doors. If we manage to disable the ship's shields, Marina will finish it off and everyone will get their rewards. If we don't manage, the Qualian reinforcements will arrive and the raid will be over. It's not much of a choice."

"Take my armor suit, don't leave it here and get behind cover." Graykill waited until I hid around the corner and began to prepare. First, he activated all his shields, then he took something out of inventory and carefully inserted it into the slots of his armor suit. Zooming in as much as I could in my HUD, I made out oblong gray objects without any markings, and I guessed without Brainiac giving me a hint what they were. Like all players, Graykill could blow himself up if necessary, as he was about to do now, but first he added some extra pieces of raq to act as shrapnel. Shields did not work against flying physical objects. Small fragmentation particles could penetrate good armor, especially if it was located a few meters from the epicenter of the explosion.

Once he was ready, Graykill hunched like a sprinter and then rushed forward. Despite his speed, the appearance of the enemy did not come as a surprise to the colossi—they instantly aimed their cannons and opened fire at the approaching warrior. But Graykill wasn't the head of *Alexandria*'s assault force for nothing. He dodged the incoming plasma balls so deftly that my jaw dropped—I had never seen someone move so smoothly in the game! It was incredible! Graykill rolled, vaulted, dodged, bounced and immediately sprinted forward, reducing the intervening distance to thirty meters. I made the last dash mentally with him. The cannons fired almost point-blank.

My screens went blank for an instant. A bright white star was being born where Graykill had just been. I was so fascinated by the spectacle that I forgot to hide around the bend in time, and little pieces of shrapnel peppered my armor suit, leaving small dents. They could not penetrate my armor at this distance; however, all that was left of the guards and the door was two loot crates and a decorative cheese grater that had once been a door. In the foreground of the aftermath, stood Graykill's suit of armor, solitary and empty.

New items: Sapphire token (2)

New items: Powercell (2)

New items: A-class Zatrathi Beam Cannon (2)

My recently unburdened inventory easily accommodated both Graykill's suit and all the booty from the guards. There was not much of the latter.

The door, however, still held despite its myriad holes. According to Brainiac's map, I would need to take the right-hand corridor beyond it.

"Brainiac, can you unlock the door?"

"Negative. Access to the command center is beyond my permissions. You must first locate a comm nexus in the secure area. The closest one is located behind the wall."

Clenching my fist, I hit the door as hard as my suit allowed me. The door itself, for all its holes, managed to resist, yet the raq it was made of failed. The panel I struck broke at the holes left over from the shrapnel. I made it larger with another blow and was able to stick my hand through. Brainiac activated the space scanner on my glove and found the control panel. I reached my hand as close to it as I could. Then Brainiac did the rest—connecting to the network and entering the access codes. A klaxon blared and the door—with me attached to it—began to rise. I yanked with my shoulder, but I couldn't get free. Luckily the sash was so damaged that the uneven surface kept sticking. Once I had pulled my hand out, I helped the stuttering motor lift the door and entered the ship's holiest of holies.

After taking a few steps, I turned the corner and froze: a blaster muzzle at my chest. If it fires, my armor won't hold. It's too close.

"*Delnarga kurr! Irrich siu ta lorey!*" burbled the weapon's owner and pulled the trigger.

"He said: 'Die dirty filth. We never considered you sentient,'" translated the snake as I flew back to the wall. My armor had withstood the plasma shot at the cost of its control unit, which blew out. The ejection mechanism activated, throwing me out of the suit. The enemy did not expect his victim to fly out of his armor like a zombie from a casket, instead of dying as he was supposed to. My foe's surprise at this bought me a couple seconds. This was enough time for me to pull Graykill's suit out of my inventory, slip into it and then calmly restore my health. The Zatrathi atmosphere was corrosive and fatal to players. I barely noticed the second shot from close range—Graykill had excellent armor. I grabbed a manipulator and suspended the Zatrathi in the air before me, disarming him with the other manipulator.

"Engineer, translate the following: 'This ship has been captured. I demand your unconditional surrender. Otherwise, my orders are shoot to kill.'"

The snake's translated into the guttural Uldan tongue. The enemy's wings twitched to confirm that he understood everything. I regretted sending the adviser back; he would have liked this encounter. The ship's commander turned out to be an Uldan—whose mind had been swallowed by the Zatrathi consciousness. Like a parasite. Why did I decide that? Why it was simple. The head of the Uldan butterfly was covered with brown slime, his eyes rolled up, and the way he had wielded his blaster, spoke and resisted me was entirely like some puppet.

I pushed the prisoner aside and walked over to the control console. It looked completely ordinary.

"Brainiac, how do I disable the shields?" I allowed my ship computer to connect to the Zatrathi mainframe. A download progress bar appeared. Brainiac was not wasting time, pillaging any data that seemed useful.

But when the download progress reached 70%, Brainiac suddenly said:

"Shields are shutting down in three, two…Warning! Remote access detected. The captain's console has been disabled. Attention! The self-destruct protocol has been activated! One hundred seconds left before self-destruction!"

"Abort!"

"The ship is being controlled remotely. I no longer have root access. Ninety-six seconds remaining."

"Marina, get out of here ASAP! The ship is about to explode in less than two minutes! Jump to the far end of the system."

"What are your instructions for us, Captain?" Brainiac asked.

"Follow Captain Kiddo."

"And what about you, Cap'n?" interrupted the snake.

"Do as I say, or I'll send you to the scrapyard myself! Sebastian! How's it going?"

"Swell. I am currently at the hangar doors. I was waiting for your call."

"Wait for me, I'll be there soon." As I spoke with Marina, I placed my own armor into Graykill's inventory and began running at a breakneck pace back, still hauling my prisoner suspended in front of me. I couldn't abandon the Uldan here. In my rush, I did not take much care with my cargo. By the time I reached the hangar, the Uldan had lost a wing and broken a leg. One last turn—and the doors of the Zatrathi recon ship opened before me. As soon as I stuffed in my prisoner, Sebastian opened the throttle and closed the hatch as we were taking off. Like all good scouts, ours had good acceleration. We left the hangar and calmly flew through the Zatrathi fighter squadrons who took us for one of their own.

A bright sun quaked to life behind us, reaching for us with its deadly rays.

"You're better at piloting a ship than an armor suit," I praised Sebastian. "But you have to obey your captain."

"That's some gratitude," the thief grunted.

Meanwhile, the game UI informed me:

New title received: 'Scourge of the Skies'—your party was the first to destroy a Zatrathi Flying Fortress. Apply to any empire for a personal reward from the emperor.

"Captain Kiddo, we are coming in on an enemy scout. Please hold your fire. And start getting ready—we're about to persuade the Precians that maybe pirates aren't so bad."

CHAPTER FIVE

THE ROUNDTABLE NEGOTIATIONS WERE GROWING HEATED. Nobody wanted to budge—neither Kiddo, nor Gammon, nor the adviser, nor me. Everyone was looking out for their interests alone and couldn't care less about what the others wanted. Once again, everyone was waiting for me to make a decision, but I had no intention of backing down:

"I'll say it again, that scout is my legal loot. I'm not giving it to anyone."

"You don't have the resources to conduct a full-fledged study," Kiddo kept hammering my weak point.

"No," I agreed glibly. "But I know people who do. Any guild will pay me cold, hard, IRL cash to dig around a Zatrathi recon ship."

"You understand that I won't let you take that scout?" Having exhausted her more reasonable options, Marina turned to threats. "Partnership is one thing. The leading position in Galactogon is something else. I can even renege on my word over it."

"Then I'll blow it up right there in your hold," I was prepared for this move. "I'd rather no one get it, then give it away for free. And don't try to appeal to my conscience—I ain't got one. I can't afford to pass up on an opportunity worth millions of real credits."

"The Precian Empire wishes to purchase the ship from you," the adviser suggested, but a deal with them was out of the question. I could improve my financial situation in the real world, only by selling the ship for real money, not GCs. Naturally, I could exchange one for another, but the rate was very unprofitable.

"Surgeon, everyone here took part in the raid," Gammon came in from another flank. "We have rights to a part of the loot too."

"I gave you the brainworm. That's your forty percent. As agreed."

"Who'd you give him to?" Gammon said, surprised. "Personally, I did not get anything!"

"You're asking the wrong person," I nodded at Kiddo. "All inquiries about the brainworm should be directed to her now."

"My people are already working on the captain," admitted Marina reluctantly. "Once we have the findings, we will shared them with all members of the raiding party."

"You started interrogating the prisoner without me?!" bristled Gammon. "My ships provided cover for your boarding party!"

"But it was my people who risked their high-level, legendary gear to get him!" Kiddo snapped back.

"Your people were barely prepared!" I wasn't about to sit this one out. "If it weren't for me, there's no way in hell the raid would've come off! I captured the prisoner, remember?"

"I demand to be included in the interrogation!" Gammon all but jumped to his feet. "Otherwise, my ships will take the prisoner by force!"

"Are you threatening me?!" hissed Kiddo. "Have you forgotten who arranged your transfer to the Precian Empire?"

"Uh, actually that was me," I reminded Kiddo about my role, but she paid me no attention:

"If it weren't for me, where would you and your great guild be right now?"

"The Precian Empire wishes to receive the prisoner in order to examine and interrogate him," piped up the adviser, comprehending little of the players' verbal sparring. Everything that did not concern the game made no sense to him and went ignored by his AI.

"I want that ship and that prisoner, and that's it," Gammon insisted. "If you don't satisfy my demands, I'll start the attack."

"The Precian Empire officially declares that if we do not receive the prisoner and the ship, anyone involved will be declared personas non grata," the adviser in turn issued his threat.

"Well I officially declare that the ship is my property and won't let anyone set foot on her," I stood my ground, assessing my chances if the Precians came after me. There wasn't really anything scary about it. Galactogon is huge and I don't have any further missions with the Precians anyway. I had dealt with the Uldan base and I could give up the Hansa thing. Come what may—one ought to stand one's ground.

Everyone was waiting for what Marina would say. It was becoming clear that we wouldn't be able to avoid a conflict. The only question was how bad it would be.

"Guys, we're not going to agree," Kiddo sighed, closing her eyes wearily. "Adviser, if you take the ship and the prisoner, will we have access to them? As participants in the raid, we have every right, if not to conduct independent research, then at least to receive its results. You've seen for yourself that the Zatrathi ships fly in ways we'd never even dreamed of. If we figure out how they work—why for instance our EM cannons don't work on the enemy—it will become easier for everyone facing the Zatrathi threat."

"The Precian Empire does not work with pirates." After a long pause, the adviser repeated his standard argument. "The research findings will be shared with the Black Sails Guild and two private individuals: Kiddo and Surgeon. Not pirates—just people."

"Does that suit you?" Kiddo turned to Gammon. "You will get everything, but through the adviser."

"Yes, this way is fine with me, but we still have to deal with the scout," everyone looked at me again. If they were trying to make me feel awkward, it didn't work. My position remained unchanged.

"Again—I will not give you the ship. It is my rightful loot. And don't try to sign me up for your research sharing program."

"Didn't you mention ten million credits? That's a ridiculous amount either for a top guild or for me. Sooner or later, the players will capture more Zatrathi ships and your prize will be a dime a dozen. I'll pay you three million IRL credits and you hand over the ship to the Precians. You can squeeze them for something else while you're at it. Gammon, you and I will split the amount to pay Surgeon fifty-fifty. That comes out to 1.5 mill each."

"Two apiece and it's a deal," I said. There was a lot of common sense and foresight to what Kiddo had said. Any player could get lucky and steal a Zatrathi ship—their controls were no different than any other's. And if they ceased being rare, sooner or later, the cost of the scout would fall. Moreover, I had no idea how I would be able to take the ship. When we flew up to *Alexandria*, the cruiser's tractor beam had knocked out all of the scout's electronics as it dragged its catch into its hangar. I had to leave Sebastian in charge, with orders to self-destruct if something went amiss, while I went to negotiate. I understood that the ship would not be given back to me, but I was ready to bargain for it to the last penny.

"Fine. Two million apiece, but you get no access to the research," Gammon replied. "If you're selling the ship then you're selling all the rights that come with it too."

"I agree about the research from the ship, but not about the prisoner—I have a right to any info you get from the Zatrathi captain." I could consider the negotiations a success. First, I did not have a crew for the scout. Second, four million would significantly improve the girth of my wallet. Third, no one knew that Brainiac had downloaded the data from the Zatrathi ship, nor that I had a Zatrathi engineer languishing in my hold. I would quietly start a new auction, only on terms that were favorable to me and in a more suitable environment.

"Adviser, Surgeon is ready to sell the scout to the Precian Empire," Kiddo said. "In exchange, he is asking for a twenty percent discount on purchases from the Hansa Arms Corporation. The Precian Empire shall not incur any further expenses—to the contrary, it will have the opportunity to study the enemy technology and discover its workings and weaknesses."

I looked at Kiddo in surprise. The pirate was counting on getting her paws on Hansa tech through me, miraculously profiting from a concession being made to me. Frankly, I wasn't opposed to such a deal—*Warlock* needed the upgrades. Our skirmishes with the Zatrathi had demonstrated that neither our speed, nor weapons, nor shields were anything to write home about. Everything on the orbship needed to be upgraded and improved significantly.

The adviser conferred with the emperor and after a little bit, announced his terms: "If Surgeon waives his right to the research findings from the reconnaissance vessel as well as the results of the prisoner interrogation, the emperor is prepared to give him the opportunity to cooperate privately with the Hansa Arms Corporation, but a twenty percent discount is an unrealistic condition. The Precian Empire is not prepared to make such a concession. His Imperial Highness graciously agrees to a five percent discount if the above preconditions are duly met."

Three pairs of eyes fixed onto me once again. A deal with Hansa would guarantee me a steady income, albeit in GCs. If

Kiddo decides to extend our partnership though, I would get the research findings anyway. I doubt the girl will insist on the principle of the matter. Making a deal right now was much more important.

"Agreed. Send me the contract and you can take the ship and the prisoner. I have other stuff to worry about. I'll send you my account number."

Stan helped me settle all the financial formalities—the money could not be traced without a special request to the authorities, but I doubted that Kiddo and Gammon would oblige them. We were acting according to our contracts and the meeting logs were on my side. The adviser sent me a license to work with the Hansa Corp, and I went back to my ship without saying goodbye to anyone. Sebastian was right about Kiddo: She only cared about profit. A muddy way of doing business. It seemed like she had resolved the situation, but she hadn't forgotten to extract a profit for herself. I would have to keep my eyes peeled around her.

"Brainiac, we're going home!" I ordered, returning to the ship. Choosing our next destination was simple and long overdue—we were going back to our planet. I wanted to deal with the loot and bind Sebastian to the planetary spirit in a peaceful setting. After the raid, I already considered the thief a part of my crew. He had proven his worth and shown the necessary initiative. Who knows what other perks this gray-skinned creature had to offer?

I had to give Kiddo her due once again. Before the start of negotiations, she had left the empire through the sector guarded by Gammon's players, whose guild still formally belonged to two empires. We were allowed to pass without any questions, but as soon as we left the sector, the entire game was shaken by breaking news: Eleven empires at once declared war on the Qualians. The second part of the scenario had begun. In an instant, hundreds of game guilds lost their leading position, finding themselves playing for a rogue state. Even during our negotiations, Gammon started receiving non-stop calls, though he was in no hurry to disclose exactly who was calling. Maybe it was his people congratulating him. Maybe it was the heads of other guild with questions and requests for assistance. The Black Sails had soared to an unprecedented height—the game rankings now placed them in third place in the Precian Empire. That's what a good relationship with an imperial adviser got you!

None of this concerned me, however. It was much more important to understand where the developers had tucked away my planet. When I reached home, I discovered that it was now only ten minute' flight from the explored area of Galactogon, instead of the usual thirty. Technically, it was a bit risky—ten minutes' flight amounted to several months of galactic traffic, which meant there was a probability that some stubborn or lucky player would stumble on our star system. Of course, the odds weren't that great, but practice showed that at least one player in a million would act erratically and according to some rationale known only to him. We multiply this by the number of players playing in Galactogon and we get about a thousand such outliers who could stumble upon Blood Island due to insanity or boredom. Such players could re-register the planet to their name and I'd have no recourse.

"Stan, is there any way that independent players can maintain ownership of the planets they've discovered?"

"A preliminary analysis of the information suggests that there is none. Any player can become the owner of the planet by binding himself to the planetary spirit. To do this, he merely needs to enter the planetary command center. It is impossible to prohibit anyone from doing whatever they like once they're in there. The only thing that does not depend on the current owner is the name of the planet and the bonus percentages from the Discoverer Achievement. Everything else can be stolen or copied. You can increase the likelihood of keeping the planet by installing an automated security system, hiring an NPC or concluding alliances with various parties. In general, the more pixels you have guarding your pixels, the more secure your pixels will be. Nevertheless, it bears mentioning that such measures carry the risk of disclosing the planet's coordinates."

Stan was right: As long as nobody knew about my system, it was more secure. As soon as at least one player comes here, even if it's just Kiddo, confidentiality will go straight out the window and no one can guarantee what will happen afterward. Any one of *Alexandria*'s thousand crew members could leak the cruiser's homeplanet. Did I really need that? After a little thought, I decided not to call Kiddo. If she is as smart as she tries to appear, then she should understand that letting yourself trust another player is a bad idea. Once is more than enough. Therefore, if she asked to register her ship to my planet again, I would say no. That much should be obvious to her. And if so, why call and talk about the obvious? Sometimes silence is more eloquent than any words.

Blood Island, covered with forests, seas and mountains, resembled the Earth, except that the dimensions were several hundred times smaller. Game conventions had retained the typical earthly gravity, which made me feel comfortable on the surface. Brainiac scanned the planet, but there was nothing on it except for the elo deposits. If the developers once hid something here, no trace of it remained now.

After landing not far from the entrance to the command center, I decided to start by binding Sebastian to the planetary spirit. The Qualian had seen plenty in his day and now seemed unperturbed, yet Brainiac, who could read his physical metrics through his suit, noted a fluctuation in his vital stats. His pulse doubled and his breathing became shallow and irregular, while the little finger of his right hand began twitching in a nervous tic. Otherwise, he looked perfectly calm. We reached the ten-meter sphere which was the spirit's altar. Thin threads stretched out from it, connecting me and Sebastian.

Do you wish to bind Sebastian to Blood Island? The binding cost is GC 100,000 and GC 50,000 for each respawn. The funds will be deducted from your account automatically.

This message came as an unpleasant surprise to me. A quick check with Stan confirmed the cost—binding an NPC to a planet was always this expensive and as a result not many players went through with it. The advantages were undoubtedly obvious, but players were much cheaper to respawn. I was in no hurry to press the 'Accept' button, watching the thief's reaction. Outwardly, he still remained calm, but he could not hide his inner excitement from Brainiac.

"The time has come to choose," I said. "My ship with me as her captain is your safety and security. The alternative is I leave you on the nearest Confederate planet."

"What are your conditions?" Sebastian asked trying to sound offhanded.

"Five percent of the plunder is yours and you will receive it in credits. I assume you have no need for raq or elo. You travel with me, you take part in our raids, you help open everything that is locked and steal anything that's not bolted down. If you get sick of working with me, you warn me in advance, and I will terminate the contract."

"Are you a tempter?" Sebastian frowned, showing emotion for the first time. "Do I need to sell my soul in order to work under such conditions? Or will we be killing babies?"

It was only thanks to Stan that I was able to understand what the Qualian was talking about—the religion of Galactogon was an amalgam of many earthly religions with its own concepts of 'savior' and 'tempter.' My answer had to be quite serious because according to the FAQs, the NPCs were very serious about their religious beliefs.

"I take care of my crew." Sebastian had calmly waited for me to say my piece. "The well-being of each crew member is my well-being and has nothing to do with the soul. I am not a tempter, but a captain."

"I accept your offer and swear to serve you faithfully," said Sebastian solemnly, adding his name to the list of crew members:

Orbship Warlock's crew had been updated. The new crew member is Jacques Sebastian, an A-class being, a hereditary smuggler and an expert thief.

Main functions: Lockpicking, hacking, item appraisal.

"Engineer, show our supplies to Sebastian," I ordered, returning to the ship. Having completed the ritual with the planetary spirit, I was impatient to check the capabilities of the new crew member.

"Am I to understand that you risked your neck on Raydon over this?" Sebastian asked cautiously, unable to hide his disappointment.

"What's wrong?"

"It's all worth about ten million credits, nine of it for a legendary snow-maker. A cutting-edge model that the Qualians use to make ski slopes on their resort planets. Several items can be attached to my armor suit. Everything else is junk. There are plenty of affordable things of better quality and functionality on the market."

"Engineer?" Sebastian was just starting out on my ship and it made sense to check the accuracy of his appraisal.

"I confirm," the snake replied sadly. "Sorry, Cap'n, I did not know how to tell you. You were so happy about your plunder that I couldn't force myself to do it. I used what I could in the ship and the armor suits. Everything else is trash, albeit legendary trash. I say we blame the marine. It was his happy mug that made you believe that there was something useful there."

A roar of protest came surging from the ship's bowels—the rhino disagreed.

"Can we sell this junk?" I asked the thief with chagrin.

"Not openly," replied Sebastian after a little thought. "Only the snow maker has any value, but I don't think you'll find any buyers who will pay its full price. You can dump this ballast on one of the planets of the Confederation. You were there if you met with Hilvar. Its name is Qirlats."

"Very well. In that case we will head over to…"

"Alarm! Alarm!" Brainiac suddenly began screaming. "A Zatrathi scout has just entered our system!"

Oh that's all I needed!

"Battle stations!" I yelled, pushing the throttle to full power. Brainiac closed 'the hatch' and *Warlock* zoomed straight up. There was no danger of pulling too many Gs: The crew was immune and my armor suit handled the sudden force with ease.

"Status report, Brainiac!" I ordered, peering at the screen. A solitary triangular scout drifted casually through our system, making no attempt to hide itself or flee. The ship did not react to our appearance whatsoever and continued along its course.

"The bogey's velocity remains constant; its thrusters are not firing. I am observing visible signs of damage, though the nature and character of the damage remain unknown."

"Engineer, get ready to intercept any torpedoes. Gunner, fire warning shots around the scout. We need to understand whether she has shields. Don't aim at the hull. We will try to board her. Sebastian, get ready for boarding action. You've already hacked such a ship once, the second time it should be easier. Let's go!"

We flew up almost flush to the scout, yet she made no adjustments to her course. Brainiac could detect no shields on her.

"The scan is complete," he announced after a minute. "There are no active electronics on board, her reactor seems to be disabled and her engines burned out. I detect no signs of life aboard. I have determined the nature of the damage—it was inflicted with beam cannons."

"Close in. Brainiac, grab her with the tractor beam and slow her down. Sebastian, follow me. Let's see whether this is space scrap or something else."

Warlock gently shook as we caught the scout and began to slow her down. Sebastian and I popped out into open space and Brainiac ferried us to the scout using the mechanical arm. I shivered—I hadn't yet had a chance to move around open space and the fifty-meter ball of the orbship hanging over my head made me anxious. It seemed the entire time as if my ship was about to fall on my head and crush me like a pancake. Driving away my fears, I focused on what Sebastian was doing. The thief cut away the door trim to unlock the lock. Up close, the signs of damage looked much more serious than Brainiac had reported. I counted about a dozen holes through which I could peek into the hull. If someone had survived the battle, exposure to the vacuum would have long since finished them off.

"I'm entering now," announced Sebastian, disappearing

inside. I hung back, waiting for news.

"All's clear! A B-class armor suit is all that's left of the pilot. You can sell it, but it's inexpensive—about ten thousand. The hold is empty. There are no engines. Nor cargo. This is just a piece of raq fit for recycling. There's nothing of value here." Sebastian emerged from the ship in just a couple of minutes, which was enough for him to reach his assessment.

There were no doubts about the qualifications of the former adviser to the head of the thieves' guild, but I still had hopes for a different type of loot.

"Move aside," I squeezed into the ship. There was little space: Zatrathi scouts accommodated two pilots and now, a single armor suit occupied one of the seats. "Brainiac, is there a jack I can connect you to?"

"The connector on the right," said the orbship's computer. "It will be necessary to activate the computer. Replace the power unit. The panel on the left. Push—it should work automatically."

Brainiac didn't let me down—as soon as I pushed the indicated panel, it slid aside, dousing us with cold vapor. Two powercells allowed me to start the computer, and Brainiac reported with delight that he had gained access to the memory banks and was downloading the data.

"Can we land the ship on the planet?" It was a pity to throw away so much raq.

"Negative," Brainiac categorically rejected my idea. "The scout will not fit in the orbship's hold and a direct landing will burn it in the upper atmosphere. A jump into hyperspace is also out of the question—the damage to the systems is too severe.

There is the option of repairing the ship in orbit, but we would need a dock. The engineer cannot work in open space."

Negatives all around. I slapped the hull sadly—this empty piece junk was absolutely useless. The connection LED changed color from red to green, indicating that the information download was complete.

"Gunner, scuttle this trough," I ordered as soon as we had returned.

A single beam salvo sent the Zatrathi junk pile to ship heaven, but even here I got nothing—the mission counter for scouts destroyed remained unchanged. The only thing remaining of our uninvited guest was the downloaded logs and the useless armor suit.

"Brainiac, is there anything interesting about the scout in the logs?"

"The logbook data shows that the ship has been drifting for a year. She was shot down in a skirmish with the Delvians. The scout managed to destroy two of their frigates but the third managed to break through her shields. The coordinates of the scout's origin were not in her logs. And I should mention that I could not find the coordinates of the Zatrathi flying fortress in her logbooks either. Perhaps Zatrathi captains enter them manually and then delete them to hide the location of their homeworld. The remaining entries are outdated. There are data on planned attack vectors but they are irrelevant now. Apart from the very last entry. It seems the Zatrathi are plotting a massive assault on the Delvian capital in the next few days. That is all."

"Oh no! Not those Delvian foxes!" said Sebastian. "They

have cute tails. I heard that the Zatrathi were pushing them hard but I had no idea it had come to this. It would be a shame to lose such beauties. Besides…" Here, the thief suddenly fell silent.

"What?" I pressed.

"I'm not sure if I should say it or not. Although in light of unfolding events my information will not be so secret soon enough. Basically, there is a small system of twin stars in the Delvian Empire. A strange place with unpredictable gravity. Between the two suns, right in the middle, at the equilibrium point of attraction, there is a lifeless planet. A small rock with twenty discovered deposits of raq. The Delvians themselves are afraid to fly in that area, but the brave guys from the Confederate thieves' guild established a profitable business there. And this is despite the fact that only one trajectory can be flown to it. Any deviation—and you will fall into the gravity well of one of the stars and you and your ship will be toast. The thieves lose harvesters and transports all the time, but even then business is booming. A whole planet of raq—who can say no? If the Zatrathi conquer the Delvian Empire, they will certainly be interested in this system."

"Do you know the trajectory to this planet?"

"Only in theory; in practice I have never flown there."

Some idea of wealth. I don't think I'd be ready to risk burning alive for the sake of a pile of raq. But then why did the developers slip me this tub? Apart from information about the Zatrathi offensive, she had nothing of value. Perhaps this is a reminder of my mission with the Delvian princess—I have to locate Alviaan, first counselor to the emperor, and tell him that he will have a child with the princess. I still had a couple of days left to do that one. However, if the Zatrathi attacked the Delvian capital, I would probably fail the mission. It's hard to report something to a corpse. The counselor is bound to the planetary spirit, and if I were the Zatrathi, I would destroy the capital in its entirety, depriving the Delvian leadership of a chance to respawn.

Hmm. I suppose I could try to solve this problem remotely...

"Marina, do you have a minute?" My attitude towards the pirate had changed, but this did not prevent me from using her connections.

"Yes, but a short minute, we are still hammering out how to divide the loot."

Jeez! Two hours have passed since I had left and they were still at it!

"I have valuable information for players in the Delvian Empire. Do you have contacts among their top guilds? Preferably only those who can pay good money."

"Anton, don't budge an inch! I'm going to step out for a sec," Marina barked at her spouse and returned to me: "All right, Surgeon, spill the beans. Did you bed one of the devs? Again valuable information and again you have it. I'm beginning to worry."

"I wish. The conditions are as follows: The information belongs to me. The connections and the haggling is your department. We split the reward fifty-fifty." Kiddo didn't bother bartering and simply repeated what I had just said verbatim. As a contract, that would do.

IN SEARCH OF THE ULDANS

"In two days, the Zatrathi are preparing a massive offensive against the Delvian capital."

"Where'd you get this information? The reliability of the source in such cases should be confirmed by the person trying to sell the info. Me, that is."

I grunted, expressing my skepticism and then replied, "It's firsthand. You can believe it. I downloaded from the onboard computer of a Zatrathi scout."

"You broke into our ship, said nothing and now want to sell the info through me?" Kiddo blew a gasket instantly.

"Easy! Yours is not the only scout I've encountered. This comes from another one. I'll explain later. You said yourself that there isn't much time."

"You have another scout?" Well that's it. The dog's taken the spoor, now she'll hound me till the end of the galaxy. I should have played out this conversation in my mind before calling.

"No! It was an empty, derelict ship! It accidentally came across my path." I paused after each phrase to make it intelligible.

"You're a lucky son of a bitch, Surgeon. I wish such a tidbit would wander across my path. You can share the details later. It would be useful for my negotiations."

"Yes, I figured you wouldn't let it go just like that."

"So they have two days," the girl drawled thoughtfully. "It remains only to understand what to do—to defend or to flee. I will think about your information and let you know when I've arranged everything, but it'll be tomorrow. At the moment, I need to finish the talks and get some sleep. Today has been hectic."

"Hang on. I have another question. Those Zatrathi tokens, what are they for? I haven't been able to find any info about them anywhere."

"You can exchange them for credits or new equipment. They took down all the info about the tokens recently. I have no idea why. Weren't you about to go to Belket? There is a viceroy in charge there. Go meet with him. He'll arrange the exchange. The rate is the same everywhere. Don't you have about a thousand gold ones? That should be enough to get several Hansa items for free. All right. I have to run, see you tomorrow!"

Sometimes I even loved Marina—but remotely and without any conflicts of interests. Her addiction to the game had made her a living encyclopedia on the hidden possibilities of the game world. You couldn't get the same kind of knowledge from official sources or the community forums. Although the last was quite understandable—the only organizations that had taken down the Zatrathi so far were leading game guilds and they weren't about to share their discoveries in public.

Feeling a wave of drowsiness, I exited Galactogon and its galaxy of problems, for several hours of sleep. The doctor had set a regimen for me, after all…

"Brainiac, set course for Belket," I ordered, waking up and still yawning into my fist. During the 'night,' all the various factors had arranged themselves onto shelves in my head. "Engineer, do you have anything in the works that can improve our attack?"

"The choices are: Upgrades to the torpedo production system. Upgrades to the EM cannon. Upgrades to the beam cannons. I can also increase the number of beam cannons. And we can put in a mine dispenser."

"Can I get more info about the last one?" The term was familiar to me from meatspace, but I wanted to know how the game mechanic worked...The snake began explaining and I liked what I heard. If the torpedoes passed through ships' energy shields without a problem, but were easy to destroy with point defense cannons because of their size, then the mines were excellent for diversionary measures. They weren't very big. The most complicated thing was to attach them stealthily to the hull of the enemy ship. Then it was possible to blow them up remotely or with a timed fuse. A very useful thing when battling capital ships, including cruisers.

It was impossible to destroy mines with beam cannons without taking damage—they clung to the hull firmly, and thirty pieces, in terms of their payload, added up to one torpedo. I was already set on installing this system on my ship, when a problem popped up. The prisoner holding cell took too much space and I would have to choose: Either the mines or some other attachment. After installing the mine assembly mechanism, I could forget about further expanding the orbship's weapons systems.

"Let's do the mines," I ordered the engineer as the star lines outside the porthole turned to points again. We had emerged from hyperspace. The dispatcher came on the air:

"Orbship *Warlock*, welcome to the Belket system. Access to the trading planet has been granted. Would you like permission to land?"

Security in the Belket system was provided by three Grand Arbiters, spread out at different ends of the system. Against the background of these colossi, the players' gigantic cruisers seemed like minnows. It was true that an upgraded Grand Arbiter wasn't the size of a Zatrathi orbital station, but working together, the three could put up more than a decent fight. Considering that the Delvians had the same monsters, it was even scary to imagine the meat grinder that would unfold in two days. The invaders would have to first take down the Arbiters, and I doubted that those would go quietly into the night. It would be a great battle and I had no desire whatsoever to be there.

The Emperor's whim outweighed my pirate's fame and I was offered a dock from the first hundred. The berth intended for the nobility was located not far from Belket's cultural and commercial center, a few kilometers from the Hansa Corp's HQ. Perhaps in granting me this VIP dock, the Precians were simply limiting the time I would spend on their planet.

The landing was successful. The local customs officers formally checked the ship, without even glancing into my hold. Instead of an inspection, there was a brief interrogation. They frowned disapprovingly, clicked their tongues as they passed the Qualian and proudly withdrew from my ship. Before I could even set foot on the dock, giant transport robots that worked as taxis and porters flew up to me. For a certain amount, they were ready to deliver me to any part of the planet and take care of any unloading and loading.

The temptation to take a VIP taxi was great. And no wonder—an enormous flying saucer with a pool, a bar and a lounge—yet the fog of temptation cleared as soon as I heard the price: The two kilometers to the Hansa HQ would cost me 100,000 GC. Spare change to vain bastards who loved luxury and comfort. And on top of this I was forced to all but beat this quote out of the driver—the Precian pretended that he didn't speak the common tongue and had no idea what I was asking. He smiled and nodded like a dummy, inviting me to board the flying saucer. Only the threat of contacting the spaceport administration miraculously taught the driver the common language and made him name his price. One hundred thousand credits for ten seconds of flight is worse than cabbies in meatspace!

Having wished him to take an erotic journey, I set out for the Hansa HQ on foot. The two kilometers, half of which I traveled on a moving walkway, were a cakewalk. The pedestrian zones on Belket were well developed, which I put down to the cost of transport services. Players and locals alike scurried about me, deftly maneuvering in the intense flow. Valorous guards looked on, keeping order. They looked out for troublemakers and pulled them out of the crowd by air for further proceedings. Nothing should impair other creatures from spending money. Such are the laws of a trade planet.

The Precian arms manufacturer occupied a fairly large area, surrounded by a high stone wall, a sort of tribute to antiquity and the ultramodern. An opaque force field covered the Hansa HQ, protecting it from anyone who wanted to peek in from above. To get to the main building, it was necessary to go through the guard post, presenting a pass, bypass the alley and climb the high and long stairs—a good hundred steps.

I was beginning my ascent when a voice hailed me from above.

"Captain Surgeon!" An elderly man slowly descended to meet me. A player. The wind flapped his cloak, giving him the appearance of a superhero from the ancient comics. The old man had nothing on him—no armor suit, no weapon, no personal shield—nothing but a short name. Mr. Eine.

"You have kept one vaiting, Herr Kapitan," the old man said in a German accent and with grave displeasure in his voice. "You vere not pleased by ze Taxi I sent for you? You decided to take a Spaziergang—a vat do you call it—a shtroll—ja?"

"I simply decided not be taken for a hundred thousand credits," I replied, examining my interlocutor: a neat trimmed beard, dry tanned skin, piercing blue eyes, a square face with high cheekbones. Once upon a time the Aryans sought to breed a paragon of their people and they could have used Mr. Eine as their model. He'd do for a fine Aryan portrait too and I even wondered if his appearance in-game matched his real one—this avatar was just a little too, uh, exact. In real life, people like this tended to attract lots of attention. I am not a big fan of show business or a subscriber to image feeds, yet I still don't recall ever seeing such a handsome man.

"Ze Idea vas I pay for you. It vas ein Gift," the sarcasm seeped from Eine. But he went on seriously: "Your Leisure has disrupted my Plans. I vas forced to cancel an important Meeting. By your Fault."

"I cannot say I'm sorry—but I have to go." It took a couple of phrases for me to form a sufficient impression of Eine. A dealer whose only priority was his personal desires. Mentally, I christened him 'Herr Huckster.'

"There is a Misunderstanding, Herr Panzer. I wished to shpeak vit you right now. I have twenty thousand Credits and the Desire to give them to you for speaking with me. Twenty thousand real Credits vill be yours if you can spend half an Hour talking with me. Die Hansawaffengesellschaft is not going anywhere, yet my Money vill stay vit me if you refuse."

I couldn't help but grow tense. This person knew my real name and seemed to know my financial situation—why else bring up IRL money?

A now-familiar taxi descended from above. Eine scurried aboard deftly, inviting me to follow him. I hesitated for a moment. In principle, the Aryan couldn't do me any harm. I could self-destruct at any moment and respawn back on Blood Island. Brainiac can fly *Warlock* back there on his own. I might lose some armor and whatever's in my cargo hold. Damn, I'd be sorry to lose the armor though. And yet I really wanted to find out what the old man wanted with me. The meeting was supposed to be interesting, considering that this was the game's biggest collector. He hadn't been too lazy to do his due diligence about me. For twenty thousand real credits, I could hear him out. I followed after him and the taxi zoomed off with us.

"Have a Seat, please," Eine said like a welcoming host,

---

pointing to an armchair. He himself sat on a modest stool, his hands on his knees. "I do not have ze habit of going here and zere, I prefer to do Business. Vould you like a Drink? Come, come, do not deny yourself ze Pleasure. I have heard so much about you during ze past two Weeks. Every Time ze Story is more interesting. One does not know vat is ze truth and vat is Fiction. I have heard about your Adventures and now vould like an Insight into ze real Truth. You own two ZPEF-Manipulators, an Orbship mit a full Crew, a Planet and various Missions. You have been to ze Uldan base and ze Training Sector Jail. I vould like to know how you acquired all of zis. I understand that you vant payment for ze information. I have twenty thousand Credits for confirming my Searches. Vat do you have to say to zat?"

Of the list enumerated by the old man, only the manipulators really got my attention. Why would Eine mention them? Making a note of this, I began to test the waters.

"Herr Eine, I will speak openly as you do. I do not like this whole situation. Imagine yourself in my position. Suddenly, a person appears who knows my name, my financial situation and the details of my in-game accomplishments. Now he wishes to pay me for information. Experience tells me that I should run away as quickly as I can and have nothing more to do with you. What do you have to say to zat?"

"You have ze right reservations," the old man smiled. "I have not been sufficiently politic. No, I mean, courteous. Not sufficiently courteous. I vish to dispel your Fears. I learned your Name in ze official Game Portal. Such is ze Game's User Agreement. Galactogon has seventy-two Players named

Surgeon and you are in zis List. I speak vit ze others, but zey do not understand. I search further. I consider ze possibility zat you are an employee of ze Galactogon Corporation. I make official Request and receive no Answer. You are a regular Player, yet you receive vat others do not. This is ze Source of my Interest. As for your 'Financial Situation'—I do not know to vat you refer. Everyone vants Money. It is simple."

"*Stan?*" Wasting no time, I had my home AI double-check the data.

"*I confirm the information.*" It took Stan just a couple of seconds to verify what Eine had told me. My name and occupation were indeed available in public sources. "*All this can be obtained quite easily.*"

"You told me how you discovered my name. But this does not explain where you got the details about my game history."

"Zis is very easy. Information about ze Manipulator and ze Planet I receive from an informant on ze Cruiser *Alexandria*. Kapitan Kiddo vas very helpful. Information about your orbship and ze Uldan Base, I received from ze Adviser to ze Precian Emperor. I have very positive Relationships with all ze Empires. I am one who values meine Name. I am not one to get involved in dubious Business, Herr Panzer. Does zis satisfy your Curiosity?"

It all sounded so plausible that the one thing I was sure of was that this old man was lying! I just wasn't sure about what exactly. My desire to talk to him further left me completely. The less you talk, the richer you'll become.

"Just a second," I muted my suit's PA and called Kiddo on a private line.

"Yeah, what of it? I sold Eine the tip about your pacifiers. Sent him a video too," the pirate confirmed. "I've had a business relationship with him for a long time. And don't go playing the victim—you sell valuable information left and right. You never said you wanted me to keep your info confidential, so I didn't even break a promise, much less violated a deal. Anyway, as your personal pirate, I advise you to work with him. He comes in handy."

Again those manipulators. Why is everyone so obsessed with them? They seem completely ordinary. As for Marina, she had confirmed my fears at her own expense. I really needed to put a damper on my relations with her.

"Frau Kiddo has confirmed vat I say? I am not a lover of foul Play," Eine accurately guessed whom I had called. Or could it be that Kiddo had already told him?

"Yes she did. But I am more interested in your mention of the manipulators. Why are you interested in them?"

"Herr Alexis, ze Players are not allowed to use zis Device. Galactogon prohibits Players to use ZPEF-Manipulators. It is a Rule set in Stone. Yet ze exception made in your Case, attracts my Attention. I vish to understand ze Reason. I have seen ze Video of you receiving ze Manipulators, but it is another Riddle. It is not possible. Vatch for yourself."

Eine showed me a compilation. I watched as, again and again, various players tried to acquire the manipulators. There were fights, riot police in the training sector, even an attempt to seize hostages. Brainiac counted thirty attempts and they all failed—with the exception of mine.

IN SEARCH OF THE ULDANS

Eine had studied and reproduced everything to the smallest detail in my 'feat,' but he lacked one factor: Being a pawn in a game between two very bored, very wealthy men. What could I tell this 'poor' collector? That I had received the manipulators as a reward for showing ingenuity and initiative? I had better keep quiet about that.

"Now that you have seen ze Information, I have a Qvestion. I vould like to know how you managed to receive these Items. I am prepared to pay you twenty thousand Credits."

"That Information is worth more than that. I am ready to provide you videos of all my raids for ten million IRL credits. You will see my audience with the emperor, how I acquired my orbship, how I recruited my crew and, in case you are still unaware of it, my recent raid on the Zatrathi flying fortress and my capture of the Zatrathi scout." I remembered Stan's description of the collector perfectly well. The old man did not mind getting unique information for pennies on the credit and pretended to be doing me a favor.

"You are talking about a terrible Amount!" Eine cried. "You must forget that ve are in a Game. Zis is not ze real World!"

"You're right. We're in Galactogon, not reality. That's precisely why I quoted you such a low amount. Only ten million. But I can sweeten the deal. This spear here was once part of the Uldan base. I was forced to fashion it to defend myself from the Vraxis warriors. There are none like it in the game and there never will be. I am also prepared to hand over an engineer from the Zatrathi flying fortress. This creature is also unique in its own way, because before me no one had taken one prisoner."

"I vant your Orbship. Ten million is a large Amount for some Pixels. I vant to receive something substantial."

"The orbship is not for sale," I snapped. "I can grant you temporary access to the ship, give you a tour of her, show you how she is arranged, but I will not part with my ship under any conditions. If this does not suit you, our conversation ends here and now."

"A Lease perhaps? I vill pay five hundred thousand Credits. You have ze Opportunity to sell me everything you say."

"No! No leases. I agree that ten million is too much, but I will not go any lower than nine. Are we done here?"

"I vish merely to receive a decent Produkt for my Money," Eine reddened and began to tremble. "I vant to pay real Money for a virtual Record in ze Database. You must understand and should take my Offer. A million Credits! I have ze shtrong Opinion that zis should be enough!"

"You are mistaken," I sighed eloquently. "You are not paying for a virtual record in a database so much as for the satisfaction of your curiosity. It is a pleasure to have unique knowledge and items, even if they aren't real. And pleasures are always expensive."

"Wenn it comes to Pleasure, for nine million real Credits, I expect to die of Ecstasy and go to Heaven too, Kapitan Surgeon!"

"I wouldn't guarantee it but anything's possible!"

We ended up agreeing on seven million, although it was exhausting for both of us. Eine would only raise his price by five hundred thousand, each time swearing that this was his final offer and he would not go any higher. I was able to resist only thanks to my experience negotiating in Runlustia.

As soon as we shook hands, things took off at a hectic pace: Stan confirmed the receipt of Eine's payment, while Brainiac reported an access request. Having made a final decision, Eine acted swiftly like a true businessman. Our deluxe taxi hovered down next to *Warlock*, where the collector's people were already waiting to pick up the Zatrathi engineer and start examining the orbship. I didn't mind handing over the alien one bit, provided that they would send me their report as agreed. I had no desire to rummage around the slug myself. I handed over the promised videos and the Uldan spear. The collector also begged out the Zatrathi armor suit from the derelict scout. Eine didn't have such a device yet and I didn't mind making a graceful gesture at a cost of ten thousand game credits.

"Vill I be able to help you further in your Game?" The collector offered to finish our conversation on the ride back to the Hansa HQ.

"Actually, yes," I said after a little thought. "Do you know where I could find a device that will convert Uldan coordinates into ours?"

"You have Information about a secret Location?" Eine began to pry.

I briefly explained the message from the Uldan survivor on the walls of the base. Eine's people would comb through all the videos frame by frame anyway, but I wouldn't sell this mission and warned the old man accordingly. Eine agreed that our deal only extended to already completed missions and tried to launch into a new round of bargaining. But I was no longer interested. I asked Brainiac to remove the frames that showed the first half of the coordinates from my videos. The possibility of getting something worth quite a deal more than a few credits was too great. Besides, the eleven million I had made today would feed and pay my medical costs for the next year.

"I have Information about ze Owner of such a Device. However, I see a big Problem. I do not have the ability to access ze Device. The owner of ze system where ze Device is located is not my Friend."

"Is he a player?"

"Nein. Not a Player. He is an NPC. Ze Jolly Roger—ze Corsican."

"Do you think Captain Kiddo could help me get to it?" I ventured and immediately bit my tongue—I had said too much.

"Nein again. Marina is ze Corsican's right Hand, but she does not have access to ze System. No Player in Galactogon knows ze Coordinates to ze Corsican's System. Zis is a big Problem."

"In that case, we'll deal with this later. I do indeed have the Uldan coordinates but until I complete a pirate mission, the way to the Corsican remains closed to me."

"Vat is zis Pirate Mission? Must you shoot down Ships, ja? Rob and plunder zem?"

"Nah just shoot them down. A lot of ships. I still have about a hundred more fighters or scouts to go. I could of course destroy nine cruisers instead, but after the latest update…Fuggedaboutit!"

IN SEARCH OF THE ULDANS

Eine paused, looking down at his feet and thinking about something.

"I vould like to help," the old man said. "My Friends have many D-class Ships. I can talk to zem, if you promise to take my People and me vit you to ze Udans. But I do not vish to talk Business now. First I must vatch the Video. Zen ve vill make a plan. Danke for your conversation, Herr Alexis. I have had a lot of Fun. I suppose zis is ze Time to exchange Contacts. Here is my Number."

Having instilled in me the hope that I could finish the pirate mission soon, the collector dropped me off at the same place where he had picked me up. I had to admit that my first impression of this man turned out to be overhasty—Eine valued his name, did not deal in empty promises, tried to squeeze out the greatest profit for himself, yet respected his partner's opinion. In any case, these were the conclusions I had come to following our meeting. Brainiac reported that Eine's people had left the orbship without leaving any foreign objects and without digging around too deeply under the hood. Everything had been done according to our contract, clearly and honestly.

I climbed the stairs and knocked on the door. There was no answer. I saw no intercoms, knockers, buttons or other means of announcing that I was at the door. A bare wooden door with a handle. I pulled it and started from the piercing squeak. The door did not open willingly. I applied more force to crack it open and slip inside. The door slammed shut, pushing me forward and showering me with dust. A single dim lantern lit the spectacle inside. It seemed as if no one cared one bit about order in this place—everything was covered with grime, dust and cobwebs. Instead of the reception room to the leading arms manufacturer of the Precian Empire, I had found myself in some neglected barracks—a corridor that led me to a door and an intercom. I pressed the call button and received a curt response after a long ring:

"Visiting hours are tomorrow. Come back tomorrow!"

The receptionist hung up before I could say anything. I frowned and tried my luck again.

"What are you, dumb? Or deaf? I don't have any time! I told you—come back tomorrow!" the speaker's voice rattled as if he had just recovered from a long illness.

When he hung up again without giving me a chance to get a word in, I grew angry and kicked the door several times as hard as I could. Sparks flew in all directions and dents appeared in the metal. Meanwhile, the noise was so loud that my armor suit automatically dampened the sound.

This time, my attempts to get in had an effect, albeit not the one I had counted on: A machine gun opened fire from the upper right corner. If I had died here, I would have had the snake make me another battering ram and come back tomorrow! But luckily the gun was firing ordinary kinetic bullets and my A-class armor suit managed just fine.

Thanks to the inertial dampeners, I didn't even budge from where I stood. Ten seconds later there was no trace of the machine gun. My shoulder-mounted blaster popped out and zapped it in a flash.

I decided to give Hansa one last chance and again pressed

the call button. After all is said and done, I prefer the path of peace.

"You're a pesky one, aren't you? Why don't you go back to your orbship and cause your ruckus there?" came the displeased answer. "Ah all right. Come on in."

I grinned. the Hansa man knew perfectly well who I was and why I was there. What remained a mystery was why they had arranged this entire circus.

A click came and part of the wall next to the door slid upward. I appreciated the width and material of the wall—two meters of monolithic metal, decorated with a thin stone lining. Walls like this could handle an orbital torpedo if someone decided to bomb Belket. Any notions of exacting vengeance against Hansa immediately left me.

The front room in this bunker was much more like the reception room of an enormous corporation I expected. Modern and high-tech, full of surrealism and devoid of human logic, the decor caused me neither discomfort nor anxiety. To the contrary, my ape brain equated the interior chaos with comfort. I couldn't help relaxing and even began to feel sleepy. The armor suit reacted to this by injecting me with a dose of synthetic glucose.

"What'd you come here for?" asked the boorish voice from before. The hologram of a Precian appeared beside me dressed in a white doctor's tunic. The Hansa salespeople did not even bother meeting their clients in person. It was no wonder he had received me at the door the way he had—impunity gives rise to permissiveness.

"What happened to the red carpet for VIP clients?" I wasn't

about to tolerate this kind of attitude.

"Tell me which closet we threw it in and I'll apologize to your human ass," snarled the Precian. "Are you so stupid that you don't know who you're talking to?"

"I don't need you dragging your tongue all over my human ass, thank you. And I believe I'm speaking to His Imperial Majesty's subject, so I'll be happy to return to the Emperor and inquire why his Imperial Majesty's subjects are rude, obnoxious, asslickers."

The grin vanished from the stupid Precian mug and he said solemnly:

"What have we, lowly tradesmen, done to earn this great honor—a visit from the great owner of the orbship?" The hologram's tone had changed to unvarnished sarcasm. I winced at the realization that the adviser, knowing full well the attitude of this guild's employees had sent me specifically to establish business relations with them. Surely the cunning Precian hoped that I wouldn't succeed. I considered several options to how this scenario could play out and tried the first one:

"Engineer, I need schematics for something powerful and unique, which the Precians cannot replicate at their level of technology. And it has to be something we wouldn't be sorry handing over to them."

"What about silicahydralization. A process for turning sand into water," suggested the snake, sounding unsure. "I thought of it a hundred thousand years ago and even created a prototype device demonstrating the process—the silicahydralizer. Should be knocking about the ship somewhere, taking up space. I never figured out a way to integrate it into the orbship and I'd be sorry to throw it away. It'll seem like a divine miracle to them—their current tech will not account for its principles of operation, let alone allow them to replicate it."

"Send me the schematics!" I ordered and turned to the hologram: "I was told that Hansa was unparalleled when it came to recreating the inventions of ancient epochs. That you can reconstruct the most incredible devices of the past. In fact, this is precisely why I wished to meet you. I wanted to verify the rumors."

"What do you want to surprise us with? An Uldan wondercannon? A miracle shield? Or perhaps an engine of unprecedented power?" The hologram was mocking me quite openly now. I ignored the gibe and projected a hologram of the schematics I had received.

"I have a working prototype, so I can say for sure that it works. I want to understand how and why."

The Hansa spokesman glanced at the hologram scornfully, yet I almost broke into a smile when his gaze lingered, locked and melted. The disdain on his face gave way to piqued interest, surprise, shock, and, finally, utter puzzlement. The Precian wholly succumbed to his examination of the schematics. I waited a few minutes and turned off the hologram, snapping him out of his reverie.

"It seems the rumors about your capabilities were exaggerated."

"But that can't possibly work!" A nearby wall slid aside and another Precian waddled in, this time in the flesh. He wasn't the

---

same one from the hologram, but he was dressed the same way. "Let me see that again!"

"There's no 'possibly' about. It works perfectly well," I insisted, re-casting the hologram. Two colleagues joined the Precian and they began ogling the schematics, arguing and poking their hands at different places of the projection.

"Prove it or I call BS!" one of the Precians turned to me.

"Engineer?"

"Will a video suffice?"

The Hansa experts glued themselves to the holovid. The Uldans visible in the background did not really add to the realism—in fact, to the contrary, they, made the video seem like a Sci-Fi flick. But the Precians made no complaints. It was as if they did not even notice the Uldans.

"But how?! Sand cannot simply turn to water!" One of the workers muttered in befuddlement. "And 'silica-hydralization?' *Really*? What a bunch of tosh!"

"Just because you can't do it, doesn't mean no one else can," I concluded. "It's all clear now. The emperor granted me the right to one Hansa device, but I can already imagine the level of your 'celebrated' products. I don't need more junk on board my ship. I guess there's nothing for me here. Open the door."

The entrance panel slid upward and I held my breath. The moment of truth had come—if Hansa allows me to leave now, I won't be able to come back for who knows how long. And even then at the price of great shame and humiliation. I stood up and walked calmly to the door. The Hansa techs watched in silence as I disappeared in the doorway. The wall behind me returned to its original state. That's all. I suppose I had chosen the wrong strategy, yet I did not slow my gait. One must know endure defeat nobly.

"All right, we want to know the principles behind your device. What would you like in return?" They sent the same jerk from before to talk me out of leaving. The Precian's voice caught up with me as I was descending the stairs. The players and locals loitering around paid no attention to him—I believe only I could hear him. An interesting trick. I need to ask the snake to reproduce it for me.

"You have nothing to offer me, bud. Barter implies an equal exchange, but I see that you lot only deal in dishing out abuse and rudeness for free. My regards to your marketing department. They did the impossible—Hansa is a much ado about nothing on a galactic scale. They really did stir up a fuss about a bunch of mediocre upstarts."

"You forget yourself, human!" a note of steel surfaced in the Precian's voice. "We make products that you never even dreamed of!"

"I believe it's me who has a product that you haven't dreamed of. And, unlike you, I've shown you proof. Before we start comparing how cool our toys are, why don't you convince me that you have something even worth speaking about."

"Turn back. I assure you we have something to discuss with you," the voice replied arrogantly, and a part of the wall next to the door rose up. The passage led to a regular lighted corridor. I hurried to enter while the invitation remained standing. In a roundabout way, I found myself in the earlier reception room. All the same Precian engineers were still there.

"We want a prototype silicahydralizer for research."

"First you will provide me with a worthy device, as per the emperor's orders." I'd be the one making the demands now.

"An exchange?"

"No way. I get one device for free—granted to me by the emperor. It is not your place to dispute it. Surprise me, prove that Hansa is worth its marketing budget and we can continue our conversation. Or give me some trinket. I'll toss it in the trash bin and we can forget about each other for a long time. Choice is yours."

The Precians began to confer among each other, whispering in a circle. Try as I might, I could not make out anything. A minute later, the very same Precian who started the conversation announced: "Very well, we are prepared to provide you with a device, which has no analogues in Galactogon. A set of extremely powerful engines."

"But your engines are fundamentally different from the type my orbship uses."

"That problem may be solved. We need only consult with your ship engineer. Ask the dispatchers to transfer the orbship to our repair shop. We will modify it there."

"Brainiac, get on it," I ordered the ship, but instead the snake replied with indignation:

"Cap'n, I seem to have missed something. I am working hard on upgrading the engines, trying to increase our velocity and you trust these sly devils more than me? I'm not even talking about the ethical aspect, although I am hurt, I just wish to remind you of the security of our ship."

"Can we do this without the sentiments? First, you will evaluate, examine everything and draw a conclusion, and then we will make the final decision together. I know you longer than them, but they promised to surprise me. Give them a chance."

"What surprise? You've seen those so-called modern ships! They fly about as fast as you walk. But okay, let's take a look at their engines. But no advances and no discounts! I'm the one who has to pick up the pieces after your tinkering."

The orbship landed in the repair dock right through the protective dome. It looked like a celebrity surrounded by fans. The local engineers, though they really were fans, were only interested in the upgrades and research. All actions with the ship were broadcast for me on the screen in the meeting room, and the Hansa staff provided a consultant explaining what was happening. The engineer got out of the hull and began to study the submitted schematics.

"Now we are planning the modifications that have to be made," the consultant began to explain. "We have never worked with an orbship but Uldan technology is familiar to us. In fact, we need to study the assemblies for mounting the engines to the hull and ensuring that they function within their proper tolerances. Your engineer is examining our blueprints to find a way of wiring our engines to the ship's computer."

"Cap'n," the snake called quietly, without looking up from the schematics. "I was a good ship engineer for you? Right? Wasn't I?"

"What do you mean, 'was?' Are you going to resign? Get to

the point, will you?"

"As embarrassing and unpleasant as it is to admit it, my achievements are childish hiss compared to these devices. I…uh…I admit that sometimes I grumble and complain too much. Sometimes I'm a bit too pushy, but…will we install these babies or what? Our speed will match the Zatrathi ships—surpass it in fact. I mean these are some rockets! I am ready to eat my tail from envy."

"Have them installed and quit babbling. You'll do better in the future." I smiled, pleased with my foresight and relishing the snake's embarrassment. Everything turned out for the best: I got not just new equipment, but the best equipment there was.

"Oh! They have agreed on the modifications they will make," my consultant commented on the change in activity. The snake was hovering over the workers, making comments and gesturing with her little snake hands. Only fifteen minutes had passed and our engines had changed dramatically: The housing had been taken off and several compartments had been reconfigured entirely. The engineer dove into the hull and rolled out two outdated engines, then went back for the new ones.

"I'm done here, Cap'n," came her report. "Our preliminary delta v is 1.9 times the previous one. If we race the Zatrathi ships now, we'll leave them in the stardust. Even the cruisers. Although we will need to test them further. In any event, Hansa are like tech gods or something. They have my admiration."

"Start working on a prototype sand-to-water converter," I sighed. "You'll give it to your new idols."

CHAPTER SIX

"**I** WANT IT ALL!"

I barely recognized the snake anymore. She was so impressed with Hansa that even once we'd flown off, my engineer couldn't calm down for a long while. Delighted by the prototype silicahydralizer and having signed our cooperation contract, the Hansa specialists offered me a list of thirty products with detailed descriptions. There were improvements for the armor suit here, as well as new shields for the ship, an updated computer system, and even weapons. Thirty items all together, with the cheapest coming in at twelve million—a rapid-firing beam cannon for an armor suit—and the most expensive costing one and a half billion—an upgrade to the ship's armor. According to its description, the armor could withstand a direct hit from seven A-class torpedoes at once.

Seeing the list, the snake lost her mind.

"Do you know where to get three billion?" I said, quoting the total cost of all the upgrades.

"Don't look at me. I just know how to spend it. Getting it is the Cap'n's problem," the serpent said indignantly. "You can't say no! That is, I mean, it would be irresponsible towards your crew and ship if you did. Go kill someone, rob a mogul, kidnap an heiress—we need it all! Hansa are geniuses! Geniuses! I'm literally ashamed of my prior attempts. In our time, they would be priceless."

"They maybe geniuses, but they also charge an arm and a leg. You saw the price list," I looked at the list again. "Stay here, I have to go see the local viceroy. Maybe I'll manage to haggle for something else."

The imperial viceroy's residence was located next to the part of the planet that is commonly called the 'military testing ground.' This area was about two hundred kilometers in diameter and was completely devoid of vegetation, since this is where Hansa's customers tested the weapons they bought. Droids, weapons, armor suits, torpedoes, and other means of mass and individual destruction—all were brought here. The viceroy issued the licenses for the tests and monitored them. It was quite a lucrative post. If you add the other, ever-vital component of bribery, it was simply the good life. People accustomed to living according to the law in reality felt liberated from their ethical scruples in the game and sometimes let their dark side to the surface. It was like this everywhere, so why not give them the opportunity to fool around in Galactogon as well?

In any case, I needed to see the viceroy for another reason—I wanted to exchange the tokens I had accumulated. I knew where to go as soon as I entered the building. A crowd of players was milling at the entrance to a big hall. From the snatches of their conversation, I deduced that some guild had shown up en masse and kicked everyone out so that its players could cash in their tokens in peace and without waiting in line. Working through the crowd with my elbows, I snuck up to the entrance and looked inside. The room looked like an ordinary school gym. A Precian was sitting in its center, counting a heap of golden tokens on the table before him. Next to him stood ten players in legendary marine armor. There was no one else there—if you ignored the dozens of expelled onlookers staring daggers at the whole scene from the lobby.

"Wait your turn!" My appearance did not go unnoticed and I was instantly warned. I held my ground.

"One hundred seventy-two gold and forty-three silver tokens," the Precian concluded and addressed the tokens' owner: "Would you like credits or gear?"

"Credits." The marine looked like he was about to be rewarded for slaying some rare and dangerous beast. Despite his average height, he looked around himself haughtily.

"A silver token is worth a hundred credits, a gold one—five hundred. In total, you are entitled to ninety thousand three hundred credits," the Precian entered something in his tablet and added: "Done. The funds have been transferred to your account."

Another Precian swept the tokens from the table and into a box, clearing the space for the next marine.

"Did you not understand something, you piece of a moron?" The marine from before bristled at me again. "Get outta here!"

"Stan look up a guild named 'Fighting Breed' for me ASAP. Who, what, how and where they're from."

"The Fighting Breed Guild is listed tenth in the Precian Empire rankings. They specialize in ground operations. They recruit players to the guild exclusively out in reality, focusing primarily on the physical parameters of their candidates. They are known for their aggressive behavior. Their assets include three populated planets, three cruisers, twenty-three carracks..."

Stan went on listing the guild's goods, but I could no longer listen to him. The arrogant marine was monopolizing my attention.

"Do you hear me, shithead? If you don't scram this instant, my entire division will come down on you. Don't you know who we are?" The marine took several decisive in my direction.

"Baby, I don't care who you are," I shut the doors behind me and beelined for the two-bit game bully. "I see you've raided a Zatrathi daycare. What are you, heroes now? I won't even ask which one of you got it from the Zatrathi while you were harvesting your tokens. That's clear as things stand. Does your rear still itch? Or does it seek further adventures? Don't be shy. This is a game, everything is allowed here..."

I spoke the last words already mid-scuffle. Insulted in front of his comrades, the marine rushed forward bellowing, using his mass instead of his head. He wanted to simply knock me down and trample me—which is what I had counted on when I switched my logorrhea switch to full blast. This fool did not even have time to touch me. Cloaked up until the moment, the security guards lifted the bully into the air and dragged him away. This is a trading planet, 'piece of a moron!' You can't assault other players here.

"Next!" The Precian reminded everyone why they were there in a demanding voice. The remaining marines had a problem, requiring all their CPUs' cores to solve—reduced to two words it amounted to: What do? The musclehead tribal code clearly stated that I was to be punished immediately, while the guards hovering overhead were proof that no action was possible. Amid the heavy silence, pregnant with their contemplation of this paradox, I approached the desk.

"Here?" I asked the Precian, skeptically examining the cleared part of the table. He nodded. Having estimated that its surface would hardly accommodate a thousand tokens, I unloaded the lot of them. To the exclamations of the stunned onlookers, who had made their way into the hall to see my fight with the marine, I dumped all of my black, silver and gold tokens. The ensuing pile was my height.

"612 silver tokens, 96 black tokens and 12,025 gold tokens." The count came in fifteen minutes later and only because the head Precian called for help. "Would you like to redeem them for credits or equipment?"

"Hansa equipment. Hold up...do you accept these as well?"

I placed the two sapphire tokens I received for killing the guards at the Zatrathi base on the desk. The marines had forgotten all about their revenge and huddled up to the table gawking at my loot. Apparently, they'd never encountered creatures like that before.

"Two sapphire tokens worth one hundred thousand credits

---

each," the Precian did not react at all to my 'raise.' It was like he did this every day. But his assistants had already joined the marines and the crowd was loudly discussing this new development—no one had ever brought in tokens like these.

"Cool. What about these?" I placed one of the tokens I had received in the Uldan base on the table. These did not faze the head Precian either.

"Yes. These are ancient tokens but we don't accept them. The bone one is worth fifty credits, the gold one with a border, eight hundred. They hold more historical value than material."

"Will anyone give me more?"

"No, these tokens are outdated, but not rare."

"I see. Take your antiques then." I was pleased to rid myself of dead weight. Another mountain appeared on the floor, though half the size of the first. The Precians again began to count.

"Five thousand and four rimmed gold tokens and four hundred twenty-one bone tokens. Would you like to add something else?"

"Not, that's all," I replied with undisguised pleasure. The marines stood there silently watching what was happening. And yet the crowd of onlookers was burbling with questions that should have tormented the marines: Who the hell was this guy? Where did I get so many tokens and why did nobody know anything about the battle in which I had earned them?

Still, no one bugged me with questions, which was perfectly fine with me.

"Thus in total, you are entitled to GC 10,336,050. This is your certificate for any Hansa item worth GC 20,672,100. People who redeem Zatrathi tokens receive a fifty percent discount from Hansa."

I took the certificate and the list of equipment appeared before my eyes. For twenty million I could afford to completely upgrade the beam cannons on my ship. All I had to do was speak to the Hansa Corp and install the upgrades.

"Hold it right there, Surgeon," one of the marines, whose name was Dantoon, made his way to me. The rest surrounded me in a tight circle. "We have a score to settle. And the time has come to settle it. Hand over the certificate and get the hell off our planet. If you do that, we can call it even."

"You're threatening me?" I glanced at the guards hovering nearby. The marine knew that the merest touch would be deemed an act of aggression. "You can't do anything to me here. I will not give you the certificate. But I'll remember you and your gang. I'm going to go now—enjoy tormenting yourself over who I am and what I can do to you. However…if you like, I can forget about you for only thirty million."

No one said anything, nor moved. It took Dantoon some time to ponder what I had said and understand the main gist— right now, in here, these guys really couldn't do anything to me.

"We're leaving," the marine announced, indicating that he was the leader of the gaggle. "We'll remembered you, dickface. Keep an eye over your shoulder. Galactogon isn't so vast that this'll just blow over."

"Are you saying you won't pay me?" I continued mocking the dummy. I know, it's low of me, but it felt so good too. "Consider, marines, at the moment it's a mere thirty. Later, it'll be a hundred."

The meatheads fixed me with all the contempt they could muster and, trying to keep their pride at least in their postures, withdrew from the hall. The public triumphantly surged forth to redeem their tokens.

I never bowed or buckled under bullies like the marines and I wasn't about to now. You couldn't help encountering these boys either in VR or meatspace from time to time and the only way to deal with them was to speak their language—with threats or brute force. More often than not, they seemed formidable only in words.

Now expelling them from my head entirely, I hurried to the Hansa HQ to get my upgrades. Everything went off without a hitch and in half an hour, as we emerged into orbit around Belket, I could already boast of new and powerful armament.

The plan for the near future was extremely simple—I had to finish the pirate mission, eke out access to the coordinate converter, and then zoom off to collect the Uldan treasures. Set course for Daphark!

"A jump into hyperspace is not possible at the moment," said Brainiac. "Our vessel's hyperdrive is being disrupted by a beam."

I peered at my screen with a nasty premonition. Now, which of the ten cruisers currently in the system was risking its health and keeping me from jumping. There was nothing to be afraid of in the system itself—as soon as even a single torpedo flew in my direction, the three Grand Arbiter's would intervene to restore order, and yet the hyperdrive disruptor was not considered a

---

form of attack. Just a bit of griefing, no more. There was no punishment for it.

"Bring the throttle up to 20%. We'll leave the system. Brainiac, who's painting us with the beam?"

"The cruiser *Smasher*. She is registered to the Fighting Breed guild. She is a class B vessel."

So (and no surprise here) the bullies were vindictive! Analyzing their tactics, I couldn't help but feel some respect. They had passed, as they say, from words to deeds, without clogging the air with stupid insults and pointless threats. They just held us with their beam and stayed silent. Meanwhile, the situation around my ship was heating up—without any overt aggression, I was encircled by ten frigates and twenty fighters, all from the same guild.

Wow, they really had taken offense and approached the issue of punishment very seriously.

The engineer had finished installing the minelayer. We hadn't tested the weapons we got from Hansa yet and it would be nice to see the full power of the new engines in action. In general, there was no better way to test the ship than to get into a good scrap. Ready or not, here I come!

"Hi ladies!" The first thing to do is deprive the players of their self-control by some tried and true method. "Did your mommies let you out to play today?"

There was no answer.

"Brainiac, throttle to forty. Let's see what they can do. Circle the system, without leaving the Grand Arbiters' coverage zone."

None of our pursuers fell behind, yet the impression that the fighters were giving it their all refused to leave me. The frigates coped with our velocity just fine. Constantly swapping positions, they swarmed around us, staying on our wings. Without knowing my capabilities, the players had assumed that *Warlock* had a standard weapon configuration in which the beam cannons were mounted at the bow and stern. The truth will come as an unpleasant surprise for them—but a little later.

"Speed to sixty. Set course along the system's outer perimeter."

The fighters fell behind, but the frigates still managed, though with a struggle. Only three truly held on—they had good engines that allowed them to keep up. The cruiser had remained in place the entire time, turning its bow to follow our maneuvers and ready to pounce at any moment.

"Prepare to attack. Gunner, at my command, destroy the frigates. Brainiac, keep that planet between us and the cruiser." I pointed to a lifeless giant in the system's outer orbit. "Keep maneuvering, so that they cannot paint us with their disruptor beam. The objective will be to sink the cruiser before they can summon reinforcements. No messing about. Engineer, you take care of point defense. Make sure that not a single torpedo gets through. Are these objectives clear to everyone? Let's go then! Throttle to seventy!"

My plan was a resounding success. Ducking behind the gas giant blocked the disruptor beam. Two frigates managed to match our speed giving it all they had and took up positions on either side of us. Very good—they had showed that they also hadn't been running at full throttle. The cruiser set a course on a

---

tangent to the planet, simultaneously approaching and closing the disruptor's 'blind' zone. I had about thirty seconds to act and set a course to leave the system. It was impossible to move in a straight line—I had to keep drifting to one side in order to keep the gas giant between myself and the cruiser. The frigates did not lag behind, and as soon as Brainiac reported that we had left the Belket system, I ordered:

"Gunner, destroy the enemy!"

"What the?!" At long last a voice broke over the air. The frigates simply did not expect our cannons to shoot from our sides. There's that promised surprise! Despite their shields and considerable size, the enemy was destroyed in a couple of seconds. The EM cannons stripped the frigates' shields almost instantly and two shots from the beam cannons finished them off. The upgraded beam cannons pierced straight through the enemy ships. With one volley, the gunner destroyed the engines, with another the fusion reactors—turning the frigates into useless space debris. Then the snake ended the fight by launching a torpedo at each one. We were ahead. Score: 2-0.

The third frigate, which had fallen behind, arrived just in time. I turned around and flew at the unlucky sucker. An EM blast, two shots from the beam cannons and a parting torpedo— and the third frigate rested with her fellows. Brainiac launched the robotic arm and picked up the loot. A bit of elo and raq. Trifles, but no point in cluttering space further.

"Let's go!" I barked, moving the projection of the ship in the opposite direction. The guild did not understand the hint and rushed after us, but they were too late by ten to fifteen seconds.

In space combat, however, even a fraction of a second determined the battle's outcome.

"Our hyperdrive is being disrupted again," the snake reported. The cruiser had left the system and was now giving chase. The fighters and frigates had returned to base, unable to match their mothership's speed.

"Speed to eighty. Let's see what their tub is capable of," I ordered, watching *Smasher*'s maneuvers. Entering the field of battle, the cruiser tried to hit us with her main cannons but the distance between us gave us time to leave the line of fire. I could hardly keep myself from seeing which was better: The cruiser's cannons or the orbship's shields, but Hansa hadn't upgraded our shields yet, so it was better to save any experiments for another day. Fifty million for a new reactor and one hundred twenty for shields were not a price I could afford right now.

The cruiser was lagging noticeably behind us so I had to hold my horses and reduce speed to seventy percent. This put us on equal footing, turning the chase into a marathon. The enemy was the first to blink.

"Torpedoes. Twenty incoming. They are closing at a speed of 85% of our maximum. We won't be able to knock out all of them. Thirty seconds until contact."

"Let's go then," I stepped on the gas, driving the orbship up to the speed of the torpedoes. Their service radius wasn't that great—only a dozen or so AU. The cruiser fell behind as expected, but did not give up the chase. Ten minutes later, the torpedoes petered out. The cruiser recovered them as it flew past. No one wanted to leave expensive ordinance lying around.

IN SEARCH OF THE ULDANS

Seeing such thrift, I inquired:

"Snake, do you think if we fire torpedoes at them, they'll destroy them or capture them?"

"Don't ask me! You humans are incomprehensible and unpredictable creatures. You are asking me for advice now and then later you'll blame me for giving you bad advice. Think for yourself."

"I am. What would you do?"

"I would destroy them, obviously. I am well aware of the kind of surprises lie in store for those who recover enemy torpedoes. When a timed fuse goes off, you'll be good and sorry for your thrift."

"That's what I'm talking about…Do you think the players will take the risk or not? I'll bet two credits that they risk it. They seem like the kind that's greedy when it comes to other people's property. Load three torpedoes and set their fuse to three minutes. You can do that, right?"

"Of course. Only, three minutes is too long. It's typically set to thirty seconds. In three minutes they could send those torpedoes back to us."

"That's the idea. If the torpedoes are captured, but not immediately destroyed, they will definitely keep them away from the ship. I say two minutes at least. And then they'll drag them in. So set it to three minutes!"

"Done. Fuse set to three minutes."

"Now get ready, we will feign an attack. Engineer, shields to bow. We need to survive a direct hit from their main cannon, if we can't dodge it. Brainiac, help me with that. I trust your knowledge of the ship more than my own. If you see that I can't cope—you can take control. Let's go!"

The inertia from our abrupt change of course pressed me into the chair. The orbship was now headed directly at the cruiser. And the cruiser, without waiting for us to close, instantly answered with volleys from her beam cannons. Brainiac gently banked to the side without slowing down. The distance between the two ships was disappearing rapidly and the cruiser did not have time fire again, since the reload took ten seconds. The moment had come for both sides to fire their torpedoes.

"Now!" I ordered, banking *Warlock* sharply away from the cruiser. Their torpedoes did not have time to pick up enough speed or maneuver behind me. At 85% throttle we were leaving the enemy and her missiles far behind us.

"Brainiac?"

"They are recovering their torpedoes. They have intercepted ours," the computer announced to my jubilation. "They are keeping them at a distance."

We continued on our way, calmly, awaiting the outcome. Only at the end of the second minute did our warheads began gradually drifting towards the cruiser.

"They bought it!" Sebastian cried, delighted. This entire time he had been staring at the screens in blank boredom. The thief could do nothing to help during a space battle, but he still appreciated a good trap. It was exactly in the spirit of pirates. I don't know what cul-de-sac Dantoon had though himself into, but perhaps he figured that I was counting on hurting them with a surprise attack and underestimated how good his players were.

IN SEARCH OF THE ULDANS

Whatever it was, he ordered my torpedoes to be picked up. Thirty seconds before the explosion. I watched with bated breath as the missiles vanished inside the vessel, clenched my fists, and could not help cracking a smile at the spectacle. The cruiser's hull burst on one side, burping a fireball into space. Naturally there can be no fire in space, but the devs couldn't help but embellish their game with cinematic touches. The cruiser blinked several times and went out—the explosion had taken out its reactor.

"Close in on them," I grinned, banking *Warlock*. The damage looked serious, and I dismissed the possibility of a trap. "Gunner, shoot any objects that move in our direction. Brainiac, how are their defenses? Could they be rope-a-doping us?"

"The energy shields are down. The hyperdrive disruptor has also stopped working. It does not appear that they are feigning their damage."

"Send the torpedoes, engineer. Let's exterminate the Fighting Breed once and for all."

It all happened so quickly that the players did not have time to get their bearings. A few seconds after the torpedoes exploded, I took up a comfortable position, on the cruiser's left flank where her beam cannons and tractor beam could not reach me (these were on her keel). My torpedoes zoomed into the target and took out her engines, her hangar and the fighters in it. *Smasher* survived, but she now evoked pity instead of fear. I made a quick estimate: I still had sixteen torpedoes and the seventeenth was supposed to appear in the next five minutes. I had more than enough to finish the cruiser off, but another idea occurred to me.

"Brainiac, I want that cruiser. Can we disable her self-destruct mechanism, so that we can board?"

"Analyzing now. Such an operation must take into account a lot of factors, otherwise we will blow up the ship when the self-destruction button is destroyed."

"Do it when you're ready," I ordered Brainiac just in case.

Receiving the silent orders of the ship computer, the gunner began blasting four targets at a time with our beam cannons, incinerating the hull plating and disabling equipment and circuitry whose purpose was known only to Brainiac.

"The auxiliary power units have been located and destroyed," the computer announced after a while of sustained fire. I had even begun worrying about consuming too much energy, its reserves sinking noticeably for the sake of my whim. "The cruiser can no longer destroy itself with the self-destruct button. Even if they had a backup circuit, it won't be able to reach the payload. We severed the comm lines to the explosives. They are harmless."

"Listen up, crew. Shoot anything that comes flying out of that cruiser's hull. No one's allowed out and no one's allowed in. Brainiac, get the marine and the droids ready. We're gonna board her. Sebastian, you are with me. We will have to open her entrance hatch."

The snake fired two more torpedoes just to be safe. One hit the cargo hold, the second slammed the cruiser in her prow, depriving her of her main cannon. The captain's deck was damaged only tangentially—the electronics could cope with the hit, which could not be said for the players—especially the ones with sub-A-class armor. Naturally, the captain and his officers would be in Legendaries, but I planned to relieve them of this burden.

Brainiac took control of the ship and glided up to the cruiser's open bow. The marine went in first, then Sebastian and I. The rhinoceros has already managed to get bored in the hold and gladly rallied out to fool around on the cruiser. Up to this point, I had never used the marine for his intended purpose, forcing him to gather loot, steal items, and punch through walls, so I was really looking forward to causing some trouble with this boarding action. The rhino stamped his foot from impatience like a true bull. The gunner carefully blasted a hole for us right into the captain's deck, simultaneously destroying anyone who might have been in there. Even a legendary armor suit couldn't protect from a ship's beam cannon. The marine dived into the opening first to scout out the situation and clear the enemy. It was the first time I'd seen my rhino use his blasters. Situated in his eyes by default, they shot wherever the cryptosaur looked, turning him into some terrifying and not uncomic monster. The marine only used his blasters twice—to finish off two players who were hiding in the deck's corners. Judging by the marine armors littering the floor, the ten bullies from the viceroy's office had met an inglorious death after all.

"Sebastian, take the loot to our ship," I ordered the thief, pointing at the armor suits. These items, even if they were only A-class, would sell perfectly well at auction.

"Brainiac, how can I make myself an access key and

register the ship to myself?"

"You're looking for a reserve backup?" the snake wedged in. Apparently, Brainiac did not like the idea of me acquiring a new ship, especially one that on paper was more powerful than *Warlock*. The last thing I needed to deal with was a jealous computer.

"Don't panic. Our objective is to re-register the ship to me and strip her of her homeworld binding. Then, when she's destroyed, she will respawn outside the nearest planet. And that would be Belket—where we can find a suitable buyer for her as well as all this loot. I mean, are we pirates or what?"

"Get ready to receive the cable," the snake said relieved and after a couple of moments, a droid appeared hauling a power conduit. "You will have to power up the main computer. The power outlet is bottom right. Found it? Plug it in."

I followed the engineer's instructions and the cruiser came to life. Or at least her computer did. The captain's deck looked much more cheerful when all the consoles in it started blinking and buzzing.

"We accidentally blew all the circuits around here, so we'll have to make the access key to the cruiser on our ship. I need permission to expend a ton of raq."

"Why so much?" I asked surprised.

"Don't worry about it. It'll take me longer to explain it than just to do it."

I shook my head and granted permission. Brainiac and the engineer went quiet, working their magic on the cruiser's systems. Of course, we could simply capture her by hunting down all the players remaining on board, but that would also be very laborious and time consuming. And how many players had survived so far still remained a rather important question. How they were organized, where they were located, what they were armed with—the more I thought about it, the clearer it became that it was easier to hack the ship. Fortunately no one interfered. Sebastian finished hauling the armor suits and began exploring the area we were in. I strictly forbade him, as well as the rhinoceros, from leaving the captain's deck.

New ship acquired: Cruiser Smasher. Item class: B-61. Consult the ship log for a detailed description of this vessel. The ship's respawn location has been reset. Attention! If the cruiser is destroyed she will respawn in the nearest ship graveyard.

"You're a genius, Brainiac! You too, snake. Now tell me, how can we blow her up?"

"Only with torpedoes. About ten should be enough," the snake replied.

"Everyone off the cruiser!" I ordered. "Brainiac did you download the ship log? I need to know where the main base of the Fighting Breed is. I'd like to pay them a visit."

"Data analyzed. The main base is located in the vicinity of Galvara, the second-largest trading planet of the Precians. It is ten minutes' flight in hyperspace from here."

I looked at my watch—seven minutes had passed since the torpedoes had exploded aboard the cruiser. If we assume that Dantoon immediately asked for help and got an immediate reply, we should have guests soon. Which means we should get out of here before it is too late.

"Snake, sink that tub," I ordered as soon as I set foot on my orbship.

There was an explosion. Another. And another. And another. The engineer had miscalculated—we were forced to use all our torpedoes. Post-update, the cruisers were too strong and *Warlock* had no weapons of a larger caliber. At least I got a mission progress update for the Hilvar quest—destroying my own cruiser had counted toward my killcount. Obviously, I wasn't expecting to complete the mission by sinking cruisers, but it couldn't hurt, could it? Eight more and I'd be a bona fide pirate lord.

"The cruiser's holds were not empty," said Brainiac when the visual effects of the ship's destruction disappeared along with it. I cautiously flew up to the huge shimmering creates and brought them in with the robotic arm. A list of available items appeared on the screen, and Sebastian whistled in shock—the marines were preparing for serious combat. Ten legendary armor suits, one hundred tons of raq, twenty of elo, about a dozen armored vehicles and even one huge mech—a fighting robot for five people.

"Brainiac, can we take the lot of it?" I asked, gulping.

"The armored cars are junk," Sebastian interfered. "The mech is a good one. I've never seen this model before. I reckon we could offload it for about thirty million. The armor suits...I don't even have the words. So many Legendaries in one place! Each worth ten million. It is a pity we have no use for them: They are designed for fighting planetside and in the open. You won't be able to move around in one in the orbship."

"Even if we leave the armored vehicles, we still have to choose between the elo and the raq. I can accommodate seventy tons."

"Take the raq then. We have enough elo," I had no doubt which was more important.

"The cargo has been stored. Attention! We are being painted with a hyperdrive disruptor beam."

"Throttle to eighty and set course for Belket," I ordered, assessing the situation. As I had expected, the help had arrived. The other two Fighting Breed cruisers had arrived to seek revenge. The orbship zoomed off, leaving the cruisers far behind. Brainiac announced that we had entered the Belket system, which gave me the opportunity to rest quietly—we were again under the protection of the Grand Arbiter. Now, whatever the Fighting Breed tries, the NPCs will cover us.

"Stan, run a forum scan—how much does an upgraded C-class cruiser cost?"

"Between nine hundred million to two billion Galactogon Credits." I was stunned by my smart home's reply. "It all depends on the configuration and equipment aboard the ship."

After brief reflection, I called Gammon.

"Hey ya! Do you need a C-class cruiser? Being old friends and all, I'll make you a deal."

"Surgeon?" Gammon did not immediately understand who was calling him. Or perhaps he was taken aback by the generous offer.

"Uh-huh. A couple of minutes ago, I ganked a cruiser from

the Fighting Breed guild. It's currently in the Belket graveyard, but only I have the access key. If I recall you have eleven already. This one will make it a pretty dozen. It's a good offer."

"All your generous offers sure do hurt my wallet," said Gammon. "The guild budget won't allow me to spend such money right now. How much are you selling it for?"

"Oh come now, come now. You just sold a bunch of planets as well as the info about the Zatrathi. 1.5 billion. I can't go any lower. I have my eyes and heart set on this one thing Hansa has in their catalog. I want it on my ship."

"You're dealing with Hansa now?" Gammon's second name could as well be mistrust.

"It was hard, but yes, I have a list of goodies and a five percent discount. Five seconds, I will send you the upgrades they have. Here it is! I really want item number twelve."

"Seven torpedoes at once?!" Gammon again grew flustered. If we continue in the same spirit, I am afraid that I will have to shell out for his therapist fees.

"Ok, I understand, you're not interested. I'll look for other buyers."

"Wait!" As I imagined, Gammon began to fret once he saw that I was determined to get my 1.5 billion. "Let's suppose that your offer interests me. But 1.5 billion is much too much."

"I can't do less—you've seen the Hansa prices yourself. Considering that I'm going to be a target now, I need armor like I need air. Sorry, but I can't haggle on this one. I called you purely because we fought the Zatrathi together. I'll ask Kiddo for her contacts. Surely I can sell the cruiser for what she's worth."

IN SEARCH OF THE ULDANS

"All right. 1.5 billion it is," Gammon gave in. "With one condition. You will introduce me to Hansa. I also want that armor."

"I don't have permission to do that, so that won't work. But there is another option. My contract with Hansa states that I can only install their equipment on my ships. If you want the upgrade, lease me your ship temporarily, I will update it at your expense plus a small commission and return it to you. There's no other way. I'm not going to risk my connections with Hansa because of you."

"I see you've thought everything through in advance." A note of irritation sounded in Gammon's voice.

"That's true. And so! One and a half billion for the ship. A billion five hundred and seventy five million for the new hull. If you agree, call your lawyers. We can sign the contract stating that the transfer of your ship is fictitious and purely for upgrading out in meatspace."

"Where did the seventy-five million come from?"

"My commission is five percent. Keep in mind, I'm charging the minimum, as an old friend. You're paying exactly the price that Hansa offers to other players, when they get the opportunity. Surely you've seen the market and know the prices, right? Hence your surprise when I showed you my price list. You can't get this in the open market."

"Where are you anyway?"

"I'm just approaching Belket. With two cruisers full of baddies on my ass. I'm not planning on landing just yet. I want to set them up with the Arbiters. I don't like this Fighting Breed guild."

"You be careful with them. If they can't get at you in game, they'll try in meatspace. They take their losses very seriously. Especially this kind."

"Uh-huh. They'll find me and punish me," I grinned. "Do you know how many such punishers I've met in my life? Why I couldn't count the lot of them. I'll be waiting for you on Belket."

"Thirty minutes. I have to decide where to get so much money and have the contract drawn up. I don't trust you," said Gammon, gaining my utmost respect. I like people who are frank.

Unfortunately, reason prevailed over testosterone among the captains of the cruisers pursuing us. The hyperdrive disruptor remained on our ship, but no one opened fire, wary of the Arbiters. I flew near the cruisers several times, testing their patience, but got no reaction. No one even tried to radio me. Realizing that there would be no scuffle, I asked for permission to land closer to the Hansa HQ. If Gammon comes through, my ship will be due a significant upgrade.

"Stan, how much money can I transfer into the game without killing the family budget?"

"Three million, five hundred thousand. I have taken the liberty of paying for five months' treatment for Eunice and you, and I have started a savings fund that should be enough for another five months as well as half a year of living expenses at the average rate. The remaining budget of four million has been reserved for covering risks. Five hundred thousand is more than enough to do so; therefore you can afford three and a half million at the moment."

What would I do without Stan?! He managed not only to think for me, but also took care of all the necessary paperwork, eliminating the burden of routine. Eunice would return to Galactogon in a week and a half. I should prepare a worthy welcome for her.

"*The official exchange rate is one to a thousand*," Stan concluded his report. A list of Hansa equipment appeared before my eyes. The total value of the items was three billion. If Gammon buys a cruiser for one and a half, I only need to transfer one and a half million into Galactogon. Although I had better give myself a buffer—who knows what else Hansa would offer.

"Transfer two million—try and invest the remaining 1.5 for the next six months so that we make some good interest. It's not good business letting money sit idle."

"Done. The exchange application has been generated and is being verified. I have received a request for confirmation— please provide a digital signature."

I put my finger to the PDA, and a message appeared:

Thank you for using the official Galactogon store. You have acquired GC 2,000,000,000. To commemorate your first deal, we will give you a 10% bonus. Have a nice game!

Two billion two hundred million! My heart skipped at the realization of the crazy amounts of money flying around Galactogon. Of course, these weren't real credits, just gaming ones, but still it was impressive.

"Stan, what is the reverse exchange rate?"

"*One to twenty thousand,*" my home AI reminded me of harsh reality of life. If I need to convert my money back to real credits, I will receive twenty times less than what I invested. Not a very bright prospect. Two hundred tons of raq amount to five hundred real credits. And here I was rejoicing at having found the opportunity to earn my bread and butter. Hah! The emperor's generous gesture in granting me so much raq, turned into complete zilch if I thought of it in real numbers. I wonder how Eunice's financial affairs are?

Gammon reappeared exactly thirty minutes after our conversation, as if he had waited for the indicated time to expire. I was sitting on the steps in front of the Hansa HQ, looking at the players and NPCs running to and fro. I couldn't help notice my friends: Like hulking breakwaters in the current of creatures moving past me, five marines from the Fighting Breed guild stood in the crowd staring at me. I guess in order to increase the intimidation factor, they did not bother hiding and stood like statues.

"What's up!" Gammon came up to me on the steps. "I decided to immediately take the bull by its...Hmm, hang on, I gotta answer this call."

A minute later, the head of the Black Sails happily declared:

"Did you know that you've been declared a dead man? The head of the Fighting Breed just called me and strongly recommended not to buy your cruiser. Are you being watched?"

"Yeah, they're right there," I pointed at the silent marines.

IN SEARCH OF THE ULDANS

"Why are you so happy? Have you changed your mind about the deal?"

"Are you nuts? To the contrary! What could be better than to screw your closest competitor? Losing that cruiser has already dropped these guys from the top hundred in the rankings. No one will have anything to do with them until they clamber back up. They wouldn't touch me—even they're smarter than that. But you they will hound to the ends of the galaxy. Both in little ways and big ways. So why shouldn't I be happy? I'll get a cruiser, new armor, and you have to deal with the problem of fighting these guys off. It'll do you good—you're too greedy and too lucky."

I smiled back, recognizing the sense in what Gammon was saying. I didn't worry too much about being on some guild's blacklist. This is a game. Those who get in too deep are sick. What's there to be afraid of? Gammon allowed me to consider the situation and went on:

"All right. Let's start with the purchase. Where is my access key?"

The deal did not take much time. I received one and a half billion, Gammon received the access key and sent an aide to the ship graveyard to pick up the purchase. The crew for the new ship was already waiting. Then began the second, but no less important part—the transfer of Gammon's cruiser to my name. I poured over the prepared contract long and hard, looking for loopholes. I didn't find anything—everything seemed by the book—so in the end I felt secure accepting the transfer of Gammon's ship.

After re-transmitting the access key, the system announced that from now on I am the owner of the A-class cruiser and a huge amount of money, of which five percent was intended only for me. The Hansa employees greeted me like family and when they learned that I had brought in a deal worth a total of 4.5bn GC, they grew positively generous and hospitable. None of this, however, extended to Gammon, who effectively didn't exist for Hansa. A call from Kiddo interrupted my enjoyment of being treated like a VIP client.

"What's the deal, partner?" Instead of greeting me, Marina opened up with complaints.

"And hello to you. What's the problem?"

"Gammon's bragging all over Galactogon about his new armor! Why did you give him access to Hansa?"

"You okay in the head, Marina?" Kiddo had decided to interfere with who I worked with. I wasn't about to tolerate this. "Gammon and I reached a deal. He paid the full price and now everyone's getting what they want. He gets an upgrade and I get credits."

"You owe me half. That was our agreement."

"The deal was you get half from clients that you bring in yourself. I didn't go looking for anyone, but if someone comes to me without your involvement, why should you get anything? Sorry, partner, but this is my business. I'll pay you when you bring me the business."

"What did he get?"

"Armor. Here's the list. You can see the properties yourself. By the way, this is all the equipment that Hansa has offered me."

IN SEARCH OF THE ULDANS

"I need everything." I had no doubt that Kiddo would want to upgrade her cruiser to the point that no one could catch her or damage her, and upgrade her armor suit into a walking bunker in the process.

"Not even a question. You know the price and my conditions are the same—five percent and you transfer *Alexandria* in my name. I can only upgrade ships that belong to me."

Here, Kiddo hung up without answering. Well, her emotions are her problem; professionals don't act like that. Five percent for me is one hundred fifty million. Seven and a half thousand real credits. Am I ready to make her a present worth that much? Nope!

I found my ship at the drydock. The orbship's re-armored hull shimmered in the sun like a rainbow.

"Your upgrades have been installed." One of the Hansa workers approached me. It was odd—it seemed like whoever was closest was in charge.

"I don't even have anything else to fantasize about," I smiled, examining the changes to my armor suit. It was effectively an entirely new armor with the old name. Firstly, it was legendary again. Secondly, two wrist blasters had been added to the two upgraded shoulder cannons—plus one EM blaster with autoaim. They had also updated the energy shield, the computer hardware and software and adjusted the jetpack to save fuel tenfold. Thirdly, the armor was made of the same metal as the ship's armor. It couldn't handle a direct hit from a torpedo of course, but if it were to explode nearby, for example, there'd be a chance of survival.

"Why not? There's always more," said the Precian and handed me a paper. "The possibilities are limitless, you just have to use your imagination."

The new list of thirty upgrades—fifteen for the ship and fifteen for the armor—spoiled all my fun. I even grew upset. I hadn't even had time to enjoy my recent purchase. In total, the new list amounted to nine billion. Three times more than the first. At the same time, the equipment on it was much more powerful—even though it dealt with other areas.

For example, the torpedo production system produced a legendary projectile every five minutes, cost five billion and was the guarantor of a quiet life, because the produced torpedoes had their own radar jammers and active protection against the flycatcher. To catch one, you need to use not one, but three beams at once. Not every cruiser can boast such a number of flycatchers. Given the destructive power of these missiles, a ship with such a system would be invincible in any battle. But five billion! That the equivalent of five million in real money! A year's worth of a carefree life! Galactogon really was a commercial project, even if not everyone understood this. Since not everyone had a ton of money. What had Reynard said back there? In the game, everyone was equal, except those who paid good money. Now that I had something to fantasize about again, all I had to do was find a good source of income.

Kiddo did not call back. Although I gave her an hour to make a decision before heading off to test the ship. Brainiac and the engineer were singing songs, celebrating the latest updates. Fifteen new toys from Hansa, three billion game credits, and instead of an orbship we now had a true pocket cruiser.

Fighting Breed could not anticipate my launch from the Hansa drydock because the dome hid it from prying eyes. When they realized it, I calmly flew across the prow of one of their cruisers and disappeared behind the nearest planet. Using the planet to screen me from their beam, I opened the throttle and zoomed away from the system at full speed. Brainiac began a countdown—one minute before our jump to Daphark. I needed to meet with Tryd, Hilvar's contact, as quickly as possible, so that I could join the pirates.

"Warning! Our ship is being painted with a hyperdrive disruptor beam. The source of the beam is the cruiser *Inevitable* straight ahead."

"Surgeon, this is Aalor. You won't leave the Belket system until you return what you stole from Fighting Breed."

"Stan—who the hell is Aalor?"

"Captain of the cruiser Inevitable from the Liberium guild. An independent guild without allegiance to any empire. Liberium is the number three guild in Galactogon's overall guild rankings."

Serious guys. The third guild in Galactogon is quite a deal more formidable than the tenth guild in the Precian Empire. These are birds of another feather altogether, which makes their involvement here entirely incomprehensible to me.

"Respectfully, I disagree. Fighting Breed provoked a conflict, I responded and punished them."

"I do not care. You must return their cruiser and all their cargo to them. You will not be allowed to leave Belket otherwise."

"Full throttle, Brainiac. Let's keep going. We'll see what *Inevitable* is capable of."

In terms of speed, the orbship was comparable to a cruiser, but the hitch turned out to be something else entirely. Aalor didn't bother messing around and immediately started to beat up on the babies. After just three minutes of flight, the snake began screaming in a wild voice, urging me to return to the area protected by the Grand Arbiters. Because it's scary when a 5bn GC torpedo launcher starts shooting its missiles at you. Our beam cannons and tractor beams were useless against them, and the engineer was forced to try and hit their torpedoes with ours. The enemy torpedoes came out faster than we could manufacture ours, so the struggle was a hopeless one. Aalor did not even shoot his main cannon as if to demonstrate that he could destroy my ball at any time. Either way, sinking us wasn't his objective. He wanted to force me back to Belket.

I banked sharply, returning to the system. The *Inevitable* stopped hurling torpedoes at us, but maintained the disruptor beam.

"You are free to sit in the system for as long as you like," Aalor said at last. "If you want to leave, return the cruiser and the armor suits to Fighting Breed. If you blow yourself up and return to your homeworld, I'll still find you. Galactogon isn't as big as you imagine. Only next time, I will act differently. You will lose the orbship for good. Over and out."

The disruptor beam from the *Inevitable* disappeared once I was intercepted by the beam from the Fighting Breed cruisers. I felt awful. I had just started thinking that I was the boss with my upgraded ship when I ran into an enemy superior to me in every way.

Grudgingly, I dialed Kiddo's number on the PDA.

"No, Surgeon, your problems are your problems. I'm not about to pick a fight with Liberium, they're out of my league. I don't know what deal the Breed have with Aalor, but if he himself is engaged in your public flogging, then it's either a very unique deal indeed or they enjoy some close relationship in real life. I'll have to pass. Return their cruiser."

"It won't work. I already sold It to Gammon."

"Buy it back. Buy a new one. Steal another one. There is no other option. These guys won't joke around. I have to go."

My prospects looked bleak, but Kiddo was right. The reasons for the involvement of a player of Aalor's stature could only be some unique arrangement or close personal relationships in meatspace. I could only hope it was the former or I really would have to buy the cruiser back from Gammon. It's not like I could lose my orbship...

"Brainiac, you're our only hope. Did you find anything valuable in the information you downloaded from the Zatrathi ship? Some reference to resource-rich planets or strange anomalies? Anything at all that could buy us our freedom. A cafeteria menu won't cut it this time."

"Yes. I am not certain what fits your search query, but I can try. There is a Zatrathi planet that is located apart from any other. It is orbited by a number of asteroids that are quite obviously artificial in nature. There are no further data, but judge for yourself—six asteroids occupy the same orbit yet never collide. One cannot help wondering what lies on the surface. I have its coordinates."

Five minutes later I was at the edge of the system, once again facing the barrels of the cruiser *Inevitable*, and sending a bribe to Aalor. For convenience's sake, he even shuttled over to my ship and carefully studied the information. Brainiac made the right choice. In addition to the planet, I offered to furnish Aalor with the findings from the brainworm interrogation.

"I am prepared to provide your guild with coordinates of a strange planet. You have already seen the video of the captive. I will send you all the information extracted from the brainworm. Perhaps there will be nothing interesting among it, but then again it could be the opposite case."

"And in exchange you want us to forget about your existence?" Aalor understood me correctly.

"Yes," I confirmed. It seemed like maybe personal meatspace relationships weren't a factor here after all. "What I offer you is worth much more than a cruiser. I could sell this information to any guild, get a cruiser in return or buy a new one. However! This is a matter of principle. I refuse to give Fighting Breed so much as a credit. The bullies should be punished. Virtual games were invented for people to enjoy as entertainment, not to harass others with impunity. That is my position. And since the Breed have gone so far, I would like to propose to you a little excursion to their base. They have two cruisers left, I want to relieve them of this burden."

"Your proposal is an interesting one, but I have a contract with the marines which I must honor. There is nothing to discuss here. They have already paid for our services, which means that the players must receive their cruiser. You can save your principles for meatspace—we don't care. But we can discuss working with you once we have settled the Breed account."

So, the guild did not wish to lose whatever the marines had offered. I had only one thing left:

"Do you have a C-class cruiser?"

"You must return a B-class cruiser," Aalor corrected. "When you stole *Smasher*, she was class B."

"I didn't steal her. I captured her. What is this crap anyway? I was playing the game the way it's meant to be played. If I hadn't killed them, they would've killed me."

"In that case you could have hired us and Fighting Breed would have issued you a public apology. Perhaps even paid you compensation. Instead, it was they who hired us so now you owe them a B-class cruiser."

"I think we can wrap it up here," I concluded. A B-class cruiser started at three billion and I wasn't ready to part with such money. Especially since I didn't have it. "Belket is a great place. I'm sure I can set myself up quite nicely on it. Godspeed, Aalor."

The captain of the *Inevitable* shrugged, recognizing my right to make my own decision. Each one of us had stated his positions. I considered the possibility of calling one of the two top guilds for helping me against Liberium but ultimately decided to put it off for better times. It was too obvious of a move and would therefore be accounted for somehow. I had to find a way out of my current predicament on my own.

Stan had assembled a complete dossier on Aalor and the Liberium guild and I sat down to pour over it, looking for the solution. Aalor was an excellent captain who did not take stupid risks. He was one of the few players who has never been downed in two years of play. Accordingly, he occupied his deserved place among the best. One could discount any surprises from cropping up in any conflict that Aalor was involved in. Whoever first paid for *Inevitable*'s services would be the one to win. Basically, either my ship would be blown up or I would settle down on Belket until I scraped enough GC together to buy a B-class cruiser.

"There's some business, Cap'n," the engineer appeared unexpectedly.

"Mmm…is it urgent?" Frustrated, I was still looking for a way out.

"Yes. I'm just not sure whether it's a good thing or a bad thing. In short, Hansa isn't as amazing as everyone thinks, the snake announced smugly.

"What? Why? Did you find a bug in our hardware?" I began to fret about the money I had just spent.

"Yes, but not in ours," said the snake and began explain the problem to me.

"Brainiac, head for Belket. Request permission for landing at the Hansa HQ."

By the time we held our meeting with the Precians, Brainiac and the engineer had rendered a model of the 5bn GC torpedo launcher and isolated the flaw in the prototype. It turned out that having their own shields, the torpedoes became like nimble fighters, which could be easily neutralized with EM cannons—otherwise useless in a fight against conventional torpedoes. If you fried the high-tech torpedoes' electronics, they would become nothing more than tubes of explosives tumbling in space. Instead of testing our theory in practice and risking the orbship we hurried back to Belket to get Hansa's confirmation.

"Indeed, such a problem exists," admitted the engineers. "But it will be solved in the immediate future. We have obtained a Zatrathi scout, which can resist electromagnetic pulses. We will present the solution and upgrade the system. We take pride in the quality of our products and want them to be the best the market."

"I see. I will wait a bit to purchase this system then. One more question. What will happen to a torpedo that is hit by an EM pulse?"

"It will explode. We do not want our designs to find their ways to third parties. If the torpedo loses control, it self-destructs."

"And your customers know about this?" I asked the most important question.

"If the buyer asks a question before purchase, he receives a complete answer," the Precian pursed his lips, unwilling to answer openly.

"And do many buyers ask questions?"

The Precian considered for a long time whether he should continue this conversation or not.

"No. But those who have encountered this problem after purchase receive good compensation and continue to use the launcher system with no complaints!" He admitted the obvious. Hansa had buttered up those who could ruin its reputation. But who will start carving the goose that laid the golden eggs?

"Last question, and it concerns a customer. Does Captain Aalor know about this malfunction?"

"Captain Aalor is not one of our customers," the Precian frowned. "If he has one of our weapons systems, it means that he purchased it through an intermediary on the secondary market. This is not forbidden, but such equipment has no warranty and is not updated. May we assist you in some other way?"

I was still thinking about the odd mining planet that Sebastian had mentioned and decided to try and pump the inventors for some info.

"Maybe—but strictly in the capacity of analysts. Imagine the following hypothetical: A system that consists of two stars. Between them there is a planet that balances the stars' gravitational wells and keeps the system in a state of equilibrium—a 'keystone planet' in other words. Two questions. How would one calculate the approach trajectory so as to avoid the gravity wells of either star? And what would happen to the system if you blew up the planet?"

"This is an interesting hypothetical…We can understand what is being asked but there is not enough data in the input… Are the diameters of the stars known?"

"Nope. The sizes of the stars, as well as the planets are unknown variables. But couldn't one find a relationship in which the system will be balanced and stable? Imagine that you are the creator and are going to build such a model."

"You are not considering a hypothetical system?"

"Of course not. If you solve the problem, I will show you this system. It really exists."

"We accept your challenge," the Precian rubbed his hands, anticipating a good mental workout. "I will have an answer for you tomorrow."

It was a bit of silliness, of course, but logic suggested that Hansa needed to be constantly stimulated. Items, problems, riddles. Anything at all to force them to strain their minds, making you a useful and interesting customer in the process.

"One more thing. Is the current speed of my ship the maximum, or is there a way to increase it by twenty percent?"

"Everything can be increased, given time, resources and money," answered the Precian, not bothering to hide his smile.

"How much would such a service cost?"

"Solving your problem will require a turnkey approach, for which, unfortunately, we lack the resources at the moment. So far all that we can offer you is in the list of devices known to you. All the best," the Hansa employee bowed and quickly ran away.

For my next step I decided to play it safe and taking Sebastian with me, went to the NPC equipment vendor, or the local huckster as I liked to call him. The armor suits and the mech that I had plundered from *Smasher* took up too much space in my cargo holds and were much too valuable to lose them at respawn. It wasn't the right time to look for buyers, so Sebastian haggled with the NPC huckster until both were foaming at the mouth and a deal was reached. The huckster got a ten percent discount on the market value of the armor suits and the mech. He refused to even entertain a smaller discount. Once the lump sum of 157 million GC settled into my gaming account, I sighed with relief. The die, as they say, has been cast and there is no turning back. Fighting Breed would not recover their property, no matter whom they contracted. If you want to be respected, you need to be able to defend your own interests. Since I am stuck in Galactogon for the next six months, I will invest in my good, pirate's name.

"Brainiac, we're taking off. Let's get out of Belket, shall we?"

"Surgeon, is this your decision? There will be no further negotiations," Aalor made his last warning when he saw me crossing the system boundary. Both of the Breed's cruisers remained in-system, waiting for Big Brother to do all the work for them.

"Yes," I replied, and repeated: "There will be no new negotiations. Over and up!"

Under Brainiac's control the orbship zoomed forward. We rushed headlong into the vast unknown and hoped only that death did not lie in wait ahead. And if it did, we would fight to our last.

CHAPTER SEVEN

S PACE COMBAT, LIKE ANY OTHER FORM OF DUEL, is no different than a game of chess. The most important factor is having a plan. Naturally the captains' reactions play a significant role—as do the ships involved and the weapons and defenses they have available—but all other things being equal, space combat is a contest of minds in which success depends on one's ability to calculate accurately. The main difference from chess is that a player can make a move or make a hundred moves, but he can also make no move at all and still retain initiative in the battle.

Every Galactogon warship has at least three types of weapons in its arsenal: torpedoes, beam cannons and EM cannons. Cruisers were also outfitted with main cannons, but these were basically just larger versions of the beam cannons that everyone had. And then there was the case of Kiddo who had managed to somehow attach a mysterious prototype supercannon that remained unproven and that was capable of blasting right through a cruiser's hull. But such cases were rare.

Beam cannons were used in close combat against other small ships. They did a good job of knocking down fighters or scouts by blowing up their reactors or engines. Beam cannons weren't good for handling destroyers, carracks or frigates because these ships were already too big. This is where torpedoes came in—missiles with their own guidance systems and engines. Passing calmly through the shields which only blocked plasma, the torpedoes detonated near or inside the targets' hulls, filling the area around them with raq shrapnel. Torpedoes could be diverted by hacking their navigation systems or shot down midflight with beam cannons. In that case, the self-destruction mechanism would trigger and the torpedo would explode. Hansa's new torpedo models eliminated this defect by carrying shields which protected the missile's vulnerable components. And yet, despite this unique solution, there was one big flaw in this approach: The torpedoes now depended on their advanced defensive systems. EM cannons were rarely used in serious PvP combat. It was simply too expensive to expend all that energy to knock down the enemy's defenses for a short space of time. Besides, larger ships had redundant systems which would kick in the moment the primary ones failed. Meanwhile the shields of fighters and scouts were much easier to take down using beam cannons. As a result, some players deliberately refused to install EM cannons at all, replacing them with further beam cannons or other useful ship systems. Any way you approached the problems, all vessels were limited by their equipment slots. And any gun took up one such slot. My orbship, for instance, had four and they fired very rapidly.

My adrenaline rush suppressed any thought of self-preservation, while leaving my mind lucid. It takes a good deal of experience in virtual battles to develop this condition and any professional gamer worth his salt knows the value of this state of mind. The feeling was pleasant—I was filled with anticipation, a clarity of perception and a precise order to my thoughts. This was all exactly what we pro gamers play for!

My strategy was as follows: Take advantage of the fact that the *Inevitable* had its bow pointed at the Belkel system and fly straight at it. The cruiser would not fire at me from its main guns, wary of a stray shot crossing the system and entering the area guarded by a Grand Arbiter. This would be fraught with a hefty penalty to Liberium's rapport with the Precians. Aalor would therefore have to resort to his advanced torpedoes, smaller beam cannons and swarms of fighters that had so far remained inside the *Inevitable*'s hangars. At the very least he would have to wait until I changed course to go around him. This was the first part of my multi-stage plan.

"I am detecting a hyperdrive disruptor beam. Warning! Ten torpedo launches detected. ETA twenty seconds. These are advanced torpedoes."

"Maintain course straight at the cruiser. Gunner, fire at will. Engineer, shields full front. Don't let them knock us down."

"Target hit! One more! Another one! Torpedoes destroyed!"

"Full speed ahead. Gunner destroy anything that gets close. Snake, start working on the hull as soon as we get within range."

We rushed at the still-motionless cruiser. A moment of

confusion cost Aalor his strategic initiative. Before he could react, we entered the perimeter of the cruiser's shields, snuggling up as close as possible to her hull, right next to her immense engines. The snake fired three torpedoes. Two were immediately destroyed by the point defense guns, but the last one hit its targets—the cruiser lost one beam cannon on its stern. Neither the hull nor the engines were damaged—Aalor had stayed on top of his upgrades. A few broadsides from my beam cannons later, a single tail turret remained on the cruiser's stern—the one I had plans for.

"Torpedoes inbound!"

The new wave consisted of thirty missiles. The gunner tried his utmost, squeezing the most out of the guns, but Brainiac summarized sternly:

"Two torpedoes cannot be destroyed."

It was a shame of course, but at least we were about to find out whether Hansa was worth the money it charged.

"Brace for impact! Brainiac—keep the orbship next to the cruiser's hull! Impact!"

The blow sent the ship tumbling along two axes a once. Inside, it was like being on a space themed roller coaster.

"Brainiac, report!"

"Hull integrity is 100%. All systems nominal. We lost two sensor antennae. I am picking up multiple bogeys. The enemy cruiser has scrambled her fighters."

Aalor understood that torpedoes wouldn't cut it. Or, rather, they would cut it eventually but it would cost him too much. It was much easier to scramble your bored fighter pilots, telling them to go nuts and boosting their morale in the process.

"Phase two! It's your turn, gunner!"

Despite the absurdity of my attack, I wasn't acting on instinct but according to common sense. Stan even assessed a thirty percent chance of success once I had explained my plan in detail to him. So what did we have? The cruiser *Inevitable* was a cutting-edge, fully-modernized ship with the best equipment available. The Liberium guild was too strong for others to stand up to it, so Liberium ships did not take part in active hostilities against players. Typically, their mere presence was enough to mediate any conflict. Accordingly, their crew's reflexes and readiness wasn't up to snuff. Aalor mostly focused on his new torpedoes, which were truly formidable weapons. I doubted that Aalor had had the opportunity to test them in battle against other players. So what would happen if a player who was used to always winning, discovers that his favorite weapon is useless? He will be stumped—maybe for no more than a few moments, a single heartbeat. And in doing so, he will lose his initiative. This moment of confusion would be enough for me to implement my idea: Stan had pointed out that the tail section of the cruisers contained one of the cargo holds—large enough to accommodate my orbship several times over. Having cleared the hull of the beam cannons and hoping that the confusion would delay the fighters' arrival immediately after the second wave of torpedoes, I ordered the gunner to burn through the hull of the cruiser. I needed an opening about seventy meters wide.

In order to scramble out of the cruiser, fly around it, and gain speed and fly up to me, the fighters would need between ten and twenty seconds. The snake fired five torpedoes in the direction of the fighters, more to divert attention than to kill them. The missiles were shot down as soon as they came in range of the other beam cannons. However, this gifted me another five seconds. And this proved enough time for the gunner.

"Ready!" Brainiac reported cheerfully. No matter how well the cruiser was protected from torpedoes, she was helpless against our beam cannons at this range. We were within the area protected by her shields and so it was a cinch to burn a perfect square into her hull. Now came the third phase of our operation.

"Push in!" I ordered, and the orbship crashed into the cruiser. There was a metallic screech and part of the hull collapsed inward. With it came my ship. Bulkheads crumpled all around us and we collapsed into the empty void of the cargo hold. Like any other self-respecting player, Aalor did not bring valuable cargo on his missions. The breach we had made in the hull now shimmered over with a force field—Aalor had a second hull upgrade that reinforced his external hull with a forcefield in case it was breached. A cool trick that I should consider getting as well.

"Get to work, Brainiac! Hack their engine controls! Gunner, blast anything around us."

Phase four now. Now that we were inside the cruiser, I could not allow Aalor to jump into hyperspace. If he jumps to some Liberium base—I will have to self-destruct. But I still had time—a minute at least. At this point an epic contest broke out between two computer systems: *Inevitable*'s Advanced Hansa

IN SEARCH OF THE ULDANS

Ship Mainframe (nicknamed 'Bunny') vs. *Warlock*'s Advanced Hansa Ship Mainframe—grafted onto an Uldan matrix—(nicknamed 'Brainiac'). Personally, I'd bet on the latter. My droids pulled out the cable, hooked the orbship up to the cruiser and the AI battle got under way. The players who came rushing to us were instantly sent to respawn—the gunner was shooting to kill. A pair of fighters passed through the force field but met the fate of their fellow crew. There was no headway to be made in the face of our beam cannons.

"Snake, fire the torpedo."

"Fuse set to three minutes," the engineer reported. Since torpedoes in Galactogon flew only in conditions of complete weightlessness, it was impossible to shoot them on a ship with artificial gravity. But it was possible to hand the torpedo to a couple of droids and tell them to kamikaze in the right place.

Two of the robots picked up the missile that fell out of the orbship and marched forward. The gunner swept the way before them and in three minutes the droids managed not only to reach the other edge of the cargo hold but walked straight out of it, heading into the cruiser's bowels to deliver their pill. I glanced at the timer. Three. Two. One! Ba-da-boom! Smoke flooded the cargo hold as showers of sparks and fragments rained all around.

"Success!" Brainiac said to my delight. "I have taken control of the cruiser's hyperdrive system. She can no longer enter hyperspace. Now taking control of the tail turret—success! Rerouting turret control to the gunner."

As Stan predicted, the torpedo exploding inside the cruiser

had damaged the central data bus. There were backup contours, of course, but they could not cope with the hacking onslaught emanating from *Warlock*. The cruiser's entire stern compartment now belonged to me.

"Fire the second and third torpedoes!"

I launched the other missiles more as a diversion. I understood that, even after separating the tail section, I would not be able to destroy the entire cruiser. I didn't have enough torpedoes or energy for that. Meanwhile, all the fighters aboard the *Inevitable* had scrambled. The frigates couldn't squeeze through the breach and the fighters no longer dared risk it—four kills had made it clear that I had become master of the cargo hold.

"An interesting move, but foolish," Aalor's didn't even sound upset. "You lack the ordnance to destroy me from inside. Once you try to leave, it'll be respawn time for you. You don't have the marines on board to seize the ship. You can blow yourself up, but in any case, consider that your ship will be my compensation for all this anxiety you're causing. Were your principles worth it?"

I said nothing because now was not the time to be distracted by idle talk. The final phase of my plan began. The engineer was the first to report:

"Second and third torpedoes launched. Fuse set to five minutes."

The captured tail turret allowed us to orient ourselves. Once again, having made sure that the cruiser *Inevitable* was still facing Belket, I ordered:

"Brainiac, launch the tub. Block any attempts to seize

control. I need thirty seconds!"

The cruiser shuddered and slowly, lazily, began creeping in the direction of Belket. The bow thrusters which we couldn't control began firing to slow us down, but they were no match for the main engines. All they could do was delay the inevitable…hah. Several interceptors broke through to us through the force field, but the gunner remained attentive—the fighters did not have time to release their torpedoes. Amazingly—Aalor decided to blow a couple of torpedoes inside his ship. Without having understood what I was trying to do with the reasonable part of his brain, he nevertheless sensed the threat perfectly well.

Instead of using the thrusters to turn his cruiser away from the system and head into deep space, Aalor only tried to brake with them. This was a major error on the captain's part. He was right—I didn't have enough torpedoes or energy to blow up his ship. My orbship was a mosquito buzzing around an elephant's ear. The slightest wrong move and the elephant would swat me with its trunk. Only Aalor did not understand that my buzzing was no more than a diversion. The mosquito was weak, but he knew who was stronger than all on Belket.

"We have entered the Belket system," announced Brainiac.

"Fire at will, gunner!"

"You son of a…" Aalor screamed over the comms, but it was too late. A bolt of plasma from the cruiser's tail turret went flying at the nearest Grand Arbiter, turning the *Inevitable* into an aggressor. By giving me the time, Aalor had sentenced his ship to death. Fighters rushed forward, trying to knock down the gun, but they were too late—I managed to fire two more times before they could silence their own turret.

"We're out of here!" The orbship took off, emerging back into space among the swarm of interceptors. Only now nobody could attack me—they had been immobilized. With one enormous EM blast, the Arbiter fried all the electronics that weren't shielded by the cruiser's hull. Even the cruiser had a hard time—the energy shields were still holding against the onslaught from the Arbiter's main beam cannons, but without proper control of the engines, Aalor could no longer maneuver. Another Arbiter moved to join the battle and now the outcome was certain. *Inevitable* was doomed.

"Surgeon, you're a dead man!" yelled Aalor before his cruiser turned into a beautiful fireball. That's minus one class and, as a result, minus several equipment slots. Yet the Arbiters did not stop there—the interceptors belonged to the outlaw cruiser and had to be destroyed too. I did not intervene, despite my desire to get more kills for Hilvar's mission. I left the mopping up to the Arbiters. From their perspective, I was no more than an innocent bystander. I hadn't attacked anyone after all.

The two Fighting Breed cruisers drew closer, but didn't dare do anything to me, trying to figure out what happened. From the outside it must have seemed like *Inevitable* had caught a flea and then went haywire, first drifting aimlessly and then attacking a trade planet.

Brainiac announced several times that enemies were locking onto us, but no one fired. For the locals, I was merely an incidental gawker observing their security operation. Making sure that no one survived, the Arbiters returned to their positions, watching over the peace and security of the system. But now it was my time—the time of looting and plunder.

I didn't care about the fighters. The most I could get from them was a bit of raq. All my attention turned to the huge crate left after the cruiser. The fact that one of the holds had been empty did not mean that all others would be too. A ship of her class would have had four or five. The robotic arm opened the flickering crate, and Brainiac displayed a list of the contents.

"What do you think, Sebastian?" I asked just in case, although the thief was already immersed in studying the list.

"One hundred and twenty armor suits. They're A-class, but you've seen yourself how much they fetch. I'd say on average 8 million apiece. Right, now then, what else is in here? These blasters are trash. Cheap Precian knock offs. And here's more junk. Ah! Now this is interesting. These look like Zatrathi ship parts! And not from their interceptors or scouts either...These are beam cannons, and these are some type of reactors. I wonder where they got these from? I've been keeping up with the war news and there was no mention of Liberium being involved in any boarding action. These parts are new. Some are still in their packaging—you could only get these straight from the stockpiles."

"Braniac, can we fit the lot of it?" I could guess where Liberium had gotten these parts. They were the true reason for why the high-ranked guild had stood up for Fighting Breed. The marines had captured a Zatrathi repair base and looted it. They had no use for these parts themselves—their focus was ground combat—so they had sold it to Liberium in exchange for my punishment.

"Yes, we can take all the parts, but nothing more."

"Sebastian, is there anything here that is worth more than ten million?"

"Two harvesters, a marine landing craft, an assault mech and three hundred tons of raq."

"Brainiac, load up the parts and let's land on Belket. We'll show our haul to Hansa and see if there's anything valuable among it."

We had barely left the site of Aalor's defeat when my PDA began to buzz. It was Gammon.

"Pirate Surgeon at your service!" I happily answered the call. Despite all the potential problems down the line, the taste of victory was overpowering. My plan had succeeded, the enemy was defeated, I had made a good penny—what could be better? That's what Galactogon was for—a game to enjoy yourself in.

"May you escape a ship-less, agonizing death. Vargen wants to speak with you. I'm putting him through."

"Greetings, leader of Liberium! How may I be of assistance?" I was expecting a call but had thought it would be Aalor instead of the head of Liberium himself.

"I want your footage from the moment the battle began until it ended," Vargen's tone could not be called friendly, but he didn't threaten me openly either. That in itself was a good sign.

"Sure. How should I send it and to whom?" I saw nothing odd about the request. The guild head needed to figure out how one of his officers had been sent to respawn and I didn't mind

---

making Aalor's life a little more difficult. After all was said and done, he had made several errors that had cost his ship her legendary class.

"Stay on Belket. You will be contacted. Give me your comm number."

"Here you go," I was all courtesy and generosity.

A pause followed in which Vargen did not hang up, as if wondering how to talk with me further. Maybe he had expected to hear anything but consent or cooperation from me.

"Do not talk to anyone, do not make any deals, do not answer any calls. I will be on Belket myself in twenty minutes. Wait for me at the Seven Beauties club. There will be a table there in my name. You will be taken to it. Over and out."

The dispatcher gave me permission to land on dock number ten—an honor in which I saw Vargen's involvement. Before I could leave the ship, we were surrounded by engineers with Hansa patches on their coveralls who began to repair the hull damage. Although we did indeed need minor repairs, I hadn't requested anything of the kind. Only the appearance of a system notification that the first ten docks came with free ship maintenance dispelled my puzzlement. A taxi hovered over to the dock too—and even turned out to be free of charge. Even though it wasn't Eine's luxury saucer, it did the job of taking me to the Seven Beauties just fine.

Vargen's chosen establishment resembled an ancient amphitheater from the inside. The tables were set up along the different levels to maximize the view of the stage in the center. At the same time, it was a bit difficult to spy on the other guests to see what they had on their plates. Vargen still hadn't shown up, so I indulged in the establishment's offerings: Seven semi-nude Precian acrobats were tumbling above the stage.

Vargen appeared exactly as their performance ended. I couldn't make out his face. Like mine, it was completely concealed by his armor suit's visor.

"The video," he said at once. There was no objection on my part, so as he watched I turned back to the enchanting magic of the dance of the seven beauties. Vargen watched my battle with Aalor through my eyes, without looking up. Finally he turned back to me:

"You must return the Zatrathi ship parts," Vargen did not conceal that his people had already reached the flickering crate and made a list of the missing inventory.

"That is my loot. I have every right to it," I replied without looking away from the show and demonstrating that my cooperation had its boundaries.

"It would be foolish to hand that equipment over to Hansa. You cannot give it to anyone else, but I can."

I turned and leaned forward.

"Buy it back. I'm happy to sell my property at the right price."

"What about this? Will this suit you?" Vargen placed a small silver badge on the table. "The insignia of a Liberium officer."

"I spent many years as an officer in a leading guild. I play alone now. Don't waste time on listing the benefits of joining your guild. I know very well the kind of workload an officer has to deal with. Don't do this, don't do that, don't go there, file a loot report and don't forget to turn everything over to the vault keeper.

Thank you, but freedom and independence are more important to me. I can make you a counter offer, however."

"Let's hear it."

"You officially declare me a friend of your guild. That will be more than enough for everyone, including Fighting Breed. A guild doesn't harass its friends. In exchange for this guarantee, I forget about the video of my battle with Aalor. And we agree on a different price for the Zatrathi ship parts. The game is a means to make money for me. Pay me three million real credits—and they are yours. If not, I can find other buyers. It really would be foolish to hand them over to Hansa, but I have other plans. Most importantly, you give me the opportunity to deprive the Fighting Breed of their remaining cruisers. I am not vindictive. If they wish to punish me so much, let them do it themselves, without outside help."

"The Zatrathi ship parts are not subject to negotiation," Vargen snapped. "You must return them. Further, Fighting Breed paid us to get their cruiser back. There is nothing to discuss there either. The cruiser must be returned to them."

"Then I don't understand what the hell you are doing here." I said, baffled. "Did you show up to twirl that officer's badge under my nose? I could not care less about you and your guild. If you start any trouble, I will sell all the items to the NPCs, delete my character and make a new one. You really think that an independent player will go along with your guild BS?"

"As I said, the cruiser must be returned," Vargen continued, as if nothing had happened. "Only I did not say what cruiser it should be. Fighting Breed still has two B-class cruisers. I imagine you can figure out the rest yourself. Liberium takes its obligations seriously, so I will assist you in returning the cruiser to Fighting Breed, informally at least."

"Works for me. When will I get the money for the loot?"

"That issue is not under discussion. The guild's interest trumps everything else."

"Vargen, you have a lot to say about Liberium's interests, but not so much about the interests of the player named Surgeon. That would be me. I don't care about your guild. I'm more interested in my own affairs. No money—no equipment. That is my position. There won't be another one. Three million."

"Another offer," Vargen handed me a sheet of paper. "We cannot investigate this. You can."

"Planets like that are a dime a dozen in my mission logs," I snorted, reading the description. Pretending to remain calm was the hardest part here, yet I managed. "Aalor should have told you what planet I offered him almost for free. So I'm not interested."

Admittedly, Vargen had caught me off guard—he was offering me information about an anomaly which could easily be related to the Uldans. A mysterious nebula that sent any ships that entered it to the graveyard, regardless of their size. Only *Inevitable* had managed to survive. Aalor had entered the nebula and discovered a planet within it. He hadn't learned anything else though—his cruiser's hull was deteriorating rapidly and the captain had had to flee urgently. Only thanks to Hansa's enhanced armor was he able to hold out in the nebula for some time and then emerge alive. But the most interesting thing was that his sensors picked up several orbships like mine shadowing him. They escorted him the entire way, without getting involved, waiting for Aalor to leave the nebula.

Vargen had expected another reaction from me, so he kept his silence. I was forced to prompt him now:

"Let's get back to the equipment. Will I get my three million?"

"Do you want war? We will keep you on this planet and forbid anyone from working with you."

"It's time to wrap this up then, Vargen. We are going in circles. If you want to cause me trouble, I'll have something to say about it. You're the only one in the red right now—you don't have your ship parts and your rep has just taken a hefty blow. You've seen the video of Aalor's demise. You think I'm so generous that I won't share it with anyone else? I showed it to you so you could be the first to appreciate how your officer handled that battle. But if you insist on your position, I'll be happy to upload it to the forums. How long will it take your guild to regain its current reputation—if at all? Who will contract a guild that can't even deal with a single lone player? Don't threaten me. I thought that we would be able to come to an agreement. I was mistaken. We can wrap this up the way we started and go one with our game."

"You will receive 200,000 for the equipment," Vargen also understood the need to agree in an amicable way. My position was stronger. "And we will sign a non-disclosure agreement."

"Three million and not one credit less," I snapped. "Official status as a friend of your guild, help in the fight against the

Fighting Breed and the nebula's coordinates. In exchange you get the Zatrathi parts, the coordinates to the planet I mentioned and, most importantly, my silence. There were no player witnesses. Without the video, everyone will assume the *Inevitable* was destroyed due to navigation and equipment failure. No more. And you give me any B-class cruiser, so that I can pay Fighting Breed back and you can hold up your deal with them. Either way, we'll take the three cruisers back from them later. And your reputation won't suffer."

Vargen was silent, but the fact that he didn't simply get up and leave told me more than any words. The head of Liberium was ready to pay and was merely considering how.

"I need guarantees of your silence. We will sign a contract. Three million is too much. I am ready to offer 500,000."

Several sets of 'seven beauties' had had their turn on stage before Liberium and Surgeon came to an agreement. I had Stan hire me a competent and very expensive lawyer who justified all the money invested in him. The first thing he did was tear the contract sent over by Vargen to little pieces, calling it legal shackles. Then Vargen's lawyers showed up to defend their terms and a real battle broke out—no smaller than the one that had recently taken place at our roundtable aboard *Alexandria*. Only now all kinds of penalties and limitations started appearing alongside the terms. Finally, when all the legal details had been hammered out and the parties had signed, Vargen and I said goodbye.

"I cannot say it was nice to meet you, Surgeon, but I gained some good experience from it. We will fulfill our obligations under the contract and then our paths will part."

"I'll go explore the nebula in a couple of days," I pretended not to hear anything. "I can sell you two spots on my crew."

Under the agreement, I had received the nebula's coordinates, the money, and a joint raid with Aalor against Fighting Breed. However, Liberium refused to recognize me as a friend of the guild. When it came to the raid, I had my doubts until Vargen revealed his reasons for being involved: the Breed hadn't handed over all the Zatrathi parts and he wanted the full set. As a result the contract prohibited me from sharing any information. Regardless of how he feels about me, Aalor would do his job. Vargen did not demand being included in the research expedition, so I offered Liberium front row tickets with a clear conscience.

"Three. Your orbship has room for five passengers. Your Qualian will take up one, the other three will be my people. Eine will receive the findings but he will not participate."

"He offered me half a million real credits for a spot and completely refused any share of the loot," I improvised. Vargen wanted to impress me with his connections and knowledge of my affairs, but the move didn't come off so well. I knew his informant—Kiddo. More of a leaky sieve than a partner, that one.

"I cannot grant you such conditions," Vargen did not hide his displeasure. "Twenty thousand real credits for two spots and a third of the loot. Do not forget that the coordinates were ours. If we agree and the mission is a success, you will get another planet."

"No, these conditions don't suit me," I said without the

slightest hint of politeness. Since there are several such planets, it means there is nothing unique about them. "One hundred thousand real credits from each and the opportunity to be the first to participate in the auction. If we find something, Eine will also want it."

"When can we pick up the ship parts?" Vargen decided that these details were not important. I was completely certain that a task force of 3–4 cruisers would remain on duty in the system with the strange planet to keep me from getting close. Giving me the coordinates was one thing. No one had promised to give me access though.

"Right this instant. Dock ten."

Vargen departed without bothering to say goodbye. I hadn't managed to eke out a 'friendship' status with his guild and could safely assume that Liberium would continue to treat me like a dangerous freak that was to be eliminated at the first opportunity. The hell with it. The terms of our mutual neutrality were clearly spelled out in the contract. If someone from the guild or in its pay attacked me, the contract would be terminated and I would be free of my nondisclosure obligations. Accordingly, Vargen's feelings did not bother me. It was much more interesting to decide what to do next. The idea of hanging around Belket and selling access to Hansa upgrades was out of the question—all the guilds who could afford the expensive upgrades had already acquired them long ago. My only clients would be minnows like Gammon or freelancers like Kiddo, but I doubted I'd make much money from them.

I returned to the orbship and ordered Brainiac to set course for Daphark. This was my third attempt to get in touch with Hilvar's aide and become a pirate. This time nobody bothered me: No disruptor beams, no hostile cruisers, no weird meathead bullies. For the next few days, the player named Surgeon had become extremely uninteresting to everyone. After weighing all the pros and cons, I finally decided to call Wally, who was flying somewhere around Galactogon on my *Space Cucumber*. The frigate, in which I invested a lot of my own and other people's money, was the first ship I received in the game, so I was still interested in her fate.

"Wally, hello! This is Surgeon. How are you? How's it going?"

"Hi," came the terse reply. "I heard that you were back online. Was wondering when you'd call."

"Relax. I wasn't planning on taking my ship back. I'm curious about your progress with Hilvar's mission. I need help getting in touch with Tryd, his intermediary. Who is he? What can I expect with him and what shouldn't I do around him?"

"Eighty-seven fighters, forty-two scouts, twelve shuttles," answered Wally. "Thanks to you running your mouth, we still have a lot of work ahead of us. *The Space Cucumber* has reached class A. I've upgraded her a bit with Kiddo's help. All in all, we're keeping our heads down, doing our job. The crew is all the same; there've been no changes."

I estimated that Wally and the crew had completed half the mission requirements over these two weeks. I had no idea why he sounded unhappy—the potential rewards were worth all the grinding.

"As for Tryd, he's an ordinary local. A Delvian. His missions are classic—deliver a letter, pick up a package, go here, fly there. Nothing complicated. It's a chain of twenty missions altogether. We completed them in two days. There is one detail. Daphark is a planet of rogues and criminals. Even the locals tried to steal my ship there, several times in fact."

"Not your ship—my ship," I corrected Kiddo's officer.

"Yours. Anarchy reigns on Daphark, the law of the jungle. There's no security, no police. All power rests with the local warlords and moguls. It's a true Eden for the riff-raff of Galactogon. Keep your bits about you if you go there." Wally paused and then changed topics abruptly. "Surgeon, since you called, let's get down to brass tacks. I want to buy *The Space Cucumber* from you. You have your own ship now and I don't want to spend my money investing in someone else's property. But I need to upgrade the frigate too. The Zatrathi are kicking our ass all over this quadrant. I can hack the mainframe and re-register *The Space Cucumber* to myself but I want to do this by the book."

As I expected, Wally did not like to be in a state of uncertainty. Who knows when I would call and demand my frigate back? Kiddo didn't work with dependent people.

"What do you propose?" Obviously Wally had prepared himself for this conversation in advance.

"You gave me a B-class frigate. Kiddo paid for a ton of upgrades and we grinded her up to class A. I am ready to pay you the market value of a B-class frigate, plus ten percent on top. I was thinking that 110 million GC would be fair."

"Stan, I need a price check urgently…"

"I confirm Wally's estimate," the answer was not long in coming. "The cost of a frigate of this class starts at 80 million."

"Pay me 150 and you can have her," I decided. Those who cling to the past have nothing in the present and are terrified of the future. *The Space Cucumber* is gone. I should recognize this and move on.

We agreed on one hundred and thirty. As soon as the money appeared in my account, I received a notification that the frigate was no longer mine. Wally did not wait for me to send him the access key. He had long since cracked the ship's security and the only reason *The Space Cucumber* had remained mine was his principles. Such people are rare. I'll be sure to invite him on any raids. Having one of my people working for Kiddo will come in handy anyway.

"Warning! We are under attack!" cried Brainiac as soon as we emerged from hyperspace. The orbship appeared in the Daphark system and was instantly locked onto by the orbital station. The locals weren't sleeping on their watch and rolled out the carpet for us.

"Twenty torpedoes inbound," the engineer piped up. "We are being tracked by EM cannons. 150 small bogeys incoming. None of them are larger than a frigate."

"We're leaving," I ordered. "Torpedo speed?"

"Sixty percent."

"Maintain speed at sixty then. We'll wait for them to run out of steam. Hold your fire. We did not come here to fight."

The locals swarmed us in their fighters but they did not open fire either. Everyone waited to see how I would react to the torpedoes. I made no aggressive moves and once the torpedoes petered out and stopped trailing us, I contacted the system dispatcher:

"This is Orbship *Warlock* requesting permission to land."

"What the hell do you want in these parts?" came the rude response. The station was still locking onto us, but there were no further torpedoes. This in itself was a positive sign.

"I have some business with Tryd."

"Does he know you?"

"No, Hilvar sent me."

"So you want to become a pirate?" the dispatcher's voice suddenly grew a lot warmer. "Why didn't you say so right away? We are always happy to welcome new brethren! Follow descent corridor 4-7-23. Prepare for inspection. Not just anyone can land on Daphark."

There were two inspections. Initially, the orbship was scanned for unregistered life forms, or at least that was the official explanation. In fact, the locals were making sure that any arriving ship wasn't carrying law enforcement agents from some empire. The law with its long arms had no business on one of the few pirate planets. The next inspection took place in person and was more scrupulous. They not only examined my ship for prohibited items, but also called Hilvar to check my story. The Pyrrhenian looked at me from the screen and admitted that he did send me to meet Tryd a couple of weeks ago but added that had no idea where I had been this entire time and why I hadn't tried to complete his mission earlier. In parting, he strongly

---

recommended running an additional background check on me. I was forced to prove that I had no links to law enforcement agencies and then explain where I had been this entire time. The locals turned out to be meticulous investigators—they got to the bottom of every detail and demanded confirmation of every word. At long last, they accepted my story.

"Tryd is waiting for you. We'll be watching you. One wrong move and we'll send you packing from this planet. And you won't be allowed to come back. Statist spies have no business here!"

Having ordered Brainiac not to let anyone close to the ship, I headed to my meeting. Daphark was a strange planet indeed. Ruin and poverty reigned on the streets, against a backdrop of spaceships and apartment blocks. The locals were all dirty, angry, sullen or completely sick—a state I had never encountered on any other planet. Beggars scurried everywhere, begging for alms in the various languages of the Confederation. Waste was dumped directly into the streets and the sewers were clogged with litter. A stinking slurry flowed along the pavements, turning the road into a slow-flowing river. The locals deftly jumped along makeshift stepping stones, not noticing the stench. The sensory filters in my armor suit were a real life saver here. At times, I encountered the wrecks of machines littering the streets. They had not worked for a long time and had become rusty monuments to a time when life was better on Daphark.

Tryd had an office (if you could call a tiny room with holes where the windows were supposed to be an office) on the upper floor of a high-rise building. The windows and doors throughout the building had been busted a long time ago. The stooped old fox stood by a large window opening and gazed down on the dark gray city. There weren't any street lights and what illumination there was came from burning rubbish and ships' spotlights, which only really illuminated small areas around the pirate vessels. There was no electricity. Daphark suffered from serious shortages of elo.

"So you've decided to become a pirate?" The Delvian barked, turning in my direction. A terrible scar gashed across the fox's face, depriving him of his right eye and part of his cheek, which twitched to reveal yellowed fangs. Tryd flaunted his terrible appearance, enjoying his visitors' reactions. I immediately got the urge to start asking the NPC about his scar. Such features usually indicated that some prying would be rewarded with a mission.

"You are unconcerned by the alien invasion taking place?" continued Tryd. "Instead of fighting the Zatrathi for the sake of all of Galactogon, you want to rob and kill the defenders?"

"Defending Galactogon doesn't earn me anything but trophies and honors," I answered the old fox. "I handed the Precians a Zatrathi flying fortress and a scout on a platter, and in return I received a paltry five percent discount with the Hansa Corp. Being a hero is noble and all, but it's not profitable. I prefer to combine these two concepts."

"Combine, eh? Here's a mission then. There is a certain Ruandr who lives on the planet Hillstock in the Rell system. Your job is to find him, give him a letter from me, get an answer and come back. You can combine what's good for you and pleasant for me. Now scram! You got three hours. Hillstock ain't far."

IN SEARCH OF THE ULDANS

New mission available: Planet Express. Description: ...

"Seriously?" I didn't feel like spending two days running around like a messenger boy. "I'm supposed to become a pirate, the terror of Galactogon by doing stupid delivery missions? You think if I start at the very bottom of the career ladder, I'll climb my way up rung by rung?"

"Eh? What ladder?" Tryd replied, taken aback. "What are you talking about, small fry? You were ordered to deliver a letter—why are you still here?"

"First of all, you didn't even give me a letter. Second of all, why can't you just call the guy? Do you not have his number? Does he not have a phone? Does Ruandr perhaps have some religious objection to answering the phone on...what day is it today anyway?"

"So you don't like to follow orders, eh?" Tryd came to his own conclusion, and a notification about a penalty to rapport flashed before my eyes.

"When have you seen a pirate running errands?" I stood my ground. "A pirate either thinks for himself or ends up a corpse. Anyone who thinks otherwise is a spy for the statists."

"Did your homework, I see..." A grin appeared the on fox's face, turning the already ugly mug into a mask of horror. The good news was that my rapport with Tryd had returned back to neutral. "In that case, here is another assignment for you, worthy of a real pirate. If you want to be one of us, kill ten creatures on this planet. Anyone you want! Because you can. Once you've killed them, come on back to see me. I'll be waiting for you here."

Tryd returned to his contemplation of the slums before him, as if forgetting about my existence.

New mission available: The Killer. Description: ...

"Stan?"

"According to the fora and information received from player Kiddo, one of the missions issued by Tryd involves killing ten random creatures."

I grinned at the phrase 'information received from player Kiddo.' At the very beginning of our relationship, Marina had made the generous gesture of giving me a summary of what it would take to become a space pirate. In fact, it turned out to be a slightly more detailed compilation of official and well-known information. While the official FAQ mentioned that Tryd was a contact of Hilvar's, Kiddo's info stated that Tryd was 'a contact of the Pyrrhenian Hilvar.' In other words, there was detail, but it was useless. Kiddo had taken care not to provide any extra info.

"What about the creatures? Are there no restrictions at all?"

"Absolutely none. Some of the players even tried to kill Tryd himself, others attacked random bystanders and still others asked the warlords that run Daphark to serve as executioners. There are very many options for completing this mission. You need to choose an acceptable one for yourself. "

"Tryd, I refuse to do your mission," I said, confident that it would be more interesting this way. "First you want me to be a messenger boy, now you want me to be a sociopath. I want to be a pirate, not a murderer. What the hell is the point of killing those who could be profitable later and who pose no threat now? And 'because you can' isn't a good reason. I can pick my nose too, but doing it won't make me a pirate."

"So what do you want from me?" Tryd replied to my objections.

"A mission. A real one. One that is worthy of a pirate."

"You're not a pirate!" the fox cut me off, turning his back to me. "And you don't want to do anything to become one!"

"Sure I do. But not this way! Those who want to be pirates love freedom and stealing stuff. They are not servants, delivering messages for their masters; they are not murderers, spilling blood because they can! A true pirate's blood boils from adventures!"

"Oh. Why didn't you say so from the get go? You're a romantic, eh?"

"There are a few of us," I admitted. "I spoke to some who have done your tasks. They talked about strange missions: take this thing there, hide that thing there, jump and crawl. Truly great missions for prospective pirates! They teach exactly what pirates shouldn't have: obedience, humility, and timidity. Thank you, Tryd, but that's not for me. I will pass your greeting on to Hilvar."

"You'll still have plenty of time for that," smirked the fox. "So you don't like my assignments? Then here is a worthy task for you—steal the Lara crystal from Derval the Fierce, one of the local warlords. It is the symbol of his power—he values it more than his own eye! If you steal it, I will call you a thief and a brother. If you fail, you may as well get off this planet now! You'll never be a pirate!"

Tryd left the room, slamming the door, which already hung loosely on one hinge, behind him. The door couldn't bear such abuse and crashed to the floor, stirring up a cloud of dust. The old fox swore bitterly, spat, kicked the sash, and vanished in the neighboring room.

A couple of minutes later Stan sent me a summary report about Daphark. A huge city covered the entire land mass and was divided into districts each of which had its own overlord and standard of living. The Pyrrhenians ruled all of it—the flying fat men had taken all the power in their little hands, eliminating any competition and stabbing each other in the back without the slightest hesitation. It was utter chaos. Wars over territory could break out at any moment and yesterday's allies could turn on each other over something as minor as another mansion. When hostilities broke out, the civilians huddled deep in their burrows, waited for things to blow over and then crawled out to rebuild their hovels—though, just the walls, since there was no point in putting glass in the windows. It'd only get broken again soon enough.

Derval the Fierce controlled a sector of the city known as the Red Rose. This contained the city's central neighborhoods and the main attraction—Daphark's first ten docks. Nine of these were arranged around the tenth, giving rise to a floral design from above. Although it wasn't a rose, so much as a daisy. Whether this fact was related to the name or not, no one knew, but Derval maintained tight control on his 'Rose' and didn't hesitate to crack heads to ensure order. Within its confines, the

IN SEARCH OF THE ULDANS

Rose's districts were fairly tranquil, which allowed its residents to enjoy windows with real glass.

Taking a step forward, I tumbled out of Tryd's 'window' and turned on my suit's stabilizers. It was easier to get to the Rose by air. My thrusters carried me away from Tryd's lair. From a bird's eye view the landscape was depressing: Everywhere I looked, all I saw were ruins, dirt, gloom and complete desolation. The locals did not even glance up at me, unwilling to demonstrate any interest in someone who could be dangerous. Several times, I spied movement among the high-rise buildings and my suit announced that I was being locked onto. No one opened fire, however, and after a few seconds I flew beyond the range of the missile launchers anyway.

"Surgeon, where are you?" As per usual, Kiddo called at a bad time and with a demanding tone in her voice. "We had a meeting scheduled outside the Hansa HQ!"

"I think perhaps you scheduled it in your head and forgot to tell me about it." I did a barrel roll, landing on the roof of the nearest building. Arguing while in midflight was annoying. "I'm no longer on Belket."

"You set out your conditions and I agreed. I came all the way over to Hansa but you're not here. You're wasting my time, partner!"

"You know, Marina, it's time to set boundaries to our partnership." To my surprise, I felt no anger towards Kiddo. Instead, I felt a kind of serenity. "I'm not interested in a relationship in which you leak information about me right and left. You're guided only by your own interests and make up all kinds of complaints about nothing. We agreed to work together on the Hansa project. Let's stop at that. Notify me in advance if you have a player looking for Hansa upgrades so that I can schedule my plans accordingly. And make sure to negotiate their ship's transfer right away so that there are no stupid questions later. I need between six and twelve hours to reach Belket. Keep that in mind when discussing timeframes with the clients. As for the upgrades to your ship—I will be free in twelve hours and I will call you. If you still want the upgrades, we can meet then. I don't have time right now."

I hung up and looked at the crowd of ragged people gathered around me. Initially frightened by my appearance, the locals soon got over their fears and their instinct for self-preservation and decided to check out the miracle that had fallen on their roofs. Who knows, maybe I'll decide to stretch my legs and leave my armor suit unattended.

I didn't bother messing with them. Firing my thrusters and making the rabble scurry back into their corners, I headed for the city center. A few minutes later, skyscrapers with real windows appeared, along with a warning in my HUD that I was being tracked by a surface-to-air missile battery.

"Surgeon, flying is not permitted over the Red Rose," the dispatcher's voice sounded in my earpiece. I was being tracked the entire time, without a single lapse. "Land your suit or we will attack. I repeat, the Red Rose is a no-fly zone. Await the arrival of a patrol once you have landed. You do not have permission to enter this area."

Three small escort cars surrounded me, forcing me to do as

---

the dispatcher ordered. I did not argue. Raising my hands to show that there were no weapons in them, I slowly began to descend to the ground. Of course, you can't fool experienced soldiers—everyone could see the blasters on my shoulders, but I figured that a peaceful gesture would set them at ease.

I was not allowed to touch the earth. Using advanced manipulators, the patrol grabbed me while still in midair and began dragging me to the center of a secure area. Twenty minutes later I was being interrogated in a dark and cramped room. A fat detective floated past me with a folder that turned out to be my 'case' and took a seat across from me. The Pyrrhenian slowly looked through the folder's contents, getting acquainted with the list of my crimes. Finally, shutting the folder, he turned to me:

"Well, well, well! An offender? Disturbing the peace? Are you trying to earn ten years in the slammer? Well, we can arrange all that! We will send you to the mines. You will become one of our valued employees. Was this what you had in mind when you attacked the Red Rose?"

"I did not attack the Red Rose," I snorted. "I am here because I would like to meet Derval the Fierce to offer him my services."

"Offer? You want him to hire you?" the detective asked.

"Yes. I heard that the Lara crystal wasn't secure enough! I decided to check and offer my services. I imagine Derval will be interested in a third-party opinion about his security system. After all, a symbol of power must have the best protection."

At this point, a voice came on over the room's speakers:

"We don't need the services of random rabble! The crystal's security system was designed and installed by the Hansa Corporation itself!" As I had assumed, our conversation was being monitored. "Who are you to think you can do better than Hansa?"

"Someone who knows the weaknesses of the Hansa guys perfectly well. I can provide evidence. This video will help you make the right decision."

Brainiac put together a video showing the shameful destruction of the Hansa torpedoes in less than a second. I sent the file to the detective and waited. I had no doubts that the video would be passed on to all interested parties. After a couple of minutes, the detective gave way to another flying fat man who introduced himself as Reon, the head of the Red Rose's security. Having ascertained that I was not going to turn in my informants, the Pyrrhenian asked the main question:

"Why do you think you are qualified to test our security system? Maybe you discovered that vulnerability in your video by accident. We have hired more than a dozen experts, and they all confirmed the quality of the work. What do we need another verification for?"

"One coincidence is an accident, but two or three are already a norm," I said meaningfully. "No one else in all of Galactogon managed to infiltrate the Zatrathi flying fortress, reach its command center and download the ship's data. But I could. No one else in Galactogon could crack the security on the aliens' ship and steal it from under the enemy's alien nose. Yet I did. All this makes me superior to your testers. They check reliability whereas I look for vulnerability. You're confident in your system? So what's stopping you from hiring me? What do you have to lose?"

"Time. Why should I waste time on some braggart?" The Pyrrhenian remained unimpressed.

"You can check my every word. Surely you have your spies among the Precians—ask them who sold them the Zatrathi scout they're currently taking apart piece by piece. I can wait. As for the data, I can provide it. Not all of it, of course, but I can share plenty. I'm really the one I say I am. I don't have anything to hide. I can make your security system better and make some money in the process. Let us help each other."

"We've already checked it," Reon said. "You had an audience with the emperor, but you were banished for being a pirate. This smells like a setup. You're working for the Precians. This is confirmed by the fact that right after being 'banished,' you traveled to Zalva's moon with an imperial adviser in tow. The moon's off limits to anyone the Precians don't truly trust. And the adviser was with you when you attacked the Zatrathi flying fortress. You're no pirate—you're a statist spy!"

These were serious accusations, but I was in no hurry to make excuses. They hadn't killed me on the spot, so I had a chance. For the moment, I simply shrugged:

"You are free to refuse. If you think the crystal is well-protected, well that's up to you. When it gets stolen—and I do mean, 'when' not 'if'—you can remember me."

"It's not possible to steal the crystal! You are nothing but a smug braggart!" Reon cut me off.

"Want to bet on it? You are right. Before I prove my usefulness as a security analyst, I'm ready to prove that you actually need my services. I'll steal the crystal myself!"

"Have you lost your damn mind? Surely your previous employers fired you and you are trying to bluff your way into another job," the head of security exclaimed in shock, but I went on plying my line:

"If I succeed, you will pay me for the theft and pay me to find further vulnerabilities. If I fail, you can kick me out in disgrace, and I will give you ten million credits for your wasted time."

"Ten million, you say?" frowned Reon. "For an attempted theft? And then we can kick you out?"

"Almost. My task is not to steal the crystal, but to find vulnerabilities, to prove to you that they exist and to eliminate the holes. Ten million is your insurance in case I fail. I may as well say now that I do not work for free. If I get into the room, take the crystal and get out safe and sound, the cost of my services to upgrade your system will be fifty million."

"Now this is interesting," Reon grinned. "Faith in charity vanished from this planet many millennia ago. Everyone here knows to expect trouble if someone wants to do something for free. Fifty million is too much for the security system. Even Hansa only charged us forty."

"Well, I ain't Hansa," I said. "You overestimate their abilities! I am offering you an extraordinary product and therefore the price is extraordinary too. I don't want to brag, but...have you seen my ship? Surely you know that she is an Uldan vessel! Hansa still has some ways to go before they reach the level of our winged ancestors. Just today I handed over some of my inventions on the basis of Uldan technology to those vaunted geniuses at Hansa—and they had no idea what they were dealing with! Fifty million is the price of peace and security. Take some time to think it over. I won't rush you."

"I need to discuss this with the boss. Wait here," Reon flew out of the room. Long minutes of waiting followed, accompanied by the anticipation of a breakthrough. My plan for completing Tryd's quest was entirely improvised, a true game, an adventure. You could call it whatever you like, but the bottom line is that I didn't take it seriously. That is why the progress I had made so far was a complete surprise for me.

Reon appeared an hour later, by which point I had managed to calm down and even sleep a little.

"The boss wants fifty million if you fail," said the Pyrrhenian. "If you are so confident in your abilities, you shouldn't care what this amount is anyway."

"Agreed," I said simply. "For me, the cost of failing really does not matter."

"What do you need to start work?"

"Not much. A contract that you are hiring me for a test theft with the amounts we discussed included in it. It's not that I don't trust you, but I want confirmation that everyone is ready to fulfill their obligations. I want to do my work fairly and honestly!"

Reon nodded his head respectfully. The gangster did not expect anyone to want to work with them officially. Of course, if they had the desire to get rid of me, there wasn't a contract in the galaxy that could save me because on this planet every boss was a law unto himself. Nevertheless a contract would make the business seem legitimate outwardly.

"You will get your contract. It should be ready in two hours. When will you start?"

"As soon as we sign all the papers. You will show me the crystal itself so that I don't confuse it for another."

"Are you so confident in your abilities?"

"I would not be here if I weren't. In my line of work, you either know what you're doing or you don't—in which case you keep your head down and learn until you do. There is no other option."

Reon did not answer my grandiose reply and an hour later handed me a contract. The small print included everything we had agreed on, plus minor legal details, such as force majeure, third-party liability, and other verbiage designed to fill the empty space and transform the contract from a two-line list into a serious document with a secret meaning. Glancing over the main points and not seeing anything important for me, I made a show of signing it, not forgetting to cough self-confidently.

"You have three days to complete the task," Reon rubbed his hands, leading me to the crystal. I had no doubts that the Red Rose's entire armed force would spend the next three days standing around the Lara with their eyes glued to the crystal. Silly NPCs.

Reon escorted me to Derval's residence, where, in the second basement level, behind massive doors made of raq, in an immense vault equipped with a modern security system, stood the object of my heist. The Lara was a pristine diamond about half a meter in diameter. My former game, Runlustia, was rich in various gems, but even there I never saw a beauty like this. It seemed that the purest light in the world had concentrated itself in the Lara, refracting across the diamond's facets with all the colors of the rainbow. The crystal buzzed and vibrated, as if overwhelmed with the energy it contained. A huge power cable snaked along the floor, forcing me to wonder whether its purpose was to discharge the energy or, on the contrary, to supply the strange crystal...If its purpose was the former, then what was this Lara crystal anyway?

"As you can see, our security system is cutting-edge." Reon did not hide his glee at my imminent failure, as if part of the money I would pay was his already. "You have three days to prove otherwise. Get to work."

If he was expecting me to do something right now, then he was deeply mistaken—I was not going to risk it. The reason was pretty basic—ten beam cannons had me in their sights. The underground bunker was chock-full of various traps. I managed to identify several. Pits, ampoules of acid, beam and EM cannons, powerful magnets—Hansa had gone all out. And that was only what was visible to the naked eye. I could only guess what remained hidden in the walls.

Before proceeding with the theft, I decided to go back to the planetary command center. Amazingly, even on such a decentralized planet, there was one that was responsible for all the flights in Daphark's star system. No matter how hot the turf wars grew, the various factions understood that without a single facility coordinating the movement of spacecraft, life would be difficult.

"What is the purpose of your visit?" a droid greeted me, kindly offering me clean water. On this polluted planet, clean water was valued more than tea and coffee.

"I need to set up the date and time for a mock heist," I handed a copy of my contract with the Red Rose to the droid. "I have a contract with Derval to test his security system."

"This lies beyond our jurisdiction. What is the purpose of your visit?" the droid repeated, having familiarized itself with the contract.

"The Red Rose area is a no-fly zone. However, in order to perform my obligations under this contract, I will need to fly in it. Since my task is to test the facility's security system and not the response time of the control tower, I would like to avoid dealing with the air defense systems. They may prevent me from fulfilling the terms of the contract. Let's coordinate my flight over the residence of Derval the Fierce."

"Allow me to see your contract once again." One of the wall panels opened ushering in a command center employee—an Anorxian synthoid. A bright red mark of paint smeared on one of the cube's faces indicated that this specimen was no longer linked to the Anorxian Motherboard. Having scanned the contract, the robot buzzed, processing the information.

"The Red Rose has confirmed its contract with you to test the security system," the dispatcher informed me. "What is your desired date?"

"Today, in four hours," I estimated the most optimal time for myself.

"Negative. Cargo ships have been scheduled to land at docks two and seven for that time frame. The Red Rose territory will be closed to flights at that time."

"I don't need much," I said with a sinking heart. "I just need to make one short flight and show Derval that I have fulfilled my part of the contract. I won't interfere with the cargo ships."

"I can only provide you with a window of ten minutes."

"That would be more than enough," I couldn't help but smile. My closed helmet kept the robot from seeing it. "When can you frant me that window?"

The next two hours passed hectically for me. The officer in charge of the Red Rose air defenses confirmed that they would not shoot me down with missiles if I appeared over the city at the specified time. The head of the orbital defense did not quite understand why I came to him, because he was not responsible for the actions on the surface of the planet, but confirmed that they were not going to attack me either. Even Reon, the head of security, assured me that I would not be charged for damage to the property or manpower of the Red Rose, given that everyone already knew the time of my attempt. Each of the parties issued confirming papers, turning me into a messenger boy between various offices. Even the head of the firefighters signed a document certifying that his unit was ready to extinguish a sudden fire, if it were to break out in a couple of hours.

All of the various services were preparing for my attempt to steal the Lara crystal, and I did not disappoint them.

"Brainiac, let's take off," I ordered, returning aboard my ship. "Set course for the Red Rose."

"Orbship *Warlock*, your takeoff is not authorized. Return to your dock immediately," the dispatcher wasn't sleeping on his job, tracking the movement of ships.

"I refer you to flight permit number 25.12," I declared, checking my papers. "I have permission to take off."

"Just a second...Pursuant to this permit, permission was granted only for flying in an armor suit..."

"Tower—I am looking at the paper here—there's no mention of forbidding me from flying my ship!" I said, forcing the robots to shut up. Bureaucracy in all its glory: The more official papers you have, the cooler you look.

"Cap'n, we are being tracked by surface to air missiles," the snake said. "Are you sure that everything will be fine?"

"Brainiac, patch me through to the head of the Red Rose's aerial defenses," I ordered, and as soon as the call went through I fell upon the unsuspecting NPC: "What the hell? I am not going to risk my ship! Stand down or the contract will be terminated because of you! Didn't I show you the signature of Derval the Fierce himself on the contract?"

"We had discussed an armor suit." I had deliberately misled the officer, but I was not going to admit that. Brainiac was about to reach the desired location and my objective right now was to confuse everyone. I hadn't sat in line in all those office reception rooms for nothing.

"I have a copy of the contract here before me. Find the words 'armor suit' in there and I'll pay you a hundred million! If you don't stand down in ten seconds, you'll be paying the boss out of your pocket. I refer you to clause thirteen—'force majeure.'

IN SEARCH OF THE ULDANS

I do not intend to work in conditions that are not close to realistic. This is a test, so I told you in advance what I was going to do, but a true thief won't grant you that luxury!"

"Orbship *Warlock,* this is tower! Your flight has been cleared," the dispatcher finally gave up and granted me permission. I had the right to be here in my ship.

"Missiles are standing down," the security officer grunted, hearing dispatcher's words. "Get on with your work!"

"Brainiac?"

"We are in position, altitude is two kilometers. We are not being locked on. What's next?"

I rechecked all the systems. Everything was nominal and we had elo up to the eyeballs.

"On my mark, we will dive and destroy any defenses we encounter. Snake, keep us safe. Gunner, I need you to blast a pit at these coordinates. That would be the second basement level of the compound. Keep one cannon free for any defenders—we can't afford someone to hit us with a missile. Sebastian, you will have ten seconds to get down and grab that crystal. Be careful, this plan was designed with you and your amazing thief skills in mind. Is everyone ready? Then let's do it!"

I lost my breath when *Warlock* plummeted. I only had time to note the bright flashes on the screens—the defense of the Derval residence began at an altitude of one and a half kilometers. The snake didn't risk it, raising the shields to full power and absorbing all the AA fire which caused our ship to burn like a beautiful falling star. Closer to the surface, the gunner opened up with his cannons, clearing the way before us.

"We are now ten meters above the roof," said Brainiac, abruptly bringing the ship to a standstill. Pieces of concrete and melted metal flew around us—*Warlock*'s five cannons began to blast the building, boring their way to the vault. It took no more than ten seconds for the upgraded beam cannons to burn a hole wide enough for the orbship to pass.

"Go, go, go, Sebastian!" I yelled, jumping out of the ship. The thief was beside me, holding my hand—it was impossible to see anything in the cloud of dust and smoke.

"We're in position! Sebastian, grab the crystal! Move!"

The pedestal holding the Lara was covered with a hollow metal dome—a defensive measure I had not reckoned on. Sending the thief to deal with this surprise, I turned to more important matters—namely the local security that was beginning to clamber out of the ruins. Reon and his squad of loyal fighters, personally took positions on the last line of defense. A salvo from my ship broke their formation and scattered the defenders around the vault, but not all were killed—at least five remained alive, including Reon, who was reeling. The head of security was unarmed but this did not make him a harmless enemy. Who knew what that flying barrel was capable of?

"Hope you're in tight with the local planetary spirit, bud," I said, firing my blasters.

"Got it!" exclaimed Sebastian with delight in his voice. The metal dome rose two meters and hovered. Sebastian did not climb inside. Instead, he grabbed the nearest hunk of concrete and hurled it as hard as he could at the pedestal. The pedestal rocked slowly and then keeled over, dumping the crystal to the floor. I was about to object but as soon as the crystal came off its stand, an energy grid fell down from above, melting not only the stones but also the pedestal in its path. One more layer of security. Sebastian took out some long tongs and lifted our booty into the air. He did not dare touch the Lara, and rightfully so—the tips of his tongs instantly began to heat up and melt. The Lara almost slipped out, but I managed to catch it with a manipulator. There was no defense against my favorite weapon—the manipulator coped with the crystal with ease.

"Let's go!" I barked, assessing the effects of our raid. Derval had a tempting vault, but the longer we lingered, the less were our chances of getting off Daphark alive. Meanwhile, I couldn't stuff the Lara into my inventory, nor put it on the floor of my ship for fear of it melting everything it touched.

"Here, take it! Don't let go! I handed the manipulator to Sebastian and hoped that the engineer would come up with a way to store the crystal. "Brainiac, head to Tryd's place! Snake, get ready to take on a passenger. The old fox won't be pleased to see us!"

I did not have time to complete the mission, so I decided to kidnap the pirate and deal with the further formalities aboard my ship.

"Orbship *Warlock* you have violated the agreement!" The personnel responsible for the aerial defenses were just beginning to figure out what I had done, yet they still tried to act according to the contract.

"I refer you to item 14.7 therein," I answered at random, peering at the screens. The Red Rose was receding behind us already.

"Orbship *Warlock*, you have entered the Cardan sector," said the dispatcher, also coming to. "You were cleared only for takeoff and landing in the Red Rose sector!"

"Tower, I request launch to orbit. I am still acting strictly in pursuance of my contract with Derval the Fierce." I didn't waste time. Tryd's building was rapidly approaching. I could even make out the small figure of an old fox standing in the window hole looking out at the city. Brainiac stopped a few feet from the building, blasting Tryd with a gust of air. Amazingly, the pirate did not even budge. Either his experience or advanced age kept him from fleeing from the orbship that almost rammed into his office.

"Your request is being processed, please stand by for a response," the dispatcher answered, as I jumped out of the ship. Tryd did not have time to react, I grabbed the old man by his arms and jumped back. The snake poked out of the hull, caught us in midair and pulled us inside. Tryd began to complain but my assistant did not waste time—an injection of tranquilizer and the old fox curled up in a ball on the floor. The engineer took his body to the medcapsule in case the old man over-exerted himself. Meanwhile, the dispatcher came on again:

"Permission to take off from the planet granted. Follow corridor 2-2-7."

"Let's go, Brainiac! Patch me through to the commander of the orbital defense."

"Surgeon?" came the voice in the speakers. "All of Red Rose is on red alert. They are demanding that you remain in the system."

"Everything is according to the contract. They are angry that I was right, and their security is crap," I replied as calmly as I could, although I was trembling from excitement. Derval's people came to their senses a bit too quickly. "I'd be worried about their hides too, if I were them. I'm going to circle around and go back to console them."

"As you say. Everything is according to the contract. Good luck in designing your security system. Come visit me—perhaps I could use your help," boomed the orbital station's commander, giving me a green light.

"Brainiac, get us out of this dreadful system. Set course for Belket," I leaned back in my chair, still unable to believe that the heist had been a success. Taking out the PDA, I dialed Marina: "I'll be there in twenty minutes. Get your money together. We're going to upgrade your cruiser."

CHAPTER EIGHT

"**Y**OU DAMNED SON OF A...you can take your...ship and shove it up your...with you and your...crew, you pathetic little..."

Tryd expressed himself in a flowery, sailor-like language. The pirate had been out for a long time. In the meantime, I had taken ownership of Kiddo's cruiser and sent it to be refitted. As soon as the old fox regained consciousness, he broke out in a stream of abuse which brooked no interruption—not that I minded, since it really was fascinating and I was having a good time hearing him go on and on.

I'll admit that my idea of kidnapping an NPC and taking him to the Precians hadn't been very well thought out. The customs officers for example, were so elated to see a wanted pirate on my ship that my rapport with the Precians jumped a hundred points. Four detectives immediately set up camp right outside the orbship. The Precians weren't allowed to board *Warlock* and take the pirate: According to them, the players' right to their property was sacrosanct. As long as Tryd remained on my ship, he was considered part of my crew. But if he stepped outside, he would immediately be subjected to the full force and effect of Precian law.

"Enough!" I snapped after five minutes. Everything has a limit. In my estimation, Tryd had already had his say and the time had come for constructive dialogue. "Let's think about how we're going to get you out of here!"

"You brought me here—you think!" the pirate replied angrily.

"I was informed that I won't be allowed to leave the planet with you on board," I sighed. "So let's decide together. This concerns you a lot more than me."

"You gut of a mole!" the fox snarled through his fangs. "You've set me up and now you want to rid yourself of me? Hilvar warned me to be careful with you. And I, like an old fool, did not heed his advice. I bought your drool about piracy."

"Will you be crying for a long time?" I interrupted Tryd. "Are you a pirate or what? I'm not going to surrender you but we do need to figure out how to get away from here. The longer you resist, the less chance we have."

"There's nothing to think about—the Precians will never let me go. Do you know how many years I've been a thorn in their sides?"

"What about an exchange? Maybe they will trade you for the Lara crystal?"

"You managed to steal it?" Tryd said, shocked. "It was protected by a security system designed by Hansa itself!"

"Yeah along with Derval's brains," I waved. "There's no

security to speak of when the dunces are in charge."

Yet Tryd would not leave me alone until I recounted how I had stolen the jewel. After this, the fox admitted that I really hadn't the time to complete the mission with him back on Daphark.

"You should have set out for Qirlats," the old man said, still in an offended yet softer tone of voice. It was not as cold and disdainful as before. "Hilvar would have gladly taken the crystal. Someone like him would know how to use it."

"By the way, is the crystal some kind of energy source?"

"Damn it all! You're not thinking about the right thing," said Tryd, indignant. "Why don't you figure out how we will get out of here? You can deal with the crystal later. And to make you think better, here's a present:"

Mission accomplished: The Heist.

Mission accomplished: Meet Tryd.

Congratulations! You have earned the first rank of pirate. Speak with Hilvar for further instructions.

"Pirate Surgeon!" the dispatcher's voice came on my headphones. "You are prohibited from taking off! Starting your engines will be perceived as a violation of this order and you will be immediately destroyed! You are to appear before the viceroy to stand trial! Pirates have no place in the Precian Empire!"

"Now I know that you are not spy," Tryd laughed, rubbing his paws in satisfaction. "Think, novice pirate, how are we going to escape. I'll take a nap meanwhile."

IN SEARCH OF THE ULDANS

"Oh, you old shit. And if I blow us all up to hell right now, will you respawn on Daphark or what?" The fox didn't so much as twitch an ear to my outrage.

"You'll lose the crystal and your rapport with Hilvar. What'll you do if I *don't* respawn?"

The cops outside the ship were now waiting for two pirates. Bristling with blasters and beam cannons, several dozen Precian soldiers had set up a tight perimeter around us. Tryd had really set me up by marking my missions complete—a good revenge for my kidnapping him.

I wasn't going to languish aboard my ship. But as soon as I stuck my head outside, I was yanked into the air with advanced manipulators, which ignored my suit's active protection. A Precian ran up and connected several cables to me. Before I knew it, I went flying out of my armor suit. It crashed to the ground beneath me, while I remained suspended. The Precians wielded their manipulators like experienced circus masters. A transport flew up to us and an escort of a dozen soldiers took me to the viceroy's office like the planet's most wanted criminal. I had neither armor nor weapons. Now I really couldn't self-destruct.

"Pirate Surgeon," the viceroy was waiting for me, postponing all his other business. It was amusing to see the long faces of the other petitioners as I was dragged past them. It's not every day that you get to see a captive pirate suspended upside down. "You have violated so many laws that I don't even know where to start!"

"Like what? What law did I violate?" I asked, rubbing my

bruised shoulder. The Precians didn't bother handling their cargo with care and every doorway we passed through had left its mark.

"You have become the foe of all Galactogon." The viceroy's monologue was prepared in advance. "You have smuggled a dangerous criminal to Belket, one who has destroyed many of our ships. You have broken a dozen laws. The emperor exiled you, yet you are still in imperial territory. Should I go on, or is it already clear to you that three years of hard labor will be mild punishment for one such as you?"

"Viceroy, let's get down to business. What do you want?" The viceroy wouldn't bother talking to a criminal if there wasn't something he wanted from him.

"I want peace and order for my empire," the official said dramatically, still beating around the bush. "Prosperity and well-being. So that our children grow up with hope in their future."

"May I somehow assist you in this difficult, but truly noble cause?" I was starting to understand what the Precian was getting at. A bribe? I was even curious how big it'd be.

"Indeed you may! That is why we invited you here instead of sending you to trial immediately." A screen behind the trade viceroy flickered to life—displaying none other than my old friend the imperial adviser. "We learned that on Daphark you stole an item that once belonged to us. We will let you go as soon as you return the Lara Crystal to us. The pirate Tryd will have to stand trial. He must answer for all the evil he has done to our empire!"

"That's not all, right?" I did not take my eyes off the adviser. "You understand perfectly well that I will not give you the pirate.

Adviser, we've been through several adventures together, let's not waste time with formalities. What does the Precian Empire want for Tryd's freedom?"

"Do not forget that from now on you are also officially a pirate and pirates have no place in the Precian Empire. Being uninitiated before, you were not a threat. We hoped that you would choose the right path, yet now…"

"Adviser, let's get to the point!" I interrupted the aristocrat. "Let's assume that you gave me a lecture on the dangers of piracy."

"Show more respect to my person, pirate Surgeon! The crystal is part of an item known as the Vengeance. The second element—a pedestal, is located on the Delvian capital. The third—the coupler unit—was lost many years ago. This time, the Precian Empire is willing to exchange Tryd for a complete Vengeance set. Such is the Emperor's decree."

"Three items for one pirate?" I asked surprised.

"Lara is the price for your neck, Surgeon. The remaining two are for Tryd!"

"It's still a bit much. You're not confusing Tryd with the Corsican by any chance? Or maybe with Hilvar..? Adviser, my answer is no. Tryd has lived a long time. If he does not have a homeworld, that is his problem. You cannot hold me indefinitely. Sooner or later you'll have to release me. And I'm not handing the Lara over for nothing. Even my relationship with the Hansa Corp isn't worth such an item. On the black market, the Lara will fetch good money."

Of course, I was bluffing. I'd trade Tryd for the crystal in a

---

second, but I was sick of the Precians' attitude too. Found themselves an errand boy!

"Then you shall become an outcast not only in the Precian Empire, but throughout the entire Alliance!" came the next logical threat.

"There's nothing to talk about. You're not getting Tryd or the crystal. All the best!"

I pulled a blaster out of my inventory, and pointed it at my head, preparing for suicide. The manipulator holding me could not control my hand. In order to snatch the blaster from it, they would have to get another manipulator which would take a few extra seconds. If I wanted to respawn, I would get my wish.

"Wait!" cried the adviser, evidently believing I was serious. The warriors arrived and took the blaster aside, allowing them to make a demonstrative shot at the furniture. Purely to be a jerk. I was disarmed and my hands were tied behind my back. So began the second round of negotiations.

"Don't worry. I have more blasters. You can't restrain me forever."

"Tryd's freedom in exchange for the crystal!" the adviser reluctantly agreed. "Will that suit you? I don't imagine Hilvar will be pleased with the person who cost him his best pirate."

"This is not enough. If Tryd were as dangerous as you suggest, your spies would have gotten him a long time ago. Everyone knew where he was. The pirate never hid himself and yet no one touched him. That means that you never needed him—that you don't need him at all. But now you want to exchange the Lara for him? The hell do I need an old fox for

---

instead? So this deal will not work, adviser. Tell me first what you need this crystal for. What is the Vengeance? Some new source of energy?"

"Leave us, viceroy," the adviser vacillated, deciding whether or not to answer. He even consulted his emperor, so serious was the matter. The Precian viceroy cast me a displeased look, but did not dare to oppose the will of the adviser. I was left alone in the viceroy's office—even the guards had to leave the room. My eye couldn't help pausing on the tablet the viceroy had left on the table. If I had my armor suit, I would definitely try to hack it right now.

"Two hundred years ago, the Confederation stumbled upon the ruins of an unknown civilization. Excavations and research led to astounding discoveries. The ruins were more than eighty thousand years old. It would seem that nothing should have survived the elements—the dust, the water, the oxygen and myriad organisms. But, in spite of everything, the ruins remained. Three items were found in perfect condition. A crystal, a pedestal and a coupler unit. Part of the archeologists instantly died from direct contact with the crystal. It turned out to be a highly concentrated source of energy. How the ancients managed to create it is still not clear. But the fact remains. You have seen it for yourself. Scientists have suggested that all three items are somehow interconnected, and decided to put them together. That day the Confederation lost a planet. It evaporated—completely and entirely. We believe its matter turned to energy and was absorbed into the crystal. What happened during the merger, we can only guess. Search parties

---

that arrived at the place where the planet disappeared, found only three floating objects. They were named the Vengeance and it was decided never to combine them again. In the following years, the Confederation continued to study the deadly artifact, but to no avail. Then, fifty years ago, the Corsican stole all three items from the Confederation. Twenty years later the Lara appeared in the possession of the Red Rose boss on Daphark, while the pedestal turned up in the palace of the Delvian Emperor. The location of the coupler unit is still unknown. Perhaps the Corsican has it. The war with the Zatrathi has brought a myriad misfortunes to Galactogon. If we could find the Vengeance, the balance would tilt in our favor."

"You want to send a kamikaze to the Zatrathi?" I guessed.

"That is correct. One small ship will be able to break through the defenses and get to the hull of the flying fortress and the orbital station and the planet. Having created the Vengeance, it is possible in one action to destroy the superior force of the enemy, without incurring irreparable losses. We are ready to bestow upon our chosen warrior binding and constant rebirth. It is impossible to destroy the items themselves. At least all the researchers working on them were unable to do so. We believe that this will bring us victory. We will let you and Tryd go in exchange for the crystal, but the emperor wishes to entrust you with a quest. Help Galactogon in the struggle against our common enemy."

New mission available: Seeking Vengeance. Description: Find the components of the Vengeance: The Lara Crystal, the

IN SEARCH OF THE ULDANS

Lira Pediment and the Lora Coupler Unit. The crystal is in possession of the player Surgeon, the pedestal is located in the main hall of the Delvian Palace, the location of the coupler unit is unknown.

"The Delvians won't let me enter their empire," I said thoughtfully, reading the system notification. Another pretentious speech which made me grind my teeth turned into an impossible quest.

"We can take care of that issue. You can leave today as a member of a diplomatic mission. How you come by the pedestal once we're there will be your concern."

"Let's discuss the details," I was in no hurry to accept the mission and feigned disinterest. "What'll I get if I complete it?"

"You will help Galactogon fend off the greatest threat the galaxy has seen!" the adviser grew all dramatic and lofty again. I needed him to calm down.

"Do you really believe that one captain will be able to defeat an entire armada? I've seen firsthand a Zatrathi flying fortress fight twelve A-class cruisers to a stalemate—and this was as the Qualians were repairing it. What will you do if there's more than one? This Vengeance weapon is good for a onetime shot at one planet. After that, you have to collect its three parts, put them together, pass them to the next kamikaze...It's too complicated and improbable. I've seen what the Zatrathi are capable of. They won't step on the same rake twice. So spare me the tales about how you're going to use the Vengeance against the enemy fleet. It'd be put to better use against the Qualians. Isn't that right, adviser?"

"Our tactics, like our politics are none of your business!" the adviser cut me off. "We are prepared to compensate you with two free Hansa upgrades and an additional five percent discount on your subsequent business with them—if you successfully complete this mission. That should be enough, considering that you have already received the second list. Do you accept the emperor's mission?"

"Sure. I will get you those items," I grinned, accepting the assignment.

"The viceroy will brief you. You will set out for the Delvian homeworld immediately!"

My rapport with the adviser fell by three points—I guess he really disliked my guess about the true purpose of the Vengeance. Then again, destroying the homeplanet of an enemy's ally isn't that bad of a move.

The screen with the adviser went out and my hands reached for the desk of their own volition. The viceroy's tablet lay there as lonely as before, begging me to do something about it. I grabbed the device and pushed the wake button—and encountered a password dialog. Behind me, I heard a door opening. The viceroy was on his way back—and the manipulator beam yanked me into the air. Having no other alternative, I quickly tossed the tablet into my inventory. Let them try and shake it out of me.

"We have received new instructions regarding you and your accomplice," the viceroy said disdainfully, sitting down at the table. "In an hour we go to the Delvians. I was advised to include you in my team, and I am partial to heeding this advice."

"I only travel on my ship," I was surprised by the viceroy's wording.

"Impossible! The instructions clearly state that you are to participate. You will be included in our embassy to the Delvians as a member of the engineering staff. There is no other way for you to enter the Voldan Alliance!"

"Is that what the adviser told you?"

"No! That is what I'm telling you!" The Precian slammed his desk so hard with his fist that several papers tumbled to the floor. "You will do as I tell you! Speak when permitted! Do not even dare to breathe without my permission! I will not allow this embassy to fail! I was ordered to take the pirate aboard and deliver him to the Delvians and this is what I will do, even if I have to chain him to my ship! Take Surgeon to my ship. Put him in the holding cell. We depart immediately!"

Somehow 'advice' had become 'orders,' but I didn't bother drawing the viceroy's attention to this inconsistency. Especially once I saw that he was now diligently looking for his tablet, turning over the papers on the desk. I wonder if he has surveillance cameras in his office?

The viceroy's problems evaporated as soon as the door descended between us. No one's a thief until they're caught. I was more worried about the current mission: Going to the Delvians without an armor suit and a ship was a bad idea, yet I had no options. I couldn't reach Brainiac on my PDA and I had no other way of contacting my ship. After a lengthy trip I found myself in the holding cell of the viceroy's cruiser—the only VIP in the place. One of the marines tossed me a Precian maintenance suit and ordered me to put it on. The ceremonial garb I had been wearing under my armor since my audience with the Precian emperor was not befitting of an engineer envoy.

"Familiarize yourself with these." The head of the maintenance service approached the cell and handed me some schematics. "This is our engine. You should carefully study its operation for your cover story. The Delvians will not be happy to see a human among the diplomatic mission. They might start interviewing you to see whether you really are who you say you are. You need to prepare. Look at the design features of our engine: Instead of the normal two modulation units, ours uses three. This allows it to…"

I can't say I enjoyed the training much. The engineer used lots of technical terms and the gist eluded me, despite his efforts. Modulations, singularities, triangulations, and other 'ulations' were Greek to me as far as I was concerned. I placed all my hope of passing the check on my game logs and Stan's assistance. If anyone can help me pass the test, it'd be him. After making sure that I was alone, I pulled out my PDA.

"Talk but do it fast!" Kiddo's greeted me.

"What happened to the information about forthcoming attack on the Delvians?"

"Not much good news there, I'm afraid. I got in touch with Ash, the head of Vanguard. They're the top guild in Galactogon. It turned out that over the past week they've captured about forty ships with the same information. The developers announced a galactic event—inviting players to participate. As Ash said, he's accepted the challenge and is organizing his forces. As far as I

---

know, so far 130 guilds have confirmed their participation. He's coordinating them himself. So I couldn't sell your tip, sorry. It just wasn't worth anything."

Marina hung up, leaving me to my disappointment. I had imagined that this was my chance to save an entire game empire and become like the Delvian messiah or something—and now it turned out that the whole thing was a marketing stunt. I wasn't about to get involved in the upcoming battle of the titans. If the players wanted to rumble with the Zatrathi, that would be the place for them. As a pirate, I was much more comfortable away from places of galactic conflict. The hull shuddered, indicating that we had emerged from hyperspace.

"Attention! Man all stations!" announced the cruiser's intercom. "We have entered the Larsi system. Prepare for inspection."

The Precian rolled up his schematics and dashed off. He was replaced by two guards. I was escorted to a hangar filled with various equipment and parts that were now vaguely familiar to me from my recent crash course on starship engineering—the parts represented a disassembled cruiser engine. A hive of engineering personnel were already busy around it, pretending to be doing repair work. Though to be accurate, they were all just turning the same nuts and welding the same parts over and over again. The spectacle in which I was to play the leading role had begun. I was led up to the engine and handed a diagnostic unit. My guide hooked it up, pushed some buttons and began explaining to me what I had to do. The graphs and tooltips on the equipment screen fascinated me so much that I lost track of time. I came to my senses only when I heard an indignant cry:

"A human?! We were not warned that there would be a human on board!"

"Certain aspects of the engine's upgrade necessitate round the clock monitoring of certain changes," the viceroy began to explain as verbosely as possible. "Engineer Surgeon is one of the few people with the requisite skills and qualifications to work on Hansa equipment and technologies."

"An ordinary human has reached certification level 2 with Hansa?" A pretty fox appeared from behind the back of the main customs officer. A segmented, metal tail, a monocle that detected hidden properties, a cybernetic left leg—her appearance suggested a passion for technology and a troubled past. This Delvian had suffered some kind of accident.

"We would not deal with any other human," the viceroy said a bit defensively. He seemed proud to have such a capable human among his engineers.

"Sounds like utter tosh," drawled the Delvian expert, causing the customs officer to turn around.

"You have reservations about this Lumara?"

"Humans aren't to be trusted," the fox grimaced. "They are frequently not who they say they are. I would like to test his qualifications."

"You may ask him whatever you like," said the viceroy, but Lumara frowned.

"I intend to, don't worry—but not here. If this Surgeon is as good as you say, he will be happy to answer my questions in a jammer field. If he answers correctly, we will clear him from any suspicion and I will issue my formal apologies to your embassy. If he does not answer—you can expect consequences for trying to plant a spy among us. In that case, I will insist on your expulsion from the empire."

"As you wish," the chief customs officer nodded in agreement and turned to us: "Did you hear? The ship's examination has been suspended. Until Surgeon has been examined, I ask everyone to remain in their places. The human comes with us."

Now I found myself guarded by the Delvians.

"Lumara is the youngest daughter of the Delvian Emperor," Stan explained after some digging around the forums. "Before her older sister's abduction, she did not take an active part in politics and was not popular among her subjects. Everything changed when her sister disappeared. She is interested in all known advanced technologies. There is no further information."

Alarm bells were going off in my head—this new character could upset all my plans. I felt naked and defenseless without my armor suit, so I did not even consider resisting. I was escorted to the Delvian ship and placed in a room full of all kinds of equipment. A pair of handcuffs fettered me securely a metal chair, and a forcefield flickered to life around me, cutting me off from the outside world. My PDA continued to function but only for calling other players: The jammer cut off my contact with Stan. I would have to pass the exam on my own without any cheat sheets or outside help.

"I'll take it from here," Lumara sent the guards out. Sitting down behind a touch panel, the fox activated some device and an unpleasant hum filled my ears. The guards retired. Either they did not dare object to the princess or they would rather be away her experiments. The fox approached the jammer field that surrounded me.

"You say that you were on Raydon and saw my sister. I am listening."

"She is holding strong, even though it's not easy for her," I replied carefully. It was unclear to me what the younger princess was interested in. My qualifications as an engineer turned out to be irrelevant.

"One more answer like that and I will send you and the Precians flying out of here," growled Lumara. "How is my sister?"

"Her bond with the planetary spirit has been ruptured. There is an explosive device around her neck. Her movement around the Zatrathi ship is limited," I related the well-known information. I am sure that the Precians already had shared this information and I was simply being checked right now. I still held onto the most valuable bit.

"How does the collar function?"

"It is unclear. I had never encountered Zatrathi technology before and my time on their orbital station didn't allow me to study this issue further."

"Why are you here?" Lumara changed the topic abruptly.

"I have come as a member of the Precian embassy," the cover story flowed easily from my tongue. "I work on their engines, since they themselves..."

"Each empire has its own Hansa equivalent," the princess cut me off. "Specialists from different empires constantly exchange information and data about the newest developments, including other capable engineers. As the chairman of the Delvian industrial corporation, I know that 32 humans have received level 2 certification from the Hansa Corp. There is no one named Surgeon among them. I will ask you again: Why are you here?"

The girl had some tricks up her sleeve.

"I am traveling with the diplomatic mission as an engineer. I am ready to be tested and prove my professional qualifications," I insisted on my cover story, ignoring the fox's words. It could well be that she was trying to bluff me.

"Like I told you, they've come for the Lira," came a familiar voice. A shadow separated from the wall and assumed the form of none other than Aalor. Liberium did not forgive its foes, especially ostentatious ones like me.

"So this is your informant?" I managed an easy laugh. "Aalor, have you apprised the princess about your cruiser's inglorious end at my hands? You've followed me seeking revenge. It is said that that is a dish best served cold."

"Revenge? Aalor, is this true?" Lumara turned around.

"It is, but my personal relationship with Surgeon has nothing to do with the Precians coming here to steal the pedestal of the Vengeance."

"Prove it," I continued to ply my line. "Princess, let's get to the testing. It is silly to trust the words of someone seeking revenge. I can easily prove that I am who I say I am. I have too little time to spend on this human's false accusations."

A long pause ensued. My words had struck home with

Lumara. Perhaps, if Aalor were not here, I would even be able to push it, but my opponent was not going to give up so easily.

"I can provide proof too! It is right here, princess. I am sending you the file now," the Liberium officer sent over a video to the fox. Puzzled, Lumara accepted it and started watching. Her face grew longer with every passing second.

"But the viceroy…" the princess began in surprise, but Aalor cut her off.

"We can discuss this without Surgeon."

Too late. I figured that the video was of my meeting with the adviser—and it was the viceroy himself who had leaked it. He was the only one who had received the adviser's instructions. Despite the bind I was in, I cast Aalor a malevolent smirk. It was impossible to see his reaction behind his visor, but I was sure he had understood me. He had just set up his entire guild, revealing their informant. I was certain that if the adviser found out about Liberium's betrayal, the Precian Empire would forever be off limits to this guild. I'll be sure to negotiate the price of my silence with Vargen.

Lumara finally watched the video and turned on Aalor:

"The pedestal was presented to my father the emperor by the head of the Jolly Roger. What is the Vengeance? Why do the Precians seek it?"

"The viceroy does not know this," Aalor no longer even bothered to conceal the identity of the informant. "But he is sure that it is a weapon to fight the Zatrathi. The entire idea is nonsense however. The third part of the weapon has disappeared."

"If the Corsican gave us the pedestal, he may know where the third item is located. I will speak with him," the princess said pensively, causing me to mentally add her to my list of important NPCs. If she had a line of communication to the Corsican, then she could put in a good word for me.

"What will happen with Surgeon?" asked Aalor.

"He and the Precians shall be expelled. The viceroy should remain. We will look out for him. The Precians would not forgive his betrayal."

"Princess, do not rush to expel me," I refused to stand by idly. "It is true that I seek the pedestal, but I am willing to exchange information to obtain it."

"What is the Vengeance?" came the counter question.

"It doesn't matter now. In two days the Delvian Empire will suffer a crushing blow."

"Do you mean the Zatrathi assault? We are already preparing for it. The enemy will not triumph."

So, Ash decided to involve not only players, but the NPCs too. A reasonable move, even if it slightly spoiled my plans.

"In that case, there are two other issues to discuss. First, I want to meet with the emperor and receive my rightful reward for destroying the Zatrathi flying fortress. Second, your sister is with child and I know who the father is."

"What?!" Lumara loomed over my dome, dumbfounded by the news. Her cybernetic body flushed the color of garland. With such nerves, she should probably avoid the poker table.

"I want the reward I earned," I repeated, as if nothing had happened. "I happen to be the first person to destroy a flying fortress. The Precians can tell you about how I did this."

"To hell with your reward! What did you say about my sister?"

"I'm not going to talk about that while he's here."

"Leave us," Lumara barked at Aalor without turning around. Not in a position to argue, Aalor had no choice but to make himself sparse. But I was not deceived. There were certain to be cloaked guards around us—no one would leave a princess, even one as odd as this one, alone. Still, this did not bother me—I had already gotten rid of the one enemy that could disrupt my plans.

"Well?" Lumara began pacing the room from impatience.

"I want three things. The first is the pedestal. Second, I must inform the father of the princess's baby of her current state. The princess asked me to tell him what happened. Third, I want you to call the Corsican and find out where I can find the third part of the Vengeance."

"How can I know that you're not lying? Why should I trust you?"

"You'll just have to. I can't send you the video of my meeting with your sister because the Precians have my ship."

"The viceroy brought it with him," said Lumara, reflecting on my demands. "The orbship is on our planet. I was saving it for later. I wouldn't mind digging in her innards. I have never had a chance to examine a ship of that class."

"And you never will," I said sharply. "She is my ship, and I won't let anyone do anything with her. Requirement number four: You return the orbship to me safe and sound. What is your decision?"

IN SEARCH OF THE ULDANS

In principle, the viceroy had acted logically enough—he was planning on betraying me to the Delvians along with my ship. All he would have to do is show Brainiac that I was aboard his cruiser and the *Warlock* would follow us. As soon as I get back, I will set up some secure line of communication with the ship. This is the second time I've lost contact with her.

"You ask too much," Lumara replied. "I can arrange a meeting with the baby's father. You can tell him about my sister. I can call the Corsican and ask about the third part of the Vengeance, but I am not sure that he will answer. I can return your ship to you under one condition—you give me a tour of her. I wish to see the orbship with my own eyes. The Hansa people speak very highly of her. As for the Lira—this demand is out of the question. It is a present to our empire. No one has the right to take it away. I would not agree to this even for my sister's sake."

It was already obvious to me that no member of the imperial family would agree to hand the Lira over to a simple player, but it was worth a try. What I need to do right now is sigh languidly and convincingly, demonstrating an epic internal struggle, and then propose new conditions more acceptable to both of us.

"I understand about the pedestal. I am prepared to offer an alternative demand. Confirm my stay on your planet as a Precian engineer. You can do whatever you like with the viceroy. I will speak to Aalor's boss about the cost of my silence. I imagine that if you work over the traitor properly, he will make an excellent spy. Surely you don't have any spies in the Precian Empire of a viceroy's rank and stature? The head of a trading planet...a once-in-a-lifetime opportunity."

"You are prepared to betray the Precians? Are you stranger to your people?"

"My people? I am a pirate!" I even injected a dose of hurt into my voice. "I have no people. My life is catch, plunder, release and catch again…to plunder once more. There is no place for patriotism or syrupy love for any one empire among these important activities. I fight for those who pay me the most."

"A pirate?" Lumara's muzzle wrinkled in displeasure. "How much do you want for information about the Vengeance, pirate?"

Lumara had understood me and the conversation turned in the right direction.

"Information for information," I made another attempt to bargain. "I am interested in anything to do with the Uldans. Finding the orbship has kindled an interest in alien archaeology within me. Their way of life, technology, records. Even just stories concerning the Uldans will do."

"So you're an archaeologist too, are you?" the fox looked surprised. "You've read many ancient tales about noble pirates that once plied space, robbed the rich and gave money to the poor?"

"That's right. I give to the poor to make them rich so I can rob them later," I said. "I think the meaning of being a pirate is constant plunder. For example, I like to steal information."

"What is the Vengeance for?" Lumara asked again, yet this time I was ready to answer her. The princess didn't say no to my request for information sharing, therefore she'd be willing to compromise. It was impossible to go too far.

"A weapon of last resort," I repeated the words of the Precian adviser.

"The Precians are ready to sacrifice their relationships over a single shot?" asked the fox, having understood the principle of the Vengeance.

"Fired at the right moment, even a single shot can bring victory," I said philosophically. "When will my audience with the emperor take place?"

"Tomorrow. My father is busy today. We are making our final preparations for the offensive. I imagine I can allow the Precians to land on our planet. We will assume that you have passed the test. You will be taken to your ship where you must remain until tomorrow. You are not allowed to enter the palace. I will come by in the morning. And I'll take a look at your orbship."

Lumara paused, drilling me with her gaze. Unable to bear it, she asked:

"What's his name?"

"Alviaan. First Councilor of the Delvian Emperor."

"What the...!" Lumara cursed. "That trifling fop! Tomorrow morning I will visit you aboard your ship with him. Get the video ready. It'll be picked up in the evening. Bear in mind, Surgeon, if you lied to me, I will do everything possible to ensure that no empire will deal with you again. Do you understand me?"

"Then I will add one more requirement," I decided to squeeze some more out of Lumara. "I want one of your inventions. Specifically, a comm unit that can keep me in touch with my ship regardless of whether I have an armor suit or not. I don't imagine that I have to prove my honesty to you anymore and I can't count on always having my armor suit with me."

"Accepted," Lumara grinned and hurried to the exit. Already at the door she added: "Take him to the ship. He is to be treated as a guest with certain restrictions."

You have been granted access to the capital of the Delvian Empire.

Another shadow split from the wall, this time turning into an android. The jammer field disappeared, giving way to a manipulator's beam. I prepared to encounter all the corners and doorjambs in the place again, but the android moved me carefully. Having safely reached my ship, I put on the suit and listened to the crew's report.

"Cap'n, I have a proposition that is almost genius," the snake declared at once. "Let's get out of here."

"What's wrong?" I sighed with relief, climbing into my metal shell. It was much safer inside than out in the open.

"It's all wrong. After they kidnapped you, they tried to hack us and then destroy us. We couldn't get in touch with you and didn't know what to do. Then they brought us here and we even decided to self-destruct just as you reappeared. Now, of course, you will start saying that everything is fine, that we shouldn't panic and all that, but I haven't told you the most important thing yet. Out of boredom, I began comparing the data we downloaded from the Zatrathi fortress from the data we got off that scout. Something doesn't add up. I can't say what exactly, but my intuition tells me that we need to get out of here ASAP.

IN SEARCH OF THE ULDANS

The Zatrathi aren't planning on conquering the Delvian Empire—they want to destroy it outright. And if so, why would they even come here? They'll simply strike from afar with some terrible weapon and—boom—no more Delvians. And they'll get anyone who works with them in the process. The Zatrathi know how to rupture planetary spirit bindings—what if their weapon can do this too? I repeat, there is little information, it is contradictory, but the general message is that we need to fly away from here!"

"I will meet with the emperor tomorrow morning and then we can leave," I agreed. If the snake was panicking, it was a good idea to heed her advice. Given the large number of derelict scouts encountered by the players, everything that was going on smelled like a Zatrathi ploy. First no one could even get close to their ships, then suddenly they were a dime a dozen. And every one carried the same data. If this was the situation, we needed to act quickly. I spent the rest of the day holding colorful negotiations with Vargen. Liberium's leader resisted to the last, trying to pay me off with GCs, but I at last forced him to put the play money away. Five hundred thousand real credits replenished my family budget.

In the evening, Lumara's people showed up and I gave them the video. Only having done that did I permit myself to exit the game. My body needed a break in the form of sleep.

"There are visitors outside, requesting permission to board. There are visitors outside, requesting permission to board. There are visitors outside, requesting permission to board. There are visitors…"

It was of course possible to wake me up in some less monotonous manner, but I guess Brainiac was taking it out on me for allowing the Delvian girl to rummage around his tender guts. Shaking my head to clear the remaining drowsiness, I ordered the guests to be permitted aboard. First came an inspection team to check whether there was any undeclared biomatter on board, then two secret service foxes stuck their noses in all the nooks of the ship, and, having made sure that there were no enemies, Lumara stepped on board along with a handsome Delvian and a ton of gadgets. Whereas the Precian adviser seemed like a kind uncle, this Delvian aristocrat tried his best to show his superiority over everyone around him.

"The princess said that you had important information for me," Alviaan's tone matched his appearance. Arrogance multiplied by vanity. I was surprised that the adviser had not seen my video but I just sent him another copy. The NPC began watching it and after the video ended, I received a notification:

Mission accomplished: The Stork and the Fox. Reward: A slight nod of gratitude from Alviaan, First Councilor of the Delvian Emperor.

IN SEARCH OF THE ULDANS

I almost laughed when I saw the reward. Alviaan cast me another arrogant look, nodded slightly expressing his gratitude, and silently left the ship. Ain't it just like this all the time though? You place all your hopes into some job and when you've done it you get the merest of nods. I had the urge to let this nodder have it in his teeth, come what may.

Lumara did not follow Alviaan, nor notice his departure, as she was engrossed with her examination of my ship.

"Cool crew you got there," the princess's eyes came to rest on Sebastian and Tryd. The viceroy had brought the ship along with the pirate. "A pirate and a thief. A Delvian and a Qualian. Outcasts and fugitive criminals. Do you go out of your way to recruit this rabble? I'm surprised you let a Qualian on board. You had a hand in turning them into the rogue state of Galactogon— yet here is one of their number traveling with you. Consistency is not your strongest trait, is it?"

"No, I just don't care what race my crew members are. Tryd's a Delvian; does it follow that all Delvians are criminals?"

"I agree. Race has no meaning," Lumara nodded, pleased. "Don't judge Alviaan too harshly. He's still not sure whether he should be happy or distraught over the news, and arrogance is his way of hiding his feelings. We are not all like that. My father recently demoted him from Councilor for having dishonored my sister. Alviaan is beginning to learn what it means to be part of the imperial family. Today, his engagement with Niola will be announced, and I will finally be free."

"The princess will be allowed to leave the planet?"

"Maybe. Here I am a princess and that's it," Lumara said.

"Out there, I am an engineer, the head of the Pamir Industrial Corporation, a Delvian, a simple creature. Anyone, just not a princess. By the way, if you hadn't arrived with your news, I'd still be stuck here. How I hate all these ceremonies. I don't intend on leaving the planet—it's not bad here, after all. But I'm not in the habit of remaining in debt. Here—this is what you asked for."

I arranged all the data in my head, finally completing the portrait of the princess. Before her sister was kidnapped, Lumara occupied herself with whatever interested her. Her soul sought technical knowledge and engineering practice, not court etiquette. Returning to her native land and the status of heiress was akin to hard labor for the Delvian. No wonder she was so pleased to hear about the birth of a potential heir. It meant her freedom. For some reason, I was filled with sympathy for the Delvian and wished she could join my crew. The snake could deal with shields and repairs, while the princess could work on new developments for the ship. Oh, daydreams!

Lumara handed me a small electronic bracelet, but I was in no hurry to accept it. Sebastian jumped up from his seat and took the device from the princess. Nothing happened. The snake popped out of the wall, drawing a cry of delight from Lumara. Ignoring the guest, the engineer hovered over the bracelet, scanning its capabilities.

"What is this circuit for?" A projection of the schematics appeared over the bracelet.

"It's a jammer field bypass," Lumara answered, regaining her composure and returning to her business demeanor. Surprisingly, the princess reacted to the snake's verification quite calmly.

"And this component?" The projection displayed another circuit.

"Allows you to communicate during an EM pulse. It restarts the system and restores the power supply. It contains inactive elo, with an electromagnetic pulse mesh. The EM pulse activates the elo which restarts the system. I stole that from the Zatrathi."

"And this bug?" The engineer asked with surprise in her voice, projecting another hologram.

"It was worth a try." A sly smile appeared on Lumara's muzzle. "What if you hadn't checked…I'm curious after all. Never seen an orbship before."

"Plenty of those who've never seen us before," the snake snarled, continuing to study the 'gift.' Ten minutes later, after removing three more bugs, she found the bracelet usable and worthy of me wearing it. Brainiac set up a link between the ship and the bracelet, so now I would always remain in contact with my crew.

"The Corsican flat out refused to disclose the location of the third part of the Vengeance," Lumara continued. "He said, if someone wants it, he can come himself in person, instead of asking his sister for favors. So that matter is between you and the rest of your pirate buddies. I'm not your messenger."

"The Corsican is your brother?"

"You didn't know? He'd never have become the head of the pirates without my technologies! Little brother was first out of the running for the throne. He quarreled with my father nice and early. But that doesn't matter now. That other thing you asked about—the Uldan fairy tales. I think you will like this for sure."

Lumara pulled out a flash drive.

"Once upon a time, our researchers stumbled upon a strange planet. It was surrounded by several mysterious orbital stations. They were quite aggressive—all our attempts to establish contact were met with silence and our scouts were mercilessly destroyed. Then they simply began to push us out of the system with waves of torpedoes. It was decided to forget about this planet for a while. When I was looking over your orbship I remembered what the orbital stations reminded me of—Uldan shipbuilding. Maybe they will take the orbship for one of theirs and won't attack it, at least right away. You can try exploring the planet. A preliminary analysis indicated that it was habitable."

The flash drive contained two viruses which Brainiac had for a snack. Lumara shrugged without a hint of embarrassment and made no further comment. We found them, so good for us. And if we hadn't, that'd be our problem. You just can't trust fox princesses these days.

"The planet is located in a remote area of Confederate space," Brainiac brought up a map of Galactogon and marked the new coordinates with a dot. "That territory is considered highly insecure."

"Everyone thinks so but the truth is that it hasn't been explored much," the princess spoke up. "Too many asteroid fields and stray comets. Anyway, we are quits now, so I can begin to explore your ship with a clear conscience. Snake, are you the boss here? Show me your possessions. I'm giddy from curiosity…"

Lumara disappeared with the snake in *Warlock*'s reactor compartment, while I had to go attend my audience with the emperor.

It didn't take long and not much happened. A crowd of high-born foxes thanked me for my active participation in defending Galactogon from the horrible foe. The emperor complained that I was a pirate who wasted his potential for personal gain and donated a legendary suit to my cause. I wanted to begin to object that I already had one and demand a different prize, but I remembered Eunice. In a week at most she would be back in the game. A good suit of armor wouldn't be wasted.

Back on my ship, I took Brainiac's advice to hightail it off the Delvian capital. It was obvious that we wouldn't be able to get the pedestal at the moment—I had been taken to the audience under heavy guard assigned by Lumara.

Sebastian and Tryd also came back with nothing. As soon as they left orbship, they were politely surrounded and firmly asked to return. Aalor had really mucked it up for us, apprising the Delvians of the nature of my visit. And although Sebastian was used to such welcomes, Tryd took to this treatment poorly. He really wanted to visit his childhood haunts.

"Tower, this is Orbship *Warlock* requesting take off."

"Takeoff is prohibited. There are no free corridors. Please await your turn. Waiting time is five hours."

My justified indignation caused the waiting time to grow by another two hours.

After some digging, Stan explained that the delay was due

to the preparations for the coming battle. More than one and a half thousand game guilds had already gathered in the system under the leadership of Ash in order to repel the attack on the Delvians. The central system of the foxes was choked by a jumble of cruisers, frigates and carracks, and leaving the planet through this throng was unrealistic. The players had started a countdown on one of their sites and now only three hours remained before the slaughter began.

And I had no doubt that it would be just that, a slaughter. Having collected so many players with expensive toys in one place, the people running Galactogon were simply obliged to reduce all their ships by one class. If anything, to encourage their subscribers to buy new levels and upgrades, injecting even more money into the venture. I really had to get out of here urgently!

"Can I sit with you a bit? Oh that's nice. Snake, climb on out here—I have questions for you!" Lumara reappeared after an hour. Busily walking around the ship, the princess was starting to issue orders as if she were in her palace.

"Shouldn't you go join your family? The battle is going to start soon," I asked in a bad humor, looking at the screen. The live broadcast was showing the preparations being made. The well-coordinated maneuvers of the giant ships were being narrated by military NPCs. Galactogon was about to broadcast a main event.

"They can do it without me," Lumara said dismissively and handed me the flash drive. "I almost forgot! The people from the Hansa Corporation asked me to tell you that they have solved your riddle. I looked through the files—do you really think that such a system can exist? It looks completely absurd! Such an ideal balance should have collapsed long ago due to the stars losing mass!"

Brainiac ate several more viruses and allowed me to see Hansa's findings. There was indeed an approach vector to the hypothetical planet; however, it depended on the mass of the stars and the type and size of the planet itself. The Precians had built a mathematical model with various trajectories dependent on these variables.

I did not bother trying to persuade Lumara. The planet was far from the center of the Delvian Empire—a flight-time of seven minutes in hyperspace or three hours at full throttle. When the battle is over, I'll go and check out what kind of present Sebastian gave me in exchange for joining my crew.

"By the way, Filte has been notified that you are here," Lumara finished examining one of the blocks and suddenly turned to Tryd. Her voice dripped with venom. "She asked if she could see you, but my father did not allow it. I am on his side—prison mines are no places for conjugal visits. I hope your little wife won't die there soon!"

Tryd's already scarred face grew even more terrifying, his one eye drilling into the princess as if wishing to bore a hole in her. The princess grinned wickedly, enjoying his reaction, and went back to the snake. This smelled like a mission if I've smelled missions before, and I had better shake the pirate down for it.

"What is she talking about?" Sebastian joined instantly,

hoping to unwind the backstory.

"Twenty years ago, my family was sentenced to a life of penal service in the mines," Tryd could control his body but not his voice, which trembled and stuttered. "My children perished, but my wife survives. The mines of Zarvalus are truly a terrible place. No one returns alive."

"Two systems from Larsi. Zarvalus is a shlir mining planet. The terrain features do not allow the use of harvesters, so prisoners are used to extract the ore," Stan helpfully clarified some points for me.

"What were they sentenced for?" Sebastian said tremulously but Tryd did not reply. He said nothing and only a nervous tick on his face betrayed the Delvian's internal struggle. Stan could not find out the reason for such a harsh sentence. Either this mission was rare or other players avoided it. But I had already made up my mind. Since a mission like this landed in my lap, I should accept it, do it and then Tryd would owe me.

"Princess, allow me to offer you a deal. I will trade you the Lara crystal in exchange for Tryd's wife. You already have the pedestal and the Corsican can give you the third component of the Vengeance. Then the Delvians will have a powerful weapon."

"You do not understand what you are asking," Lumara looked up from her conversation with the snake. "And it has nothing to do with the crystal. First find out who you are going to release! This is not some innocent, honest woman who was sent to the mine for the sins of her husband! She is a monster. One of our own, born on our planet!"

"Nonetheless," I said—whoever this Delvian was, it seemed

wrong to back down, "the crystal in exchange for the woman."

The princess didn't say anything, perhaps trying to understand my motives. The NPC was unaware of a player's logic and didn't understand that her standard algorithms had no hope of accounting for it. Having stumbled across a hidden mission, I could think of nothing but how to reunite the Delvian with his beloved spouse. Hell, were my feelings for Eunice spurring me on here?

Lumara gave up trying to understand what drove me and finally pushed a few buttons on her PDA, displaying information about the crimes committed by Tryd's wife—on *Warlock*'s screens! When the hell had she found time to link to Brainiac?! The file was full of photographs of mangled bodies.

"Read it," she nodded. Everyone, including Tryd, glued themselves to the screen. Filta turned out to be an interesting lady—for more than ten years she ruled the Larsi underworld. She dealt ruthlessly with anyone who objected or was unwilling to do business with her. Her mob killed both them and their families, sparing neither children, not the elderly. And Filta always took part in the massacre. In the end, her organizations was responsible for over a hundred murders. During the trial, the emperor had to put Filta in protective custody to protect her from mob justice. The Delvian people sought to tear the criminal apart with their bare hands.

"Do you really want to free this monster?" Lumara asked once again.

"My offer stands. The crystal in exchange for Filta," I answered firmly. There was no mention of Tryd in the article and

---

I grew curious why Filta and their children had been sent to the mines, but the pirate was spared.

"I need to discuss this with my father." The princess turned and quickly left the ship. She didn't like my decision much, but the crystal was too valuable to refuse.

"I want to hear your version of the story, Tryd." I began to pressure the pirate, but it did no good. The Delvian did not react. Having glanced at the text provided by Lumara, Tryd looked away from the screen. Neither I, nor Sebastian could get him to open up and as a result, by the time Lumara returned, I hadn't learned anything new. Tryd turned out to be a minor character in this scenario.

"Father agrees," said Lumara. "We will hand over Filta in five hours. She will be delivered directly to the ship. And I will take the crystal now. Father authorized me to do so."

The Delvian had forgotten about her desire to be an ordinary person and now looked like a high-born princess who had come down to communicate with the rabble. A proudly upturned chin, a look full of contempt, her words spoken thrown through his fangs—one could not learn this unless one were born into it.

It was sad to look at her change of masks. In the end, nothing mattered—in a few hours the Delvians would cease to exist anyway. There is no need to spend time and resources to build relationships with them, as well as worry that I gave them an item from the Vengeance set. The crystal won't do anything anyway. Brainiac knew our coordinates. Once the Zatrathi get done here, I'll swoop in and pick up the crystal and the pedestal while I'm at it from among the ruins. For now, let the Delvians enjoy the good deal they think they've made.

The transfer of the crystal occurred without incident. Lumara pulled out a manipulator and took hold of the Lara in midair, not allowing it to touch the ground. Without speaking another word, the princess left the ship, presenting me with negative rapport with her empire. A −2000 all at once.

As soon as the hatch closed behind her, two things happened:

First, Tryd finally deigned to open his mouth.

"You shouldn't have done that, Surgeon. We haven't seen each other in twenty years. It's not possible to preserve one's sanity in the mines of Zarvalus. If you expect me to be grateful for the return of a crazed vegetable who was once my spouse, you are mistaken."

Second, an extremely unpleasant message flashed before my eyes:

By giving the Lara crystal to the Delvians, you have betrayed the interests of the Precian Empire. Mission failed: Seeking Vengeance. Your relations with the Precian Empire have deteriorated. Current rapport: −100,000. You are no longer allowed to enter Precian space. Exception: You may visit the Precian trade planet Belket once a day for a period of not more than five hours.

"Why didn't you say anything earlier? Were you waiting for me to just give up the crystal?" I asked, pursing my lips in disappointment. I didn't expect this at all, nor that I would fail my mission as a result. I still had plans for the Precians. Well at least I still had my relationship with Hansa. No one wanted to strip a player of the opportunity to spend huge money on game features. "Let's deal with the problems as they come. They will bring your wife and then we can see how she is and figure out what we'll do with her. Now I want to hear your version of the story, and don't you dare stonewall me again. I'll kick you off this ship in an instant!"

The tension had gotten to me. I was almost yelling at Tryd and it did him some good. The pirate cracked.

"There is nothing to tell! We met about thirty years ago. She was already running her gang," Tryd began telling his story with displeasure. "I had just finished serving on the Corsican's ship and came back here…"

I learned some more about the leader of the Jolly Roger. The Corsican recruited various creatures to his crew, but the conditions for all were the same: twenty years before the mast. One could not leave earlier. Tryd sweated out his term, but did not wish to renew—the pirate decided to return home. Once in the capital, Tryd drew the attention of the underworld, some of whom decided to squeeze him a bit. The gangsters began hunting Tryd, but the fox was no blunderer. Twenty years of service as a marine aboard a pirate ship meant that Tryd started his own hunt after the gangsters, raising his social status among the capital's authorities. Filta and her gang wanted the head of the former pirate and came to him. A shootout broke out and turned into the melee in which Tryd received his wounds. Filta was an experienced fighter, but she lost in the end. Tryd did not turn her over to the authorities. Instead, he continued his activities, clearing Larsi of the gangsters, but not touching Filta's people. A few years later they had twins and lived a happy life. But when the Corsican broke with Hilvar, Tryd re-entered the service and was sent to Daphark. The pirate had no choice—you can't persuade characters like Hilvar. Filta visited her husband a couple of times, but refused to move to Daphark. Soon thereafter, she was arrested and sent to the mines with the children who had by that time joined their gang. Tryd remained uninvolved. He was just a former pirate who had cleared the capital of the gangsters and kept his little wife from committing further bloody madness.

"Twenty years is too long a time," finished Tryd. "I have only memories left."

"Once again, we'll wait and make our decision when the time comes," I snapped.

"Attention!" Brainiac wedged into the conversation. "The battle with the Zatrathi has begun!"

The cruisers had arranged themselves into a giant sphere and simultaneously flashed from our screens—the defense fleet had entered hyperspace. The broadcast picture changed. Thousands of spiky vessels gleamed in the darkness of space— the Zatrathi armada was terrifying in size: Four orbital stations, twenty flying fortresses and five hundred cruisers. A summary of both fleets appeared on the screen. Seven thousand cruisers had set out against the enemy. The NPCs hadn't provided their Grand Arbiters, citing the need to protect the planets, but in general, the balance was in favor of the players.

The screen shifted from the Zatrathi fleet to an empty stretch of space where the players' fleet was about to appear. Ash was leading his forces into battle.

CHAPTER NINE

"**G**alactogon's defenders have adopted a spherical formation," the first commentator began.

"The sphere's a conservative set-up that will allow our boys to defend their flanks at the expense of tactical flexibility," added the second. "Well-equipped cruisers take the brunt of the attack, providing cover for the frigates and fighters to operate in the channels that open up."

"The cruisers inside the sphere meanwhile are ready to reinforce a faltering ally on the sphere's periphery, while repair docks in the heart of the sphere can repair various types of damage in a matter of hours."

"The defenders are well prepared. Here's hoping they smash the visitors. But what about the Zatrathi anyway? What can you say about their formation, Ray?"

"Absolute chaos, in my opinion. I can't make heads or tails of it, Bobby. Four orbital stations arranged in a pyramid holding the center of the field. That's logical enough. But it's absolute chaos on the wings. Flying fortresses and cruisers spaced unevenly. Gaps everywhere. Our boys will have a field day choosing which direction to attack from. Let's turn to our 3D simulator for a better view…"

The camera zoomed out, shrinking the Zatrathi fleet and six arrows appeared indicating the players' possible approaches of attack.

"A well-coordinated strike along one of the channels should take down ten to fifty cruisers and three flying fortresses," the commentators continued their analysis. "A foolhardy decision by the away team."

I would have agreed with the talking heads if not for one 'but.' Experience showed that standard approaches didn't work against the Zatrathi. The six 'corridors' that seemed like an oversight were most likely—like with a probability of 99%—traps.

"Cap'n, something is off here," said the snake with worry in her voice. "Why would there be empty space between the orbital stations? That space is well protected, so there's no reason to leave it empty."

Indeed, fighters, frigates, and even several carracks were flitting between the cruisers and flying fortresses, while the space inside the pyramid of orbital stations remained vacant. Brainiac zoomed in, but there was nothing there. Just stars in the darkness of ordinary space.

"The stars are twinkling," noticed Tryd. "Stars don't twinkle in space."

Indeed, outside the pyramid the stars were constant points of light, whereas inside the pyramid, they flickered and varied the intensity of their glow.

Earning his claim to his name, Brainiac said authoritatively:

"The flickering of stars is an optical illusion observed on planets with an atmosphere, which refracts the rays of light, causing the flickering. There should be no such distortion in space."

"Could this distortion be caused by a cloaking field concealing some dangerous object?"

"Cloaking technology capable of concealing an object of such dimensions has not been developed yet," Brainiac began to object, but I cut him off:

"Since when are you an expert in Zatrathi technology? Let's assume the worst—there is something between the orbital stations and it is hidden by a cloak. Brainiac, how would we go about confirming or refuting this assumption?"

"Why can't we simply sit here and enjoy the show, eh Cap'n?" the snake hissed. "Here we are, perfectly comfortable, watching the broadcast along with millions of others. And everyone is happy. Everyone but you. What exactly is there to look for here? Are there options I wasn't aware of?"

"If there is indeed a cloaking field there, it would have to be generated by several devices pointed at one another and mounted on various ships around the cloaked area. We can zoom in on the orbital stations. What you need to look for are identical, codirectional antennae or projectors capable of transmitting information or energy. Moreover, they must be aligned with all the other stations in order to form a single closed contour around the empty space. Now do you understand what you need to look for?"

"Eh, you're fantasizing a bit, but I get the general gist," the snake nodded, ducking back into the orbship's hull.

It took Brainiac ten seconds to run and analysis and display the results on the screens.

"If the assumption is true, then these attachments point at each other and could form a cloaking field. As you can see, the coverage area is huge—the Zatrathi could hide up to five orbital stations in there, depending on the location and designs of their spires."

"Five orbitals or one immense titan we haven't seen yet," I added to Brainiac's analysis.

"If it's a single vessel, then the Zatrathi formation begins to make sense," Tryd jumped in. "They are spaced apart. Even if a supernova goes off in their midst, the ships won't collide with one another. While, the sphere that the defenders have set up will fall apart."

I started looking for ways to contact Ash as the commentators piped up again:

"The two sides have yet to fire a single shot. Everyone is eagerly waiting for the action to begin. Who will blink first? The players or the Zatrathi? The defenders or the invaders? Good or evil?"

"I believe that the home side will make the first move. Look over there—three cruisers have moved forward."

"Indeed. The cruisers *Guldan*, *Striking Boar* and *Colossus* are leaving the sphere's protection. The Zatrathi are also coming to life. Several squadrons of interceptors are approaching the defenders' vanguard. Something is about to happen…"

The babbling commentators turned out to be right—
something really did happen. The giant cannon Kiddo had
installed on her cruiser was not unique. The bows of the three
advancing cruisers flared brightly, each generating a miniature
sun that rushed in the direction of the Zatrathi. The space battle
had officially begun.

The Zatrathi ships surged forward like dogs let off their
leashes. The screen flashed for a few moments—the Zatrathi
had added torpedoes to the mix. The broadcast operator
corrected something and the picture came back.

Three small suns flew leisurely, as if aware of their
invincibility, in the direction of the enemy fleet. About half of the
torpedoes slammed into them, doing nothing but increasing their
size. I had seen this already when Kiddo had fired her Yamato
cannon. Unlike *Alexandria*, however, these three cruisers had to
expend all their energy on the one shot and were now being
towed back into the sphere. They could no longer move on their
own.

"They have fired into the space between the orbital
stations," Brainiac calculated the projectile's trajectories. "Two
minutes until impact."

Like us, Ash had taken note of the orbital stations'
formation. Although, perhaps, this shot into space was also
prompted by intelligence—surely the players had tracked the
Zatrathi fleet's movements. Whatever it was, Ash played his
trumps immediately, forcing the Zatrathi to reveal their hand.

The only problem was that the invaders had no intention of

doing so.

Three alien cruisers, located closest to the orbital stations, moved to intercept the incoming suns. Unlike in reality, which operates under such physical concepts as invariant mass, inertia, and other basic concepts of Newtonian physics, the huge Galactogon vessels could immediately reach a considerable speed. Of course, this greatly complicated the lives of novice or low-income players, but Galactogon was oriented towards a solvent population that could acquire and maintain a carrack or even a cruiser. Who is going to think it fun to chase an enemy at a snail's pace? Who is going to pay money for such entertainment? Who wants to wait an hour for their ship to accelerate? No one—and therefore the cruisers needed a decent rate of acceleration. So, Galactogon had to break its own rules, ignoring some of the laws of physics. Interceptors, of course, remained the fastest and most maneuverable ships in the game, but they surpassed other vessels only slightly.

"An incredible act of sacrifice!" the commentators admired the Zatrathi move. "Three-zero, the defenders are out in front! If it goes on like this, there'll be nothing left of the Zatrathi in short order. Nothing but the mystery of why everyone was so scared of them…"

The huge Zatrathi vessels entered the path of the manmade suns, taking the brunt of the blow. Ash immediately sent the next three cruisers, but now the invaders made their move: All twenty flying fortresses moved forward. Once again, the screen went white with a blinding light, and the Zatrathi fired a second wave of torpedoes. Only this time, instead of aiming at the mini-suns, the torpedoes raced straight at the sphere of the defenders.

"The Zatrathi reply seems a bit underwhelming to me. Those look like quite ordinary torpedoes."

"Let's not jump to conclusions, Ray. I imagine the torpedoes are a diversionary move. But let's give them a chance. Let's see how the defenders deal with the torpedoes."

The players' cruisers erupted in a flickering of point defense cannons as they began to clear the incoming missiles. One couldn't call the point defense effective, however, as several hundred torpedoes still broke through. It seemed the Zatrathi had come up with the same idea as Hansa and shielded their torpedoes. The few moments that the players wasted switching from beam cannons to EM cannons, cost the defenders' sphere three cruisers. The Zatrathi torpedoes turned them into flickering crates of loot. Reinforcements instantly plugged up the hole in the defense but the score was tied now. Three-three.

"Cap'n, those flying fortresses have lined up very oddly. There is some kind of plan to their formation. The outer circle is a regular pentagon, the inner circle is a heptagon, and there's one lone ship in the center. It looks a bit too threatening."

Ash was already reacting to the enemy's reorganization. Three cruisers, which were hiding within the sphere, again slipped forward. A couple of seconds of aiming—and three more suns rushed at the three flying fortresses. Ash sought to disrupt the Zatrathi formation even as they were reorganizing themselves. The screen blinked again and a salvo of torpedoes went flying from the players' fleet in the wake of the miniature suns.

The Zatrathi acted as before: Three cruisers came out to intercept the suns, while the rest of their fleet handled the torpedoes in a matter of seconds. And that included the advanced, shielded ones too. The invaders' gunners were quite a bit better than the humans in this regard. Finally the Zatrathi completed their reorganization and halted, as if waiting for something. Everyone watched the central ship anxiously as if it was about to do something decisive.

Only Ash refused to wait idly. He ordered his fleet to move forward as one. Several nimble interceptors dashed ahead of the sphere—but were immediately culled by the Zatrathi beam cannons. The sides had not exchanged broadsides of plasma up to this point. There had been six 'suns,' there had been waves of torpedoes and constant reorganization—but that was it for the space battle so far. The spectacle I expected—a disorder of ships blasting each other with all the energy they had on board— had not come to pass.

Nor would it. It was now the Zatrathi' turn. The defenders' armada had closed half the distance to the Zatrathi fleet when they finally figured out what the main weapon was. While everyone was gawking at the flying fortresses and wondering why they were lined up in such a strange order, the orbital stations entered the battle. The cloaking field vanished, revealing a true nightmare—a ship, several times larger than anything anyone had ever seen before. Cosmetically, the monster was not much different from the rest of the invaders' vessels: Its shapeless central hull was studded with countless spires and blisters. Despite any official title for this vessel, the gamers in the

---

raid chat immediately began to refer to it as the Womb: the Zatrathi flagship, the one that surely carried their queen.

A wall of text began to scroll past my eyes, full of new lore and explanations. I angrily brushed the text aside, wishing to see what would happen next. The bow of the Womb flared up, and a pillar of plasma rushed at the flying fortresses. A second later, a miniature supernova had formed where the flagship had been. The shields of the ships on the outer and inner perimeters began to flicker—acting like deflectors that directed the released energy at the players. The explosion of the Womb was so intense that, despite their shields, the flying fortresses closest to it evaporated in a matter of seconds, feeding the ball of fusion. The outer perimeter lasted a little longer—long enough to divert most of the energy towards the moving sphere.

Ash had no time to react. The plasma moved at an incredible speed, covering the distance to the players in a matter of moments. The cruisers' shields shimmered, holding the pressure, but in addition to the energy wave, the Zatrathi attack also included immense hunks of shrapnel which had been parts of their own ships. Half melted in the blast and now carried by it at an insane pace, the shrapnel pierced the players' ships without even noticing their armor. As the shield generators failed, the energy wave did the rest, tearing apart the armada. The players' organized formation disappeared into a fiery whirlwind and gave way to a terse notification that lingered on the screen for a few seconds before fading:

Defenders' losses: 100%.

The fiery whirlwind did not last long—in this, the devs had respected the laws of physics. Nor did the broadcast end there, allowing its audience to look out over the expanse of shimmering crates where all the players' ships had been. More than ten thousand cruisers had taken part in the battle. I could hardly imagine how much treasure now littered the battlefield. The Zatrathi armada, meanwhile, moved onward. The camera began to follow the invaders, but then the screen rippled and the shot changed back to the studio with the commentators. If someone had expected a subtle contest of maneuver and strategy, they were quite mistaken.

"This is…Well, I haven't the words to describe what has just happened," the commentator managed. "This is just indescribable!"

"The defenders have suffered an incredible defeat," his partner echoed. "Such an enormous fleet destroyed by a single shot! I think we should consult with our experts."

A Delvian in a military uniform appeared on screen.

"The main mistake here was the arrangement of forces. The humans gathered all their ships in one point in contravention of all astro-naval doctrine!"

"The main mistake here was advancing towards the enemy!" The broadcast cut to the next expert in line. "If they had stayed in place, they would have had more time to take evasive action."

"The main mistake here was that the Delvians trusted the humans at all!" The third expert was also the most outraged. "They should not have done so! Now we have nothing left to do

---

but flee! We must evacuate our home planet!"

As the Delvian general spoke these words, sirens started howling wistfully in the background. Something was going on in the capital and I began to worry.

"Cap'n, you need to look at this," the snake said in shock. One of the screens showed a familiar picture: The Delvian capital, its skyscrapers and skyhooks stretching like stalactites into the heavens—where, suddenly, a dark dot had appeared. At first a point, tiny, small—with every second the dark dot grew larger and larger untll I could make out the silhouette of a Grand Arbiter, burning, plummeting. Part of the ship's hull was missing and is it grew larger I could make out holes blasted by beam cannons and a dozen burning portions that had clearly taken direct hits from torpedoes and were now billowing black smoke into the atmosphere. The Delvian Grand Arbiter was falling right onto our heads.

"Brainiac, blast off!" I yelled, taking the Delvian Emperor's gift out of my inventory. "Tryd, put this armor suit on this instant!"

How glad I am that dressing in-game is instantaneous. As soon as the fox disappeared inside his metal case, Brainiac opened the throttle to full. The insane acceleration pressed us into our seats but the armor suits coped with the load. Other ships were blasting off all around us, trying to get out from under the falling Arbiter. Not everyone as lucky as we were. *Warlock*'s upgraded engines allowed Brainiac to zoom off along a safe vector, while the majority of those around us started taking hits from the falling debris. The earth shook from the impact and the part of the city that the ship fell on simply ceased to exist. The shockwave swept away the surrounding areas, increasing the area of destruction, as fires broke out in its wake.

"Brainiac, what's going on? Why has the Arbiter crashed?"

"The orbital station is falling. Two more Grand Arbiters have fallen onto the planet. The Zatrathi have entered the Larsi system."

New mission available: Delvian Dunkirk. The Zatrathi have attacked the Delvian capital. The civilian population has suffered immense casualties. Evacuate as many Delvians as possible. Reward—variable, depending on the number and rank of those you have rescued.

"How many creatures can we fit onboard?" Having read the quest description, I began to calculate our chances.

"Two in the cabin and three in the medbay," the snake's answer was disappointing. "The rest will be flattened if we enter hyperspace or climb too fast. Shall we assist the evacuation?"

"Don't forget that you promised Filta a spot," said Tryd.

"I doubt they'll give her to us now," I said to the pirate's disappointment. "I don't think the Delvians have time for any of that now."

"Then let's go get her ourselves. The Zatrathi won't bother with Zarvalus for a long time yet."

Oh how quickly Tryd changed his tune from the 'it's been twenty years' blues to the 'I ain't leaving the system without her' rag.

"They won't let us on Zarvalus," Brainiac injected. "We have no permission."

"So we'll get it!" There was no stopping Tryd. "The palace has only been partly destroyed. We'll fly there, rescue the emperor and scram! He is definitely still alive; otherwise everyone would already be yelling about his death. People like him are protected from everything."

The pirate's idea was so nuts that I agreed without hesitation.

"Brainiac, set course for the palace. We will..." I did not have time to finish. The snake, as always, played the spoilsport:

"Multiple bandits incoming at eight o'clock. Zatrathi interceptors."

"Gunner, don't let them close in on us! Brainiac, fly low and get the marine ready. There's bound to be some rubble to clear in the palace. Sebastian, you're coming with us. Here's your chance to plunder a real bona fide imperial residence. What is going on up above in orbit?"

"Two flying fortresses have entered the system and are systematically destroying the Delvian defenses. The Grand Arbiters cannot stop them."

Mission updated: A Pirate I was Meant to be. Part 1. 55 of 150 interceptors destroyed.

Planetside, the Zatrathi interceptors burned like any other ships. My upgraded beam cannons worked wonders, destroying the fighters two at a time. Of course, I had to strain and fly as close as possible to the ground, trying to get lost in the smoke, fires and ruins of the Grand Arbiter. It would be foolish to fly in the open with such a numerous enemy around. Then again, no one was looking for me. The Zatrathi were entirely occupied in shooting down the armada of transports, frigates and all the other available vessels that had rushed to evacuate the Delvians. The low-flying orbship which packed a hefty punch did not interest them much.

We reached our location almost without incident—we had more trouble with the Arbiter debris exploding all around us than the Zatrathi. Brainiac found a small burned out hollow and settled us in it, deploying the rhinoceros. We followed behind our tank, wondering at the remains of the palace. The Arbiter had fallen very unfortunately—her bow had buried the main building and the nearby buildings under it, leaving only the complex's wings intact. Fires raged all around, spewing up clouds of black smoke and completely hiding us from the Zatrathi. The marine bellowed, drawing my attention—he had managed to break through the hull of the Grand Arbiter. There were no other ways to the throne room.

"Sebastian, you know what to do," I reminded the thief and turned to Brainiac: "Send a dozen droids to haul the loot. Download all the data from the Arbiter, while you're at it. That information could be very important to us."

I hadn't had a chance to rummage around an Arbiter before and I was certain that any player would jump at the chance. The loot could be sold, but so could any data and video Brainiac uncovered. Stan confirmed my guess that there were no public sources about the Arbiters' technical specifications. Players were supposed to take it for granted that there was no way of fighting an Arbiter. And though Kiddo had already shattered this axiom— that was more as a result of good luck than study and logic. Not my preferred M.O.

"This way!" shouted Tryd, following right behind the rhinoceros. Inside, the Arbiter was no different than other NPC vessels. Bulkheads, decks, communications, corridors. There were some loot crates here and there—the Delvian crew had heroically gone down with their ship. I opened one of them—a C-class blaster, a Delvian fleet ensign's uniform and a couple hunks of elo. Nothing to write home about, in other words.

"We need a retaining wall," Tryd nodded at a large pile of rubble. The rhinoceros again smashed through the Arbiter's hull and was now resting, noisily drawing in air through his flared nostrils. His red-hot horn would not cool down, and it was becoming apparent that the marine would not be able to go on at this pace. He needed a rest, for which we had no time.

"Brainiac, send five droids here," I ordered, and having thought a bit, added: "And withdraw the rhino. Look to his recovery."

The rhino, obeying the computer's orders, began to plod back to the orbship. Five droids immediately took his place, awaiting my instructions.

"One here, the other there, the third carries the stones and the other two on the flanks," Tryd took command, understanding how to take apart the collapse better than me. I surrendered the reins and the robots got to work. Just as the work was starting in earnest a beam fell from above. We would have been flattened if it weren't for one of the droids heroically saving us just in time, by wedging himself between the beam and a ledge. The beam crushed the robot's upper torso, but his legs locked and kept the beam from crushing us too. I had to call a replacement droid and listen to the snake's moans about how tired she was of droid repair work.

Tryd went on working with more caution—the droids built columns of stones to support the ceiling and strengthened the cleared areas. Then Sebastian came back all in tears—there was nothing of value on the Arbiter. Meanwhile, Brainiac could not connect to the internal network as it had burned out. Everything that could have been stolen had been destroyed from the impact. The captain's deck was completely gone—the beam cannons had incinerated it entirely. On the whole, it was a mess. My plan of looting the Arbiter was foiled entirely.

"There is a passage here!" Tryd yelped happily. "I knew that the throne room would survive! It was built to last eons!"

Without waiting for permission, the pirate ducked into the dark corridor. My spatial scanner generated a model of the throne room in my HUD. In my opinion, the word 'survive' was quite a stretch. The columns, like the partitions, were broken. The ceiling had not collapsed solely because two long beams had come together cross-wise, retaining the slumping arch. The droids rushed in after Tryd, illuminating the hall with their searchlights. It was littered with flickering crates of loot. It seems that the Arbiter crashed during an emergency meeting convened in the wake of the players' defeat.

"This way! There are survivors here!" yelled Tryd, sweeping

the throne with his searchlight. The pirate's assumption had been correct—the Delvian emperor really was alive. A familiar spherical shield—like the one used by the Precian adviser—flickered around him, retaining a massive piece of wreckage and saving the emperor from inevitable death. Brainiac instantly ran an analysis: The shield was actually keeping the entire hall from collapsing, bearing the load of the failing structure. I really didn't like that second part—the emperor was clearly doomed. We had no means of preventing the collapse ourselves and his majesty's energy would run out sooner or later anyway. So far we had been in the room for less than a minute and the Delvian Emperor had already swapped out two powercells.

He seemed to say something to us, but sound only traveled through the shield in one direction. And it wasn't our own. Yet the Delvian refused to resign himself to his fate and nodded meaningfully into the darkness. The spotlight illuminated a pile of rocks. The emperor nodded and began gesturing for us to pick apart the heap. I set the droids to work on it and in short order they recovered Lumara from the collapse. The princess was unconscious but alive. Burned, broken, with a crushed paw, she looked more like a zombie than a living creature. Sebastian rushed to her, activating his armor suit's first aid unit. The princess's ragged breathing finally leveled off after he applied some injections and coagulating foam to her wounds.

"She has to be returned to the orbship as soon as possible!" Sebastian cobbled together an improvised stretcher and gently placed the princess on it. "The injections will only suffice for a few minutes!"

"Do it. Snake, see to our patient. Do whatever you have to, to ensure she survives. Tryd, do you understand what the emperor is saying?"

The emperor was babbling excitedly, waving his paws, pointing in one direction and then another. A lot of his gestures were directed at our feet. My lip reading skills aren't very good to begin with and when the lips to be read belong to an anthropomorphic fox—well, forget it...Luckily, Tryd came to my aid.

"Slow down, Your Highness, and repeat what you're saying. I could only understand half."

The emperor repeated his flailing. The pirate only grunted, from time to time trying to scratch his ear. It's hard to scratch anything in an armor suit, and yet his reflexes insisted on trying. Tryd looked extremely concerned.

"Nod if what I say is accurate. The general idea is: The Zatrathi have destroyed the planetary spirit and removed its binding from all the creatures on the planet. All of the Delvian aristocracy was in this throne room and, instead of being reborn, they have now departed into eternity. Did I understand you correctly?"

The emperor nodded, continuing his story. He was asking us to get Lumara out of here—since she was now the only heir to the throne. Alviaan had been one of many gathered in the hall.

"The princess is safe," Sebastian returned fairly quickly. "The snake is taking care of her. What should we do?"

"Locate the pedestal and the crystal. We have to take them with us."

IN SEARCH OF THE ULDANS

"They are not here," Tryd translated the words of the emperor. "They have been transferred to a secret treasure vault on one of the outer systems."

"In that case, I want access codes and coordinates," I said. "Otherwise, I will leave Lumara here and that'll be the end of the dynasty. I'm a pirate, not a white knight. My time costs money."

"We need access codes to Zarvalus too. I need to rescue Filta," Tryd recalled his mission, forcing the emperor to grin. Due to the armor suit, he had not recognized the pirate, assuming that he was a player. My relations with the emperor immediately collapsed—the Delvian in his bubble let us know what he thought of our demands. The only problem was he had no choice in the matter:

"Brainiac, halt the princess's treatment. We won't be taking her with us after all. The emperor does not agree to our terms."

You should have seen the look on the emperor's face. His gaze was so withering, so filled with loathing, that I began to feel a bit uncomfortable. Meanwhile, his spherical shield ebbed a few centimeters—the emperor had forgotten to replace his powercell. Dust began to sift down from the ceiling, accompanied by an eerie creaking sound, and I began to think that we had overplayed our hand, but then the Delvian gave up. His daughter's life was more important to him than access to the treasure vault. The Zatrathi might reach it first anyway.

While Tryd was recording the access codes, I walked around the hall. Leaving unopened loot crates is not how I like to do business. Sebastian pried the surviving paintings from the wall and snatched up the imperial silverware and crockery—

anything that could be sold. The droids hauled their loads back and forth, dragging everything back to the cargo holds. I had nothing to brag about. The Delvians who showed up for the emergency meeting had brought nothing: neither money, nor powercells nor raq. There wasn't so much as a blaster around here. Each crate contained one or two items from the nobles' wardrobe. Colorful, pompous, but completely useless items of clothing. Sebastian glanced at the clothes and sighed—selling these at a normal price was unlikely.

"The emperor says that he has two powercells remaining," said Tryd. "We have a minute. After that the entire place will collapse. He is begging us to save his daughter. We have to deliver her to the planet Nadin in Confederate space. There is a Delvian colony on that planet. They will know what to do with her. I have received the access codes and coordinates we need. What are we doing?"

"We're getting the hell out of here, that's what!" I ordered and then reassured the emperor: "We will do everything to save Lumara. Sebastian, wrap it up! Leave that tapestry! You won't get it out in one piece anyway."

As soon as we returned to the ship, we heard a terrible crash as the passage behind us caved in. The Delvian emperor had ended his in-game existence and joined his fallen subjects.

Mourn oh Delvians! Your emperor has died his final death!

All trade deals with the Delvian Empire are suspended for the duration of the mourning period (30 calendar days). −50%

IN SEARCH OF THE ULDANS

XP gained for all players who belong to the Delvian Empire for the duration of the mourning period (30 calendar days). −1000 Rapport with the Delvian Empire for all players.

If a legitimate heir to the throne does not appear in three days, the Delvian Empire will be dissolved!

"Brainiac, what's the situation in the system?"

"The Zatrathi are destroying all defenses. Their flying fortresses have taken up positions at the edges of the system and are in complete control of the space between them. We won't be able to get out unnoticed."

"Cap'n, we need to get off the planet at least. There are interceptors, scouts and even frigates all over the place. I've made sure to save up of course, but we won't have enough elo for everyone. We should hide ourselves and lie low until the Zatrathi are done here. Surely they'll move on in a few days."

My engineer's arguments made sense, but I had a nagging thought that we were missing something.

"Brainiac, let me see the current Zatrathi deployment in the system."

Two flying fortress had taken up positions at opposite edges of the system, while a blizzard of red dots scurried around the system in no discernable order. Every so often, a few blue dots would sally from the planets or moons and be instantly smothered by the Zatrathi red ships. The flying fortresses didn't even have to do anything—the interceptors and frigates handled their jobs easily. I frowned, trying to grasp what struck me as odd about this picture, but the snake was the first to speak up. The engineer's voice was almost hysterical:

"Cap'n, I take it all back—we need to get out of here this instant! Look at the outermost planet!"

I could understand where the snake was coming from—Larsi's star system had just lost one of its planets. Granted it was uninhabited and not very large, but the speed with which the Zatrathi turned the giant rock into nothing was frightened. Especially since it wasn't clear how they did it: There had been neither explosions, nor harvesters. The planet merely lit up, flashed and vanished.

"They have moved on to the next one!" The engineer yelled as another planet began to sparkle. It was several times larger than the previous one, so the invaders had to spend a little more time on it—about ten seconds. We were it next. Brainiac changed the feed—displaying now how all the Zatrathi ships zoomed off from the planet's surface and fled as far from it as possible. They had done the work of disrupting the evacuation and it was now time to use their weapon of mass destruction.

"Brainiac, emergency blastoff!" I ordered, noticing how the air outside was beginning to sparkle artificially. Even my ship's hull seemed to be radiating, as if infected by the imminent planetary collapse.

"Cap'n, they're disrupting the intermolecular bonds!" The engineer sounded aghast at what was happening. "I cannot even imagine how this can be done on a planetary scale. It's unnatural!"

Brainiac didn't have to be told twice. The ship's computer was well aware of the danger and the engines roared to maximum thrust.

IN SEARCH OF THE ULDANS

"We are being painted with a disruptor beam," despite the confusion and excitement, the snake went on performing her role. "We are being locked on by EM cannons. Torpedoes straight ahead. Multiple bandits incoming. Our hull's molecular lattice is stabilizing again."

The screen went black—the capital of the Delvian Empire disappeared from the face of Galactogon, giving way to the vacuum of space. I abruptly changed course, turning right around 180 degrees—the orbship allowed me to pull of maneuvers like this. The Zatrathi did not expect such agility from us and for several suspenseful seconds no one shot at us. We flew right through the spot where the planet had just been. There wasn't even any residual radiation remaining—it was like the planet had been transported to another dimension.

"Full throttle, Brainiac!" We had only one way out. To run. To run like we had never run before, squeezing everything there was out of our ship. A dozen plasma beams struck us—the Zatrathi had come to. Yet our shields held, absorbing the damage, while the interceptors circled around, making me anxious. The gunner, who had been ordered to fire at will while still planetside, was trying his best to clear the area around us, but there were simply too many enemies. They flitted all around us, trying to take out our shields with their beam cannons. At least they weren't equipped with torpedoes and their AI algorithms did not allow them to ram us. Had there been at least one player among the Zatrathi, he would have attempted a head-on collision a long time ago, turning his ship into an improvised torpedo.

"We are leaving the system. The hyperdrive disruptor beam is still on us. One of the flying fortresses is following us. Flight time is four hours twenty two minutes."

Brainiac's report was both accurate and bleak. Our improved engines allowed us to move with incredible speed when it came to other players, but for the Zatrathi, it was quite pedestrian. The interceptors had a short range and after a while they began to fall back—yet one of the system's sentries remained in pursuit, approaching inexorably.

"Can we squeeze more speed out of her somehow?" I asked, hoping against hope.

"It won't work, Cap'n," the snake answered grimly. "We are already squeezing her for all she has. I have more news. We only have enough energy for four more hours. We've used too much on our shields. I've stopped all my projects and even turned off the lights everywhere, but it won't help. We have four hours before we become jetsam...We've been hit! Shields to stern!"

The Zatrathi chasing us did not have concerns about their energy use and opened up from their main cannons. The distance between us reduced the shot's power, so our shields managed, but then we were hit a second time. And another time. And another. Every fifteen seconds, the flying fortress emitted a huge blast of plasma which went flying in our direction at an incredible speed. The shields coped with the damage, but our energy reserves dropped markedly after each shot.

"Asteroid fields, planets, other systems? Is there anything at all around us?" My hand was already reaching for the self-destruct button, yet I refused to accept defeat. I could not lose Lumara and Tryd.

"There is nothing at all. If we fly straight. We will not get anywhere. There is nothing ahead."

"I have a suggestion, Captain," Sebastian spoke up. The thief did this extremely rarely, so I decided to listen. "Remember, when I told you about the system of two stars? The one where the pirates were mining raq? It takes about three hours to fly to it, and our energy should hold out. All we need to do is adjust our course a bit. Hansa has given us its mathematical model—let's try it out."

"And that's assuming that the Zatrathi want to take us alive," said the snake. "This new vector is almost ninety degrees' deviation from our current trajectory. I won't have enough energy to deal with a direct hit. The way we're going, at least we're managing to get away. If we turn, we'll be in the palms of their hands for a full thirty seconds. That's two shots' worth. Who wants to die? Raise your hand."

No one was willing to raise anything, but Sebastian was right—the system of two stars at least gave us a chance.

"Brainiac, if we turn around completely, how long before we reach the Zatrathi?"

The computer paused processing my query and then answered:

"Taking into account their speed and ours, twenty seconds."

"Snake, how can we survive a direct hit from their main cannon?"

"We can't," the snake muttered. "That's why it's the main

cannon—it's hard to defend yourself against it. We won't survive."

I was about to despair when a mad thought occurred to me. I have already tried this tactic on the Qualians and it had worked well. Why not try it on the Zatrathi too?"

"Brainiac, what frequency do the Zatrathi use to communicate?"

"They are using a closed channel. The encryption changes daily. I won't be able to listen in."

"I don't want to hear them. I need them to hear me. Is there anything you can do?"

"To broadcast a message, yes. They do use a common channel, but it is completely silent. I have been monitoring it."

Brainiac analyzed the information downloaded from the Zatrathi—when it came to the invaders, my ship computer had already become the most knowledgeable entity in Galactogon.

"Wonderful! What language do they speak?"

"At the moment, we know of two. The common tongue which is spoken by their engineers and warriors, and the Uldan language, which the brainworm spoke. Perhaps there are others, but I have not detected any."

"Let's use Uldan in that case. What was the name of the captain of the flying fortress we sank?"

"Individual Zatrathi have no names. They use ordinal numbers that vary depending on their ranks and positions. The captain's number was 53-4477. It is unclear whether this remains that individual's number after his capture. The Zatrathi avoid identifying themselves as much as they can. There are no names, nor surnames—only sequences of numbers transmitted to each other."

"We will have to risk it," I snapped. "Send this: 'Urgent message to the captain! The queen mother is in peril! I repeat, the queen mother is in peril! This information has been provided by 53-4477!'"

The guttural Uldan language filled the ether. Fifteen seconds passed without any fire from our pursuers. Then twenty. Then one minute. There was still no shot and yet our enemies did not even think of falling behind, closing the distance between us click by click.

"What peril could possibly threaten *her*?" came the Zatrathi reply a few minutes later. Also in Uldan. It turns out that the Zatrathi ship captains are all brainworms that speak Uldan. However, I was more pleased at the mere fact that there was a response at all. If the queen, for example, controlled her subjects entirely, she would have understood very well that the captured captain had not told us anything of the kind. Since there is dialog, the Zatrathi are not as omnipotent as they seem. They are not a single organism like the Vraxis for instance. It's much easier to wage war against a society of individuals—even if it seems that society had decided to destroy all life in the galaxy.

"I cannot speak of this over a public channel. There are spies everywhere! I request permission to dock."

"There are no spies among us!" the Zatrathi responded.

"Are you sure about that? Humans boarded a flying fortress and captured its captain. How could they have done so without a traitor? Either we meet and I tell you about the peril to the queen mother or our chase will go on. You will not receive the information I have in that case."

"Slow down," ordered the Zatrathi. "We are prepared to parley."

The flying fortress began to slow down. I was not deceived: It would take the fortress half a minute to regain its former speed, so in the long run I had no chance. Here, the second part of my plan came into effect:

"Brainiac, slow down but maintain distance. Let's see what they will do."

The enemy ship stopped completely, disgorging its swarm of interceptors. I didn't take any defensive measures when the fighters reached us. The Zatrathi needed information and they would now play their role of negotiating until the last. That said, I had no doubts that they would attack us as soon as our deal was done. That was just their AI invader script.

"We are coming in—keep your interceptors out of our way," I announced, slowly moving to the flying fortress. The fighters obediently laid off, but stayed close. We were now so close to the Zatrathi that their ship had filled our entire field of view. A hatch opened in the hull inviting us inside. I flew up flush to the fortress until we were inside their cannons range. The Zatrathi did not try using tractor beams, presumably so as not to scare off their catch. On the whole, it seemed like the first talks between a player and the Zatrathi were about to take place. The only hitch was the player!

"Go!" I ordered, and *Warlock* plunged downward abruptly, the engines blasting at full thrust. At the same time, the orbship shook as all the torpedoes we had on board flew at the fortress. The moment of confusion cost the flying fortress its main cannon—half the torpedoes reached their target, turning the fortress's bow into a beautiful formless mass. The fighters rushed after me, but it was too late—I had a head start of five seconds at least.

"They're coming around," Brainiac went on tracking the Zatrathi' maneuvers. Unlike the orbship, the huge fortress could not change course so abruptly. The behemoth had to build up speed first and then come around in a circle, losing time. By the time they had returned to pursuing us, the distance between us had returned to what it had been much earlier. Assuming that we wouldn't have to deal with shielding attacks, the snake calculated that we had four hours before they caught us.

Three hours later I kept repeating the same words in my head: Damn persistent ghouls! The flying fortress squeezed everything it had, trying to crush the bug that had tricked it. It seems I'd really pissed off her brainworm captain. All the games I'd ever played limited their NPCs to a certain area or level, which they could not leave. The Zatrathi it seems were entirely unaffected by such constraints. They moved measuredly after us in total radio silence.

"Our system is up ahead," said Brainiac. "Flight time is two minutes. I am picking up a cruiser, seven frigates and forty fighters."

The confederate thieves' guild had scrambled its forces to defend its mining interests. And yet, the radios remained silent. As soon as I got within range, torpedoes came flying at me. It was crude but effective—I couldn't really do anything against twenty missiles. I had to dramatically change course, skirting the new obstacle. The pirates were about to chase me when they saw the Zatrathi. The flying fortress grew on their screens, like a demon rising from the depths of hell. A small point grew into a giant ship traveling at a blistering pace. Another wave of torpedoes came flying past us this time—the thieves didn't feel like sharing their raq with anyone. Their job was simple—protect their mining planet to the last.

"I have calculated the stellar and planetary masses and input the data into Hansa's mathematical model. A safe approach vector has been calculated. We can head inward." The orbship began to shake as soon as we approached the system. The combined gravity well of two stars was utter chaos. The Zatrathi, meanwhile, followed on our heels, paying the thieves' guild no attention. They destroyed the torpedoes and simply flew through the thieves, ramming and scattering them like bowling pins. The frigates and fighters were destroyed on the spot. The cruiser survived the blow but began to spin and shut down. I could only guess what damage this had done to the Zatrathi—we could make out dents in their hull, quite big ones actually, but they did not reduce their speed. I guess losing half their spires wasn't such a big deal.

There wasn't really a solar system as such here—merely three celestial bodies arranged along one line. Two huge stars were playing tug-of-war with a planet between them. The stars' gravities were equal, however, and the planet remained in place. The orbship was shaking as if we were driving along a bumpy road. We couldn't reduce speed so I had to endure the potholes of the cosmic hinterlands.

"Brainiac, why are we shaking so much? Are we on the right course?"

"I don't know myself, Cap'n. The calculations seem accurate, if the model is correct and the coordinates are right, then we should make it through—but the buffeting is very strong indeed. I don't understand how anyone can actually conduct mining operations in this place. By the way, the Zatrathi are falling behind. Maybe there's good reason for it?"

"Reduce speed and move forward more slowly."

"We have to back up!" Brainiac protested, over me. "If we fly straight, we will enter one of the stars' gravity wells! Hansa made an error in their calculations—their model does not work! I've already had to adjust one engine and brake. We are being pulled forward! In a couple of minutes it will be irreversible!"

"Sebastian!" I looked at the Qualian helplessly. "You said that in theory you know the way to the planet! It's your time to shine! You've gotta save us!"

"Only in theory. I already said that information about this is stored..." Sebastian began to make excuses, but I interrupted him:

"You tell Brainiac everything you know this instant! You have thirty seconds!"

"Cap'n, the Zatrathi have stopped completely. They seem puzzled by what we have in mind. They have launched their fighters."

A series of lines blinked past us on our screens—the

Zatrathi interceptors had launched so quickly that they miscalculated and overshot us. None made it back—one half hurled into one star, braking too late, while the other half turned around and opened their throttles to full, trying to overcome the stars' pull. But they didn't have enough power and as a result remained in one place straining against the inevitable.

"Head a bit left, Brainiac," Sebastian took command. "I overheard a phrase several times: Bow to the red sun. That's the further one over there."

"Does 'bow' mean to pass at a tangent? Or perhaps use it as a slingshot and accelerate?" Not understanding the enigmatic phrase, the snake began trying to prompt the thief to provide the correct trajectory.

"How do I know?!" the thief snapped. "Every captain would repeat this one phrase like some kind of mantra. We can make it up as we go along."

"Hand me that microphone!" Tryd angrily pushed Sebastian away from the control panel. "You bunch of good-for-nothings! Do you want to dump us all into the star? I'd prefer to live a little longer. Brainiac, switch to frequency 42: 'This is Grizzled Fox. Mayday! Mayday! Code 5-22-89.'"

"What does that mean?" Everyone looked at the pirate with puzzlement. Even the snake stuck her head into the captain's cabin.

"I have a stake here," Tryd admitted reluctantly. "Every month, I get five percent of their mining income. What are you ogling me for? How would I live on Daphark without money?"

"Grizzled Fox?" a surprised voice spoke up on the speakers.

"Where have you been this past decade? What can I do for you? Uh…Where are you anyway? Are you calling from the ball or that, uh, space squid…?"

"Let's do this later, Kurt. I'm on the ball, I need a pass. The space squid should be scrapped. Feed it to the stars."

"Five percent and the pass is yours." Seeing his chance, Kurt began to bargain.

"You want to bargain at time like this? Well, I got something too," Tryd was not about to surrender just like that. "Be a good boy and I'll give you an access code for Zarvalus. The emperor gave it to me personally!"

"Bull!"

"Balls to your bull! In a minute it will be too late to find out whether it's bull or not. Give me that pass or you'll regret it."

"Tryd, you know that I'll find you even if they bury you," muttered Kurt angrily. "Sending an encrypted transmission. You still remember our passwords, right?"

"Encrypted data received," Brainiac confirmed the transfer. Kurt did everything quickly—the thieves were clearly accustomed to sharing the approach vectors.

"The pass phrase for decryption is: 'A pirate's ass grows hairier with every wave!' The first letter is capitalized, the rest are lowercase. No space and no commas. And an exclamation mark at the end," Tryd sat back down in his chair and exhaled heavily: "What would you do without me, you bunch of landlubbers? It seems like these days Hilvar recruits whoever—not like before. Oh, those were the days…"

Tryd went on muttering something, but he had

accomplished the most important thing. Brainiac processed the data, generated the vectors, figured out what 'bowing to the star' meant and banked about as hard as the orbship could muster. The approach to the planet was located on the other side of the system.

"The Zatrathi are still following us," the snake reported. As soon as we moved a little further from the system in order to turn around and go around it, the flying fortress immediately rushed in pursuit. Perhaps the enemy decided that we were fleeing the gravitational chaos.

"And now we shall bow to the sun," Brainiac explained the enigmatic maneuver. The particularities of the orbship did not allow us to perform a 'bow,' as such, but we got the general gist: The ship flies up to the sun and ducks, exposing its upper side to the star. After that the ship levels off, plunges a little toward the star and then the engine comes on. The force of gravity from the neighboring star and the full thrust combine and the ship is released from captivity and falls directly to the planet. How you take off from the planet later is a different question entirely. At the moment, it was more important to escape the Zatrathi. Since the orbship could fly in any direction, she didn't have to bow to anyone. All we had to do was reach the right point in the trajectory and then open the throttle.

"I have understood the reason for these cunning maneuvers," the snake declared, when we entered the corridor. "There are strange gravitational eddies here. If we had flown in a straight line, we would have...Well, actually, that right there is exactly what would have happened..."

IN SEARCH OF THE ULDANS

The flying fortress had followed us carelessly. It seems the captain had grown tired of messing about and decided to get rid of the irritating insect (i.e. us) once and for all. First he wasted three waves of torpedoes—pumping them straight into the nearest star. Meanwhile, the plasma from his beam cannons behaved so oddly that there was no point in shooting—the probability of hitting anything was close to zero. Another wave of fighters rushed right behind us and ran into the very eddy the engineer had mentioned. The ships flattened into pancakes, as if crushed by a hydraulic press. As a result, the brainworm made an important decision—to simply ram into us and crush us into non-existence. They only problem was the brainworm's lack of brains. For when we turned the engines to full and rushed in a circle, the flying fortress swept past us, missing us by literally a few kilometers! Incredibly close in cosmic terms, but still a miss. The last I saw of it, it formed a black silhouette against a backdrop of the red giant.

Mission accomplished! A Pirate I was Meant to be. Part 1. Requirements: 556 of 150 interceptors destroyed; 1 of 1 flying fortresses destroyed

New title acquired! Grizzled Duelist You are the first to destroy a Zatrathi flying fortress in open battle. Speak to any imperial representative to receive your reward from the emperor himself.

The entire squadron aboard the Zatrathi ship had counted toward Hilvar's mission requirements. The old pirate should be pleased at the interceptor killcount.

"Follow corridor 2-12," Kurt said. "I've taken care of everything planetside. Our boys won't shoot you down. Now how about those access codes for Zarvalus, eh Tryd?"

"We'll land, have a drink and then talk," Tryd didn't like having to pay up on the spot and tried to buy time. Perhaps, Kurt would sell the codes instantly and then the Delvians would change them...Although, what am I talking about? The Delvians are gone and the heir to their throne is in my medbay. In fact, I held all the trumps and simply needed to play them properly.

The thieves' guild had built a base almost in the center of the lifeless planet. It turned out that there were no raq deposits here at all: Instead, the entire planet was one big hunk of raq. Everywhere I looked, lines of harvesters were stripping away the crust layer by layer, sending the mined ore away from the blaring suns and into the planet's interior. And here, all kinds of work was under way. The raq was sorted and shipped to transports, of which we counted about twenty in orbit.

"Five percent?" I looked at Tryd in surprise. "Every month? And you were living in a ruined skyscraper on Daphark? Why, you could have bought the whole planet!"

"And then what? What would I do with it?" the pirate waved dismissively. "Serving aboard the Corsican's ship is hard and dangerous—but the rewards are handsome indeed. He looks out for his men. Anyway, this planet is mine—I discovered it. Open the hatch. We have visitors."

I was unable to identify Kurt's race—his description was hidden and he himself was encased in an armor suit. Tryd exchanged a few words with him and the thieves began to load up *Warlock* with elo and raq. Tryd decided to share part of his monthly profit.

"Our paths must diverge here," said Tryd, as soon as the loading was complete. "You must go on without me."

"And Filta?" I asked.

"What do you have to do with her? She is my wife, my empire, my people. I am accustomed to taking care of my business on my own, without relying on others. Your reward for pulling me out of Daphark has been loaded into your ship's holds. I am not interested in the princess. What else do you want? Kurt will ensure you can leave the system peacefully. And you're now officially a pirate. Come see me when you've made a name for yourself, small fry. You already know where to find me. I'll stay here for a bit. Once you've reached the third step, come by and we can chat. Now piss off. The locals get nervous when outsiders show up at this base. And they tend to keep their fingers on their triggers anyway so…"

New mission available: Pirate University. Complete the three parts of the A Pirate I was Meant to be mission and seek out Tryd on the planet Volta.

"I'll give you a tip—head for the Delvian treasure planet. The boys and I will pay that place a visit tomorrow. If I get that crystal and pedestal before you do, you will have to work really hard to get them back."

"You're not worried that the Zatrathi now know about this

system? You've seen yourself what they can do to a planet!"

"Knowing and doing are different things. The Delvian Empire also knew about us, and what? Where is the empire now?"

"The empire didn't know how to destroy planets," I retorted.

"To destroy the planet, you need to get to it first. The stars won't allow it. The transports can jump while still in the gravity wells. You can enter hyperspace safely from here, and disruptor beams won't work from the system's periphery. Let the Zatrathi come if they like. We'll see who wins. I don't think that they managed to destroy that planet from afar. Otherwise they wouldn't have scrambled their fighters to intervene with the evacuation back on Larsi."

It was pointless to argue with the pirate—he had an answer for anything I said. Kurt gave me the coordinates to the pocket of space where I could enter hyperspace and warned that if we want to return here, we had better warn him in advance. He even gave me his comm number. For, he explained, when strange ships appear near the planet, the operating procedure is to shoot first and ask questions later. Assuring him that I would never even think of showing up here without letting him know first, I took my armor suit back from Tryd and left the planet of raq under the watchful eye of the guards. Sebastian demonstrated a large piece of raq he had thoughtfully filched while we were planetside. Ordinary harvesters mine the metal in regular rectangular blocks, somewhat resembling gold bars, so I had never seen a hunk like this before. I will have to try and offer it to Eine—what if it's a rarity?

There was no one in the treasure planet system. Neither a

Grand Arbiter nor an orbital station, but nor could we identify a habitable planet. The system consisted of two chunks of rock devoid of minerals spinning around a fading star. In fact, the system was so unremarkable that if I had not known about the Delvian treasury, I would have flown right by. I landed at the indicated coordinates and only once we were on the surface, Brainiac reported that there was an EM cannon aimed at us. The Delvians maintained their watch, even in the absence of an emperor.

"Brainiac, pass me the access code," I ordered.

When I entered the code, another EM cannon joined the first. If the Delvians accepted the code, their reaction sure was strange.

"You are using the Emperor's personal code," the guard's voice finally came on the air. "The emperor is dead! The Delvian Empire is no more!"

So that's what it is! The Delvian Emperor had set us up! He had known that he would die and that the treasury's guards would grow suspicious when someone else used his code.

"Of course," I replied. "I personally saw the emperor's demise. He was the one who gave me his access code. And the Delvian Empire is not gone—I carry on board with me Lumara, the younger princess. She is hurt and is receiving treatment. I need to deliver her and most of the treasury to the planet Nadin. Send inspectors. They can board my ship and see for themselves that I'm telling the truth."

The head of the treasury did not take my word for it. Three warriors boarded *Warlock*, conducted a standard check and knelt before the medbay. The snake only flipped the lid off the cocoon for a couple of moments, revealing Lumara. The princess's condition was stable, but still serious. In the confusion of the last few hours, we could not afford to spend energy on treating her.

"Praise to the creators, all is not lost!" A note of relief sounded in the treasure keeper's voice. "What do you want to pick up?"

"Anything that fits into my ship," I replied, hiding my bewilderment. I did not like the Delvian's question.

"The treasury access protocol, adopted many millennia ago, prohibits handing over objects to outsiders who do not know these objects' names. I can only give you what you name. You are allowed to make three errors, after which we will be obliged to destroy you. The princess is alive and therefore, our watch continues. We can't let the empire down."

I muted the comm and swore hard—remembering the emperor with an unkind word. He had known all along! He had known that we could only get the crystal and the pedestal. The protocol would not allow us access to anything else. I decided to approach from another angle.

"The pirates know about your current location. As far as I know, tomorrow they plan to raid the treasury and plunder it clean."

"It won't work," the keeper's voice exuded confidence. "You may be a pirate but you are also transporting the princess, so I will speak openly with you: The process of moving has already begun—the current base's location has been compromised and the treasury will be moved to another secret location. Only the emperor and his entourage know where. When Lumara ascends to the throne, she will be apprised of our coordinates. You have only twenty minutes to name the items you need, after which protocol number twenty-two comes into force. Then, we will be forced to destroy you in order to protect the imperial property entrusted to our care. The treasury's location must remain secret, even if there is no emperor. The Delvian Empire shall be reborn!"

"Okay. In that case, I want the Lara crystal and the Lora pedestal first," I gave up, deciding to act consistently. It was necessary to call the crystal and pedestal by their official names—the treasury guards turned out to be real pedants in this respect.

"Brainiac, two questions. First, can we survive a direct shot from the cannons aimed at us? Second, is it possible to bring Lumara back to consciousness for a couple of minutes?"

"Allow me, Cap'n," the snake, as usual, spoke for my crew. "There are two EM cannons from a cruiser aimed at us. Not only will they fry our electronics, they'll fry anything that has a powercell in it. I could be wrong of course, but in addition to the EM cannons, there are also beam cannons here, no doubt from a cruiser as well. As a result, I strongly advise you against getting involved in an open confrontation. However, you are in charge of course, so you decide. As for the second question, I can only keep Lumara alive. She will have to be taken to a hospital in order to recuperate or even revive temporarily. Her injuries are very severe."

I sighed heavily—the treasury which seemed like such a tasty morsel turned out to be nothing more than a place where I could regain the Vengeance items. Taking into account the guards' scrupulousness, it is extremely doubtful that randomly named objects will be in the treasury. However, it was worth the risk—at least one item's name was familiar to me. I would have to check:

"I need the Lora coupler unit."

"We do not have such an item. You have named an invalid item. You have two such errors remaining."

"How about an Uldan coordinate converter?" I ventured a second time.

"We do not have such an item. This is the second error. We will be forced to destroy you at the third one—despite the fact that you have the princess on board. The honor of the empire is more precious than its uncrowned empress."

"Brainiac, let's go," I ordered, realizing the futility of trying to gain anything here. Lumara's mission seemed more promising to me than messing with the treasury guards. "Set course for Qirlats. It's time to pay a visit to Hilvar. I hope the pirates will have a place in the hospital for our guest."

CHAPTER TEN

IRLATS' CUSTOMS OFFICERS TURNED MY SHIP UPSIDE DOWN, trying to find prohibited items or law enforcement officials. But this did not bother me because at the beginning of the inspection I received a call from Vargen on my PDA.

"Surgeon, you owe me half a million!" the leader of Liberium yelled into my ear instead of a greeting.

"Vargen, have you been eating funny mushrooms again?" I had to pick up my jaw to answer him.

"Give me your number, I will call you and we can arrange a meeting."

"Are you losing your grip on reality? You should be talking to your therapist instead of bothering me! What do I owe you half a million for?" I tried my best to stay calm.

"For the viceroy!" Vargen growled. "He was killed. Our contract is terminated, and you owe me!"

"You can go to hell with your power trip!" I got angry. "I wasn't the one who destroyed the Delvian planet and the viceroy. If you that's all you have to say, then bye. I don't have time for your nonsense!"

"You're on my blacklist!" yelled Vargen, before I hung up. My surprise at this call was so great that I did not immediately pay attention to the inspectors. They had finished scouring my ship and their boss had now stopped before me with his paw outstretched—I had to pay for my stay on the planet. Looking at the customs officers' shifty eyes, I did not hold back and doubled the required amount. His eyes flashed with a satisfied glint and one of the inspectors called the dispatcher:

"*Warlock* is clear. Assign her service level three. Call the medical team. There is a casualty on board."

Such are the benefits of investing in your local bureaucracy— suddenly everyone starts treating you by the rules. Not like someone with power or money, but exactly as people should treat each other in a normal society. And if I hadn't paid up, he could have entered the offended bureaucrat's mode, finding all kinds of problems with trifles like the hull's paint job and the health code compliance to demonstrate his might and my helplessness.

Seeing customs out, I sat down in a chair and stared at a blank screen. I was still worked up about Vargen's call. How is it that the head of an enormous guild has it in for me so bad? We had a deal that he would leave me alone in exchange for me keeping my destruction of Aalor under wraps. What got into him? For all my pride, I perfectly understood that as far as Liberium was concerned, I was only one of millions of players. It seemed stupid and useless to waste time on me. Accordingly, the reason had to be something else.

IN SEARCH OF THE ULDANS

"Stan, what's going on in the forums right now?"

I needed to get to the bottom of this. Stan did not waste much time and began to send me the choicest tidbits. The more I read, the merrier I became. The battle of Larsi or, as it had already been dubbed, the 'Delvian Slaughter,' cost the players ten thousand ships. All of them were supposed to be reborn in their graveyards, but the Zatrathi had other plans. The shot from the Womb dispelled their bindings, forcing the vessels to respawn in the closest graveyard. This didn't seem like a big deal however. The players just need to agree to the respawn sequence and in a week all the ships would return to service. Except there was this one catch: The Zatrathi planted a flying fortress in the system with the graveyard. With Olympic serenity the fortress was now shooting down any ship that emerged from the graveyard, sending it back and knocking another class off to boot. More than a hundred of the lucky few to go first in the respawn order had already paid the price and were now flaming on the forums about the devs' injustice, demanding that the Galactogon admins compensate them for their hard-earned in-game property. The only response to all this was an official statement reiterating that all of these events fit the scenario and were covered by the end user agreement. If the players wanted their ships back, they would need to think more carefully about their tactics and not just try to break through head on.

But in general, it was a nice move on the part of the devs—get all the top guilds in one place, send them all to the graveyard and force the players to deal with those who had not participated in the battle—those whom they ordinarily paid no attention to.

That is, guilds outside the top hundred. Those who played the game for the sake of fun instead of profit. It should be interesting to see the vast amounts of money being paid for ships to the smaller guilds. In my view, there is no other way to defeat the Zatrathi fortress guarding the graveyard and liberate the ships of the top guilds.

Vargen and his guild had participated in the Delvian Slaughter. At the moment, he as well as Aalor and a dozen other captains were frantically trying to solve this new problem. It is not surprising that Vargen turned on me when he realized that he had thrown a tidy sum to the wind. I guess I got under his skin. I certainly wasn't in any trouble legally. I had respected our contract. I had not said anything to anyone, and the fact that the viceroy had died a martyr's death alongside all the other Delvians was not my concern—I would not be returning the money. Vargen only has himself to blame. Maybe next time he'll think twice before taking on work from the bullies.

"We need a day to normalize all the vital processes and restore the patient's health. I think you understand that the quality of our work depends on the level of equipment used," said one of the medical team responding to the call from the customs officers. I would have to make a generous contribution to the development of medical facilities on Qirlats if I was truly worried about Lumara's fate. Just to make sure that she would be treated like a patient, and not as a piece of programmed meat.

Having settled all the formalities, I finally headed to Hilvar's place. As I had already learned from Tryd, the Pyrrhenian was so fond of flying that small rooms made him depressed. That said, the pirate had mentioned that this was perhaps due to Hilvar's endless wanderings around the vastness of space. The Corsican did not like it when his aides left the ship.

"What do you seek, brother of the vast dark sea?" My way was blocked by a Precian guard. There was none of the attitude I had encountered last time when visiting Hilvar with Kiddo. The guard recognized my pirate status and addressed me as one of his mates.

"I wish to see Hilvar, to report on a mission I have completed for him," I replied, peering into the darkness above me. Somewhere up there, among the rafters, sat one of the chief pirates of Galactogon. The answer did not take long in coming.

"So you showed up after all?" The Pyrrhenians' raspy voice sounded from above. "I have heard about your business, I have heard a lot about it indeed. The boss of the Red Rose has been begging, threatening and badgering anyone who will listen: He wants either your head or your ship. Hehe! It was a joy to see Derval's face so shiny with anger. It's been a long time since I've enjoyed a sight like that. Come in, let's talk. Let there be light!"

The room flashed to life with a million crystal chandeliers. My lord! From outside, Hilvar's residence looked like an ordinary barn, but when the lights came on I saw that this interior could compete with the most luxurious palaces of Earth's elite. Everything was gold, stucco, heavy velvet, marble and leather. I grinned—the pirate adored everything expensive and rich-looking, but his taste was woeful.

The Pyrrhenian gracefully settled in one of the settees and a mechanical arm immediately popped out of its back and began massaging his barrel-shaped body. Another couple of robots began to serve the table, not forgetting to feed the owner—even in such trifling matters, Hilvar strove to appear regal. The ensuing sight, however, was stupid and ridiculous.

"I wish to congratulate you, young scallywag. Tryd has already apprised me of your success," Hilvar began as soon as I sat down across from him. The robots weren't putting anything in my mouth, so I had to be old fashioned and use my own hands. "Then again, Tryd overdid it and overstepped his authority. He will be punished. He had no right to grant you the title of pirate. Yet what is done is done. You are one of us now—not only in arms, but in spirit. Pissing off those gutter rats in the Red Rose is well worth it. You have pleased me, yes you have!"

You have received a new title: Pirate Rank I.

"Now you and I can do business. Even though you are still wet behind the ears, you have much promise. So why not start right away? How are you handling my mission? What is your progress?"

Without even trying to hide my smile, I handed Hilvar a report of the ships I had destroyed. It was pleasant to watch the pirate's mocking, squinting eyes gradually round themselves off in respect. Hilvar even held the paper up to the light as if to check whether the report was fake or not or perhaps hoping to see some small print. But everything was real and official. I hadn't simply completed the mission—I had far exceeded what had been asked of me.

IN SEARCH OF THE ULDANS

Hilvar, meanwhile, played it cool. A false negligence drove the look of respect from his face and the pirate returned the sheet to me with a careless grin as if nothing special had happened.

"Well, let us assume that you coped with the first mission. Now you need to make a choice about what path you wish to take in your pirate career. Will you pillage in space or work planetside? Attack ships or search for hidden treasures. Which is your pirate's dream?"

"What's the difference?" I asked, curious. Hilvar began to explain:

"A space pirate captures ships and plunders their holds. This is how he makes his living. If you choose this path, you will be taught the weak points of all known ship classes, how to approach them better, how to board them and how to effectively block self-detonation. You, humans, are frequently guilty of this. The only catch is I won't be the one teaching you all this. To follow this path you will need to meet Brax, the Corsican's right hand man. Those two are the authorities on space piracy."

Hilvar's face flinched as he mentioned the Corsican.

"As for planetary pirates, that would be my line of work. Here you will be taught the art of finding extraordinary items in ordinary places. I will train you to look for treasuries, the hiding places used by the ancients. I will also introduce you to contacts who can help you sell stolen goods. It should be said that no one is going to forbid you from pirating ships. Selecting one path does not block access to the second. It's all about specialization. Some things will be easier, some things more difficult."

"The Corsican, of course, is an important individual, but I

enjoyed my experience stealing information and looking for stories about the ancients. It is unlikely that I will find the answers to my questions in space," I nixed one of my own earlier fantasies, trying to get Hilvar to open up as much as possible. There was no doubt which of the two options just proposed was the right one for me.

"Questions?" Hilvar swallowed the bait.

"Yes, several in fact. The first has been eating at me for a long time already. What is the KRIEG? Everyone but me seems to know and no one wants to talk about it. Second, what happened to the Uldans and where did they go? Their underdeveloped foes are alive and well, while the winged angels have not been seen for ninety thousand years. It doesn't add up. Third, why do two great pirates who have fought side by side for many decades hate each other? And fourth, when will I finally get my next mission? My armor's starting to rust from sitting in one place."

Hilvar thought for a long time, wrinkling his forehead amusingly and moving his lips. He mumbled something to himself and squeamishly twitched his upper lip when he remembered the Corsican, but switched over to another question and fell quiet again. At long last the Pyrrhenian made his decision:

"I cannot help you with your first question. I do not know anything about any KRIEG. I do know some things about the Uldans, but you will have to earn that knowledge. I don't really wish to recall the Corsican. It has been ten years...But if you are really curious, then there will be a mission for you: Go to the planet Shurtan in the Delvian Empire. There was once a pirate base there. Search it and find a video recording that was made on Galactic Date 3.33300.42. On that day, the Corsican accused me of treason and discharged me dishonorably from his service—all over something I had allegedly said on Galactogon's public airwaves. Watch it yourself and you will understand everything...For my own part, I wish to say that the Corsican was wrong. Sometimes I think that he himself invented everything to set me up! I guess he was afraid of the competition, hehe...Anyway, if you do this you will cease to be small fry. I will assign you the third rank right away. And if you don't do it...Well, you'll go on like everyone else. That's it! I have no more time for your idle conversations. Get out of here and don't come back without that recording!"

New mission available: In Search of Cause. Description: Find the video recording and find out what happened between Hilvar and the Corsican. Reward for completion: Automatic completion of A Pirate I was Meant to be. Part 3. In case of failure, you will have access to mission A Pirate I was Meant to be. Part 2.

The light went out, and Hilvar ascended up to his chambers, grabbing a tray of fruit on his way. I had to make my way out in utter darkness. As I left the place, the bodyguards returned me my armor suit and escorted me back to *Warlock*. Hilvar wanted me to start the mission immediately, so I figured we'd blast off right away—yet it was not to be. The bribe had ensured that Lumara was counted as one of my crew and now I couldn't leave the planet until my crew member had been treated. This gave me a day to calmly catch my breath and sort everything out.

The first thing I did was pull out the tablet I'd lawfully filched from the ex-viceroy of Belket (RIP). In the confusion of the last hours, I hadn't had the time to examine it.

"Sebastian, can you hack this?"

"Are you kidding me?" The thief twirled the device in his hands. "It's a standard interface. I'll need five minutes, five-and-a-half tops. Consider it done!"

The Qualian began pouring over the tablet and all I could do was grin at his grumbling: "Who does this like that? Oh users—the weakest link! What? The password is '12345?!' Amazing! I have the same combination on my luggage!" No more than a minute later Sebastian handed me the unlocked device with a sour face. His was that universal chagrin at having missed an opportunity to have a good old hacking time. It was not often that my thief got a chance to show off his skills as a black hat.

An inspection of the tablet's contents uncovered a lot of interesting tidbits. First of all, the viceroy was a real asshole who had been spying for several guilds at once. His list of clients included the already familiar Fighting Breed, which had sold the viceroy the Zatrathi equipment several times. Considering the fact that the imperial adviser had an iron grip on the scout that I had captured, no one else had Zatrathi parts. Consequently, the adviser must have had his own distribution channel for the counterfeit goods. But there was no mention of this in the documents on the tablet. I also found several working drawings of country villas. One of the projects was worked out in such detail that there was no doubt—the viceroy had decided to rebuild his family home bigger and better than ever. Sebastian looked at the floor plans and strongly recommended I find this mansion and pay its basement a visit—the viceroy had clearly designed three secret rooms to store expensive things. It would be negligent of me to leave all those goods to the traitor's widow. And, besides, the viceroy kept an archive of compromising information on his compatriots. There was no mention of the adviser in it naturally, but there were several memorable names that I had happened across among the Precians. Nothing too serious, but no one would praise them if this information were published. That was the extent of the useful info. There were no further passwords, nor bills, nor secret locations, nor contacts—the viceroy kept all that in his mind. The various trading accounts were not interesting to me as I understood little of them. But I knew who could use them. Having ordered Brainiac to erase all the personal information, I decided to sell the tablet to Kiddo or Gammon, depending on the higher bid. *Money, money, money. Must be funny in the rich man's world...*

Later in the evening, when the boredom was starting to get to me, the medics brought back Lumara. She looked all right—her various cybernetics had been removed, exposing terrible scars where her wounds had been. The Delvian did as the doctors instructed, silently and obediently, but otherwise did not react to anything going on around her.

"We have treated her physically," said the doctor who delivered the princess. "You will have to deal with her trauma yourself. There are no psychologists on this planet. Your Delvian thinks that she is a princess, the heir to the Delvian Empire, so we had to sedate her. I can recommend a good doctor. He performs an excellent lobotomy. Your crew member will forget all about her imaginary personality and generally keep her mouth shut. Obedience, politeness, joy—everything a gentleman requires."

"That's okay." The prospect of having a personal slave in Galactogon did not entice me. "When will her sedatives wear off?"

"Just inject her with this. She'll come to right away." The doctor handed me a vial and then hesitated, shifting from one foot to the other. "Since there are no further questions, perhaps we should be on our way. We have a lot of work, lots of patients."

I smiled and counted off several thousand more credits for the doctor. My 'gratitude' for the time spent on me, the attention and quality of services provided. Or simply the fact that I have too much money in my game account. By the way! An interesting thought—do the NPCs know my account balance? I don't recall them fawning over me like this before I became a billionaire…

"Surgeon?!" Lumara fixed on me in surprise as soon as the snake administered the injection. "What am I doing here? Where is my father?"

I silently pointed at the screen where Brainiac broadcast our recent adventures. The downing of the Arbiter, our excursion to the palace, the conversation with the emperor, the rescue of the princess, the collapse. Lumara watched in silence and only the tears streaming down her cheeks spoke of her inner turmoil.

"What are you planning to do with me, pirate?" Lumara regained her composure amazingly quickly. The free-spirit princess was gone, giving way to a true imperial heiress. The Delvian understood and accepted the burden of her responsibility and she decided to bear this burden with her head held high.

I could understand her attitude towards me. As a potential,

future empress, she already behaved in accordance with my current status of 'enemy of the Delvian Empire.'

"Your father instructed me to take you to Nadin," I shrugged. "If I don't do this in three days, the Delvian Empire will cease to exist."

"So what's the holdup?!" Lumara replied indignantly. "Why are we still not in space?"

"Because we haven't agreed on my compensation," I said. "We have already discussed who I am. I'm no hero. I'm a pirate. Others can rescue princesses from the clutches of space dragons. My own skin is dearer to me."

"You're just like my brother," the Delvian whispered. "He also thinks only about himself."

"Let's stick to the issue at hand. What can you offer me for my assistance?"

"You will receive the crystal and the pedestal."

"Not an option. They are already mine," I snorted, forcing the Delvian to freeze in shock. She recovered quickly enough, however:

"Everyone knows that you are looking for the Uldans. If I become the empress, you will gain access to one of the Uldan artifacts that the empire currently possesses."

"No!" I snapped. "Your capital is destroyed, the treasury can be looted or also destroyed. The Delvians are currently fragmented and scattered throughout Galactogon. In return for taking you to Nadin, I want everything that the Delvians know about the Uldans. Items, information, lore. And that's not the end of it!" I raised my voice, seeing that Lumara was about to object. "I want the empire to pay for the upgrades on this list!"

I showed Hansa's second price list to the silent princess.

"If we can see eye to eye, you get to be empress. If not, you remain an ordinary Delvian. You can keep your emotions to yourself. I'm not going to take you back from some vague, heroic motives."

"You will become the enemy of my empire!" Lumara threatened angrily.

"Am I not that now?" I asked sarcastically. "Just don't forget—it was this very enemy who pulled you from the rubble. The empire's friends weren't around for some reason. And whether your empire even exists or will exist remains an open question."

The princess tried to bargain, but I was adamant—it was either all or nothing. I knew that as a result, the Delvian Empire would be forever closed to me, but I could not act otherwise. The second level upgrades from Hansa were worth it.

"You will get what you ask for, pirate!" Lumara finally surrendered. A wall of warning text scrolled past, but there was nothing there that I objected to too much. The only upsetting thing was the time frame for the Delvians to provide me with the info about the Uldans. Whereas the Hansa upgrades were simple and straightforward (it was enough to deliver Lumara to the planet and she would pay me for the upgrades), the Uldan question remained problematic. The princess wanted a week after her coronation to gather together all the fragments of her broken empire. I had Stan rummage through Galactogon's lore, but he could not find a clear answer for when the coronation should take place: The day after Lumara reappeared or a few years after the official mourning. In the end, I was forced to agree to her terms, since it was unlikely that as soon as the new heiress appeared, she would receive all the state secrets on a silver platter.

"Brainiac, set course for Nadin!"

My words surely caused a sigh of relief from the dispatchers. I was finally doing as Hilvar had ordered.

The Nadin system in Confederate space did not stand out in any way—it was an ordinary system with two habitable planets. After undergoing inspection and landing, I presented Lumara to the locals and everyone began running about, fussing, bowing and curtseying. It was the usual turmoil caused by no one knowing how to treat the heiress of the empire. At long last, a coordinator appeared who introduced himself as the chief authority on the planet and he solemnly brought the heiress out of the ship. All I got was a letter to Hansa stating that the Delvian Empire would pay for the second tranche of upgrades as well as a small monetary reward. The *Delvian Dunkirk* mission remained uncompleted, yet the news of a new hope shook Galactogon:

Rejoice oh Delvians! The ruling dynasty has survived!
+1000 Rapport with the Delvian Empire for all players who are not enemies of the empire!

The last bit was surely a gibe directed at me—Lumara made it clear that she had not forgotten about her promises. The dispatcher ordered us to leave the system immediately, threatening to open fire otherwise. I didn't feel like ascertaining the limits of Delvian patience and decided to head back to Blood

Island to unload all the excess raq in my holds. However, as soon as our departure had been confirmed, Sebastian stunned me:

"Surgeon, wait. I want to stay."

The thief looked decisive and I asked for clarification:

"I want to stay with Lumara," he explained, "and help her rebuild the empire. We had time to talk as we traveled. She offered me a position at court and I realized that I wanted it. She knows that I am not a pirate, but a thief. She knows that I have no place among the Qualians or in space. You said yourself that as soon as I want to leave, you would not hold me. It seems to me that I will be more useful here. Nothing personal—it will just be better that way. Goodbye. I assume I've earned my armor suit."

A blow below the belt from the princess! I was well aware that it was impossible to persuade the NPC to continue on with me, he was acting according to his script. But what a sly fox that Lumara! First she tried to slip us her malware and now she poaches one of my crew! And one that any pirate would trade his best Sunday eye-patch for! I will have a tough time of it without Sebastian. I will have to steal everything myself and rely on Brainiac to estimate the price of what I come across. A sad day!

"You have my comm number," I nodded, managing my emotions. "If you get tired of working with Lumara, you can always return to *Warlock*. You know the terms. As for now—out you go!"

Brainiac opened a hatch under the Qualian, ejecting the traitor from my ship.

"Shall we head home, Cap'n?" The snake popped out of her compartment. "We are not welcome here."

"Then we shall go where we are welcome," I replied angrily.

"Brainiac, set course for Belket! Hansa awaits!"

The fifteen minutes that we spent flying to the Precians allowed me to cope with my anger and my mind eventually returned to a tranquil state. I stared at my PDA, for the hundredth time considering the pros and cons. One way or another, I had to make the call. It would be useful, both for me and for Liberium. Why not become temporary allies?

"Vargen, don't hang up! I have some business for you," I managed to blurt out before the head of Liberium realized who was calling him. The silence on the other line and the green 'call in progress' light indicated that someone was still listening to me.

"I have the tablet of the viceroy here. He used it to keep track of his trading accounts, among other things. I am sure you have people who could do something with these numbers and turn a profit for Liberium. A quick look was enough for me to see the details of various equipment shipments: who, where, when and why. And not only the current ones, but also the forthcoming ones for next year. If you act quickly, you might come by a nice jackpot. You're the first person I've offered this to and, you can imagine, it won't be free. If you are interested, I can send you some excerpts."

"Surgeon, you seem to be calling with a good offer, but I would much rather meet you out in real life and kick your ass," Vargen's voice had plenty of malice in it, yet he was restrained himself. "Where do you want to meet?"

"In real life, nowhere. In Galactogon, I will be in Hansa's office on Belket in twenty minutes. But that is not the only thing I had to offer you. Would you like to travel to that nebula planet with

---

me, while Ash is sorting out the matter of the ships? I will even cut you a deal of twenty thousand real credits for a place. There are three seats available."

"You think you've found yourself a cash cow?" Vargen could no longer hold back and lost his cool. "Well you got your sex wrong, so careful how you milk me."

"Easy Vargen. All right. Twenty thousand per place and ten percent of the loot if you want to come and take part. And if not, then see you later and bye!"

"I want half the loot!" Vargen cut me off. "We found the planet and most of the force will be our men. You're a cab driver."

"Fine. You can have half," I agreed. "But I get first choice of the loot."

"Okay. Settled," Vargen became more constructive. "How will we solve the issue of the viceroy?"

"Who told you that the viceroy's scenario ended with his death? Buy the tablet, see the data, use the name of the viceroy as the hero, untimely deceased. It's not for me to teach you how to manipulate the NPCs. I'll wait for you here at Hansa and show you what I managed to dig up. Bring your accountant with you. He should be interested."

I had no doubt that Vargen would show up to our meeting. The morsel I was dangling was simply too tasty. Of course, I could have sold this same info to Ash, but he didn't know who I was for now and that was a good thing. Maintaining acquaintances with the leading guilds is a bad habit in this line of work. Vargen was just one example of this.

"Mr. Eine, I have a unique offer for you." My next call was to the collector. "How would you feel about a chance to visit an Uldan planet?"

It took forever to talk Eine to thirty thousand for a ticket without making any mining concessions in the process. Eine resisted with every part of his body and spirit, insisting that he deserved all the loot from the venture—even though it was me who had approached him with the offer! The German was so good at haggling that I ended up all but begging him to come with us. It was a good thing that by then we were approaching Belket and I had to hang up to speak with the dispatcher. As a result of the adviser's instructions, the locals almost shot us down for being an enemy of the empire, and it was only me repeating the magic word 'Hansa' over and over again that saved us. The Precians were not happy to see me. While the customs officers were examining *Warlock*, I returned to my negotiations with Eine—though now having had a moment to sort my thoughts out. Finally Eine gave up and agreed to my conditions, though not before making me promise to sell him what we would find first. I had no objection to this—who knew if we'd find anything at all.

And finally, there was one last call to make. I was taking a big risk here. Who knows what another player might decide to do. However, I couldn't not try it.

"Hey Gammon!" I figured Gammon owed me for arranging his timely switch to the Precians, even if he had paid for it both with real and gaming credits. "No, I don't have a new ship, but I might get one with your help. Send me the logbook from the sold cruiser. I want to pay a visit to Fighting Breed and pick up their remaining cruisers. We still need to figure out who will get dibs when selling the ships. Yes, send it to my PDA, I'll figure it out. Good luck to you too!"

A huge mistake on my part—I had sold Gammon that cruiser without copying her logs first. My PDA squeaked—Gammon didn't waste time and ordered the captain of his new cruiser to send me the data. Brainiac immediately began to analyze and systematize the coordinates therein. I wanted to know not only where Fighting Breed was based, but also where they managed to get the Zatrathi equipment. Leaving my ship computer to his work, I went to visit the techies and got some nasty news:

"Two days!" the Hansa technician declared with finality upon reading Lumara's letter. "Preferably three. It's not possible to upgrade your ship faster."

I frowned. I had planned on the upgrades being done in a few hours.

"I want to note that the imperial adviser has prohibited me from providing you with the third list," the technician continued to relay the bad news. "You are not allowed to see our newest inventions. This is the imperial adviser's official position."

I could not help smiling when I heard the word 'official,' but decided to deal with this 'official' later. First I had to upgrade the ship according to the second list, and then find a way to budge Hansa from their 'official' position.

IN SEARCH OF THE ULDANS

Vargen appeared half an hour later with a bunch of bodyguards in tow. Three, including Vargen himself, were ensconced in legendary armor suits and ready to travel. Another three were accountants, judging by their uniforms. For about ten minutes, this trio poured over the info that Brainiac had extracted from the viceroy's tablet—after which they simply dissolved into thin air: Liberium's analysts exited to reality to discuss the info. I did not have access to Vargen's PDA and I couldn't make out his expression behind his visor, so all I could do was wait.

"If you give us the tablet, we can forget about the incident with the viceroy," Vargen began to aggro again.

"You can solve the question of the viceroy with Ash," I had no patience for this. "The tablet is a unique piece of loot, even if its use is temporary. Make me a better offer. What is this habit of yours to try and use your charisma stat on other players? If you don't want it, I'll find someone who does."

I knew that Vargen would argue that the information on the tablet only had temporary value and decided to anticipate this move.

"You want money again?" Vargen pouted, getting ready to blow his gasket. I didn't need to be a great psychologist to understand: Aside from the places in the expedition, Vargen would not pay me a single credit for anything. Accordingly, by offering him the tablet, I was counting on something else.

"Where did the Fighting Breed get the Zatrathi equipment?" I

---

countered his question with mine. Vargen even twitched in surprise. Brainiac had by this time already parsed the cruiser's logs and identified three planets that were the best places to look. Looking at the results, I whittled this down to one—a planet in the depths of the Qualian Empire.

"Don't stress it, I already know the answer. Actually, this will be your payment. I need some marines to help me. I won't manage alone. Give me the marines to clear the planet. Then leave me alone with the loot. What I will do with it and where I will sell it will be my business. I will give you the tablet in exchange. We can let the lawyers figure out the legal details."

"You're not afraid of making a mistake?" Vargen couldn't resist. "The Breed could have plundered all there was on that planet. What if you don't find anything?"

"In that case, I will have a good time working alongside your well-coordinated assault team," I answered calmly. "Isn't this a game finally? Where's the gameplay? I won't lose anything but the tablet and some time. We will fly on your ships. Mine doesn't have the space for the marines or their equipment."

"When do you want to do it?"

"As soon as we finish with the nebula. Why delay? Every day counts here. The sooner we get the Zatrathi equipment, the more expensive we can sell it for. Nothing personal, it's just business."

"I know NPCs and players who would be interested in that equipment," Vargen added just in case and contacted his lawyers. The long process of hammering out the details of the two upcoming operations had begun. From his former, bitter experience, Vargen even wanted to make changes to the existing contract. It was his right of course. My expensive lawyer would look out for me and mine.

"Naturally we couldn't do without this one!" Vargen quipped when Eine appeared.

"I do not understand your Surprise," the German retorted, settling himself comfortably in his chair and adjusting the screens in front of him. "I have Interest in ze uncharted Planet and have Money to pay for zis expedition. Or do you have a different, unique Offer for me?"

Eine looked at Vargen searchingly, but he only muttered something unintelligible in response, turning off the voice channel. Seeing that the leader of Liberium had nothing more to add, Eine began examining the orbship's interior. At long last, the lawyers agreed to all the details, the money appeared in my account, and the Precians grudgingly cleared us for takeoff. It seemed like a test of wills for them to tolerate a hated pirate on their planet without being able to blow him to smithereens with their Grand Arbiter.

"Are those the remnants of your fleet?" I gibed when we reached the rendezvous point. We encountered an armada of two B-class cruisers, a dozen carracks and about fifty frigates. Liberium was not taking any chances with the expedition. Although, perhaps this was just them protecting themselves from me. After all, they had the coordinates, so what kept them from flying out to the nebula and seeing it for themselves? Frankly, this idea had crossed my mind several times already, but due to constant time pressure I kept putting it away until it finally got lost in the depths of my consciousness.

"What do you think, Brainiac?" After seeing that we were not about to be attacked, I turned to exploring the cosmic anomaly. A blurry nebula wavered in the middle of Galactogon without a single star nearby. Its enormous size could easily conceal a planet along with a bunch of moons if there were any.

"I have never encountered an astronomical object of this kind before," confessed the ship's computer. "The structure of this nebula is incomprehensible. Its composition could a gas, a liquid, or even fine dust. Didn't you say it was corrosive to ships? Whatever it is, it did not exist before *Warlock* was mothballed on Blood Island."

"Move ahead slowly and monitor the hull's condition. We don't need any surprises, so be ready to take evasive maneuvers at the first sign of danger."

Everyone plastered themselves to the screens peering into the impenetrable gloom. The scanners showed nothing, as if the nebula was empty and lifeless. Brainiac brought the ship up to the edge of the cloud and halted. There was no smooth transition— the dense fog began abruptly ahead. The mechanical arm emerged holding a basket and scooped up a sample of the nebula. A moment later the basket melted away, as if dissolved in concentrated acid. The snake plunged the mechanical arm deeper into the fog and pulled it back. The fog did not affect the arm itself.

"Hmm..." the snake summed up meaningfully. "Give me five seconds. I want to try something else.

Now the mechanical arm inserted a piece of raq into the fog, then a piece of some equipment, a powercell and even the armor suit that had been Sebastian's. Everything dissolved except for the mechanical arm itself. We did save the suit—the snake declared that she needed a couple of hours to repair it. The conclusion suggested itself on its own—the nebula dissolved everything that was not part of the ship—and not just any ship, but my Uldan orbship specifically. Brainiac nudged the vessel forward crossing the nebula's border. Nothing happened. The anomaly had no effect on *Warlock*.

"Your radar is malfunctioning. Your equipment is junk, Captain Surgeon," Vargen mocked as soon as we were fully immersed in the cosmic milk. Our screens filled with ripples making it impossible to make anything out. How had Aalor even seen a planet and ships under these conditions?

"Cap'n, I am receiving a signal," the snake did not give me the opportunity to respond to Vargen. "A standard Uldan friend or foe request. What should I do? The encoding is quite standard, there should be no difficulties responding."

"Can we answer as 'friend?'"

"Done. Wow! Look, the fog has cleared!"

Indeed, our screens had cleared up. The perimeter of the area which we found ourselves in was still covered in fog, but right in front of us opened up a wide corridor leading like a landing strip to a blue planet. A dozen spherical ships hovered along the edges of this peculiar corridor. Brainiac scanned the nearest one and announced that these were automated orbital stations. They had no living beings on board them.

I decided to take advantage of the hospitality and ordered Brainiac to move forward. The fog dissipated completely at the very planet and we were intercepted by one of the stations. A standard customs inspection. I was just getting my hopes up of meeting real living Uldans when they were dashed—a red scanner beam ran along *Warlock*, changed to green and disappeared. Brainiac did not like this procedure, since it caused interference in the ship's electronics.

"But nothing bad has happened, right?" I asked just in case.

"*Warlock* has been deemed obsolete and in need of upgrades," the snake sighed heavily. "We have been ordered to replace some equipment—if not, *Warlock* will be scrapped. I'm afraid I don't understand half the components on the list they sent over. New names, new equipment, new operations. It's been twenty thousand years since our exile and the Uldans' disappearance—technology has advanced quite a bit since then. Can you believe it? Our orbship, an obsolete vessel! Why it's more advanced than the tubs currently littering the galaxy. Where can we find these parts anyway?"

"Did they give you a deadline?" I grew worried. What if they're going to blast us in ten minutes?"

"There's no time limit. They'll simply not permit us to come here a second time without the necessary upgrades," the snake finished wailing. "There are no restrictions at the moment. Shall we land?"

"Run an analysis of the planet."

"I will show it on the screen. Ten percent of the surface is landmass, the rest is ocean. The atmospheric composition is suitable for humans. I have identified a structure resembling a pyramid as well as…Attention, danger! There is a Zatrathi ship on the planet. A transport!"

"Take evasive action!" I ordered quickly. "We will circumnavigate the planet at the lowest possible altitude. Preferably under water. Brainiac keep track of the beams; make sure we're not detected. Do it!"

The orbship banked sharply, flying around the planet. The news was rather unpleasant—a Zatrathi transport had penetrated the Uldan defenses. There were so many questions piling up in my head that I brushed them aside, focusing on the main task at hand—a smooth and stealthy descent to the planet's surface. The Zatrathi don't expect us—there was no sign of security out in orbit.

"Don't you think you're being a bit too safe?" Vargen looked at the timer. Our ETA was seven hours. You can't really accelerate too much under water.

"I am not ze Owner of much free Time," Eine was also dissatisfied with my maneuver. "I am not one who pays for vaiting, I vish for Action. I believe that flying over ze Vater vould be a better use of our Time. Ze Zatrazi do not expect an Attack. As a result, ve have ze advantage."

"Brainiac, call Sebastian." My top priority was to call for reinforcements. If a transport managed to reach this place, then a flying fortress could too. And that was easily the last thing I needed.

"Cap'n, something is wrong. The nebula is blocking all outbound signals and we do not know the settings for the local hyper relays."

That was exactly what I wanted to hear. If we can't call home, then neither can the Zatrathi. So we have a chance!

"In that case, surface! Brainiac, full throttle. Head for the pyramid and make sure that the transport does not take off. Prepare the marine and the droids! The time has come to earn your ticket, Vargen. Get ready for landing!"

The three Zatrathi warriors who were guarding the transport never even understood anything. Brainiac calculated the trajectory of the marine's drop so accurately, that the flying rhino impaled the trio with his horn—and then squashed them against the pyramid's wall to finish the job. Three flickering crates was all that remained of the transport's guards. Finally, I could examine the monumental structure up close. It bore a passing resemblance to the Great Pyramid of Giza, although this stone monument stood right in the middle of a vast forest. A massive gate opened on the side facing us. The space scanner could only map a few winding corridors inside the pyramid. This was the limit of its range. Eine prudently remained aboard, suggesting that we go deal with any enemies on our own.

"Brainiac, send the droids inside the transport. Order them to clear it. Vargen, send one of your men with them. The droids could use a player to guide them. If we capture the transport, we should be able to sell her for a good price. Snake, you're in charge of hacking the ship. Sebastian's no longer with us. Can you handle it?"

"It will be done," the engineer promised, slithering out of the orbship's hull. The sight of a ten-meter snake made Vargen and his bodyguards start. It's one thing to hear the snake, another thing entirely to see her in front of you.

"The perimeter is clear! The ship is clear! The hacking

procedure is under way, ten minutes remaining," the reports started filing in one after the other. The rhino made a circuit around the pyramid, but encountered no one. There was no one in the transport either. Even the holds were empty.

"Well those three didn't just come here alone for no reason," I frowned. This seemed frighteningly simple.

"In my estimation, such a ship should fit about one and a half hundred of those guys," Vargen seemed as suspicious as I was. Indicating the open passage, he added: "I'd bet they're all inside. We'll need to smoke them out. I will call my people. They'll have a landing force at the edge of the nebula in no time."

"It won't work." I was forced to reveal my discovery that our communications were blocked. "We can only rely on ourselves."

"Give me control over your droids," Vargen demanded. "I have more experience. Join our comm channel while you're at it. I don't want to speak in the open. Here's the password. Can the rhino be controlled or is he like part of the ship or something?"

A disgruntled bellow sounded from my marine. He did not like Vargen's question.

"I see," concluded the head of Liberium. "Yeah, add him to our party too. That's it. Take two minutes and then we head out. Get to it! The Zatrathi won't kill themselves on their own."

Vargen not only loved to command, he also knew how to do it. I had to give him that. The droids transferred to him began scurrying back and forth, dragging stone blocks to the entrance and blocking the doorway. If the door shut randomly, our plans could quickly evaporate.

"The first thing to do is to scout out the place. Surgeon, how many droids can you spare? It's not possible to go in guns blazing."

"The droids are clumsy. They won't be much good," I said. "The recon drones would work better."

"You have those?" Vargen asked, surprised. "How many?"

"As many as you need. Brainiac send the recon drones into the pyramid. I want to know what's inside. Display what they see on the screens."

A buzzing flying thing flashed past us and disappeared into the depths of the stone colossus. A few turns, empty corridors and, finally, the drone emerged into a large, well-lit room.

"I am counting forty Zatrathi engineers," Brainiac reckoned up the slugs crawling around the floor. They paid no attention to the drone, going about their business. Frankly, their movements interested me. The slugs were dragging oblong metal boxes, very similar to coffins. They were using an elevator to raise them or lower them between the levels—somewhere nearby there had to be a whole host of other engineers.

"Those are prison capsules." Brainiac exclaimed in surprise. "How did they get here?"

The drone flew closer to the prison capsules yet the slugs still did not respond to it.

"Scanning now," said Brainiac and the drone began running green lasers over the capsules. "Those really are prison capsules. In our day, criminals were kept in them. Specifically, this particular prisoner was imprisoned for life for having perpetrated an unauthorized genocide of three planets. He lost his mind from solitude seventy thousand years ago and was automatically frozen by his capsule."

"When, um, you say 'unauthorized,' does that mean that there were authorized ones too?" Vargen listened to Brainiac's report attentively.

"Yes, the Uldans could apply to use a planet for an experiment and if approved, they did whatever they wanted with it. It was infrequent for the application to be rejected—there are simply too many inhabited planets. Galactogon doesn't have enough resources to sustain everyone. Yet this particular prisoner did not feel like waiting for the decision about his application. He went ahead without it and was punished as a result."

"Is he alive?"

"More likely no than yes. The body is alive, the mind is gone. When an Uldan goes mad from loneliness, his personality is erased. Such is their nature."

"I know ze Source of ze Captains of ze Zatrazi Ships," Eine piped up. Like us, the German was closely following the drone's feed.

"Yes, it looks like they get them from these prison capsules," I agreed. "But why Uldans? Do the brainworms only work on them? Or maybe only the captains of the flying fortresses are Uldans?"

"This could only be the case if the flying fortress is a creation of the Uldans. And that is not the case," Brainiac came to the defense of his creators. "Uldan ships have a spherical shape, such as the orbital stations we saw coming in here. The Zatrathi ones are shapeless blobs. The Uldans would not come up with such a design."

"What about the base on Zalva's moon?" I replied. Vargen

demanded I tell him about that adventure but I declined, pointing out that that had nothing to do with the current situation. Although, it seemed to me that the Zatrathi really were somehow connected to the Uldans. And not just because they used Uldan zombies to command their ships. Everything was much more complicated.

"Spatial scan complete," Brainiac announced and brought the drone back. "I have located a door that leads to another level, but it is closed and the drone cannot open it. Your intervention is required."

"Move forward in close formation. Aalor, you're on shields. Kart, man the rocket launcher. Surgeon, follow behind us. Shoot anything that moves in our direction but fire only on my command. Move out!"

I finally learned the names of Vargen's silent bodyguards. I nodded, agreeing with the plan, especially with the part where we would only shoot at aggressive NPCs. The slugs did not seem aggressive and it was possible that they were generally neutral. It might be possible to study the Zatrathi engineers in their natural environment.

A few minutes later we were standing at the entrance to the hall awaiting an attack, bristling with blasters and a rocket launcher. The slugs were busily crawling back and forth, hauling the capsules and paying us no attention.

I could now see what they were doing a little better: after some minor manipulations of the prison capsules, the lights came on. If the color was green, the capsule was carefully placed in a separate pile. If it was red, the capsule was dumped into a heap at the far wall like trash. The trash heap was much larger than the 'good' heap.

"Tactile contact! No aggro!" Kart reported, touching an engineer that crawled past him. There was no reaction, except that the slug came back in an arc, avoiding us. Not everyone likes being touched.

"Second phase," I said, pulling out the manipulator and lifting the engineer into the air. The dangling slug's fellows did not hurry to his aid, nor whipped out their blasters, and went on behaving as if nothing had happened.

"Brainiac, we're sending a guest your way. Have a chat with him," I handed one of the droids the manipulator and ordered him to deliver the slug back to *Warlock* alive and in one piece—and then to come back and return my manipulator. I can't imagine playing this game without such a useful device. Both Eine and Vargen had offered me a lot of money for it, but I never batted an eyelid—I needed it more than they did.

"I have received the prisoner. Establishing communication now," the ship computer reported.

"Cap'n, we have a problem the size of Galactogon," said the snake. "Our guest's name is Nal-rog-Shar."

"So what's the problem?" Vargen frowned, but I understood the snake. The engineer we had captured was not Zatrathi.

"I know a Bit about ze Zatrazi," Eine who was well-versed in the intricacies of Galactogon replied to Vargen. "Zey do not use Names. Only Numbers."

It made no sense to maintain combat readiness further— there were no aggressive NPCs on this level. Vargen and his men began exploring the hall, looking for anything that was worth hauling back to the ship.

Not wishing to miss out on a good opportunity, Eine left the safety of the orbship and joined us. Then again, there was really nothing to plunder here—aside from the slugs and the prison capsules, we found nothing.

"Cap'n, I couldn't get too much from our guest. The slug is sentient but not high-functioning. This building is their home—the slugs are born and die on the lower tier. Sometimes the 'others' come and make them do various tasks. Either they take a batch of slugs specially grown for the purpose with them or, as today, they order them to sort the capsules. The 'others' will return in a week to pick up the next batch, so no need to hurry. The guest really wants to return to work and at this point he begins to repeat himself, talking in circles. What are your orders?"

"I vould like to take him," declared Eine. "If ze Slug is sentient indeed, ve can hold a Discussion vit him."

"Brainiac, knock the slug out and store him in the medbay," I ordered, agreeing with the German. We needed to examine this gastropod more closely.

Vargen pulled one of the 'dead' capsules out of the pile and tore off the cover. The slugs scattered away from the player, as if from a leper, and the air sensors indicated the presence of toxic gases. I looked inside—if there had been an Uldan in there at some point, there was practically nothing left anymore. Several wires and a handful of dust at the bottom. Over the intervening millennia, the prisoner had decomposed to toxic gases.

"Brainiac, send the droids over and have them take one of the capsules back to the ship. We will study it closer. Vargen, there's nothing more to do here, let's move on."

There was no objection. We gathered up and approached the door.

Aalor opened it abruptly and we adopted a triceratops formation: An energy shield covering our body and the muzzles of our blasters protruding like horns. But all we encountered was peace and silence—like we were in a graveyard.

"Move," Vargen ordered. The spiral staircase descended steeply, making it difficult to maintain our order. We tried our best—if some enemy attacked us right now, he would encounter an impenetrable wall. A few turns and we arrived at a small platform. This offered a good view of the pyramid's interior.

"Goddamn!" I exclaimed once I had grasped the scale of the structure we were in.

"We have discovered an industrial Complex!" Eine rejoiced behind us. "It is marvelous! It is amazing! You must take care not to touch anything because I must touch it all myself!"

Eine's excitement was quite understandable—an immense industrial facility stretched out not a dozen meters below us. It was divided into many areas, most of which were occupied by slugs growing on perches. The difference between the Zatrathi engineer slugs and these ones was that the former were darker and had various protrusions on their bodies. Some of the areas were closed, some were empty, some contained raq, elo, and other metals. There was even ordinary stone here.

"Look over there!" Aalor pointed to the left. I gulped—at the far end of the facility stood ten metallic orbs. The Uldan orbships were awaiting their captains in solitude. It was stupid of me to imagine that *Warlock* was unique. Here they are, all here. Ripe for the picking.

"Enemy detected," Brainiac jarred us from our euphoria, forcing us back on alert. "Projecting enemy position now."

A red dot appeared on one of my screens. A small office, towering over the facility like the platform we were on contained a Zatrathi—or rather, an Uldan with a brainworm on his head. He hadn't paid any attention to us yet, going about his business—he was overseeing the slugs who were dragging prison capsules to the elevator.

We tracked the movements of the engineers and solved another riddle—the prison capsules were coming out of the closed areas.

"Brainiac, send the drone over here. We need to inventory this place," Vargen ordered. "Surgeon, take the brainworm alive."

"I don't think that's a good idea," Aalor spoke out against his boss. "What if this place is rigged to blow and goes off if we get too close? Look down—the loot here alone will be worth a heap of credits. Why risk it?"

"Brainiac, run a quick analysis of the place. Could there be mines here?" Vargen showed amazing restraint, heeding his officer's objections but also insisting on his initial plan. The part that I didn't like was the way he addressed Brainiac directly.

"There is no need to conduct an analysis," the ship computer did not keep us waiting. "The pyramid above us is composed of concentrated elo. If it is activated, half of the island will simply evaporate."

"If there is a detonator, it could be linked to the brainworm's vital signal," I made a logical assumption. "If we kill him, we might blow ourselves up."

"Kart, take care of him," Vargen ordered, making the final decision. "Plan 212."

I frowned when Kart disappeared into the air, a personal cloaking device making him invisible. The second Hansa list made no mention of such a suit capability. It stood to reason that perhaps the third list did. I really need to bring something amazing back to Hansa so I could bargain for the next upgrade list.

"Target captured. All's clear!" It took Kart only a few minutes to neutralize the threat. Activating our thrusters we ascended to the 'manager's' office. The brainworm was on the Uldan's head and the Uldan was on the floor snoring his brains out. Kart had managed to tranquilize both.

"Engineer, get over here as fast as you can!"

"I just get done working on the ship and he already wants something else! Oh my poor legs!" the snake muttered discontentedly, but obeyed my order. Squeezing into our office, she bent over the brainworm.

"Right. This collar here links the Uldan to the pyramid. If the body leaves the room, the elo will go off. Notice that chain fettering the Uldan. This body is not supposed to leave this room. The brainworm came here alone. The body's like his office cubicle or something."

There followed an awkward pause. It was a bit unpleasant thinking of a living body as a 'cubicle' of another being.

"Shall I disconnect him?" continued the snake. "The Uldan will not be harmed, but the Zatrathi might. I haven't messed around with these yet."

"Do it!" Vargen was determined to prevent the possibility of an explosion. The snake bent over the sleeping Uldan, pulled out a small scalpel and with a pair of quick movements separated the brainworm from its host. Pieces of the Zatrathi fell on the floor—the snake was a bit clumsy. These parasites attached themselves directly to their hosts' brains through a hole carefully bored in the head.

"Hmm...I have failed," the snake said apologetically. The brainworm flopped to the floor, flickered and turned into a loot crate. "Cap'n could I have a word? Privately."

I grunted. This was an unusual request from the engineer. She typically said what was on her mind. I flew back to the platform, waited for the snake to join me and took off my helmet. The engineer wanted to talk directly, without any devices.

"What I want to talk to you about is..." the snake even hesitated. "Well, I found ten orbships here."

"Yes I saw them. Over there, by the wall. Get on with it. What do you want?"

"They are updated. Brainiac scanned them with a drone—he even checked inside—their access codes are written on the stand. Anyway. These are cutting-edge ships. One of them would run circles around us even with our new upgrades from Hansa's second list. They are absolutely unreal. Their speed is almost one and a half times faster than our current maximum, their beam cannons use some new prismatic principle that makes them incredibly powerful. They come with two types of torpedoes, both the shielded and the unshielded kinds. They are one and a half times larger than ours which would allow us to integrate another ten systems or so. We talked it over, the crew, I mean, and we want you to consider changing ships. Brainiac will copy himself to the new ship. I will get a handle on all the systems in a couple of days. And then we'll be able to smash Galactogon to bits. Even their cargo holds are twice as large as ours. That should be important for you."

"What's the downside?" I had no doubt that there would be some con.

"It's not certain that Brainiac will be able to copy himself. The new orbships likely have newer ship computers that are more advanced. Brainiac might be erased and then we'll lose him entirely—even on our current ship. We are all ready to risk it of course, but the decision is yours to make. Should we try it or not? We need about three minutes to start the procedure."

I knew damn well that I would agree but I decided to pause for suspense anyway.

The snake was staring at me too searchingly. Even hopefully. Giving her the go ahead at last, I returned to the rest of the raiding party.

Vargen was busy downloading all the data from the facility's mainframes to his PDA. Eine stood beside him, impatiently fidgeting with his flash drive. The players had moved on to their favorite part of raiding—the looting.

I could of course object and demand that the German put away his flash drive—after all, under the contract, he had no right to download the data—but I didn't say anything. Nodding to Eine's unspoken question, I hooked up Brainiac. While the snake was making her preparations, Brainiac could download and analyze the base data.

"What is required to pilot such a ship?" Vargen correctly assessed the actions of my engineer who had crawled over to deal with the new vessel. Plus, the drone was whirling nearby.

"Find a crew," I admitted honestly. "These are ships for one player, all the work is done by the NPCs. Three crew members. Brainiac, are there any orbship crews in this facility?"

"Negative. My available information suggests there are no other crews here."

"Can I pilot her without a crew?" Vargen tried another angle.

"Negative. Humans cannot interface with orbship systems."

Vargen cursed—the opportunity of getting a ship that no one had, had passed tantalizingly close and vanished with a coy wave. I can't say that I felt for him. All of a sudden, my ship communicator began vibrating:

"Captain Surgeon, this is the AI of orbship model X-34-56 speaking. Would you like to customize the matrix parameters?"

My face contorted from the unpleasant news. I felt disgusted and crestfallen. I was so used to Brainiac by now that the idea of starting all over again with a new computer…

"Relax, Cap'n! Don't worry! We're only joking," the snake snickered. "You should see your face!"

My sour mug appeared on one of the screens. If there were a prize in this game for best emotional expression, I'd win hands down. I reckon I had used all 56 of my facial muscles to express my disappointment.

"The ships were empty," Brainiac reassured me once he had

---

transferred to the new ship. Then he added on the public channel: "These orbships do not have their guidance computers. They are empty vessels. It is impossible to fly them even with a crew. Captain, I request permission to depart. It is necessary to transfer all the materials, prisoners and equipment from the old vessel to the new one."

"Don't forget to take the ship into account when we start dividing the loot," Vargen could not avoid spoiling the moment, reminding me of our agreement.

"Absolutely. Brainiac, what are the most valuable things in this base?"

"Information," the computer replied true to form. For a computer system, there is nothing more important than information; all the devices and gadgets are secondary. One of the metal orbs soared into the air and disappeared under the ceiling. I could not see whether it passed through the ceiling or a special hatch in it, but a few moments later it came to rest beside my old ship. The differences were quite evident, above all in their size.

"While the transfer is underway, I must mention that we have a problem," Brainiac clearly didn't want to broach the subject but he couldn't not warn us either. "I have decrypted the data from the captured Zatrathi transport. We have 32 minutes before a Zatrathi flying fortress enters the nebula. The system was automatically configured and managed to send out a distress call. Our new capabilities allows us to send signals through the nebula too. We should leave in twenty minutes."

I looked at the generated list of materials on the base.

Standard items, nothing of value. The base was dedicated to growing slugs and ship captains, not storing unique equipment or treasure. And if so, then:

"Vargen, take the transport and let's rendezvous on Belket. Brainiac send him the access codes to the Zatrathi ship. Eine, you have ten minutes to stuff your pockets. The base is at your complete disposal. Vargen, you can do the same thing, load that transport. Do you want some droids to help you or will you do it yourself?"

"Send the droids over. Aalor, take the right, Kart, take the left. I'll handle the center," the head of Liberium did not refuse my offer.

"Brainiac send a droid over here and program him to start opening the dead capsules ten minutes after our departure. Let's not leave this facility for the Zatrathi."

The players did not object to this. The Zatrathi would increase security here after our raid so it wouldn't make sense to come back again. And if so, we may as well destroy everything. We will live by the principle of 'If I can't have it, no one else can either.'

A minute later, Brainiac called me up on our private comm: The computer wanted to speak to me without intermediaries, but hesitated:

"Captain…I have this issue…I do not even know how to start. I know why the Zatrathi managed to travel through the nebula. I also now understand the composition of the nebula's fog. I have discovered a lot of useful information in the facility's database."

"Give me the rundown of the basic points. I can think of the rest."

IN SEARCH OF THE ULDANS

"Okay. First. The nebula is actually composed of nanites that analyze the material moving among them and attack anything that is banned by their code. Second. There are at least three such planets available to the Zatrathi. The transport's logs contain their coordinates. They use two of the planets for growing their warriors—this one they use for engineers and captains. Third. The Zatrathi can travel through the nebula unimpeded because they are themselves Uldan creations. The engineer slugs, the brainworms, the warriors—they are all Uldan creations, created eighty thousand years ago to fight the Vraxis. You were searching for the Uldans and you have found them. This is precisely why only Uldans can captain Zatrathi ships—the vessels wouldn't accept any other species. The orbship was transferred to you formally by one of the last Uldans. Had you captured *Warlock* by force, you would not be able to fly her. We are not fighting a mysterious enemy—we are at war with the Uldans, the progenitors of all life in Galactogon. The same ones who created me and our entire crew. I am conflicted. To fight my creators is a grave decision and I need to further analyze the information I have received. This should take me three days."

"I hope you're not going to consider the meaning of life?" I did not like what Brainiac had said. This was mutiny!

"No, first of all, we need to leave this planet as fast as possible. The transfer is complete. We are free to go."

I looked at the players of Liberium, flying between the different areas, dragging out boxes and forcing the droids to haul them out to the transport. The players carried the heavier crates themselves, pushing their armor suits' thrusters to their limits. It would seem that only a few minutes had passed, but we had already plundered a third of the entire complex. Naturally, no one bothered with the slugs and prison capsules.

"Vargen, can you handle it on your own from here?"

"You're trying to get out of here?"

"I have nothing more to do here. We can divvy up the loot on Belket and decide what to do with the transport there too. I need to go take care of some business for a few days, but I'll be in touch, so you have free reign when it comes to selling the loot. You can give me my share later, just make sure to make all transactions only through official contracts. Let the lawyers take care of the details. The game will generate the loot list automatically. I'd say the raid was a success. Eine, are you coming with me or are you staying? Keep in mind that you can keep only what fits in your inventory."

"I vould like to remain," the German responded, stuffing another piece of equipment into his inventory.

"In that case, good luck to everyone."

I didn't want to risk a ship that was not yet bound to a planetary spirit. The new captain's cabin could hold up to ten creatures, which would really make things easier when planning subsequent raids.

The first thing I did was destroy the old ship, sending her to my planet's graveyard. Vargen could easily load my old orbship into the transport. And I'd rather keep her around for a rainy day. Who knows how this game will play out?

Placing my hand on the control hologram, I began to pilot my new ship. The controls were the same, but the sensation of acceleration had changed—that is, there was none. This vessel had inertial dampeners built in, which allowed creatures without armor suits to survive high-g maneuvers while on board. Our speed was also much higher—we zipped through the nebula in a matter of seconds. The planetary defense system congratulated Brainiac on having upgraded our vessel as per the latest regulations and assured us that we could return without any problems if we so desired.

"Brainiac, let's head home. We'll bind ourselves to the planetary spirit and deal with your concerns," I ordered, happily reclining in my new captain's chair. The raid really had been a success. And yet, I couldn't enjoy it for very long—a minute, no more. Suddenly, the air just in front of me shimmered and began to thicken, taking form. I cocked my blasters, ready to defend my ship.

"Lex?" came a painfully familiar voice. Something clicked in my head, and I rushed forward to embrace the unexpected guest—and not at all to strangle her.

"Whoa!" Eunice croaked, trying to escape from my tenacious paws.

"I was expecting you in a week!" I placed my hands on my wife's shoulders and looked her over at arm's length. She did not look much different than she had out in reality, except that here she was maybe a little more prim.

"The baby is doing well, so I was allowed to enter Galactogon early. I see you've upgraded the ship? Cool. I like the new model better. Listen, let's get down to business right away, all right? We can deal with the rest later. How did it go with the prize check?

What did the emperor say? Did you discover the coordinates of the planet?"

I stared at her blankly. The prize check? Did they not tell her that the contest was terminated?

"You signed the contract," my wife sighed. "A pity. We'll have to settle for one billion."

"You didn't sign? Give me the details!"

"There are no details. I came to on a beach, alive and well. I understood right away that I was in a medcapsule. I talked to the lawyer they sent. I know how to act in those situations. I demanded a doctor and a full report of my condition. He tried stonewalling so I started to cite various laws and statutes. This made them start scurrying about. The doc popped up instantly, along with all the information about our condition. Basically, everything that a mother should know about her child and herself. When that Reynard fellow showed up, I was ready. I refused to sign anything."

"Did they threaten you?"

"Of course not. What are they going to do to me? I am a pregnant woman with injuries. According to our medical laws, the doctors are under so much liability that they wouldn't let anyone close to me—even the three-time president and owner of Galactogon. Moreover, the clinic is not in our country. They explained everything and tried to persuade me, but I gave them an ultimatum: Pay me the billion or give me the chance to find it in the game. Actually, I would have been here earlier if not for the ensuing negotiations. They chose the second option, and here I am, on your ship, to continue the search. You dropped out as did all the other contestants, so no one except for me can receive that check. In other words, Lex, drop everything and take me to the Precian Emperor. He knows where my billion's buried."

"I'm afraid there might be a problem there," I grinned when all the parts of the puzzle had fallen into place. "The Precians don't like me very much. As in, not at all. And now they will simply loathe me."

END OF BOOK TWO

Want to be the first to know about our latest LitRPG, sci fi and fantasy titles from your favorite authors?

Subscribe to our *New Releases* newsletter:
http://eepurl.com/b7niIL

Thank you for reading *In Search of the Uldans!*
If you like what you've read, check out other sci-fi, fantasy and
LitRPG novels published by Magic Dome Books:

In order to have new books of the series translated faster, we need your help and support! Please consider leaving a review or spread the word by recommending *In Search of the Uldans* to your friends and posting the link on social media. The more people buy the book, the sooner we'll be able to make new translations available.

Thank you!

Till next time!